Lavondyss

Robert Holdstock

Lavondyss

Journey to an Unknown Region

William Morrow and Company, Inc.
New York

For George, Dorothy, Douglas,
Mercy and Rita –
fine storytellers all!

You are not far away.

Copyright © 1988 by Robert Holdstock
Illustration copyright © 1988 by Alan Lee

First published in Great Britain by Victor Gollancz Ltd., 1988

Library of Congress Cataloging-in-Publication Data

Holdstock, Robert.
Lavondyss: journey to an unknown region/Robert Holdstock.
p.   cm.
Originally published: London: Gollancz, 1988.
ISBN 0-688-09185-7
I. Title.
PR6058.0442L38   1989
823'.914—dc20

89-31587
CIP

Printed in the United States of America

First U.S. Edition

1 2 3 4 5 6 7 8 9 10

Contents

Darest thou now O soul,
Walk out with me toward the unknown region,
Where neither ground is for the feet nor any path to follow?

Walt Whitman
Darest Thou Now, O Soul

Part One

Old Forbidden Place

A fire is burning in Bird Spirit Land.
My bones smoulder. I must journey there.
Shaman dream chant, *ca. 10,000 BC*

[GABERLUNGI]

White Mask

T he bright moon, hanging low over Barrow Hill, illuminated the snow-shrouded fields and made the winter land seem to glow with faint light. It was a lifeless, featureless place, and yet the shapes of the fields were clear, marked out by the moonshadow of the dark oak hedges that bordered them. Distantly, from that shadow round the meadow called The Stumps, the ghostly figure began to move again, following a hidden track over the rise of ground, then moving left, into tree cover. It stood there, just visible now to the old man who watched it from Stretley Farm; watching back. The cloak it wore was dark, the hood pulled low over its face. As it moved for the second time, coming closer to the farmhouse, it left the black wood behind. It was stooped, against the Christmas cold, perhaps. Where it walked it left a deep furrow in the fresh snow.

Standing at the gate of the farm, waiting for the moment he knew, now, must surely come, Owen Keeton heard his grandchild begin to cry. He turned to the dark face of the house and listened. The sobbing was a brief disturbance; a dream perhaps. Then the infant girl was quiet again.

Keeton retraced his steps across the garden, stepped into the warm house and kicked the snow from his boots. He walked into the parlour, prodded the log fire with the metal poker until the flames roared again, then went to the window and peered out at the main road to Shadoxhurst, the nearest village to the farm. He could just hear, very distantly, the sound of carols. Glancing at the clock above the fire he realised that Christmas Day had begun ten minutes before.

At the parlour table he stared down at the book of folklore and legend that lay open there. The print was very fine, the pages thick and of good quality paper; the illustrations, in full colour, were exquisite. It was a book he loved, and he was giving it to his granddaughter as a present. The images of knights and heroes inspired him; the Welshness of the names and places made him nostalgic for the lost places and lost voices of his own youth in the mountains of Wales. The epic tales had filled his head with the sound of battle, war-cry and the rustle of tree and bird in the glades of haunted forests.

Now there was something else in the book, written in the white spaces around the print: a letter. His letter to the child.

He turned back to the beginning of that letter, where the chapter on Arthur of the Britons began. He scanned the words quickly:

> *My dear Tallis: I'm an old man writing to you on a cold December night. I wonder if you will love the snow as much as I do? And regret as much the way it can imprison you. There is old memory in snow. You will find that out in due course, for I know where you come from, now . . .*

The fire guttered and Keeton shivered despite it, and despite the heavy coat he wore. He stared at the wall, beyond which the snow-covered garden led to the fields, and that hooded figure, coming towards him. He felt a sudden urgent need to have done with this letter, to finalise it. It was a sort of panic. It gripped his heart and his stomach, and the hand that reached for the pen was shaking. The sound of the clock grew loud, but he resisted the urge to stare at it, to mark the passage of time, so little time, so few minutes . . .

He had to finish writing the letter, and soon. He bent to the page and began to squeeze the words into the narrow margin:

> *We bring alive ghosts, Tallis, and the ghosts huddle at the edge of vision. They are wise in ways that are a wisdom we all still share but have forgotten. But the wood is us and we are the wood! You will learn this. You will learn names. You will smell that ancient winter,*

so much more ferocious than this simple Xmas snow. And as you do so, you are treading an old and important pathway. I began to tread it first, until they abandoned me . . .

He wrote on, turning the pages, filling the margins, linking his own words to the unconscious child with the words of fable, forming a link that would be of value to her, one day in her future.

When he had finished the letter he used his handkerchief to blot the ink then closed the book. He wrapped it in heavy brown paper and tied it with a length of string.

On the brown paper he wrote this simple message: *For Tallis; for your fifth birthday. From Granddad Owen.*

He buttoned up his coat again and went back out into the cold, silent winter's night. He stood outside the door for a moment feeling frightened, very disturbed. The hooded figure had come all the way across the fields and was standing by the gate to the garden, watching the house. Keeton hesitated a moment longer, then trudged over to it.

Only the gate separated them. Keeton was shivering inside his heavy overcoat, but his body burned with heat. The hood was low over the woman's head and he could not tell which of the three she was. She must have been aware of his unspoken thought since she looked up slightly, turning to regard him. As she did so, Keeton realised she had been staring past him. A white mask gleamed from below the woollen cape.

"It's you, then . . ." Keeton whispered.

Distantly, moving down the slope from the earthworks on Barrow Hill, he saw two other hooded figures. As if aware that he had noticed them, they stopped and seemed to shrink into the whiteness of the land.

He said, almost bitterly, "I was beginning to understand. I had begun to understand. And now you're abandoning me . . ."

In the house, the child cried out. White Mask glanced towards the landing window, but the cry was another transient moment of disturbance. Keeton watched the ghost woman and couldn't help the tears that surfaced to sting his eyes. She looked back at him and he thought he saw some hint of her face through the thin holes that were the eyes.

"Listen to me," he said softly. "I have something to ask you. You see, they've lost their son. He was shot down over Belgium.

They've lost him and they'll grieve for years. If you take the
daughter, now . . . if you take her now . . ." he shuddered, wiped
a hand across his eyes and took a deep breath of the frozen air.
White Mask watched him without movement, without sound.
"Give them a few years. Please? If you don't want me . . . at least
give them a few years with the child . . ."

White Mask slowly raised a finger to the lips of the chalk-
smeared wood which covered her face. Keeton could see how old
that finger was, how loose the skin on the hand, how small the
hand.

Then she turned and ran from him, her dark cloak billowing,
feet kicking up the snow. Half way across the field she stopped and
turned. Keeton heard the shrill sound of her laughter. This time,
as she ran, it was away to the west, towards the shadow wood,
Ryhope Wood. On Barrow Hill her companions were running
too.

Keeton knew the country well. He could see at once that the
three figures would meet at the edge of Stretley Stones meadow,
where five ogham stones marked ancient graves.

He was both relieved and intrigued, relieved because White
Mask had agreed with his request; he was certain of it. They would
not come for Tallis, not for many years. He was certain of it.

And he was intrigued by the Stretley Stones, and by the ghost
women who were moving to rendezvous there.

The child would be safe . . .

He glanced round, guiltily. The house was in silence.

*The child would be safe for a few minutes . . . just a few minutes
. . . he would be back at the house long before Tallis's parents returned
from the Christmas service.*

Stretley Stones beckoned him. He pulled his coat more tightly
around him, opened the gate and waded out into the deep snow of
the field. He followed White Mask's tracks, and soon he was
running to see what they would do in the meadow where the
marked stones lay . . .

[THE HOLLOWER]

Earthworks

(i)

"So you still don't know the *secret* name of this place?" Mr Williams asked again.

"No," Tallis agreed. "Not yet. Perhaps not ever. Secret names are very hard to find out. They're in a part of the mind that is very closed off from the 'thinking' part."

"Are they, indeed?"

They had reached the bottom of Rough Field, walking slowly in the intense summer heat, and Tallis clambered over the stile. Mr Williams, who was an old man and very heavily built, manoeuvred himself across the rickety wooden structure with greater care. Half way across the stile he paused and smiled almost apologetically. *Sorry to keep you waiting.*

Tallis Keeton was tall for her thirteen years of age, but very thin. She felt helpless, watching the man; she felt certain that any steadying hand which she might offer would be useless. So she thrust her hands into the pockets of her summer dress and kicked at the ground, scuffing up the turf.

When he had crossed into the field Mr Williams smiled again, this time contentedly. He pushed a hand through his thick, white hair and rolled up his shirt sleeves. He was carrying a jacket over his arm. They began to walk on, then, towards the small stream which Tallis called Fox Water.

"But you don't even know the *common* name of the place?" he said, continuing the conversation.

"Not even that," Tallis said. "Common names can be difficult too. I need to find someone who has been there, or heard of it."

"So . . . if I understand correctly . . . what you are left with to describe this strange world which only you can see is your *own* name for it."

"Only my *private* name," Tallis agreed.

"Old Forbidden Place," Mr Williams murmured. "It has a good sound to it . . ."

He broke off, about to say more, because Tallis had rounded on him, a finger to her lips, dark eyes wide and concerned.

"What have I done now?" he asked, prodding the ground as he walked beside the child. It was high summer. The animal droppings in the fields buzzed with flies. The animals themselves were gathered in the shade beneath the trees which were grouped about the field. Everything was very still. The human voices seemed thin as old man and girl walked and talked.

"I told you yesterday, you can only say a private name three times between dawn and dusk. You've said it three times already, now. You've used it up."

Mr Williams pulled a face. "Terribly sorry . . ."

Tallis just sighed.

"This business of names," Mr Williams persisted after a while. They could hear the stream, now, tumbling over the stepping stones which Tallis had placed there. "*Everything* has three names?"

"Not everything."

"This field, for example. How many names?"

"Just two," Tallis said. "Its common name—the Hollows—and my private name."

"Which is?"

Tallis grinned, glancing up at her companion. They stopped walking. Tallis said, "This is Windy Cave Meadow."

Mr Williams looked around, frowning. "Yes. You mentioned this place yesterday. But . . ." He raised a hand to his forehead and shaded his eyes as he looked carefully from right to left. After a moment he said dramatically, "I see no caves."

Tallis laughed and raised her arms to indicate the very spot where Mr Williams stood. "You're standing in it!"

Mr Williams looked up, looked round, then cupped his ear. He shook his head. "I'm not convinced."

"You *are*!" Tallis assured him loudly. "It's a big cave and goes into the hill, only you can't see the hill either."

"Can you?" Mr Williams asked from the scorched meadow, in the middle of a farm.

Tallis shrugged mysteriously. "No," she confessed. "Well, sometimes."

Mr Williams regarded her suspiciously. "Hmm," he murmured after a moment. "Well, let's get on. I'd like to dip my feet in cold water."

They crossed Fox Water by the stepping stones, found a suitable, grassy piece of bank and slipped off shoes and socks. Mr Williams rolled up the legs of his trousers. They flexed their toes in the cool water. For a while they sat in silence, staring back up across the pasture, Windy Cave Meadow, to the distant dark shape of the house that was Tallis's home.

"Have you named all the fields?" Mr Williams asked eventually.

"Not all. The names for some of them just won't come. I must be doing something wrong, but I'm too young to work it out."

"Are you indeed?" Mr Williams murmured with a smile.

Ignoring the comment (but aware of its wry nature) Tallis said, "I'm trying to get to Ryhope Wood on my own, but I can't cross the last field. It must be very well defended . . ."

"The field?"

"The wood. It's on the Ryhope estate. It's a very old wood. It has survived for thousands of years according to Gaunt—"

"Your gardener."

"Yes. He calls it *primal*. He says everyone knows about the wood, but nobody ever talks about it. People are frightened of the place."

"You're not, though."

Tallis shook her head. "But I can't cross the last field. I'm trying to find another way to get there, but it's hard." She stared up at the old man, who was watching the water, lost in thought. "Do you think woods can be aware of people, and keep them at a distance?"

He pulled a face. "That's a funny thought," he said, adding, "Why not use its secret name? Do you know its secret name?"

Tallis shrugged. "No. Only its common names, and it has hundreds of those, some of them thousands of years old. Shadox Wood, Ryhope Wood, Grey Wood, Rider's Wood, Hood Trees,

Deep Dell Copses, Howling Wood, Hell's Trees, The Graymes
. . . the list is endless. Gaunt knows them all."

Mr Williams was impressed. "And of course, you can't just *walk*
across the field to this name-thronged forest . . ."

"Of course not. Not alone."

"No. Of course you can't. I understand. From what you told me
yesterday, I understand very well." He turned round, where he sat,
to peer into the distance, but there were too many fields, too many
slopes, too many trees between himself and Ryhope Wood for him
to have a view of it. When he looked back, Tallis was pointing
beyond the trees.

"You can see all my camps from here. In the last few months I've
heard a lot of movement in them. Other visitors. But they're not
like us. My grandfather called them *mythagos*."

"An odd word."

"They're ghosts. They come from *here*," she tapped her head.
"And here," she tapped Mr Williams's. "I don't understand
completely."

"Your grandfather sounds like an interesting man."

Tallis pointed to Stretley Stones meadow. "He died over there,
one Christmas. I was only a baby. I never knew him." She pointed
in the opposite direction, towards Barrow Hill. "That's my
favourite camp."

"I can see earthworks."

"It's an old castle. Centuries old." She pointed elsewhere.
"And that's Sad Song Meadow. There, on the other side of the
hedge."

"Sad Song Meadow," Mr Williams repeated. "Why did that
name come to you?"

"Because I can hear music sometimes. Nice music, but sad."

Intrigued, Mr Williams asked, "Singing? Or instruments?"

"Like—like wind. In trees. But with a tune. Several tunes."

"Can you remember any of them?"

Tallis smiled. "There's one I like . . ."

She "tra-la-laad" the melody, beating time with her feet in the
water. When she'd finished, Mr Williams laughed. In his own
gravelly voice he "da-da-daad" a similar tune. "It's called *Dives and
Lazarus*," he said. "It's an exquisite folk song. Your version,
though . . ." he frowned, then asked Tallis to hum the theme
again. She did. He said, "It sounds old, doesn't it? It's more

primitive. It's lovely. But it's still *Dives and Lazarus*." He beamed down at her. He had a twinkle in his eye, a way of raising his eyebrows that had made Tallis laugh since the first time she had met this man, two days before.

"I don't want to boast," he whispered, "But I once composed a piece of music based on that folk song."

"Not *another* one," Tallis whispered back.

"I'm afraid so. I've had a go at most things in my time . . ."

(ii)

They stood among the alders by the wide stream which Tallis called Hunter's Brook. It flowed from Ryhope Wood itself, then followed the shallow valleys between the fields and woods, coursing towards Shadoxhurst, where it disappeared into the ground.

Ryhope Wood was a dense tangle of summer green, rising distantly from the yellow and red of the brushwood that bordered it. The trees seemed huge. The canopy was unbroken. It stretched over the hill in one direction, and in the other was lost in the lines of hedges that extended from it like limbs. It looked impenetrable.

Mr Williams rested a hand on Tallis's shoulder. "Shall I take you across?"

Tallis shook her head. Then she led the way further along Hunter's Brook, past the place where she had first met Mr Williams and to a tall, lightning blasted oak that stood a little way out into the field from the dense tree hedge behind. The tree was almost dead, and the split in its trunk formed a narrow seat.

"This is Old Friend," Tallis said matter-of-factly. "I often come here to think."

"A nice name," Mr Williams said. "But not very imaginative."

"Names are names," Tallis pointed out. "They exist. People find them out. But they don't change them. They can't."

"In that," Mr Williams said gently, "I disagree with you."

"Once a name is found, it's fixed," Tallis protested.

"No it isn't."

She looked at him. "Can you change a tune?"

"If I want to."

Slightly confused, she said, "But then it isn't . . . it isn't the *tune*. It's not the first inspiration!"

"Isn't it?"

"I'm not trying to be argumentative," Tallis said awkwardly. "I'm just saying . . . if you don't first accept the gift as it is—if you change what you hear, or change what you learn—doesn't that make it weak somehow?"

"Why should it?" Mr Williams asked softly. "As I believe I've said to you before, the gift is not *what* you hear, or learn . . . the gift is being *able* to hear and learn. These things are yours from the moment they come and you can shape the tune, or the clay, or the painting, or whatever it is, because it belongs to you. It's what I've always done with my music."

"And it's what I should do with my stories, according to you," Tallis said. "Only . . ." she hesitated, still uncertain. "My stories are *real*. If I change them . . . they become just . . ." She shrugged. "Just nothing. Just children's stories. Don't they?"

Looking across the summer fields at the tree-covered earthworks on Barrow Hill, Mr Williams shook his head minutely. "I don't know," he said. "Although I would think that there are great truths in what you call children's stories."

He looked back at her and smiled, then leaned back against the split trunk of Old Friend and let the intense gleam settle in his eye. "Talking of stories," he said, "And especially of Old Forbidden Place . . ."

He slapped a hand to his mouth, realising what he had done as soon as he had spoken the words. "I'm terribly sorry!" he said.

Tallis rolled her eyes, sighing resignedly.

Mr Williams said, "But what about it, what about this story? You've been promising to tell it to me for two days now—"

"Only one."

"Well, one then. But I'd *like* to hear it before I have to—"

He broke off, glancing at the girl apprehensively. He suspected he would make her sad.

"Before you have to what?" Tallis asked, slight concern on her face.

"Before I have to go," he said gently.

She was shocked. "You're going?"

"I have to," he said with an apologetic shrug.

"Where?"

"Somewhere very important to me. Somewhere a long way away."

She didn't speak for a moment, but her eyes misted slightly. "Where *exactly?*"

He said, "Home. To where I live. In the fabled land of Dorking." He smiled. "To where I work. I have work to do."

"Aren't you retired?" Tallis asked sadly.

Mr Williams laughed. "For goodness' sake, I'm a composer. Composers don't retire."

"Why not? You're very old."

"I'm a mere twenty-six," Mr Williams said, looking up into the tree.

"You're eighty-four!"

His gaze reverted to her in an instant, his expression one of suspicion. "Someone told you," he said. "No-one could guess that well. But in any case, composers do *not* retire."

"Why not?"

"Because the music keeps coming, that's why not."

"Oh. I see . . ."

"I'm glad you see. And that's why I have to go home. I shouldn't be here at all. No-one knows I'm here. And I'm meant to be resting my bad leg. And all of this is why I'd like you to keep your promise to me. Tell me the story of . . ." He caught himself in time. "Tell me all about this strange place that is so forbidden and so old. Tell me about OFP."

Tallis looked concerned. "But the story isn't finished. In fact, there's hardly any of it at all. I've only learned little bits of the tale."

"Well, just tell me those bits, then. Come on, now. You promised. And a promise made is a debt to be paid."

Tallis's face, fair, freckled and full of sadness, seemed very child-like now. Her brown eyes glistened. Then she blinked and smiled and the child was gone, the mischievous young adult returned. "Very well, then. Sit in Old Friend. That's right . . . Here we go. Are you sitting comfortably?"

Mr Williams wriggled in the embrace of the tree, thought about the question and announced, "No."

"Good," Tallis said. "Then I'll begin. And no interruptions," she said sternly.

"I shall hardly breathe," he said.

She turned away from him, then slowly came round to face him again, a dramatic look in her eyes, her hands slightly raised for emphasis. "Once upon a time," she began, "there were three brothers—"

"So far very original," Mr Williams murmured with a smile.

"No interruptions!" Tallis said sharply. "That's the rule!"

"Sorry."

"If you interrupt at a crucial point you might change the story. And that would be disastrous."

"For whom?"

"For *them*! For the people. Now. Keep very quiet and I'll tell you all that I know about Old Forb—" She stopped herself. "About OFP."

"I'm all ears."

"Once upon a time," she began again, "there were three brothers. They were the sons of a great King. They lived in a big fortress and the King loved them all very much. So did the Queen. But the King and the Queen didn't like each other and he locked her away in a high tower on the great north wall . . ."

"So far, very familiar," Mr Williams interrupted mischievously. Tallis glared at him. He asked, "Were the sons called Richard, Geoffrey and John Lackland? Are we speaking of Henry the Second and Eleanor of Aquitaine?"

"No we are *not*!" Tallis declared loudly.

"My mistake. Do continue."

She took a deep breath. "The first son," she said, with a hard, meaningful look at her audience, "was called Mordred—"

"Ah. Him."

"In the King's language, a very old language, this name meant 'The Boy who would Journey'. The second son was called Arthur—"

"Another old friend."

"*Which*," Tallis said with a furious look, "in that same forgotten language meant 'The Boy who would Triumph'. The third son, the youngest, was called Scathach—"

"The new boy you mentioned."

"Whose name means 'The Boy who would be Marked'. These three sons were good at all things—"

"Oh dear," Mr Williams said. "How tiresome. Weren't there any daughters?"

Tallis almost shrieked her irritation with the impatient man in the tree. But then she looked confused. She shrugged. "There may have been. I'll come to that later. Now *don't* keep bursting in!"

"Sorry," he said again, his hand raised appeasingly.

"These three sons were good at sport, and at hunting, and games, and at music. *And,*" she said, "they loved their little sister very much. Although hers is a *different* story than this one!" She glanced at him sharply.

"But at least we know there was a sister."

"Yes!"

"And her brothers loved her."

"Yes! In different ways . . ."

"Ah hah. What different ways?"

"Mr *Williams!*"

"But it might be important . . ."

"Mr Williams! *I'm* trying to tell *you* the story!"

"Sorry," he said for the third time, in his smallest, most conciliatory voice.

Again the girl composed her thoughts, grumbling all the while. Then she raised her hands for total silence.

But even as she was about to speak the change went through her, the brief shuddering, the sudden whitening of her face which Mr Williams had witnessed just the day before. It was what he had been waiting for and he leaned forward, watching curiously and anxiously. The possession of the girl, for possession is what he imagined this to be, disturbed him no less now than it had before, and yet he was helpless to intervene. Tallis looked suddenly ill, rocking on her feet, looking so wan and gaunt that she might have been about to faint. But she remained standing, although her eyes became unfocused, staring straight through the man in front of her. Her hair, long and very fine, seemed to drift in an unfelt breeze. The air around her, and around Mr Williams, grew slightly chilled. Mr Williams could find no better word to describe this change than: eerie. Whatever possessed her would not harm her because it had not harmed her yesterday, but it changed her totally. Her voice was still the same girl's voice, but she was different, now, and the language she used—usually quite sophisticated for her age—suddenly became dramatically archaic.

He heard the slightest of movements in the underbrush behind him and twisted awkwardly where he sat to glance at the trees. He couldn't be sure, but for an instant he imagined he could see a hooded figure standing there, its face white and expressionless. Cloud shadow altered the quality of light on the face of the wood and the image of the figure had gone.

He turned back to Tallis, holding his breath, shaking with anticipation, aware that he was in the presence of something beyond his reason.

Tallis began to speak the story again . . .

The Valley of Dreams

Forty years the King lived and his sons were men, now. They had fought single combat and won many honours. They had fought in battle and won distinction.

There was a great feast in honour of the Ear of Corn. Ten stewards carried the mead to the King's table. Twenty stewards carried the quarters of the ox. The Queen's lady made bread that was as white as snow, and was scented with the autumn land.

"Who shall have the Castle?" asked the eldest son, emboldened by wine.

"By the Fair God, none of you," said the King.

"How so?"

"Only my body and the body of the Queen shall live in the Castle," said the Lord.

"That is a bad idea," said Mordred.

"On my word, it shall be that way."

"The broken haft of my seventh spear says I *shall* have a Castle," said the son, defiantly.

"You shall have a Castle, but it will not be this one."

There was a great argument and the three sons were made to stand on the flame side of the table and eat only with their shield hands. The King's mind was made up. When he was dead he would be buried in the deepest room. The outer chambers and all the courtyards would be filled with earth from the field of the Battle of Bavduin, from that great time in the history of the people. The fortress would become a huge mound in honour of the King. There would be one true way to the heart of the tomb, where the heart of the King could be found. Only a Knight of five chariots, a seven-speared, coldly-slaying, fierce-voiced Knight could find that way. For the others there would be only battle with the warrior ghosts of Bavduin.

In all of this, who gave a thought for the Queen? Only Scathach, the youngest son.

"In all this blood-earth," he said, "where will the heart of our Mother lie?"

"Unless my word dishonours me, where it falls!" said the Lord.

"That is a cruel thought."

"By the cauldron's thousand, put there by my own hand, that shall be the way."

Oh, but the Queen's heart was black. Black-hating, black-raging, black-furious for all but her youngest son. With a mother's kiss, this is what she said to Scathach. "When the time for my death is here, place my heart in a black box, which will be made for me by a wise woman."

"I shall do that gladly," said the son.

"When the heart is in the box, hide it in the Castle in an earth-filled room where the autumn rain can saturate it and the winter wind can move it as it moves the earth itself."

"I shall make sure of it."

She was a dark-hearted beauty, a rage-filled mother, wife of a great but cruel man. In her own death she would haunt that man, even as far as the Bright Realm.

At the time of the Bud on the Branch there was another great feast, and the King gave his sons Castles in the realm. For Mordred there was the Castle known as Dun Gurnun, a massive fortress built among the rich beechwoods in the east of the land. There were forty turrets on each wall. A thousand people lived within Dun Gurnun and none was ever heard to complain. The woods teemed with wild boar as tall as horses, and plump doves, and all of this hunting was for Mordred alone.

For Arthur there was the Castle in the south of the land, known as Camboglorn, high and proud turreted among the dense oak woods. It was built on a hill and there was a full week's riding around the winding road that led to its great oak gates. From its high walls there was nothing to be seen except the greensward, bloated with red deer and wild pig, sheltering crystal waters that were fat with silver salmon. All of this was Arthur's alone.

But what of Scathach, the youngest son? At this time he was away at war, fighting for the army of another king in a great, black forest. When he returned home his father hardly knew him. His scars were terrible, although his beauty was the same. But there are scars that cannot be seen and this son had been deeply wounded.

Now, when he saw how his elder brothers had been given fine
Castles with good hunting, he asked for his own. The King gave
him Dun Craddoc, but it was too draughty. He offered him Dorcic
Castle, but there were strange ghosts there. He suggested the
fortress known as Ogmior, but it stood on the edge of a cliff. The
youngest son rejected all of these and the King in a fury said this to
him. "Then you shall have no Castle made of stone! Anything else
is yours, if you can find it."

And from that day Scathach stood on the flame side of the table
and ate only with his shield hand.

Angrily, Scathach went to his mother. She reminded him of his
promise to help her to haunt the spirit of her husband in the Land of
the Fast Hunt, or in the Wide Plain, or the Many Coloured Realm,
wherever the King, in his death, should flee. Scathach had not forgotten and told her so with a son's kiss. So the Queen sent him to a
wise woman, and the wise woman kept him with her for thirty days,
between one moon and the next, while she sought in her ecstasy
among the Nine Silent Valleys for a Castle that would satisfy him.

At last she found it. It was a great and dark place, made of that
stone which is not true stone. It was deep in a forest, hidden from
the world by a circle of gorges and raging rivers, a place of winter.
No army could take that Castle. No man could live there and keep
his mind alive. No man could return to the world of his birth
without first transforming into the animal in his soul. But the
youngest son accepted it and travelled to Old Forbidden Place, to
mark its highest tower with his white standard.

Many years passed. Years without vision. In those years
Scathach's mother passed, by use of masks, into the realm of Old
Forbidden Place. And his brothers too, although they came only
as close as the closest gorge and peered at the Castle from that
distance, watching their sibling at the hunt, pursuing beasts that
are beyond description, for all things in this world were born from
the minds of men and since all men were mad, they were mad
creatures, madly running.

(iii)

It took a moment for Mr Williams to realise that Tallis had
stopped speaking. He had been staring at her, listening to the

words, to the story—which reminded him of the Welsh mythological tales he had often read—and now he saw how the colour flushed back to her cheeks, and awareness settled in her vacant gaze. She folded her arms and shivered, glancing round. "Is it cold?"

"Not really," he said. "But what about the rest of the story?"

Tallis stared at him, as if she didn't understand his words.

He said, "It's not finished. It was just getting interesting. What did the son do next? What happened to the Queen?"

"Scathach?" she shrugged. "I don't know yet."

"Can't you give me a hint?"

Tallis laughed. She was suddenly warm again, and whatever event had overtaken her had passed away. She jumped to a low branch and swung from it, causing a small shower of leaves to descend upon the man below. "I can't give you a hint about something that hasn't happened yet," she said, returning to the earth and staring at him. "It's a strange story, though. Isn't it?"

"It has its moments," Mr Williams agreed. Then quickly he asked, "What's so special about a Knight of five chariots and seven spears?"

She looked blank. "His number of single combats. Why?"

"Where was the battle of Bavduin?"

"Nobody knows," she said. "It's a great mystery."

"Why would the sons be made to eat with their shield hands?"

"They were in disgrace," Tallis said and laughed. "The shield hand is the coward's hand. That's obvious."

"And what exactly is a son's kiss?"

Tallis blushed. "I don't really know," she said.

"But you used the words."

"Yes, but they're just part of the story. I'm too young to know *everything*."

"What is 'that stone which is not true stone'?"

"I'm getting frightened," Tallis said, and Mr Williams smiled at her, raising a hand, ending the inquisition.

"You're a fascinating young woman," he said. "The story you have just told me is no story that you made up. It belongs in the air, in the water, in the ground . . ."

"Like your music," Tallis said.

"Indeed yes." He turned where he sat and glanced at the wood behind. "But *I* don't have a shadowy figure whispering to me when

I compose. I caught a glimpse of her. Hooded; white mask." He looked back at Tallis, whose eyes were wide. "I could almost *feel* the breeze between you."

He slipped from his uncomfortable perch in the heart of the dying tree. He brushed bark and insects from his trousers and then looked at his watch. Tallis stared up at him, suddenly gloomy.

"Is it time to go?" she asked.

"All good things," he said kindly. "This has been a wonderful two days. I shall tell no-one about them except *one* person, and that person I shall swear to secrecy. I have returned to one of the places of my first real vision, my first real music, and I have met Miss Tallis Keeton and heard four wonderful stories." He extended his hand towards her. "And I would like to live another fifty years, just so that I might know you. I'm like your grandfather, in that."

They shook hands slowly. He smiled. "But alas . . ."

They walked back across the fields until they came to the bridleway into Shadoxhurst. At once Mr Williams picked up his pace, raising his stick in a final farewell. Tallis watched him go.

When he was some distance away he stopped and looked back at her, leaning on his stick. "By the way," he shouted. "I've found a name for the field, the one by the wood."

"What is it?"

"Find Me Again Field. Tell it that if it argues, the old man will come and plough it up! It won't argue long."

"I'll let you know!" she shouted after him.

"Make sure you do."

"Write some nice music," she added. "None of that noisy stuff!"

"I'll do my very best," his voice came to her as his figure diminished, dwarfed by the trees that lined the bridleway.

"Hey!" she yelled.

"What now?" he called back.

"I haven't told you four stories. Only three."

"You're forgetting Broken Boy's Fancy," he shouted. "The most important story of them all."

Broken Boy's Fancy?

She saw him out of sight. The last she heard was his voice intoning the melody which he had earlier called *Dives and Lazarus*. What did he mean, Broken Boy's Fancy?

Then there were just the sounds of the earth and Tallis's laughter.

Broken Boy's Fancy

(i)

The child was born in September, 1944, and christened on a warm, clear morning at the end of the month. She was named Tallis in honour of the Welsh in the family, in particular of her grandfather, who had been a fine storyteller and who had much enjoyed the comparison of his skills with those of *Taliesin*, the legendary bard of Wales. It was said of Taliesin that he had been born from the earth itself, had survived the Great Flood, and told fine tales in the winter lodges of the warlord, Arthur.

"Why, I remember doing the very same thing myself!" her grandfather had often said to the younger, more easily influenced members of his family.

No-one had been able to find which woman's name was the same as that romantic figure of the early days, so "Tallis" was coined and the girl was christened.

This was only the first naming. It had been performed in the church at Shadoxhurst, an ordinary ceremony conducted by the old vicar. When it was over the whole family gathered out on the village green, around the hollow oak that grew there. In the bright day a picnic blanket was spread out and a frugal but enjoyable feast consumed. Wartime rationing had not affected the availability of home-fermented cider and eight flagons were emptied. By evening, Grandfather's spiky and amusing tales of legend had degenerated into a confused and incoherent sequence of anecdotes and recollections. He was led home to the farm in disgrace, and put to bed, but his last words on that last day of September were, "Watch for her second name . . ."

He had prophesied well. Three days later, at dusk, a commotion in the garden brought everyone running from the house. There they saw the great lame stag, known locally as Broken Boy. It had stumbled through the fence and was trampling over the autumn cabbage. In its panic it ran towards the apple shed, butted against the wood and snapped off a fragment of tine from its right antler.

All the adults had gathered on the lawn, watching the tall beast as it struggled to escape, but when Tallis's mother appeared, holding the infant, it became suddenly subdued, marking the ground with its hooves, but staring at the silent child.

It was a moment of both fear and magic, since no stag had ever come this close to them before, and Broken Boy was a local legend, a great hart of well in excess of fourteen years. What caused the creature to be held in such awe was that it seemed to have been known in the area for generations. Some years it would not be seen at all, then a farmer would notice it on a high ridge, or a schoolboy on the bridleway, or the hunt as it crossed farmland. The word would go out: "Broken Boy's been seen!" The hart had never been known to shed its antlers, and the velvet hung on the tines like filthy strips of black rag.

It was the Ragged Hart. The rags of velvet were rumoured to be shreds of grave shroud.

"What does it want?" someone murmured, and as if brought back to life by the sound of the words the stag turned, leapt over the fence and vanished into the gathering darkness, away towards Ryhope Wood, across the two streams.

Tallis's mother picked up the fragment of antler and later wrapped it in a strip of the infant's white christening robe, tied tight with two pieces of blue ribbon. She locked it away in the box where she kept all her treasures. Tallis was named Broken Boy's Fancy and was toasted as such well into the night.

When she was ten months old her grandfather sat her on his knee and whispered to her. "I'm telling her all the stories I know," he had said to Tallis's mother.

"She can't understand a word," Margaret Keeton replied. "You should wait until she's older."

That made the old man angry. "I *can't* wait until she's older!" he stated bluntly, and returned to the business of whispering in the infant's ear.

Owen Keeton died before Tallis had become aware of him. He had walked out across the fields one Christmas night and died, huddled and snow covered, at the base of an old oak. His eyes had been open and there had been a look of gentle rapture on his frozen features. Tallis remembered him in later years only in the family story of her name, and in the photograph that was framed by her small bed. And of course in the volume of folk stories and legendary tales which he had left for her. It was an exquisite book, finely printed and richly illustrated in full colour. There was an inscription to Tallis on the title page, and also a long letter from him, written in the margins of the chapter on Arthur, words conceived one winter in a desperate attempt to communicate across the years.

She did not read that letter with any real understanding until she was twelve years old, but one word caught her eye early on, a strange word—"mythago"—which her grandfather had linked by pen to Arthur's name in the text.

The Keetons' farm was a wonderful place for a child to grow up in. The house stood at the centre of a large garden in which there were orchards, machine sheds, greenhouses, apple sheds and woodsheds, and wild places hidden behind high walls, where everything grew in abundance and in chaos. At the back of the house, facing open land, there was a wide lawn and a kitchen garden, fenced off from the fields by wire designed to keep out sheep and stray deer . . . all except the bigger harts, it seemed.

From that garden the land seemed endless. Every field was bordered by trees. Even the distant skyline showed the tangled stands of old forest that had survived for centuries, and into which the deer fled for protection in the season of the hunt.

The Keetons had owned Stretley Farm for only two generations, but already they felt a part of the land, tied to the community of Shadoxhurst.

Tallis's father, James Keeton, was an unsophisticated and kindly man. He controlled the farm as best he could, but spent most of his time running a small solicitor's business in Gloucester. Margaret Keeton—whom Tallis would always think of as "severe but strikingly beautiful", after the first description of her mother she ever overheard—was active in the local community, and concentrated on managing the orchards.

The main running of the small farm was left to Edward Gaunt, who tended the garden and greenhouses too. Visitors always thought of Gaunt (he himself preferred the bare name) as the "gardener", but he was far more than that. He lived in a cottage close to the Keeton house and—after the war—owned much of the livestock on the farm. He was paid in many ways, and the best way—he always said—was from the sale of cider made from Keeton apples.

Tallis was very fond of Mr Gaunt, and in her early childhood spent many hours with him, helping in the greenhouses, or about the garden, listening to his stories, his songs, telling him stories of her own. Only as she grew older did she become more remote from the man, as she pursued her own strange interests in a secretive way.

Tallis's earliest memory was of Harry, her twice-lost brother.

He had been her half-brother, really. James Keeton had been married before, to an Irish woman who had died in London, early in the war. He had married again, very quickly, and Tallis was born shortly after.

Tallis had memories of Harry which were of a loving, gentle and, to a delightful degree, teasing man; he had fair hair and bright eyes, and fingers that never failed to find her funny-bones. He had returned from service action unexpectedly, in 1946, having been reported as 'missing, presumed dead'. She remembered him carrying her on his shoulders across the fields that separated their garden from Stretley Stones meadow where the five fallen stones marked ancient graves.

He had sat her in the branches of a tree and teased her with threats of leaving her there. His face had been burned—she remembered that blemish vividly—and his voice, at times, very sad. The burn had followed the crash of his aircraft when fighting over France. The sadness came from something deeper.

She had been just three years old when these memories became a part of her life, but she would never forget the way the whole house, the whole land, seemed to sing whenever Harry visited the farm; joy, perceived in her own childish way, despite the shadow which he carried with him.

She remembered, too, the angry voices. Harry and his step-mother had not been at ease with one another. Sometimes, from her small room at the top of the house, Tallis would watch her father and Harry walking arm-in-arm across the fields, deep in conversation, or deep in thought. During this time, which the child found immensely sad, the sound of the sewing machine, downstairs in the workroom, was like an angry roar.

Harry had come to the house at dawn, the summer of Tallis's fourth birthday, to say goodbye. She remembered him leaning down to kiss her. He had seemed hurt. Hurt in his chest, she thought. And when she asked him what was the matter he smiled and said, "Someone shot me with an arrow."

In the half-light his eyes had glistened and a single tear had dropped on to her mouth. He whispered, "Listen to me, Tallis. Listen to me. I shan't be far away. Do you understand that? I shan't be far away. I promise! I'll see you again, one day. I promise that with all my heart."

"Where are you going?" she whispered back.

"Somewhere very strange. Somewhere very close to here. Somewhere I've been looking for for years, and should have seen before now . . . I love you, little sister. I'll do my best to keep in touch . . ."

She lay there without moving, without licking away the salty taste of his tear on her lips, hearing his words again and again, marking them forever. Soon she heard the sound of his motorcycle.

That was the last she knew of him, and a few days later, for the first time, mention was made in the house that Harry was dead.

(ii)

Tallis became the tiny, confused witness of a terrible grief. The house became like a tomb, cold, echoing. Her father sat alone by the woodshed, his body slumped forward, his head cradled in his hands. He spent hours like this, hours a day, days a week. Sometimes Gaunt would come and sit with him, leaning back

against the shed, arms folded, lips moving almost imperceptibly as
he spoke.

Harry was dead. He had been an infrequent visitor to the family
home, although he didn't live far away, estranged by arguments
with his stepmother, and by something else, something which
Tallis did not understand. It had something to do with the war,
and with his burned face, and with the woods—with Ryhope
Wood in particular—and with ghosts. It was beyond her
understanding at this time.

Tallis found very little comfort in the house, now. When she
was five she began to create secret camps, a precocious activity for
one so young.

One hidden camp was in the garden, in an alley between two
brick machine sheds; a second by Stretley Stones meadow; a third
in the tangle of alder and willow that crowded part of the bank of
the stream called Wyndbrook; the fourth and favourite camp was
in a ruined sheep shelter among the earthworks, up on Barrow
Hill.

Each camp seemed to attract Tallis at a different time of year, so
that in summer she would sit and look at picture books by Stretley
Stones meadow, but in the winter, especially in the snow, she
would make her way to Barrow Hill, and huddle in the enclosure,
staring across Wyndbrook at the dark and brooding face of Ryhope
Wood.

Often, during these long months, she would see the black shape
of Broken Boy in the distance, but if she followed him he always
eluded her; just occasionally—always in spring—Tallis would
find his spoor close to her house, or see his furtive, lame movement
in the nearer fields and copses.

During these early years of her childhood she missed her parents
very much, missed the warmth that she had known so briefly.
Where once her father had talked to her when they had walked
together, now he strolled in thoughtful, distant silence. He no
longer remembered the names of plants and trees. And her
mother, who had always been so joyful and playful with her,
became pale and ghostly. When Margaret Keeton was not working
in the orchards she sat at the dining table, writing letters,
impatient with Tallis's simple demands upon her attention.

So Tallis found refuge in her camps, and after her fifth birthday
she took with her the book which her grandfather had left for

her, the beautiful volume of fables and folklore. Although she could not read the print with any great facility, she consumed the pictures and invented her own simple stories to go with the images of Knights and Queens, Castles and strange Beasts that were contained there.

Sometimes she stared at the closely packed handwriting that she knew was her grandfather's. She could hardly read a word of it, but had never asked her parents to read the letter to her. She had once heard her mother refer to the scrawl as "silly nonsense" and propose that they throw the book away and buy Tallis an identical copy. Her father had refused. "The old man would turn in his grave. We can't interfere with his wishes."

The letter, then, became something private to the girl, even though her parents had clearly read the text. For a few years, all Tallis could read was the beginning, which was written across the top of the chapter, and a few lines at the end of a chapter where the writing was larger because there was more space.

My dear Tallis: I'm an old man writing to you on a cold December night. I wonder if you will love the snow as much as I do? And regret as much the way it can imprison you. There is old memory in snow. You will find that out in due course, for I know where you come from, now. You are very noisy tonight. I never tire of hearing you. I sometimes think you might be trying to tell me your own infant's stories, to make up for all the tales I've whispered to you.

After that, the writing entered the margin of the first page and became cramped and illegible.

At the bottom of the page she was able to read that

He calls them mythagos. They are certainly strange, and I am sure Broken Boy is such a thing. They are . . .

And the text became illegible again.

Finally she was able to read the closing words.

The naming of the land is important. It conceals and contains great truths. Your own name has changed your life and I urge you to listen to them, when they whisper. Above all, do not be afraid. Your loving grandfather, Owen.

These last words had a profound effect upon the girl. A few days before her seventh birthday, while she was sitting in her camp by the clear water of Wyndbrook, she began to imagine she could hear whispering. It startled her. It was like a woman's voice, but the words were meaningless. It might have been wind in the branches, or the bracken, but it had a disturbing human quality; a voice for sure.

She turned round, where she sat, and peered into the bushes. She saw a shape moving quickly away and rose to her feet to follow it, trying to discern some form. She was half aware that the figure was small and seemed to have a hood over its head. It was walking swiftly towards the denser wood that led to Ryhope itself; it moved among the trees like a shadow, like cloud shadow, distinct, then indistinct, finally gone completely.

Tallis abandoned the chase, but not before she had noticed with satisfaction that the ferns close to the river bank were trampled down. It could have been the spoor of a deer, but she knew with certainty that she had been pursuing no animal.

By returning along the Wyndbrook, to her stepping stones, she could make her way across Knowe Field up to her camp on Barrow Hill. But as she reached the crossing place of the wide beck she hesitated, feeling cold and frightened. The trees were thinner here. Ahead of her was the rise of land, reaching up to a bare ridge, sharp against the blue sky; to the right, marked by a thin track, was the knoll of Barrow Hill, its summit thrown up into irregular grassy humps.

She had crossed Wyndbrook many times; she had walked that track, that field, many times. But now she hesitated. The wind-voice was gusting in her consciousness, that eerie whispering. She stared at Barrow Hill. It was its common name; it had been known as Barrow Hill for centuries. But it was not the *right* name, and Tallis felt a strong sense of dread that if she stepped on to that familiar turf she would be stepping somewhere that was now forbidden to her.

Clutching her book beneath her arm she crouched down and brushed her hand through the cold water of the brook.

The name came to her as suddenly as the dread she had earlier felt. It was Morndun Ridge. The name thrilled her; it had a dark sound to it, a storm-wind sound. With the name came a fleeting sequence of other images: the sound of wind gusting through hides, stretched on wooden frames; the creak of a heavy cart; the swirl of smoke from a high fire; the smell of fresh earth being thrown up from a long trench; a figure, tall and dark, standing, dwarfed by a tree whose branches had been cut from the trunk.

Morndun. The word sounded like *Mourendoon*. It was an old place, and an old name, and a dark memory.

Tallis rose to her feet again and began to step forward, out on to the stepping stones. But the water seemed to mock her and she drew back. She knew at once what was the cause of her concern. Although she knew the secret name of Barrow Hill, she hadn't yet named the stream. And she couldn't cross the stream without naming it or she would be trapped.

She ran back to her house, confused and frightened by the game she had started to play. She would have to learn *everything* about the land around the house. She had not known, until now, that every field, every tree, every stream had a secret name, and that such names would only come with time. Before she had found those names she would be a prisoner; and to defy the land, to cross a field without knowing its true name, would be to trap her on the other side.

Her parents, not unnaturally, considered the game to be "more silly nonsense", but after all, if the game stopped her going too far from home, who were they to complain?

During the course of that year, Tallis managed to transform the land around her house, pushing back the borders week by week. Each season she was able to go a little further from the house, further into her childish, dreamlike realm.

She soon found a route back to Morndun Ridge—Wyndbrook's secret name was Hunter's Brook—and the animal enclosure which was her favoured hide-out.

Now only a single field remained between her own realm and the dense tangle of dangerous woodland on the Ryhope estate which had so fascinated her brother Harry. The field's name defied her. She stood at the edge of Hunter's Brook, beyond the thick cluster of alders that formed her camp, and stared up that ramp of verdant land at the dimly seen darkness of the far wood.

The name would not come. She could not cross the pasture.

Each day, after school, she walked about the ramparts on Morndun Ridge, weaving between the thorns and hornbeam which grew there, each tree tapping the deep soil of the high banks. And it was here that she felt most at peace, now. The shadowy figure which she had seen those several months ago still prowled behind her, and her head reeled with strange thoughts: sights and sounds, smells and the touch of wind; she was never far from the borders of another land as she came up on to the breezy knoll and spent time in the enclosure built by ancient hands for a forgotten purpose.

It was here, too, that she first saw White Mask, although she didn't apply this name to the mythago until later. Glimpsed from the corner of her eye, the figure was taller than the first, and quicker, moving more rapidly through the trees, stopping then running on in an almost ghostly way. The white mask caught the sun; the eyes were elfin, the mouth a straight gash, sinister.

But when this figure came close to her, one Sunday afternoon, Tallis dreamed of a castle, and of a cloaked figure on horseback, and of a hunt that took this knightly man deep into a dank and marshy forest . . .

It was the beginning of a tale that would build in her mind over the weeks, until it almost lived within her.

The field by Ryhope Wood continued to defy her. Day after day she stood by Hunter's Brook, eight years old and drawn to the dark forest by something deeper than reason, struggling to find the *name* for the swathe of land that prevented her from crossing to the trees.

Then, one August evening, a tall, dark stag broke cover in the far distance. Tallis gasped with delight, stretched on to her toes for a better view. She hadn't seen the beast for two years and she shouted at it. Trailing rags of velvet from the great cross of its antlers, the proud creature raced over a rise of land and out of sight, but not before it had hesitated once and glanced her way.

(iii)

"I've seen Broken Boy," Tallis said that evening, as the family sat at the table and played a game of ludo.

Her father glanced at her, frowning. Her mother rattled dice in the cup and threw on to the board.

"I doubt if you did that," James Keeton said quietly. "That old boy was killed years ago."

"He came to my christening," Tallis reminded him.

"But he was wounded. He couldn't have survived the winter."

"Mr Gaunt told me that the stag has been seen in the area for over a hundred years."

"Gaunt is an old rogue. He likes to tell stories to impress children like you. How could a stag live so long?"

"Mr Gaunt says that it never sheds its antlers."

Margaret Keeton passed Tallis the cup of dice, shaking her head impatiently. She said, "We know full well what silly nonsense Gaunt spreads around. Now come on. It's your go."

Tallis just watched her father, though. He was looking better, these days, not so pale, although his hair was almost totally grey now, and his eyes had a watery sadness about them. "I'm sure it was Broken Boy. It was limping as it ran. And its antlers were covered with rags. Death shrouds . . ."

"Will you *play*, girl?" her mother said irritably. Tallis picked up the cup and shook out the dice, moving her counter around the board. She looked back at her father. "Couldn't it have been him?"

"Broken Boy was wounded the last time we saw him. Arrow shot."

Arrow shot. Yes. Tallis remembered the story. And she remembered something else.

"Like Harry," she whispered. "Arrow shot, like Harry."

James Keeton stared at her sharply and for a moment Tallis thought that he was going to start shouting. He remained calm, however. He suddenly sat back heavily in his chair, hands resting on the table. He looked into the middle distance. Margaret Keeton sighed and cleared the board away. "It's no fun playing with you two." She glared at Tallis. "Why did you bring the subject of Harry up? You know how it upsets your father . . ."

"I'm not upset," the man said quietly. "I was just thinking . . . it's really time we went to find that house. I've been putting it off, but maybe we'll learn something . . ."

"If you think it will help . . ." Tallis's mother said.

Tallis asked, "What house?"

Her father glanced at her, then smiled. He ignored the question. He said, "How would you like a picnic tomorrow?"

"I'd like a picnic tomorrow," Tallis agreed matter-of-factly. "What house?"

He winked at her and raised a finger to his lips.

"Where are we going?" Tallis insisted.

All he said was, "Across the fields and far away."

The next day, being Sunday, began with the early morning service at the church in Shadoxhurst. At ten o'clock the Keetons returned home and packed a picnic hamper. Shortly before noon the three of them set off across Windy Cave Meadow, towards Fox Water and beyond. They followed a dry track along the dense hedgerows between adjacent farms, and very soon Tallis realised, with a combined sense of fear and excitement, that they were walking towards Ryhope Wood.

Because she was in company she realised that she could enter the Nameless Field between Hunter's Brook and the wood itself, and she stepped on to the forbidden grass with a sense of great triumph. Half way across she started to run, leaving her parents behind. As she came closer to the dense and formidable wall of thorn and briar that was the wood's scrub, the ground became marshy. The grass here was tall and straw-like, almost as high as her shoulders in places. It rustled in the summer breeze. She moved steadily and carefully through this silent undergrowth, almost lost in it, until the high wall of oaks loomed over her. She stood and listened to the sounds in the darkness beyond the trees. Although she could hear bird song there were other noises that were more enigmatic.

Her father called to her. As she turned she glimpsed something from the corner of her eye, a human shape, watching her. But when she looked more closely it had gone.

She felt an instant thrill of fear. Her mother often lectured her about the "gypsies" who inhabited the woods, and how dangerous it was to talk to strangers, or walk alone after dusk. But the only gypsies Tallis had seen had been Romanies, in colourful wagons and colourful clothes, dancing on the village green.

That shadow, that briefly glimpsed shape, had not been colourful . . . it had been dun coloured and tall . . . odd in every respect.

She waded back through the long grass, took off her canvas shoes and squeezed the water out. Then she followed her parents further round the wood.

Soon they came to a narrow, bumpy road, bordered by high hedges and banks and flanked by two wind-blasted beeches where it came over the horizon. At some point, distantly, it must have connected with the main road between Shadoxhurst and Grimley. But here, where it entered Ryhope Wood, it was cracked and overgrown, as if it had been suddenly torn apart by a violent earth movement.

"Good God," James Keeton said, and added, "This must be the old road, then. Gaunt's 'rough track'."

At the woodland edge a thin fencing of barbed wire had been erected. The KEEP OUT notice was prominent but weathered.

Tallis was aware that her father was concerned. Margaret said to him, "You must have made a mistake. Perhaps it's further on . . ."

"I can't have made a mistake," her father said, exasperated. He stood by the barbed wire holding on to it, looking up at the trees, staring into the darkness. Finally he drew away and looked around at the farmland.

"There was a house here, once. I'm sure of it. A lodge of sorts, called Oak Lodge. Gaunt assured me that there was. At the end of the rough track, he said."

He paced along the weathered road, then turned back to look at the thick woodland. "It's where Harry came. It's where my father came before the war. To visit those historians . . . Huxley. And the other one . . . Wynne-Jones."

"Before my time," Margaret said.

They stared at the broken road, where it vanished into the dense growth. Tall oaks, crowding together, cast an unwelcoming darkness on the tangle of haw and blackthorn and rose briar below. The high grass growing among the edgewood waved in a gentle breeze. The notice rattled on its perch and the rusting wire shook.

A strange expression touched James Keeton's face and Tallis realised that her father had suddenly become very frightened. He was pale, his eyes wide. And his breathing was quick, nervous.

Tallis stepped right up to the wire and stood there, staring through the gloom. As she watched that earthy darkness so she began to see a gleam of light, sunlight in a clearing a long way beyond the outer line of trees.

"There's a glade in there," she said, but her father chose to ignore her. He was walking away from the wood. He stood on the earth bank lining the road and stared into the distance. Her mother had spread out the picnic cloth below a solitary elm and was unpacking the hamper.

"There's a glade in there," Tallis repeated loudly. "The house might be in the glade."

Her father watched her for a moment, then stepped off the bank, ignoring his daughter. He walked towards the elm, saying, "Gaunt must have been mistaken. You're right. But I can't believe it . . ."

"Daddy! There's a *glade* in the wood," Tallis called.

"Don't go too far away," he called back, and Tallis, her body tense with excitement, sagged a little.

He was not listening to her. He was so wrapped up in his own thoughts, his own concerns, that the fact that the house might be abandoned in the wood was refusing to register.

There had been a house here, and now it was gone. Tallis stared at the road, at the way its rough concrete surface was sheared off, as if by a knife, as if it had been consumed by the wood, eaten whole. Perhaps that same bite had swallowed the lodge, an entire house overwhelmed by trees.

Where this strange thought came from she didn't know, but the image was there, as clear in her mind as the images from the fairy-tales she had read all her life.

Dark forests, and remote castles . . . and in the yellow, sunlit glades, there were always strange treasures to be found.

She trod on the lower wire and cautiously lifted the barbs above it, ducking through as best she could. She looked back at her parents, who were sitting on the rug, sipping tea and talking.

Turning, she started to walk through the undergrowth towards the patch of brightness ahead of her.

She could still feel the cracked and fragmented road, hard beneath her thin shoes. Roots sprawled across the concrete and low branches had to be brushed aside as she stepped cautiously forward in the gloom. She came closer to the glade and was able to see that it was a small clearing, enclosed by enormous, dark-trunked oaks. Dead branches, cracked and twisted by winter winds, rose starkly above the foliage.

She could also see the sheer rise of a brick wall. There were two windows on that wall, the glass in them long since gone. Branches of the overwhelming wood hung from them, like dead limbs.

She took another step, pushing aside a sprawling web of

red-berried thorn. Now she could see that in the centre of the clearing, in front of the house, was a tall, wooden pillar. Its top was carved in the vague semblance of a human face, simple slanted eyes, a gaping mouth, the slash of a nose. The wood looked rain-blackened and rotten, split vertically and crumbling. Tallis felt deeply uncomfortable as she stared at it . . .

Edging her way around this hideous totem pole, she stepped into the garden of what had once been the house called Oak Lodge. The first thing she saw was a shallow fire-pit, cut into the wild turf that was all that remained of the lawn. Animal bones were scattered around and she saw the burned remains of sticks which had been used in the fire.

She called out nervously. She had the strongest sense of being watched, but could see no betraying detail or movement. Her voice, when she called, was almost dead in the confined space; the heavy trunks of the besieging oaks absorbed her words and replied only with the quiver of bird life in their branches. Tallis patrolled the small garden space, observing everything: here, the remains of a wire fence; there, impaled by roots, several slats of wood which might have come from a chicken coop, or kennel.

And dominating all, casting its sombre shadow over the small clearing: the carved trunk, the totem. Tallis touched the blackened wood and it broke away in handfuls, exposing seething insect life beneath. She stared up at the angry features, the evil eyes, the leering mouth. She could see how the shape of legs and arms had been added to the column, now corroded almost into obscurity.

This ancient effigy watched the house; perhaps it was keeping guard on it.

The house itself had become a part of the forest. The floors had burst open under the pressure of trees growing up from the cold earth below. The windows were framed by leafy branches. The roof had been punched through in the same way and only the high chimney stacks rose above the tree tops.

Tallis looked into two rooms; first, a study, its French windows hanging loose, its desk covered with ivy, its space dominated by an immense V-shaped oak trunk. Then, the kitchen. There were the mossy remains of a pine table in this small room, and an old cooker. Branches stretched like vines across the ceiling. The pantry was completely empty. When she picked up a cast-iron saucepan from the hook on the wall she nearly jumped out of her skin as the twig that had burrowed through the brick beneath it sprang out, released from its confined space.

When she peered into the parlour she was daunted by the tree growth that occupied every foot of the room, crushing furniture, embracing walls, penetrating the faded, framed pictures.

Tallis returned to the garden. The sun, high overhead, made it difficult for her to look up at the grinning totemic figure carved on the immense trunk of wood. She wondered idly who had erected the statue, and for what purpose . . .

Everything about the clearing by the ruined house suggested to her that it was a *living* place, that someone used it. The fire-pit was old; the ash had been compacted by many rains, and the bones had been dragged about the garden by animals. But there was a sense of occupation, not unlike the occupation of an occasional camp—a hunter's camp, perhaps.

Something moved past her, swiftly, silently.

She was startled. Her eyes were still dazzled by the brilliance of the sun, glimpsed partially against the corrupt outlines of the wooden effigy. She had the idea that it was a *child* running past her. But it had swiftly vanished into the undergrowth, the same patch of wood from which she had earlier made her cautious entry into this small, abandoned garden.

All around her there was movement in the woodland, an enigmatic and frustrating flickering at the edge of her vision. It was a sensation with which she had become quite familiar, and it did not alarm her.

She must have *imagined* the child.

She felt suddenly very calm, very peaceful. She sat down by the immense carved trunk, glanced up at the jagged outlines against the bright sky, then closed her eyes. She tried to imagine this house when it had been used. Her grandfather would have told her about it. Perhaps his words could be made to surface from the primitive, infant parts of her mind.

Soon she imagined a dog prowling the garden; chickens pecking the ground, roaming free. There was the sound of a wireless drifting through the open door from the kitchen, where a woman worked on the pine table. The French windows were swinging free; she could hear voices. Two men sat around the desk, examining the relics of the past they explored through their own minds. They were writing in a thick book, scratching out the words . . .

A young man walked by the garden fence, fresh-faced, tanned from the sun.

Then the sun paled and a biting wind chilled her. Snow piled high; black clouds swirled above her. The snow drove at her remorselessly, freezing her to her bones—

Through the storm a figure walked towards her. It was bulky, like a bear. As it came into vision she could see that it was a man, heavily clad in furs. Icicles hung from the white animal's teeth that decorated his chest. His eyes glittered like ice, peering at her from the blackness of hair and beard.

He crouched. He raised his two hands, holding a stone club. The stone was smooth and black, brightly polished. The man was crying. Tallis watched him in anguish. No sound came from him—the wind and the snow made no sound—

Then he opened his mouth, threw back his head and screamed deafeningly.

The scream was in the form of a name. Tallis's name. It was loud, haunting and harrowing and Tallis at once emerged from her daydreaming, the perspiration breaking from her face, her heart racing.

The clearing was as before, one side in deep shadow, the other bright with sun. Distantly her name was being called, an urgent sound.

She walked back the way she had come, glancing into the ruined study where the oak tree filled a room whose cases, cabinets and shelves were shattered by time and weather. She noticed the desk again. She thought of the dream image of the two men writing. Had her grandfather whispered to her about a journal? Was there a journal to be found? Would it mention Harry?

She retraced her steps to the edge of the wood. At the last moment, as she walked through the darkness, she saw a man's figure, standing out on the open land. All she could see of him was his silhouette. It disturbed her. The man was standing on the rise of ground, immediately beyond the barbed-wire fence. His body was bent to one side as he peered into the impenetrable gloom of Ryhope Wood. Tallis watched him, sensing the concern . . . and the sadness. His whole posture was that of a saddened, ageing man. Motionless. Watching. Peering anxiously into a realm denied him by the fear in his heart. Her father.

"Tallis?"

Without a word she stepped forward into the light, emerging from the tree line and stepping through the wire.

James Keeton straightened up, a look of relief on his face. "We were worried about you. We thought we'd lost you."

"No, Daddy. I'm quite safe."

"Well. Thank God for that."

She went up to him and held his hand. She glanced back at the wood, where a whole different world was waiting in silence for the visitors who would come to marvel at its strangeness.

"There's a house in there," she whispered to her father.

"Well . . . we'll leave it for the moment. I don't suppose you saw any sign of life?"

Tallis smiled, then shook her head.

"Come and eat something," her father said.

That same afternoon she made her first doll, compelled to do so, but not questioning from where that compulsion might have come.

She had found a piece of hawthorn, twelve inches long, quite thin; she stripped off the bark and rounded one of its ends using a knife which she'd borrowed from Gaunt's workshop. It took some effort. The wood was unseasoned, but still very hard. When she tried to carve the eyes she found that even making simple patterns was strenuous activity. The end result was recognisably anthropomorphic, but only just. Nevertheless Tallis felt proud of her Thorn King, and placed him on top of her dressing table. She stared at him, but he didn't mean anything. She had tried to copy the hideous pole in the garden-glade, but she had come nowhere close. As such, this, her first experiment with woodcraft, was empty; meaningless.

But an idea came to her and she went to the woodshed, picking her way through the cut elm until she found a thick log. It was still in its bark. This, she carefully detached and cut in half, to make a curved sheet that she could fashion into a mask.

Back in her room she worked into the evening, cutting the rectangular wood down to a roughly face-shaped oval. Elm bark is hard and she found, again, that her tiny strength, even with the sharp knife, could only make slow progress in chipping and slicing. But soon she had gouged out two eyes, and scratched a smiling mouth. Exhausted, sitting among the shards, she took out her paint box and painted concentric green rings about each eye, and a red tongue poking from the scratch of the lips. The rest of the bark she painted white.

When she placed this on the dresser, and stared at it, she decided to call it the *Hollower*.

When her father entered the room, a few minutes later, he was surprised and shocked at the mess. "What on earth . . . ?" he said, brushing the wood shavings from Tallis's bed. "What have you been doing?"

"Carving," she said simply.

He picked up the knife and checked the edge. He shook his head and looked at his daughter. "The last thing I need now is having to sew your fingers back on. This is terribly sharp."

"I know. That's why I used it. But I'm careful. Look!" She held up two bloodless hands. Her father seemed satisfied. Tallis smiled because, in fact, she had cut the *back* of her right hand quite badly, but had a plaster on the gash.

Her father came over to the two monstrosities on her dressing table. He picked up the mask. "It's ugly. Why did you carve this?"

"I don't know."

"Are you going to wear it?"

"One day, I expect."

He placed the mask against his face and peered at the girl through the tiny eyeholes. He made low, mysterious grumbling sounds and Tallis laughed. "You can hardly see anything," he said, lowering the bark face.

"It's the Hollower," she said.

"It's the what?"

"The Hollower. That's the mask's name."

"What's a Hollower?"

"I don't know. Something that watches holloways, I suppose. Something that guards the tracks between different worlds."

"Gobbledegook," said her father, though he sounded kindly. "But I'm impressed that you know about holloways. There are several around the farm, you know. We walked along one today . . ."

"But they're just *tracks*," she interrupted impatiently.

"Very *old* tracks, though. One of them runs through Stretley Stones meadow. Stretley, you see? It's an old word for street. The stones probably mark a crossroads." He leaned forward towards her. "Men and women dressed in skins and carrying clubs used to walk along them. Why, some of them probably stopped right here, where the house now stands, to eat a haunch or two of uncooked cow."

Tallis pulled a face. It seemed to her that the notion of eating raw meat was silly. Her father wasn't a very convincing storyteller.

"They're still just old roads," she said. "But some of them . . ." she lowered her voice dramatically. "Some of them led away deep into the land, and wound around the woods, and suddenly *disappeared*. The old people used to mark those places with tall stones, or great pillars of wood carved into the likeness of a favoured animal, pillars made out of whole trees . . ."

"Did they indeed?" her father said, watching his daughter as she prowled about the room, hands raised, body tensed, as if she was stalking an animal.

"Yes. Indeed they did. These days we can still see the stones, out in the fields and on the hills, but the old gates have been lost. But hundreds of years ago, when you were still young—"

"Thanks very much."

"*Thousands* of years ago, those places were forbidden to anyone except the Hollowers. Because they led to the kingdoms of the dead . . . And only a *few* ordinary people could go there. Only heroes. Knights in armour went there. They always took their dogs, enormous hunting dogs, and they pursued the great beasts of the Underworld, the giant elks whose antlers could scythe down trees, the huge, horned pigs, the belly-rumbling bears, the man-wolves which walked on their hind legs and could disguise themselves as dead trees.

"But sometimes, when one of the hunters tried to get back to his own Castle, he couldn't find the holloway, or the stones, or the wood, or the cave . . . and he became trapped there, and ever more ghostly, until his clothes were like ragged grave-shrouds on his body, and his swords and daggers were red with rust. But if a man had a good *friend*, then the good friend would go and rescue him. *If* . . ." she added with a final dramatic flourish, raising the wooden mask to her face and imitating her father's jokey growl, "*if* . . . the Hollower would allow it . . ."

Eight years old and she had shamed his "raw haunch of cow". James Keeton stared at his daughter in astonishment.

"Where on earth did you get all that from? Gaunt?"

"It just came to me," she stated honestly.

She was without doubt her grandfather's girl. Her father smiled and conceded defeat.

"Did you enjoy the walk today?" he asked by way of changing the subject.

She stared at him, then nodded. "Why didn't you come with me? Into the wood?"

Her father just shrugged. "I'm too old to go gallivanting around in woodland. Anyway, there was a KEEP OUT sign up. Can you imagine what would happen to my business if I was prosecuted for trespassing?"

"But the *house* was there. You came all that way to see the house, and then gave up! Why?"

Keeton smiled awkwardly. "KEEP OUT signs mean what they say."

"Who put the sign up?"

"I have *no* idea. The Ryhope estate, I expect."

"Why didn't they rescue the house? Why did they just leave it? All overgrown, all run down. But it still has furniture in it. A table, a cooker, a desk . . . even pictures on the wall."

Her father stared at her, frowning slightly. He was clearly astonished by what she was telling him.

"Why would they do that?" Tallis persisted. "Why would they just leave the house to be overgrown?"

"I don't know . . . I just don't know. Really! I have no idea. I have to admit, it seems very strange . . ."

He went over to the window and leaned heavily on the sill, looking out into the clear evening. Tallis followed him, thoughtful, then determined.

"Did Harry go to that house? Is that where Harry went? Is that where you think he died?"

Keeton drew a deep breath, then let it expire slowly. "I don't know, Tallis. I don't know anything any more. He seems to have told you far more than he ever told me."

She thought back to the evening when Harry had said goodbye to her. "I told you everything I remember. He was going away, he said, but he would be very close. He was going somewhere strange.

Someone had shot him with an arrow . . . that's all I remember. And he was crying. That too."

Her father turned and dropped to a crouch, hugging her. His eyes were wet. "Harry didn't say goodbye to us. Only to you. Do you know something? That has been hurting me more than anything, all these years."

"Perhaps he didn't expect to be gone very long."

"He was dying," James Keeton said. "He must have thought he was protecting my feelings by not saying goodbye. He was dying . . ."

"How do you know?"

"I just do. There was something about him, those last few weeks . . . something resigned."

When Tallis thought about Harry, she couldn't imagine him as dead and cold in the ground. She shook her head. "I'm sure he's still alive. He's just lost, that's all. I'm sure he'll come home to us."

Her father said kindly, "No, darling. He's in heaven now. We shall all have to come to terms with the fact."

"Just because he's in heaven," Tallis protested, "doesn't mean to say he's dead."

Her father straightened up again, smiling and resting his hand on her shoulder. "It must be a wonderful world in there . . ." he tapped her head. "Full of giant elks, and knights in armour, and dark castles. A hundred years ago they'd have burned you as a witch . . ."

"But I'm not a witch."

"I don't suppose any of them were. Come on. Supper time. And you can tell us another story before you go to bed."

He laughed as they walked from the room. "It's usually the parents who get pestered to tell the bedtime stories to their offspring, not the other way round."

"I've got a good one," Tallis said. "It's about a man whose son goes for a walk in the woods, and the man is so certain that his son has been eaten by wolves that he can no longer see the boy, even though he's right there, in the house."

"Cheeky little devil," her father said, tugging her hair before racing her down to the parlour.

(iv)

Some of the tension in the house faded, after that. James Keeton seemed a little brighter, more cheerful, and Tallis imagined this was because he had finally expressed his feelings about Harry to her. She remained puzzled by his apprehensive behaviour outside the wood, but her mother said simply, "He thought he *needed* to see the place where Harry went; now he realises he doesn't *want* to."

It was a confusing and unsatisfactory explanation, but it was all she got.

Nevertheless, Tallis herself felt considerably more at ease, now, and after school she continued to explore and to name the territory around the farm. She also developed her skills in carving the masks and small wooden dolls which had become an obsession. She was continually aware of the fleeting figures which pursued her when she journeyed across the meadows, but they no longer startled her, nor worried her. Whenever she was close to the enclosed pasture known as Stretley Stones, her peripheral vision seemed to have a life of its own, a flowing, quivering world of movement that could never be observed directly, but which hinted at strange human shapes, and lurking animal forms.

And there were sounds: singing, from the field known as The Stumps, but whose secret name now became Sad Song Meadow. Tallis never saw the source of the singing, and after a while stopped searching for it.

More dramatically, one day, sitting and daydreaming in the field by Fox Water, she woke to find herself in the mouth of a wide, windy cave, staring out across a lush, dense forest towards high mountains where a blazing wall of fire and smoke could be glimpsed distantly. The strange dream lasted for a second only, and thereafter she was aware of the windy cave only fleetingly, the merest touch of an alien breeze on an otherwise perfectly still, hot day.

She soon established that there were three of the cowled, female figures which seemed to haunt the edge of her vision, hovering in the denser woodland thickets, watching her through painted wooden masks. Tallis began to get an idea that the strange things happened to her whenever one of these women was close

by. When White Mask was hovering her mind filled with fragments of stories and the land seemed to speak to her of lost battles
and wild rides. When the woman with the green mask was around
she got ideas for carving, and about carving, and saw odd shadows
on the land. The third figure, whose mask was white, green and
red, made Tallis think of her own "Hollower"; this figure she
associated with such strange glimpses as the windy cave and the
sad song.

It made little sense beyond the idea of being "haunted", and for
a while she was not concerned by it. But she fashioned masks to
copy those of the "storyteller" and the "carver". As she did so, so
names came to her . . .

The white mask she called *Gaberlungi*, an odd name, but one
which made her smile as she said it. Gaberlungi was *memory of the
land*, and sometimes when she wore or carried the crudely
fashioned oak-bark the stories crowded and jostled her mind with
such intensity that she could concentrate on nothing else. The
third mask, made from hazel and painted green, she called
Skogen, but this, too, had a second name, *shadow of the forest*.
It was a landscape mask; when she held it to her face, the
cloud shadow on the land seemed different: it cast patterns
that might have been the shadows of higher hills and older
forests.

Over the years she became an expert at the craft; she worked
masks from different wood, became skilful at trimming down the
bark and cutting the holes for eyes and mouth. She developed, or
purloined, a number of tools to make the crafting easier, even
using differently-shaped heavy stones as hammers, chippers and
gougers.

To the first three she added four more. *Lament* was the simplest;
a few days after carving this from willow bark she heard the first of
several songs from the field called The Stumps; she was also aware
of the haunting presence of the female "hollower", her white and
red mask catching the grey light of an overcast day as she watched
Tallis from the hedges. Lament was a sad mask, its mouth sullen,
its eyes tearful; its colour was grey.

More exciting, more intriguing to her, were the three journey
masks which she was inspired to carve. *Falkenna* had a second
name: *the flight of a bird into an unknown region*. She disliked carrion
birds, but was fascinated by the small hawks which preyed above

the grass verges of the country roads. So Falkenna was painted in such a way as to suggest a hawk.

Then there was the *Silvering*. Patterned with the dead features of a fish, painted in coloured circles, this mask had a quieter name, a name associated with an unconscious image: *the movement of a salmon into the rivers of an unknown region.*

Finally there was *Cunhaval: the running of a hunting dog through the forest tracks of an unknown region.* She used snips of fur from the family dog to fringe the elder wood.

She had made seven masks and ten dolls; she had invented several stories and named most of the fields, streams and woods around the farm. She had her hideouts, and an association with the ghosts that hovered at their edges. She was happy. She was still very anxious to return to the ruins of Oak Lodge, but the field between the wood and her farm, and the stream that bordered it, still defied her efforts to discover their secret names.

But all of this was a game to her, a part of growing up, and whilst she approached the game with the utmost seriousness, she had never given a thought to the consequences of what she was doing . . . or of what was being done to her.

All that changed shortly before her twelfth birthday, an event, an encounter, which disturbed her deeply.

On a bright and stiflingly hot July morning, she smelled woodsmoke as she walked through her garden. Woodsmoke, and something else. She smelled winter. It was a scent so familiar it was unmistakable, and she followed the trace to the narrow alley between the brick machine sheds, where she had her garden camp. She had not used this camp for a while and the alley was gloomy and choked with nettles. At its far end it was blocked by the filthy glass of one of the greenhouses that backed on to the sheds.

She was about to force her way along the passage when Mr Gaunt appeared in the garden, coming from one of the orchards. He stopped and suspiciously sniffed the air.

"Have you been playing with fire, young madam?" he asked quickly.

"No," Tallis said. "Not at all."

He came right up to her, his brown overalls heavy with the smell of freshly dug earth. He wore these overalls in all weathers and must have been roasting in them on a hot day like today. His forearms were bare and burned brown, covered with a thick down of white hair. His face was very lean—he was well named—but flushed with bright red blood-vessels that seemed to trace a path to his thin hairline. Great beads of sweat rolled across the craggy contours of his face; but his eyes sparkled, a mixture of kindness and mischief.

Tallis stared up at the tall man. Gaunt turned his grey eyes upon her. "I smell woodsmoke. What have you been up to?"

His accent was a rich, almost incomprehensible country sound, which Tallis had to listen to quite carefully. She herself spoke "very well", which is to say she took elocution lessons at school to lose the rough, rustic corners of her speech.

"Nothing," she said, then elaborately repeated, "Nuth'n!"

Gaunt looked along the nettle-way between the buildings. Tallis felt her face flush. She didn't want the gardener going down there. The dark alley was her secret place and in some way, after the brief and disorientating experience of a few moments before, it belonged to her even more.

It was with relief, then, that she watched Gaunt turn away from the alley. "I can smell burning. *Someone's* burning something."

"Not me," Tallis said.

The gardener drew a filthy rag from his pocket and mopped his face, squinting up into the sun and drying the creases of his neck. "It's a hot day all right. I do believe I shall have some cider." He looked down at the girl. "Come and have some cider, young madam."

"I'm not allowed."

The man smiled. "'m allowun un," he said softly.

He led the way to the row of wooden sheds at the far side of the garden where a rickety bench leaned against them in the shade. Tallis followed him into the cool apple shed and past the racks of rotting apples. She liked the smell here. It was damp and mouldy, but tinged with a fruity odour. The apples were brown and shrivelled and covered with a fleecy mould. Water dripped somewhere, a tap not turned off tightly enough. Rusting fragments of old farm equipment were scattered around the walls, mostly swathed in lacy cobwebs. Light broke into the sheds through splits and cracks in the ancient slatted roof.

At the far end of the shed, in the light-tinged gloom, was a tall barrel, covered by a heavy stone lid. China flagons lined the walls. Tallis had often been here, but had never seen inside the barrel. Gaunt slid the stone lid aside and peered at the contents. Then he looked at Tallis with a smile. "This looks like good cider. Try some?"

"All right," she said, and the man chuckled.

"Got a good fermentation going," he murmured, then reached in and drew out an enormous dead rat. Liquid drained from its fur as he swung it before the girl's horrified eyes. "Him'll rot right down soon. Give extra taste. But the cider'll be drinkable by now. Now, young Tallis, how much would you like?"

She couldn't speak. The black monster dangled from his fingers and he dropped it back with a splash, the age-old tease repeated with great success. Tallis shook her head. Gaunt chuckled again.

She couldn't believe it was really cider in the barrel. It was almost certainly rainwater and the rat was just one of Gaunt's many victims. But she couldn't be sure . . . she couldn't absolutely convince herself. So when he filled a pewter mug from one of the china flagons she refused that too, backing out of the apple shed.

Gaunt looked puzzled. "Good cider, young Tallis. Nothing wrong with it at all. Rat's all dissolved away nicely." He peered into the mug. "Just a couple of teeth, one of its feet, but that's all right. Pick those out, no trouble."

"Nothing for me, thank you."

"Please 'nself."

They sat outside the woodshed, in the shade, watching the wide garden, the shadow of clouds. Gaunt drained his pewter tankard and smacked his lips. Tallis kicked at the shed below the bench, trying to think of something to say, wondering if she should risk asking about the vanished house in the wood. Gaunt knew about it, but she had never dared broach the subject. Something, some fear, held her back.

She was suddenly aware that he was looking at her. She glanced up and frowned. His stare was intense, searching, and she thought he was about to quiz her further about the woodsmoke. But he said, "You ever seen a ghost?"

Tallis tried to hide the sudden alarm she felt; she watched the old man carefully, her mind racing; what should she say? Finally she shook her head.

Gaunt didn't seem satisfied. "Not down by Stretley Stones?"

"No."

"Not down by Shadox Wood?"

"No . . ." she lied.

"I seen you playing by the meadow . . ." he leaned close and whispered, "I heard how you went to find the old house in the Shadox . . ." Straightening up: "And you're telling me you an't ever seen a ghost? Don't believe 'n."

"An't no such 'n thing as ghosts," Tallis mimicked in the strong Gloucestershire dialect. "What'n seen bin rayle."

"Don't you make fun of me, young Tallis."

Tallis couldn't help smiling. "What I saw was *real*," she repeated. "No ghosts, just shadows."

Gaunt chuckled, then nodded. "What else to see in Shadox Wood than shadows?"

"Why do you call it 'Shadox Wood'? It's Ryhope Wood . . ."

"It's called a thousand names," Gaunt said bluntly. He waved his hand around, then banged the bench. "This was *all* Shadox Wood once. Even this, where we're sitting. It was once the wood. This seat, this garden, this shed, that damned house . . . all made from Shadox Tree." He looked down at Tallis, thoughtful. "It's the old name for the whole area, you should know that. Not just the village but the whole land. Shadow Wood. Been called that for centuries. But not shadows like sun shadows, more like . . ."

When he had hesitated for a few seconds, Tallis ventured, "Moonshadows?"

"Aye," said the man softly. "More like that. Shadows in the corner of the eye. Shadows that creep out of the dreams of sleeping folk, folk like you and me; people who live on the land."

"Moondreams," Tallis whispered, and at once, without her bidding, a mask formed in her mind's eye, an odd mask, an eerie picture that she thought should be carved from . . . should be carved from . . .

Before the species of wood which would be appropriate for the mask could come to mind, Gaunt had interrupted the moment of creation.

"So you seen real things, eh? Down by the Shadox."

"I've seen hooded figures—"

She was instantly aware of Gaunt's startled reaction, but she chose to ignore it. She went on, "There are three of them.

Women. They keep to the hedgerows, the undergrowth. And I've seen other things; men with twigs in their hair, and animals that look like pigs, but are too tall and have black hides. I've heard singing, I've felt wind on windless days, and I've seen tall trees carved into horrible faces." She looked up at Gaunt, who was staring fixedly ahead, into the garden. "And I've felt snow in the middle of summer, and heard bees in the middle of winter—"

This last was a lie; just this. She waited for a response, but Gaunt was quite still.

"Sometimes I've heard horses," she said; well, she had *imagined* horses, just once, about a week ago. "Knights on horseback, riding on the other side of the hedges. That's about all. I keep hoping to find out something about Harry."

Gaunt did rise to that last, pointed little statement. He said, "You ever hear the growlers?"

"Growlers? No."

"Roaring? Like bulls?"

"No."

"A man screaming?"

"No screaming. Not man, not woman, not child. Not laughing. Just singing."

"People see all kinds of things out beside the Shadox," Gaunt said after a while. "And by Stretley Stones. By the stream. All the trees there link up with the Shadox . . ."

"If they're ghosts," Tallis ventured, "whose ghosts are they?"

Gaunt said nothing. His arms were folded, the empty tankard held in his right hand. He was staring vaguely across the garden to the distant meadows.

Tallis said, "Have you ever been to the old house? The trees have grown right through it. People live there."

After a moment Gaunt said, "Nothing lives there. That old house is dead and gone."

"But Grandad visited the man who owned it . . ." Gaunt twitched but remained silent. Tallis went on, "And Harry visited the place. That's where he went the night he disappeared . . ."

Gaunt slowly turned to look at her, watery eyes narrowed, expression one of alarm, then suspicion. "You really been to Oak Lodge?"

"Yes. Once . . ."

"You see the writing?"

She shook her head. Gaunt murmured, "The man who lived there wrote things down. That's why your grandad went to visit. He wrote things down, but no-one believed what he wrote . . ."

"About the ghosts?"

"About the ghosts. About the *Shadox*. They say the word 'shadox' is as old as the first folk who walked up the rivers to settle here. So our village has the oldest name in England. It's no wonder people see ghosts around. The man at Oak Lodge, he called them something else . . ."

Tallis remembered the odd word from what little of her grandfather's letter she had bothered to read. "Mythagos . . ."

Again, Gaunt was startled, but all he said was, "They come from dreams. From shadows, moonshadows. That's what you said. You were right. He wrote about them. I didn't understand what your grandfather was talking about. Things from the unconscious. *Symbolic* things. Ghosts that we all carry. Ghosts that can be brought alive by trees . . ."

"People are living in the house," Tallis said again, quietly. "I saw their statues. I saw their fires. I dreamed about them . . ."

Abruptly, Gaunt turned his tankard upside down so that the dregs dripped on to the lawn. He rose to his feet and disappeared into the apple shed again. When he emerged he was buttoning up his brown overalls. "Cider needed topping up," he said, and Tallis grimaced with disgust, causing the old man some amusement. He sat down again, folded his arms and leaned back against the shed, his eyes narrowed. His whole attitude changed suddenly; Tallis could feel both the awkwardness in him, and the menace.

In a low voice he said, "I seen you making dolls, young Tallis. Wooden things. I seen you carving them . . ."

He seemed to be accusing her of something terrible and this confused her, silencing her for a few moments as she watched the far side of the garden and thought what to say.

"I like making dolls," she murmured after a while. She looked up at the solemn face of the gardener. "I like making masks too. I make them out of bark."

"Do you indeed," Gaunt said. "Well, I know what they're for. Don't think I don't."

"What *are* they for?" she muttered irritably, still looking away from him to where the family's dog prowled by the far brick wall.

He ignored the sullen question, asking instead, "Who showed you how to carve? Who showed you the making?"

"No-one!" Tallis said sharply, confused again. "No-one showed me."

"Someone must've showed you. Someone whispered to you . . ."

"Anybody can make dolls," Tallis said defiantly. "You just take a bit of wood, and a knife from the shed, and sit down and cut. It's easy."

Even as she spoke, she had an image of Green Mask, but she struggled hard not to let that enigmatic figure confuse her conversation, now.

"It's easy for them as knows," Gaunt said quietly. Then he stared back at Tallis, who met his gaze unflinchingly for as long as she could bear. His grey eyes, dark-rimmed, stared so hard at her from the flushed, weatherbeaten face that at last she gave in and looked away.

He said, "There's dolls for playing with, young madam. And there's dolls for praying with. And as sure as pigs have ticks you don't play with the dolls you make."

"I do. I play with them all the time."

"You hide them in the ground. And you give them names."

"All dolls have names."

"Your dolls don't have Christian names, and that's for sure."

"My dolls' names are my own business," she said.

"Your dolls' names are the devil's business," Gaunt retorted, and added almost inaudibly, "Broken Boy's Fancy . . ."

He rose stiffly from the bench and rubbed the lower part of his back. As he walked away across the garden Tallis watched him, puzzled by what she felt to be his sudden anger, saddened by it. She couldn't think what she had done. He had been friendly, chatty, then abruptly turned hostile; just because of her dolls.

Gaunt called back, "You're your grandfather's girl, all right."

"I don't remember him," she said, kicking beneath the bench, her knuckles white where she gripped the seat.

"Don't you just . . ." Gaunt said, then turned in the middle of the lawn to stare back at the girl. He thought hard for a moment, then came to a quick decision. "All I want to know is . . . if I ever ask you for help . . . and I don't mean now, not yet, not for a while . . . but if I ask you for help . . ."

He hesitated and Tallis thought that he looked nervous, more uncomfortable than she had ever seen him, watching her in a knowing, almost fearful way. "If I ask you for help," he repeated, "*will* you help?"

"Help what?" she said back, equally nervous and very puzzled. She really didn't understand what he was talking about.

"Will you help me," he said again, putting strange emphasis on the words. "If I ask for help . . . will you help me!"

She didn't answer for a moment. Then, "What killed the rat?"

After the briefest of pauses Gaunt smiled thinly, shaking his head as if to say, "Clever little so-and-so". "You'd bargain with me, would you?"

"Yes," Tallis said. "I'll bargain with you."

"Water," he said quietly.

"I thought so," Tallis said. She shrugged. "Yes. I'll help. Of course I'll help."

"That's a promise then," he said, and wagged a finger. "And a promise broke is a life choked. We'll call this one 'Gaunt's Asking'. Don't forget."

Tallis watched him go, her small body shaking, deeply disturbed by his words. She liked Mr Gaunt. He was disgusting, and he teased her, and he always smelled of sweat; but he was a comforting presence and she could not imagine life without him. He told her silly stories and showed her bits and pieces of nature. Sometimes he got irritable with her, sometimes he seemed unaware of her. But until today he had never confronted her.

She liked him and of course she would help him . . . but in what way? What had he meant by that? *Help* him. Perhaps he had meant help him to make dolls, but that seemed unlikely. And why had he been so *upset* by her dolls (and where had he seen her making them?). Her dolls were things that were special to her, part of her game. They had meaning for Tallis Keeton, but for no-one else. They were fun, and they were magic, but their magic was a special magic and had nothing to do with the gardener, or her parents, or anyone else.

A few minutes later, when she went back to her camp between the sheds, the smells of woodsmoke and winter had gone. Perhaps she had been mistaken. And yet the thought of a fire, burning somewhere out of sight, intrigued her.

She found a stick of firewood and took it back to her room.

Using her own tools she blunted the sharp edges, rounded the head and cut a deep gouge for the neck. She carved eyes that were closed and a thin mouth that smiled, adding two hands and crossed legs. She patterned the hair as flame. She returned this fire doll to the alley, throwing it to the far end, close to the grimy greenhouse glass.

She waited at the end of the alley for a while but the doll did not call back the fire: that scent of snow and woodsmoke had slipped away, out of the summer's heat.

Someone—an invisible someone. The whole conversation with Gaunt became very meaningful suddenly. He had referred to Tallis as 'her grandfather's girl'. He had echoed something that she had read in her grandfather's letter in the book of legends: *I urge you to listen to them when they whisper . . .*

She walked slowly back to her room. She sat on the bed, her masks around her, the book on her lap. She peered at the book through the eyes of each mask. She felt most comfortable with the Hollower, her first mask and the crudest. How many masks would she make, she wondered? Perhaps there would be no end to them. Each time she went to the enclosure on Barrow Hill she came back with the idea for another mask. Perhaps she would be inspired to make them all her life.

She opened the book of folk-tales. She turned slowly through the pages, looking at the knights and heroes, the castles, the gorges and forests, the wild hunts. She lingered on the image of Gawain, his clothes like a Roman tunic, his helmet oddly skull-like and made of burnished bronze. She turned to the picture called The Riders to the Sea, which had been marked in pen with a large exclamation sign. It showed four knights on horseback, riding hard, bent low over the withers of their mounts, cloaks streaming as they escaped a terrible, dark storm.

Eventually she turned to her grandfather's letter. She felt strongly that it was time for her to read the words. It was seven years since it had been "given" to her, four years after the old man's death.

My *dear Tallis*
I'm an old man writing to you on a cold December night

She forced herself to read the most legible parts of her grandfather's message to her, even though she was familiar with them already. She hesitated at

there is old memory in snow
And stared for a long time at
*I sometimes think you might be trying to tell me your own infant's
stories, to make up for all the tales I've whispered to you.*

Frowning, she began to unravel the whole of the text, which
she had ignored for all these years.

(v)

*My dear Tallis: I'm an old man writing to you on a cold December
night. I wonder if you will love the snow as much as I do? And regret
as much the way it can imprison you. There is old memory in snow.
You will find that out in due course, for I know where you come from,
now. You are very noisy tonight. I never tire of hearing you. I
sometimes think you might be trying to tell me your own infant's
stories, to make up for all the tales I've whispered to you.*

*Your mother says you cannot understand a word. I think differ-
ently. White Mask; and Ash; and the Bone Forest; and the Ragged
Tree. Do they mean anything to you? I'm sure they do. I'm sure as
you read these words you are seeing images. One day you will
understand completely.*

*Tomorrow is Christmas Day. It will be your second yuletide, and
it will be my last. I've known seventy Christmas nights. I can
remember every one of them. I can remember goose stuffed with fruit;
and partridges as fat as pigs; and hares the size of deer; and puddings
that cracked oak tables. I wish you could have been there with us, in
those lovely days, before this war. We are rationed now. We have
one chicken and five sausages, and that is our yuletide fare, although
Gaunt, who works for us, has hinted at eggs. For all of this poverty, I
wish you were here now, aware and alert. I wish I could know you in
days to come. It is agony, to an old man like me, to imagine how you
will be just ten years on, a noisy child I expect, and mischievous, and
imaginative. I expect you will look like your mother. I can almost see
you. But long before you read this, long before you are grown up, I
shall be in the shadowlands.*

*Think kindly of me, Tallis. Someone has played a mean and brutal
trick upon us, sending one to the hidden places of the earth before they
have sent awareness to the other. But there will always be a link*

between us, just as there will always be a link between Harry and myself, and perhaps you and Harry too. Harry was flying over Belgium. He was shot down. Everyone believes he is still alive, but for myself, I fear the worst. We have heard nothing of your brother for four months, now. If he does come back, I shall be gone, I fear; and if it is true, if the worst is true, then only you are left. Only you.

How do I explain something to you that I hardly understand myself?

They first came to the edge of the wood four years ago. There were three of them. They tried to teach me but I was already too old to learn. I could not grasp their ways. But I learned the stories. I have kept this quiet, of course, although Gaunt suspects. He is a local man. In his own words: half this bedammed land is growin' on the ashes of us Gaunts! That may be true, but he did not call them to the edge.

Harry went away to war. So they lost him too. But now that you are here they have started to come again. They will tell you the other stories, all the stories. I know so few. But they will show you more than they have ever shown me, I'm sure of that. Who are they? Who knows! There is a man living on the other side of the wood who has made a study of them. He calls them mythagos. They are certainly strange, and I am sure Broken Boy is such a thing. They are perhaps from some mythological place, long forgotten. They are like ghosts. I expect you will see them before long. But do not think of them as ghosts. Do not think of them as spiritual forces. They are real. They come from us. Again, how and why I do not know with any real understanding. But I have given you a book, this book, whose pages I am completing with my letter to you, and when you read it, when you read these fairy tales, these stories of brave knights and sinister castles, you are reading about them, only you will not recognise them at first.

If it happens to you as it has happened to me, then everything in the wood that is strange is you. You are the beginning and the end of it, and there is a purpose which perhaps you will discover. I have lived in fear of what would happen to me. They were coming closer; I had begun to smell a terrible winter, far more terrible than this snowy Xmas eve. I was close to being taken to that forbidden place . . . and then you were born and the wood pulled back. I was abandoned. It is all around us, Tallis. Do not be deceived. Do not think of open land as open land, or a brick house as something permanent. The Shadow

Wood is all around us, watching, biding its time. We bring alive ghosts, Tallis, and the ghosts huddle at the edge of vision. They are wise in ways that are a wisdom we all still share but have forgotten. But the wood is us and we are the wood! You will learn this. You will learn names. You will smell that ancient winter. And as you do so, you are treading an old and important pathway. I began to tread it first, until they abandoned me.

Look at Broken Boy. I have made my own mark upon that ragged tree. When you have done the same it will mean that you are ready for the riders. Look at the picture in the book. Have you heard them yet? Have you heard the horses? Count the figures, and count the hooves. Did the artist know? All things are known, Tallis, but most things are forgotten. It takes a special magic to remember them.

You are Tallis. You are Broken Boy's Fancy. These are your names. All things have names, and some things more than one. The whisperers will teach you. The naming of the land is important. It conceals and contains great truths. Your own name has changed your life and I urge you to listen to them, when they whisper. Above all, do not be afraid.

Your loving grandfather, Owen.

It was late evening. Tallis finished the letter and rubbed her eyes, weary with the effort of translating the old man's scrawl. The words of his message were at once sinister and reassuring. Her own grandfather had somehow *known* of the strange life that his granddaughter would lead! He had implied, indeed, that for a while at least he had lived a similar life.

Tallis ran her fingers over the tightly packed words; once so meaningless, now she could recognise meaning in every shaky line.

It was as if she had been holding back. This letter, with its odd and enticing content, had been hers for seven years, but she had resisted reading it. Perhaps she had known that the contents would make no sense until certain of the patterns had begun to repeat for her. She would never have understood the letter when she had been five years old; nothing had *happened* to her when she had been five years old . . .

But now. Like her grandfather, she had heard horses, riders . . . Like her grandfather, she had seen figures at the edge of vision, and the three figures at the edge of the wood, the masked women

. . . they had come for the old man first. He had known them; they had retired; they had come again.

And grandfather Owen, too, had experienced a strange winter. An ancient winter, he had called it, and Tallis was disturbed by that allusion.

For the first time in her short life it came home to her that something was being *done* to her. She was playing games, but there was more to it than that. Her games had a purpose. Everything, suddenly, seemed to have a purpose . . .

These ghosts—the mythagos—they had been here when her grandfather had been alive, watching him, *doing* things to him, whispering to him . . .

Do not be afraid.

Now they had returned to watch Tallis herself. There was something in the thought that made her apprehensive, but she was at once calmed by the very presence of the letter.

Do not be afraid!

What could their purpose be? To show her the making of masks? Of dolls? Of stories? Of names?

But *why*?

The wood is us and we are the wood.

Everything in the wood that is strange is you. You are the beginning and the end of it.

Then had *she* made the masked women? Out of her . . . out of her moondreams? Then how could they have known her grandfather? Had she also made the song, the twiggy figures, the riders, the cave . . . the smell of snow? Perhaps she had simply remembered her grandfather's stories to her, whispered when she was a child, unconsciously remembered when she was grown up.

Or was it true what Gaunt had said, that *everyone* carried such ghosts in their heads? These symbolic things, fragments of a past, carried forward in the moonshadows at the back of the thinking mind . . .

Moonshadows.

Dreams.

Harry . . .

When you were born I was abandoned.

Tallis stared at the last page of writing, then turned back to the picture of The Riders to the Sea. She counted the figures—four knights riding like the wind—then counted the hooves.

There were eighteen in the picture!

So that is what he had meant. Four riders but five horses, the riderless animal shown only by its extended front legs as it raced in tow with the others.

All things are known, but most things are forgotten. It takes a special magic to remember them.

She read these words again then closed the book and shut her eyes, leaning back against the pillow and letting the images and voices of her brief past flow through her mind . . .

As she drifted into sleep she was remembering Harry, leaning close, his eyes glistening with tears . . .

I'll see you again one day. I promise that with all my heart.

In the middle of a summer night, an ancient winter began to blow. At first there was just the cold breeze, the crisp smell of snow; then there was the sound: a storm raging. Then the feel, an icy touch on her face, a snowflake blown from a time ten thousand years lost, eternally forgotten. The flakes came through from the other world like frozen petals, instantly destroyed by the humid heat of the August night.

Tallis watched them without moving. She was on her knees between the brick sheds, her garden camp, called there by a voice from her dreams. The fire doll was buried in the ground before her. She was quite calm. The wind from that icy hell gusted into the still summer and caught her hair, made her eyes water. She watched the thin line of grey, storm grey, a vertical slash in the dark air before her, half her standing height. From this unguarded gate came the sound of people, the wailing of a child, the nervous whinny of a horse. And the smell of smoke, a fire burning to keep the warmth in the bones of those who waited.

Darkness; except for that strip of pale winter, a thread of the past hovering before her wide, unfrightened eyes.

The wind whispered, and on that wind came the hint of a voice.

"Who's there?" Tallis called, and at once there was confusion beyond the gate. A torch flared—Tallis could see its brilliant yellow flicker—and someone came close to the gate and peered through. Tallis almost believed that she could see the gleam of firelight in the eye that watched her. The horse, several horses, became restless. And then a drum began to beat, a rapid, frightened rhythm.

The human shape in the winter world shouted. The words were like nightmare speech, familiar yet meaningless.

"I don't understand!" Tallis called back. "Are you one of the whisperers? Do you know who *I* am?'

Again there was just the confused gabble of words. A child began to laugh. On the cold wind came the smell of sweat and animals, like the smell of hide taken from a deer. A woman started to sing.

"My name is Tallis!" the girl called. "Tallis! Who are you? What's your name?"

Her words were met by the sound of anguished cries. The dark shapes moved in that other world, blocking out the light of the torch, then exposing it again. The flame guttered in the fierce, freezing wind, and even as Tallis listened so she heard the distant fire begin to roar, and wood crackle; the darkness beyond the gate began to glow with the faintest hint of burnished gold.

Riders were coming. She could hear their rapid clatter on loose stones, their angry cries, the noise of horses, forced to scramble on dangerous slopes.

She tried to count them. Four horses, she thought. Four animals. But she quietly acknowledged that she had no real way of telling; more than one . . . not more than a lot!

She listened carefully. The arrival of the riders had caused movement, shouting, chaos. One of them—a man—cried out, angrily. A dog barked, panic stricken. The wailing child wailed even louder. Wind, gusting coldly, made the bigger fire suddenly roar and flare so that frantic dark movement became fleetingly visible against the brightening glow of the sky glimpsed through the gate.

And it was at that moment that she heard her name shouted.

For a second she was almost too stunned even to think. Then the man's voice began to familiarise itself to her. She remembered her early childhood and Harry's laughter. She heard again his teasing words as he imprisoned her on the lower branches of the oak by Stretley Stones field. The two voices danced around each other: that from the summer of her past; that from the fire-raging winter of the underworld.

And instantly they fused, because they were the same.

"Tallis!" her brother shouted, from a place that was so close yet so far. "Tallis!"

And his voice thrilled her; there was desperation in it; and sadness. And longing; and love too.

"Tallis!" for the last time: a lingering cry, shouting to her through the strip of no-place that separated her from that forbidden place of winter.

"Harry," she screamed back. "Harry! I'm here! I'm with you!"

Snow gusted through the gate. Acrid smoke made her choke. One of the horses screamed and Tallis could hear the way its rider urged it calm.

"I've lost you," Harry called to her. "I've lost you, and now I've lost everything!"

"No!" Tallis shouted back to him. "I'm here . . ."

The cold wind blew her back. She could hear the storm beyond the gate, and the restless sounds of the frightened people who gathered there. She looked up, looked around. If only there were some way of opening this narrow strip of contact!

And even as she shouted, "I'll come to you, Harry . . . wait for me!" Even then, the gate was fading.

Had he heard those last words? Was he waiting there, crouched in the cold, watching the thin-space, the thread of contact, still rejoicing at the glimpse of his fair-haired, freckled sister? Or was he weeping, feeling abandoned by her?

She felt her own tears rise to sting her eyes, and she rubbed them fiercely. Taking a deep breath she sank back on her ankles and stared at the darkness, listening to the silence. There was the briefest of movements on the other side of the greenhouse glass, and Tallis glimpsed the white flash on the mask she called the Hollower. The figure had been there all the time, then.

Her hand was cool with her smudged tears, but there was a deeper cold, the cold of the snow that had settled on her flesh. This vision had been no dream. And if the snow was real, then so had been her brother's voice, and the contact with the forbidden world in which he wandered, lost, lonely, and from the sound of him : . . very much afraid.

Lost. In a world whose name she did not know. She called it Old Forbidden Place. Everything was right about that private name.

Tallis stood up and went out into the garden, balancing on the lower bars of the gate to the fields. It was a bright, starlit night. She could see clearly Morndun Ridge and the clustered trees on the earthworks of the old fort. In the stillness she could hear the faint sound of water running, probably in Fox Water. All around her, in fact, she could see hints, or hear sounds, of the night life that existed on the land . . .

All around, that is, save in the direction of Ryhope Wood, the wood which was the source of Harry's sadness. There, that sombre forest was a void within the darkness, a dizzying black emptiness that seemed to suck her towards it, a small fish to a great and all-consuming mouth.

(vi)

The clatter of a pot in the kitchen of the house disturbed Tallis's reverie. She didn't know how long she had been standing at the gate, staring across the silent land, but it was dawn, now, and the sky was rich with colour over Shadoxhurst village.

Her body felt fresh and energetic, almost excited, and she ran to the back door, bursting into the kitchen. The action was so sudden, so startling, that her mother dropped the pan of water she was carrying to the stove.

"Good God Almighty, child! You've taken ten years off my life!"

Tallis made an apologetic face, then stepped round the great spill of water to pick up the copper pan. Her mother was up earlier than usual. She was still in her dressing gown, her hair held inside a red head-scarf. She wore no make-up and her eyes were bleary as they watched the girl.

"What on earth have you been doing?" her mother asked, drawing her robe tighter. She took the pan from Tallis and passed her one of the ragged and smelly floorcloths.

"I stayed up all night," Tallis said. She got down on her knees and started to help soak up the cold water.

Her mother regarded her cautiously. "You've not been to bed?"

"I wasn't tired," Tallis lied. "It's Sunday, anyway—"

"And we're going to Gloucester, to the Cathedral, and then to Aunt May's."

Tallis had forgotten the annual outing to Aunt May and Uncle Edward's. It was a visit she did not relish. The house always smelled of cigarette smoke and sour beer. The kitchen was usually full of washing, hanging on lines strung across from wall to wall;

and though the bread they served for tea was always crusty, the only spread they ever used was a lumpy, yellow mayonnaise. Her cousin Simon, who also went to visit on these occasions, called it "sick spread".

They cleared up the mess. Tallis could hear her father moving about in the bathroom. She wished he was here too when she spoke for the first time about the strange and wonderful thing that had happened. But then, as she watched her mother draw fresh water for the eggs and set it to boil, she was glad of these few moments alone.

"Mummy?"

"You'd better go and wash. You look as if you've been dragged through a wood by your ankles. Pass me some eggs, first."

Tallis passed the eggs, shaking each one to make sure there was no rattling sound, the sure sign of a beak, according to Simon.

"Would you be angry if Harry came home again?" she asked eventually.

Her mother didn't falter as she placed eggs in water. "Why do you ask a silly thing like that?"

Tallis was silent for a moment. "You used to argue with him a lot."

Her mother glanced down, frowning; an uneasy look. "What's that supposed to mean?"

"You and Harry didn't like each other."

"That's not true," the woman said sharply. "Anyway, you're far too young to remember Harry."

"I remember him very well."

"You remember him leaving because that was a sad time. But you don't remember anything else. You certainly can't remember any rows."

"I do," Tallis insisted quietly. "They used to make Daddy very sad."

"And *you're* making me very angry," her mother said. "Cut some bread, if you want to be useful."

Tallis walked to the breadbin and drew out the huge cob with its burned crust. She started to scrape the charred top, but the action had no heart in it. She was never able to talk to her mother about important things, and that made her sad. She felt tears rise to her eyes and she sniffed loudly. The sound drew a puzzled, slightly regretful glance from her mother.

"What's the sniffing for? I don't want to eat bread you've sniffed over."

"Harry spoke to me," Tallis said, her eyes very watery as she watched the stern woman. Margaret Keeton slowly scraped butter from the solid lump, but her eyes lingered on her daughter's sad face.

"*When* did he speak to you?"

"Last night. He called to me. I called back. He said he had lost me forever, and I called back that I was close and would come and find him. He sounded very lonely, very frightened . . . I think he's lost in the wood, and making contact with me . . ."

"Making contact how?"

"Through the ways of the wood," Tallis mumbled.

"What ways of the wood?"

"Dreams. And feelings." She was hesitant to talk about the masked women and the clear and vivid visions she occasionally received. "And in stories. There are clues in the stories I make up. Grandad understood," she added as an afterthought.

"Did he, indeed. Well I don't. All I understand is that Harry went away, to do something very dangerous . . . he never told us what . . . and he never came back again, and that was years ago. Your father thinks he's dead and I agree. Do you seriously believe that if he were still alive he wouldn't have sent a letter to us?"

Tallis stared at her mother. How could she tell the woman what was on her mind? That Harry was not in England, probably not in the *world* as anyone understood the world . . . he was *beyond* the world. He was in the forbidden place, and he needed help. He had made contact in some magical, unimaginable way, and that contact had been with his half-sister . . . there were no letter boxes in the otherworld. In heaven . . .

"I didn't dream it," Tallis said. "He really *did* call to me."

Her mother shrugged, then smiled. She placed the butter knife on its plate and leaned down towards her daughter. After a moment she shook her head. "You're an odd one and no mistaking. But I don't know what I'd do without you. Give me a hug."

Tallis obliged. Her mother's embrace was uncertain at first, then became more urgent. Her hair, below the scarf, smelled of shampoo.

Drawing back slightly, Margaret kissed her daughter's upturned nose; then she smiled.

"Do you *really* remember me rowing with Harry?"

"I don't remember what about," Tallis whispered. "But I always thought he made you angry."

Her mother nodded. "He did. But I can't explain it. You were very young. I had a very difficult time with you. When you were born, I mean. It upset me for a long time afterwards. I wasn't myself. I wasn't anybody *else* of course," she smiled at the slight joke, and Tallis smiled too. "But I lost something . . ."

"A marble?"

"A marble," her mother agreed. "Or perhaps two. I was very angry. I can't remember how it felt, now, but I can see myself—as if I was *outside* myself. I was very unreasonable. And Harry . . . well, with his talk of ghosts, and lost lands, he just managed to rub me up the wrong way—"

Harry had known too!

"—And Jim . . . Daddy . . . always took his side. And why not, indeed? He was his father. Harry was the first born. When Harry went away, when he disappeared like that, I felt so upset about it that I found my marbles again."

She leaned down once more and gave Tallis an affectionate squeeze. Tallis saw the moisture in her mother's eyes, and the drip on the end of her nose.

"Unfortunately," Margaret Keeton whispered, "at the same time your father lost one or two of his."

"I remember that too," Tallis said. Then brightly, "But you're happy now . . ."

But her mother shook her head, then wiped her eyes with her knuckles. She smiled, picked up the butter knife and began to work at the pat from the fridge.

"One day," she said. "One day it will come right again. We *are* both happy. And we are *especially* happy with you. And if you want to go and look for Harry in the woods, then please do. Just don't talk to strangers. Don't go near the water. And if you hear people talking, either run away or hide. And be back here before tea-time every day or it'll be *you*, young madam . . ." She waved the knife in mock warning. "It'll be *you* who will be calling for help!"

"And if I bring Harry home?"

Her mother smiled, then crossed her heart. "No more rows," she said. "On my word of honour."

It was a particularly unpleasant visit to Aunt May and Uncle Edward. Uncle Edward had discovered a brown cigarette paper which, he told them at great length, improved immeasurably the taste of the rough tobacco that he could afford. He and James Keeton had sat and smoked for over an hour. The small parlour had become heavy and thick with the aroma.

In the car going home Tallis heard her father say that he couldn't stand this annual visit. He complained in exactly the terms that Tallis herself might have complained.

But it was a duty done.

At home again, Tallis asked for an hour to play. "Are you going out to find Harry?" her father enquired with a smile. She had told him about the encounter with Harry the night before, and he had explored the alley with her and made his own chalk mark on the brick wall, a little encouragement for Harry to communicate again.

Tallis realised that he wasn't taking her fully seriously.

"Not yet," she said. "I'll have to wait for the proper time."

"Well . . . don't go too far. And keep your eyes open."

"I'm going up to Morndun Ridge. Perhaps Harry will contact me there."

"Where in the name of God is Morndun Ridge?" Keeton asked, frowning.

"Barrow Hill," Tallis explained.

"You mean the earthworks?"

"Yes."

"That field belongs to Judd Pottifer, and I wouldn't like to be in *your* shoes if he catches you chasing his sheep."

Tallis watched her father very hard, very angrily. When her stare, and her silence, made him look uncomfortable she announced with great control, "I have better things to do than chase sheep."

It was a lovely evening, cool and clear, just beginning to fall towards dusk. Evensong was being tolled from the church at Shadoxhurst, the sound of the bell a faint and pleasant chime on the summer's air. Tallis went down to the Wyndbrook, Hunter's Brook, and moved slowly among the trees. She wondered whether she should take a chance and cross the unnamed field to Ryhope Wood. She longed to visit the ruined house again and she was often strongly tempted to risk that visit. But against that thought was the feeling that the house was something . . . something *not* of her. Whereas Morndun Ridge, like the alley, like Windy Cave Meadow, was a place of her own creation.

She had already concluded—during that interminably boring afternoon in the Gloucester suburbs—that the places which would be of importance to her were those places that she had made into her camps. Her interest in the ruined house in the wood was twofold: first, that it was the place from which Harry might have ventured into the otherworld, into Old Forbidden Place. And secondly, that it was the place where two men had studied the "mythagos" of the forest. They had kept a record of them, according to her grandfather—and perhaps her vision too—and that record, that journal, might still be there. Clues, anyway, as to who and what these mythagos were. They had fascinated her grandfather, and her grandfather had passed on that fascination to Tallis.

She and he were two of a kind. She was *his* girl. That was a fact, firm and hard. Everybody knew it. What had begun for her grandfather was continuing for her; they shared a *purpose*. And although that purpose could not involve the search for her brother Harry—Grandfather Owen had died *before* Harry had disappeared for the second and final time—they were sharing a common experience. Tallis was now convinced that this experience was designed to show them the way *into* the strange wood, into the unnamed but forbidden place that had snared her brother and which seemed to exist within the same space as the world of Shadoxhurst, but could not be seen.

This evening, in the hope that Harry would call again, she made her way towards her camp on Morndun Ridge. But when she arrived at the Wyndbrook she crouched among the trees opposite Knowe Field, listening to the sounds of the water as she watched something that delighted the innocence in her: two fawns drinking from the still pool where the stream widened.

They were beautiful creatures, one slightly smaller than the other. When Tallis dropped into position, hiding behind a fallen tree to watch the animals, the taller and more nervous of the two perked up and stamped its feet. Its ears were pricked, its huge, dark eyes bright and alert. As its companion continued to drink, this more canny animal began to trot along the stream's bank, then stopped and listened. Beyond them, the field stretched up to the ridge beside the wooded earthworks. The sky was a fabulous, evening blue as the sun began to set. Tallis could see dark birds walking along the bare part of the ridge, pecking at the ground. The evening was so clear that she felt she could see every detail of their bodies.

Below them, the deer had both reacted to a sound, even though Tallis had been stiff and silent.

Are you the children of my Broken Boy, she asked silently? Is he close by? Are you creatures from the storybooks and not of this world at all?

In that place, the stream among the summer trees, it was easy to forget that these simple creatures were part of the herd that grazed the edge-woods on the Ryhope estate. They could have come from any place in any time, from the fairylands of old, from the earth before humankind, from the dreams of a young girl who was now finding, in their dun-coloured bodies, a beauty that went beyond the animal in them, into the realm of the magic that they countenanced.

To Tallis's left, a twig snapped. The air was split by the hissing sound of a stone, or a missile, some object thrown with great force.

She was overwhelmed by the suddenness of events.

Her attention, distracted for that moment, failed to locate the source of the sound; a second later, when she looked back at the stream, it was to witness the agony of the taller, more cautious fawn, as it kicked in the air. It was half in, half out of the stream, struggling to stand again from the water. An arrow had pierced its eye and cracked through the back of its skull, forming an ugly and terrifying blemish on its screaming beauty.

The animal made the sound of a child, crying out for its parents. Its companion had already bolted. Tallis noticed its sleek shape moving among the trees, further along the stream. She felt instantly sick. The blood that poured from the wound in the deer below her had begun to swirl in the crystal water. It staggered to its feet, then collapsed on to its forelegs, as if kneeling in honour of some icon. It turned its head slightly and its tongue appeared, touching the water into which it slowly and gracefully subsided.

Tallis was about to run from her hiding place, to go to the dead animal, when a part of the woodland floor before her rose, straightened, stretched out to become, to her astonished eyes, the full figure of a man wearing the skin of a stag.

He had been crouching within her field of vision all the time and she had not noticed him. No doubt it was he who had shot the arrow and that too she had failed to see, but he was carrying a bow that was stretched taut and already had a second arrow nocked and ready. Indeed, as Tallis saw him, she gasped . . .

And instantly he had turned, staring at her through the flapping mask of the stag's facial hide that covered his own face.

Tallis felt wind on her cheek. When she ducked and looked round she saw the arrow quivering in the tree behind her, its flights cut from white feathers, its shaft painted in green and red stripes.

The man watched the place where she crouched. When she lifted her head slightly he saw her, held up a hand, fingers spread. It was a small hand, delicate fingers. In the instant before he turned to run to the stream Tallis formed the impression that he was young and unlikely to attack her further. His head and shoulders were covered by the stag's hide, and the antlers had been cut down to two stubby projections. He had watched her through the dead holes of the eyes, but the eyes of the man had been bright, catching the sun's dying light. His legs had been clad in hide boots, reaching to the knee and tied with crossed leather. A sheathed knife was strapped to the outside of his right leg.

These head and lower leg coverings apart, he was quite naked. His body was slender, tautly muscled, very pale. It contrasted astonishingly with the body of her father, who was the only other man whom Tallis had seen naked. Where her father was darkly haired, heavily built, large in stomach and leg, this strange apparition was in all ways slighter and lighter; a boy, perhaps, and yet the contours of his body were the contours of a man, the lines that defined the muscles held hard, the mark of an athlete.

All of these thoughts, all of the sensations, were contained within a moment.

The stag-youth was upon the fallen fawn, dismembering it, slitting its belly so that the steaming entrails, a glistening purple sludge, drained from the corpse into the water.

A knife cut, then a second, and the mass of guts had fallen away. The stag-youth slung the body across his shoulders and picked up his bow. He ran along the stream, bent low, and disappeared into the concealing darkness of the woods further along the Wyndbrook.

For a while there was a stunned, uncanny silence. Tallis watched the stained water. She kept thinking: Hunter's Brook. I named it years ago. I named it for this very moment . . .

Then she saw the movement of the smaller fawn as it came back to the place of death and quickly sniffed the air.

Tallis stood. The animal saw her and bolted, gambolling away from the stream, up the field to the stark ridge where the carrion birds pecked for worms. Tallis followed it, wading across the stream and calling to the creature.

"It wasn't me! Wait! If you're Broken Boy's I want to be able to give you my scent! *Wait!*"

She ran up the hill, stumbling and grabbing at the tight grass. The fawn vanished over the ridge, bob tail high, hind legs kicking in sadness and determined escape.

Tallis did not give up the pursuit. She was almost at the top of the field, where it flattened out before dropping towards Ryhope.

She could see the line of the land, hard against the glare of the blue-grey sky behind.

A black spread of enormous wings rose suddenly against that sky. Tallis gasped and dropped to her knees, her heart pounding.

They were not wings. They were antlers, a broad and terrifying sweep of dark and ancient horn. The huge beast stepped on to the horizon and stared down at her, its forelegs braced apart, the breath pouring from its flaring nostrils. Tallis could not take her eyes from those antlers: immense, horizontal bone blades, ten times wider than a red deer's; like scimitars, curved up at the ends, hooked and pointed along their length.

The Great Elk towered above the land, higher than a house, its eyes larger than rocks, its whole shape fantastic, unreal . . .

As Tallis watched, so its features blurred, changed. It had been a vision; the vision faded and a real view of the great hart replaced it. Yes. This was Broken Boy. The cracked tine showed clearly against the grey sky; its antlers, perennial, unreal, were broad, but that abominable hugeness of a moment before had gone away and this was just the strange beast, the undead stag, facing her down the hill. Watching her. And perhaps wondering whether it should charge and kick, or butt, or impale, or leave her for the innocent she was.

Yet it could smell the sour smell of guts and blood, and its offspring was dead. Tallis *knew* that it knew. Her face blanched with fear. It looked beyond her, to the wooded stream. Perhaps it saw the ghost of its child. Perhaps it was waiting for the spoor of the killer. Perhaps it was waiting for the smell of the fire smoke, and the fire flesh, the flesh consumed, its ghost-born eaten by the hunter with the stag fur.

"It wasn't me," Tallis whispered. "I had nothing to do with it. I love you, Broken Boy. I was named for you. I need to mark you. Before I can go for Harry, I need to mark you. But I don't know how . . ."

She stood up and walked towards the beast. It let her approach to within an arm's length, then it threw back its head and roared. The sound made Tallis scream. She stepped back, tripped, and fell to the ground. Looking up, braced on her elbows, she watched Broken Boy pace, limping, down towards her, straddle her, tossing its head so that the black rags of skin, hanging from its antlers, flapped on the bone.

The stink of its body was sickening; it was a corpse; it was dung; it was the wood; it was the underworld. The air was heavy with its stench and liquid dribbled from its maw as it looked down, snorting, sensing, thinking . . .

Tallis lay below its legs and felt suddenly at peace. She relaxed her body, lay back on the earth, arms by her sides, staring up at the silhouette of the stag against the evening sky. Her body hummed with sensation. She thrilled in her chest, in her stomach. The stag's saliva caressed her face. Its eyes gleamed as it blinked and stooped closer, to peer at this, its namesake, its fancy . . .

"It wasn't me," Tallis whispered again. "There is a hunter in the woods. Beware of him. He will kill your other ghost-born . . ."

Such an odd expression. And yet, when she said the words, they sounded right. She might have had them in her mind for all of her life. Broken Boy's *ghost-born*. Yes. His ghost-born. Mothered among the herds that roamed the Ryhope Estate; fathered from the underworld: but solid flesh and blood, and good to eat for the hunter who had come to the land.

"I will find him and stop him," Tallis said as the stag loomed above, silent, watching . . .

"I will kill him . . ."

The stag raised its head. It looked towards the dark wood that was its true home, and Tallis reached out a hand to touch the mud-matted hide of its hoof. It raised its leg and shook off the touch, then backed away, an oddly ungainly motion.

Tallis sat up, then stood. Her clothes were wet; the wetness on her face cooled as it dried. The smells in her nostrils became marked upon her. She adored them.

Broken Boy turned and cantered awkwardly to the ridge above the field. Tallis watched its tall, sinuous body as it walked a few paces to the west, towards the fading sun. The broken tine was a gap on its great head and she thought guiltily of the fragment that lay at home, hidden in her parents' chest of treasures, part of the remembered childhood of their own precious offspring.

"I can't replace it," Tallis called. "If it hasn't grown back then it wasn't meant to grow back. What can I do? I can't *stick* it back on. It's mine, now. The tine belongs to me. You can't be angry. Please don't be angry."

Broken Boy roared. The sound carried across the land. It drowned the sombre tone of the Shadoxhurst bell. It marked the end of the encounter.

The stag walked out of sight across the hill.

Tallis did not follow. Rather, she stood for a while, and only when darkness made the woods fade to black did she turn for home again.

[FALKENNA]

The Hollowing: Bird Spirit Land

She had felt abandoned by her ghosts during the winter, but now, early in May, the red and white mask of the Hollower seemed always to be watching her from the hedges. The figure, swift and shadowy, dogged Tallis's journeys about her land, but would never let the girl approach.

Where it had been, however, the air always smelled of snow.

Prompted by Gaunt's words of the summer before, she finally made a mask which she called *Moondream*. She used old bark from a round of beechwood, and painted moon symbols on the face. For a while it didn't feel right and over the weeks she worked on the wood, a touch here, a chip there, a line across the features: trying to let the true name emerge.

One evening it came to her: *to see the woman in the land*. When she placed the mask against her face she sensed a strange and haunting presence—a ghost—like the ghost in the glade of Oak Lodge, when she had explored the ruins a few years ago.

She now had eight masks. But the Hollower began to intrude its power, and the woman watched from the woods . . .

The Hollower was the vision-maker and Tallis began to prepare for the vision that would come to her, sensing intuitively that such was the meaning behind the constant, watching presence. Nevertheless, the vision, when it came, took her utterly by surprise, not so much by its nature as by the profoundly disorientating effect it had upon her.

She was running along the tree-line by Stretley Stones meadow, trying to hide from her cousin Simon with whom she was adventuring. Simon, at fifteen, was two years older than Tallis and was an inconstant companion. They usually adventured together —they hated the word "play"—every fortnight, mostly on Sunday afternoons while their parents walked and talked around the farm. They went to the same school but kept very different company there.

As Tallis edged around the large, gnarled "grandfather" oak in the hedge, hoping to squeeze her thin frame into the bushes behind, she heard an intriguing and disturbing sound that made her skin prickle with cold. It had been a human cry, she was sure of that. It had seemed to come from beyond the tangle of briar and thorn, from the meadow, but had somehow filtered through the branches of the tree.

She went immediately to the gate and looked into the thistle-littered meadow. It was a very peaceful place. It was full of stones. When the grass was long and the cow-parsley high, and the wind blew, the field seemed to flow like a sea-tide, waves of leaning pasture rippling across the hummocky ground.

For a while Tallis could see no sign of life, but then, in the distance, in the dark hedge, the Hollower shifted, the sun catching the white and red clay of the mask.

A memory came to her: a walk, with her father, a few years ago. They had come to the meadow. He had seemed sad. He had lingered by the tree which Tallis, in a future time, would seek to use as a hiding place. It had been here, at the tree's base, that grandfather Owen had died, crouched, as if watching . . . eyes open, his face smiling. Facing the stones.

Perhaps affected by the grief that was briefly resurrected in her father, Tallis had begun to imagine the presence of a sad ghost. The conversation was crystal clear in her mind as she looked back:

"There's a funny feeling here."

Her father frowned, rested a hand on her shoulder. "What do you mean? A funny feeling?"

"Something unhappy. Someone crying. Someone very cold . . ."

Perhaps he was trying to comfort her. "Don't think about it," he said. "Your grandfather is happy, now."

He walked to one of the overgrown stones and tugged the grass

and clover aside. He smoothed the crumbled grey surface. Along
the straight edges were notches, still visible. "Do you know what
this is, Tallis?"

She shook her head.

"It's *ogham*. Old writing. The scratches make different letters,
see? Groups of twos and threes, some at different angles. There are
five stones like this in Stretley meadow."

"Who wrote on them?"

A lark was ascending, its song a delightful and momentary
distraction. Tallis watched it fly high into the air. Her father
watched it too, saying, "People of old. Long lost people. Gaunt
says that a fierce battle was fought here, a long time ago." He
glanced down at his daughter. "Maybe even *Arthur's* last battle."

"Who's Arthur?"

"*King Arthur!*" her father said, looking surprised. Tallis was
always reading books of legend and folklore. She knew the
Arthurian romances very well. She just hadn't made the immediate connection when her father had been speaking.

It wasn't Arthur's name on the ogham stones, however. Several
of the words—which had been translated years ago—made no
sense. The sound of them, her father told her, was unpleasant and
seemed linked to no language, although one of them honoured
"kin of the wanderer", and another "spirit of the bird".

They had been left to nature, their enigmatic script covered by
grey lichen and green pasture. Like bodies, they swelled the
ground. They were known as the Stretley Men, the grey stones
that gave the field its name.

She returned to the sprawling oak and shinned up its rough trunk
to the lower branches. Sitting here, in the heart of the tree, she
could hear Simon calling to her as he hunted her. A moment later
the strange cry came again, a chillingly mournful sound, almost
final. There was another noise as well, a dull striking sound. The
cry had been as haunting as the night cry of a badger, full of
sadness, full of loss.

Tallis immediately thought of Harry and her pulse began to
quicken. Was it Harry on the other side of the tree? Was this his
second contact?

She squirmed out of the oak's heart and along a branch, peering
into the meadow below, searching for the source of the distress.

She saw summer sunlight on long, lush grass, dappled with yellow and white flowers. There was no-one to be seen, not even the Hollower. Tallis sniffed the air: no sign of winter. Still intrigued, though, she climbed higher into the branches. One of them leaned out over the meadow and she crawled carefully along it. Soon she was right over the field. She squirmed a foot further along and something strange happened. The light changed. It became darker. And the warmth in the summer air was suddenly chill. She could smell burning, but not the pleasant smell of woodsmoke. This was choking and unfamiliar.

All her senses told her that she was suddenly in a land of early winter.

The leaves below her were dense clusters, a sharp and vibrant summer green. She reached down and pulled the thin twigs aside and was able to see the field again.

Her gasp of shock, her cry, was so loud that Simon, approaching, heard it clearly. He ran rapidly towards the tree and must have seen Tallis spreadeagled along the branch because he sent two apples—his hunting ammunition—hurtling into the foliage. The second fruit found its mark, striking her side a bruising blow.

"You're dead! You're dead!" the hunter cried in triumph.

Tallis slithered back down to the heart and climbed from the tree. She dropped to the ground, her face ashen as she stared at her cousin. Simon's smile faded and he began to look puzzled.

"What is it?" he asked. When she said nothing he looked guilty. "Did that apple hurt you?" He passed the apples towards her. "Throw one at me. I shan't move, that's a promise."

She shook her head. Her eyes were glistening and Simon shuffled uneasily, conscious that his cousin was crying but not at all certain that he understood why. "Is it the game? Shall we adventure up at the fortress?"

"In the meadow," Tallis said softly. "He looks so sad."

"*Who* looks so sad?"

"I thought it was Harry, but it isn't . . ."

Simon dropped the apples which he had carried from the shed and climbed up the grandfather oak. Tallis watched him as he edged along the same branch in which she had been hiding. He jumped into the meadow, kicked around among the long grass for a while, then ran round to the gate.

"There's nothing here," he called.

"I know," she said quietly.

She wondered where the Hollower was hiding.

Tallis was upset for the rest of the day. She refused to adventure with Simon any more, and would not tell him what it was she had seen from the tree, so eventually he wandered off. Tallis hid in the oily gloom of one of the machine sheds for a while, when her father came looking for her to help with the clearing of nettles, then returned to Stretley Stones meadow.

She swiftly climbed the grandfather oak, sitting in its heart for a moment, hoping that she would hear the secret name of the tree, but nothing came. No matter. She was certain that the name would speak to her before she returned to the land.

She edged out along the branch until the light changed and the air grew cold, then reached down to part the leaves, snapping several twigs away so that her view was clear. Then she rested her head on her hands and lay there, staring into her other place and at the young man below her and the terrible scene around him.

She wanted to speak to him but the words caught in her throat. He was sprawled on his side, propped slightly on one arm, clearly in great pain. He was shaking slightly and when he turned his head Tallis could see the blood on his cheeks. He had about him a recognisable flush of youth, but he looked strong, he looked as if he had lived well. His hair was very yellow and very long, his beard fair and trimmed short. The pain-filled eyes that stared from the ashen face were as green as the oak leaves which filtered the light to him.

On his chest, the blood from a wound had formed a spreading pattern where his hand had clutched and wrenched at the short blade which still impaled him.

Tallis thought how knightly this young man was. His mouth was small, his nose very fine. He looked wild, mischievous, yet gentle. She could imagine him laughing, reminding her of Harry. But this was not Harry. He reminded her of the picture in her grandfather's book of legend, the picture of Sir Gawain in the story where he fought the Green Knight. But Sir Gawain had been in bright metal armour and this warrior was dressed more like a scarecrow. His clothing was more like the picture of Peredur, the brave, wild, adventuring knight from Arthur's court. He wore a loose brown tunic and a green and bloody sleeveless shirt. Around his arms and waist were bright yellow bindings. His trousers reached to just below his knees and were tight and coloured in brown and dull red squares. His boots were black and decorated with bits of tarnished metal.

As he lay below her, shaking with pain, Tallis could see the short red cloak he wore, tied on each shoulder with a gleaming yellow brooch. Every so often the warrior touched the brooch on his left shoulder and closed his eyes, as if thinking hard about something or someone.

She knew he was a warrior, partly because of the way he was dying and partly because of the simple, blood-raw sword that lay beside him. In the storybooks—and Tallis had by now read a great many of them—swords were always bright steel, and their hilts were worked about with gold filigree and topped with green jewels. This sword was dull iron, about the length of an arm, and was badly dented on its edge. The hilt was bound in dark leather. It was as plain as that.

She craned her neck to see beyond the tree. She shuddered at what she saw, the shattered chariots, the scatter of men, the pennanted spears jutting from the ground and from the sprawled corpses. Fires burned. The field no longer existed, only open land, a wide river marking where the Hunter's Brook flowed in Tallis's world. There were dead men there, and black shapes moved among them. Beyond the river she could see smoke and other fires bordering the dense woods that stretched, beyond this place, for as far as she could see. It was a winter wood, earth-coloured now, crowded and grotesque, a swathe of forest on an untrodden land.

And above that forest, a sky that was as black as night, sweeping towards the river, towards the scene of the slaughter. Below the storm, dark birds circled.

Tallis knew immediately what the tree should be called, and she named it there and then: Strong against the Storm.

She couldn't sleep. It was a hot, humid night, utterly still. Her window was open and she lay on the bed, staring at the stars. She wondered if her warrior was watching the same stars. The storm she had seen had not materialised, not in Tallis's world. But perhaps where her warrior lay in such pain, already his fine hair was being drenched by the downpour. The fires were out. She imagined the field hissing to nature's drowning, blood draining into grass, earth reaching up to enfold the dead and their weapons, and their cold spirits.

Gaunt says that a fierce battle was fought here, a long time ago . . .

Had the Hollower showed her how to *envision* that great battle, or rather, its aftermath? Tallis's mind reeled with images, with story. She got up from the bed and looked out of the window. Was that a figure, lurking in the shadows by the fence? Was it White Mask, whose presence encouraged the tales and the imagined adventures to fill her head?

A youngest son, youngest of three . . .

The story that began to form was almost frightening to her. It consisted of a confusion of images. A castle—high-turreted, thick-walled—being filled with earth, a thousand men carrying the dark soil with which to block the corridors and the rooms. Fires burned about the land and two knights, armoured and fierce, rode around the castle, pennants streaming.

An image of three young men, arguing with their father, and being banished from his hall.

Images of castles in the land, some among oakwoods, some among elmwoods, some by winding rivers and steep hills. Images of hunting.

An image of the youngest son, banished to a world created by the dreams of a witch. There, in a castle made of some strange stone, he lived a cold and miserable life, barred from return by the immensity of the gorge on whose northern wall the castle grew, a ragged stone palace rising from a ragged winter wood.

Images of wild hunts, the creatures of the forest rising like giants against the moon; boars, the spines on their backs like jousting lances; stags with antlers made from the wind-shattered limbs of oaks, their bodies crushing the forest as they ran from the angry hunter . . .

Finally, the image of a battle in black woods; the flickering movement of torches in the darkness; the cries of dying men; bloody bones and broken armour slung in the bare branches of trees . . . a sinister, fleeting image of what might have happened just days before this pleasant and proud young prince had crawled to the bole of the oak, to find shelter, to find safety . . . to find Tallis . . .

Story . . . vision . . . and a stranger sense, the sense of somehow having *been* to that ancient land. The air had chilled her, the smoke had choked her, the blood stench had sickened her. She had *been* there. She opened the *way* to Gaunt's "fierce battle". She had changed the landscape, bringing the old winter to her modern summer.

The Hollower was with her, she realised. All of this was for the purpose of showing her another facet of her power, her skill. Tallis: mask maker; mythago maker; her grandfather's child.

But by midnight she was distressed. Because, for all of the insight—whether right or wrong—she felt most strongly for the dying man.

She stood by her window, a frail shape in a thin nightgown. She stared across the night land to the silhouette of her tree. Tears came and she imagined she could hear her warrior crying too. She didn't know his name and she desperately needed to call to him. She should try and help him. She should take him bandages, and food, and antiseptic ointments. She should jump from the tree into the field and comfort him, tend to his wounds.

Her warrior had crawled to Strong against the Storm; perhaps he had heard her as she had adventured with her cousin! He had called to her, and for help. And what had she done? Nothing. Made no sound; only watched him and wept!

Angry with herself she pulled on her plimsolls, then crept downstairs into the garden. On impulse she tore a wide strip from the hem of her nightdress for use as a bandage. She thought about going back to the house for food and medicines, but changed her mind. By starlight she ran towards the Stretley Stones.

She had expected that night would have fallen in the forbidden place as well, but as she crawled along the branch she passed suddenly back from darkness into the winter daylight. Below her the young man was exactly as she had last seen him. The storm was still a distance away. The fires were the same.

For a moment this confused Tallis. Then she realised that her warrior was staring up into the branches of Strong against the Storm. He was murmuring words that were too faint for her to hear.

"What's your name?" Tallis called. And again, more loudly. "What's your name? I'm Tallis. *Tallis.* I want to help you . . ."

At the sound of her voice the young man's gaze hardened slightly. A frown touched his pale skin. Then he seemed to smile, just briefly, as if amused, and his eyes closed.

"Tallis . . ." he murmured.

"What's *your* name?" the girl insisted from the tree.

All he said was, "Tallis . . ." And then a desperate cry of strange words, words which fled through the branches of Strong against the Storm, meaningless, eloquent, elusive. Tallis threw down the strip of gown; her bandage for the young man's wound. For a second she lost sight of it, but then there it was, unfurled, fluttering down to the reclining man. He saw it fall. He reached for it, tears of joy in his eyes, his mouth, till now a grim slash of pain, becoming a wide smile of hope.

He clutched the rag and held it to his lips. He shook violently and the blood on his body gleamed where the flow began again. "Tallis!" he cried, and then shouted the word, "Scathach!"

He fell back, arm outstretched above his head, nightgown fragment fluttering in his fingers. Tallis watched in shock. His eyes remained open but a dullness appeared there instantly. The smile on his lips faded and he became utterly still. For a moment Tallis thought he had died, but then she thought she saw movement in his hand. He wouldn't die. He couldn't. She had saved him. Whoever he was, he had heard her voice. The Hollower had helped, of course; or perhaps Tallis's own talent for *hollowing*. But he had heard the voice and perhaps imagined that she was a goddess, or a tree spirit. It had been a sign of hope for him and now he would live. He would live for her, for Tallis. He would stay by the tree. When he was well again he would build his house there, and perhaps climb the wide trunk of Strong against the Storm. Or perhaps . . .

Yes. She would climb down to *him*. When she was older. When the time was right to join the spirits of two worlds. She was not ready to climb down yet.

"*Tallis!*"

The angry voice ripped through the moment of joy. She slipped on the branch, kept her balance, but the forbidden place had gone.

A torch shone brightly from the ground beyond the field where the Stretley Stones had fallen. When her name was called again she realised it was her father.

He knocked on the door of her room, then opened it. Tallis remained by the window, staring sullenly out across the dawn. She was wide awake, even though she had had no sleep. She was dressed in her dungarees, a white blouse, gym shoes. She had refused to wash her face, content to let the tears remain, a reminder of her anger.

"Tallis?"

"Go away."

He was gentle, now. He had been upset at midnight, and frightened too. Now, he explained to her, he was just anxious. There was something wrong with his daughter and that worried him. The way she was behaving was so unlike her. Whatever had upset her was very real to her. He had decided to do a little probing for the source of the concern.

"Why were you in the tree? What were you doing there?"

She didn't answer.

"Tallis? Talk to me. I'm not angry any more."

"*I* am. You sent him away."

"Him? Who did I send away?"

She looked at her father, furious, her lips pinched, her eyes narrowed as if to challenge his stupidity. He smiled. He was unshaven and his greying hair, usually so neatly combed back, was unkempt. It gave him a wild look, an odd look. He was still in his pyjamas. Now he reached out, gently touching his daughter's arm.

"Help me understand, Tallis. *Who* was there? *Who* was in the tree?"

She looked back towards Stretley Stones meadow. She felt her tears again and a deeper longing than she had ever known. She wanted her warrior, wanted to be there, looking at him. In her young mind she had grasped a strange truth: that time, for her wounded hero, existed only when she was watching him. The storm was coming. With it would come the rain.

In a way which went deeper than simple consciousness she knew that when the storm came so her romance would be finished. It was as if a part of her knew the truth behind the dulling of her young man's eyes, and that cry, so final, so full of relief . . .

Yet she refused to acknowledge it. He was *not* dead. He would live again.

Something, though . . . something terrible . . .

She had been thinking of it all night, all the early hours during which she had stood here, staring out to where Strong against the Storm waited for her. She was afraid to go back. Afraid to look at him. Each minute which she spent with him was a minute more of his own life, and the storm would be a minute closer.

She was alarmed by that storm. She had seen the sombre shapes of carrion birds, circling closer, just below the clouds. It was no ordinary storm. It was a wind from hell and it was sweeping the land of her hero, gorging on the dead, the dying. She had read about such storms. She knew all the names of the hell crows, the scald crows, the scavengers, the ravens . . .

Her father was still speaking to her. Without looking at him she cut in abruptly. "What is written on the Stretley Men? On the stones?"

He seemed surprised by the question. "It makes very little sense. Didn't I tell you that once?"

"But there must be *something*. Other than the 'wanderer' and the 'bird'. Isn't there *one* name?"

He thought hard for a moment, then nodded. "I think so. Several names. Odd sounding names. I've got them all written down somewhere, in a book on local history."

Excitedly she said, "What are they? What are the names? Is one of them *Scathach*?"

His frown was almost of recognition, but then he shrugged. "I can't remember. Where did *that* name come from, anyway?"

"He's there. His name is Scathach. He's one of the old people, only he's just a young man. I've seen him. He's beautiful. He's like Gawain."

"Gawain?"

She ran to her bookshelves and pulled the leather-bound volume from among the piles of storybooks. She leafed quickly through the pages and placed it down upon the bed, open at the picture which reminded her of the man in the meadow. Her father stared at the figure for a moment; then he turned the pages, finding the letter which had been written by his own father, several years before. "This is your grandfather's writing. Have you ever read it?"

Tallis wasn't listening. She stared towards the meadow and her eyes were wide, her whole face radiant with pleasure. She was sure she knew his name, now. He had called it to her. And it was certainly one of the strange names on the stones. An odd name, but a lovely one to her ears. *Scathach*. Scathach and Tallis. Tallis and Scathach. Scathach and the Tree Spirit. Scathach's stone, a monument to a great hero, a youngest son, left in the field where he had found life and love with a strange and slender young princess from another world.

She clapped her hands. She had to see him again. Then she remembered the storm and she felt afraid and helplessly young. She was not old enough to be of true assistance to him. Not yet. She must bide her time.

"Tallis! *Who's* in the tree?"

It was her turn to be gentle now and she brushed her fingers across her father's face, trying to reassure him.

"He's not in the tree. He's *below* the tree. Scathach. That's his name. He's very young, very handsome, and one day, a long time ago, he was a very great warrior. He was wounded in battle, but a tree spirit came to him and saved him."

Frowning, her father said, "Take me to see him, Tallis . . ."

She shook her head, placing her finger on his lips. "I can't do that, Daddy . . . I'm sorry. He's mine. Scathach is mine. He belongs to me, now. That's why the Hollower let me see him. It's part of my training, don't you see? The stories, the masks . . . I have to do what I'm told, and see what I see. I mustn't resist. And I have to save Scathach before the storm comes. I'm sure that's what my function is. Before the storm comes. Before the crows come. Don't you understand?"

He brushed his hand through her hair and concern glistened in his eyes. "No, my darling," he said softly. "No, I don't understand. Not yet." He hugged Tallis quickly. "But I will. I'm sure I will."

He stood up from the bed and left the room. When he looked back, Tallis was facing the window again. She had her eyes closed. She was smiling. She was whispering.

> *I out-last feather*   ·
> *Haunter of caves am I*
> *I am the white memory of life*
> *I am bone.*

The crows were coming. And the screech owls too, and the blood ravens. All the birds of prey. All the birds of hell. Coming to gorge upon the dead, to become fat with flesh. She had to stop them.

She had to protect him. She had to find the spells to turn them back. She had to find their bones.

She cleared one of the walls of her room, taking down the bark masks that she had hung there, all except Falkenna, because the hawk was a hunter; she was a hunter; Scathach was a hunter; and through the hawk's eyes she might see the hated birds which preyed upon the dead.

Around Falkenna she painted crows and ravens, using water-colours and charcoal. As each was finished so she blinded it with a knife, cutting deep slashes across the cold, piercing gazes. She made models of the birds, from straw, from paper, from clay. She buried these in Stretley Stones meadow, face down towards the bedrock. She marked each of these graves with the feathers of dead birds which she found in the hedgerows. She tied black feathers and strips of her white nightgown to each of the oaks that bordered Stretley Stones meadow. She made a daub of her own blood (squeezed from a graze on her knee) mixed with brook water and the sap of thistles and nettles. With this she painted the oaks around the field, painting birds whose bodies were split in two, painting arrows in the clouds, where the birds hid, and painting beaks that were broken.

Finally she painted the two masks on Strong against the Storm, one facing out from the meadow, one facing in. They were *triumph* masks, and they were both shaped like hawks.

In this way, then, she had turned the meadow into a cemetery for the consuming birds. Yet *still* she felt the crows circle closer. So she gathered the skulls and bones of birds wherever she could, plucking the feathers away from the maggoty corpses and stripping the flesh away with pincers. She kept the bones in a leather bag and each day ran around the meadow with them.

As the summer heightened Tallis felt a growing need to see Scathach again, just once, just a glimpse of him to see her through to the new term at school, to give her strength to last until Christmas, closer to the New Year, closer to an age at which she might really help him.

She walked across the fields. She sat below Strong against the Storm and read books. She loved to go into the hidden meadow and stretch out below the oak, arm above her head, body twisted just so, just as Scathach was even now lying there. He was staring up, as she stared up, and perhaps what he could see was what she was seeing—the tangle of leaves, the darker form of the branch. But there was no smiling face for Tallis, no tree spirit for her as there was for him.

She was aware, over the weeks, that the cowled women who haunted the woods were moving with increasing agitation through the concealing undergrowth. She scarcely bothered with them any more. The image of that young man, Scathach, grew to consume her. She forgot about Harry.

One day, when she heard horses, she tried to follow their movement but soon gave up. More of Scathach's story, which she now called Old Forbidden Place, began to crystallise. He was not just a lost son, his tale had been lost too, forgotten by the tongues and minds that had preserved so much else of legend. She struggled to make sense of the thoughts, the sensory excitement, the glimpses of a strange land and a mound-covered fortress, the wild sounds of the cycle of adventure that was the Tale of Old Forbidden Place.

She stopped going to school. This made her parents angry, but she had no time for them, now. Sometimes she was aware that her mother was crying. Sometimes she would wake from sleep to find her mother sitting in the room, watching her from the darkness. This all made her feel sad, but she crushed the feeling; she had no time for it; whatever the Hollower was doing to her she had to be receptive to *everything*. But she could not fail to be aware of the arguments. Her behaviour had precipitated a crisis in the house. When she heard her parents talking about Strong against the Storm she listened intently through the door. Margaret Keeton wanted to cut the tree down. But James said no. If they did that they might lock Tallis in this summer madness forever. They had lost Harry . . . he couldn't cope with losing Tallis too.

Summer madness? What madness could they mean? She listened more. There was talk about 'dreamstate' and 'fantasy' and 'hallucination'. No mention of what she was doing for Scathach. No mention of her fear that the carrion eaters would attack him as he lay unconscious. She scowled, closed her ears to the gabble of the adults. Was it madness to try to understand how to protect the wounded man? Was it madness to make her charms and spells? She had the books, the story books of wizards and witches, and the magic ways. In all of them she had read that *belief* was the greatest ingredient of any spell and now she focused her young mind on *believing* in her ability to keep the crows at bay. It didn't matter *what* she did, there would be power in all her acts, all her words, all her talismans.

Almost at once she knew how to make her ninth mask. Cut from the bark of a young wych elm, fallen in one of the hedges, it was painted first white, then with azure blue around the eyes to give a look of innocence. This was *Sinisalo*, and made her think of shimmering blue forests; but its secret name was *seeing the child in the land.*

In Stretley meadow, between the fallen ogham stones, she found other stones, small, hand-sized rocks that were smooth to the touch. She gathered as many of these as she could carry, then returned for more, piling them up below the oak. When the stones had been cleaned she fetched brushes and paints from the house and took a few of the pebbles up to Morndun Ridge, where she sat on the earthwork bank, facing Ryhope Wood, trying to imagine the black sea of forest that had once existed here.

She painted the Killing Eye on some of the stones, the sign of the Bird of Prey on others, the crosses, circles and spirals of olden times on still more. She scoured the books in her collection, and on the family shelves, for suitable charms. She copied the blind faces of the victims of Druids, the lifeless stone heads of Celtic times, and sensed at once the energy of otherwordly life imbued within them. She created her tenth mask, dead from the front, but so alive from behind. It was called *Morndun*, which made her look with puzzled eyes at the earthworks on the hill. Its second name, a secret one to her, was *the first journey of a ghost into an unknown region.*

Finally she painted *Leaf Man* and *Leaf Mother*, each on separate stones. She painted them in green, and then added red eyes, red blood for her own blood, the common bond with Scathach.

She tied strings around Leaf Man and Leaf Mother and climbed to her branch. It was not something she felt wise in doing. She had not been here for eight weeks. She had decided not to look at Scathach until the first day of the autumn term. If he lived only when she looked at him then she would have to stretch his life out over several years.

She was powerfully taken with the idea of her stone faces, however, and wanted them to protect her young man. So she edged forward from summer into the early winter of the forbidden place. She peered down at the sleeping warrior.

He was just as he had been those few weeks before. Nothing had changed. She smiled at him, called to him, then lowered the guardian stones from the branch. She lost sight of them, and then they appeared again. She could see how the string from her branch vanished, appearing in thin air a few feet to the south, but this illusion didn't bother her. The two leaf faces dangled above Scathach's body, turning slowly this way and that. She tied them to the branch, secured the knots, and leaned down to call to him once more—

And that was when she saw them.

She had been almost too anxious to look at the distant, dark clouds. But she glanced that way, across the river and the dark woods and saw how the black shapes of the birds were more numerous, now. But it was not the birds that made her cry out, it was the carrion eaters who were crossing the river and beginning to prowl around the land at the bottom of the hill, where in Tallis's world Knowe Field bordered Hunter's Brook.

There were four of them, stooped, old figures, dressed in black rags. Tallis knew at once that they were women, but beyond that she could see no details, except that their hair was long and grey beneath the dark shawls. They were not the whisperers, not the masked women from the edgewoods. One of them pushed a cart, a ramshackle structure on two huge, solid wheels.

Their voices, their shrill exclamations and laughter, carried across the field of slaughter where they had come to loot the dead.

Tallis called urgently to Scathach. He didn't stir. The strip of white nightdress fluttered in his fingers. A stronger wind was blowing in that other place, the beginning of the storm. Tallis suddenly felt frantic. She had two of the small stones in her pocket and she dropped them on Scathach's unconscious form. She aimed for his legs but as the stones vanished they reappeared above his chest, knocked off target during their transition between the two worlds. Tallis gasped as she saw them strike, but they rolled harmlessly off the warrior's body. Scathach remained unmoving.

Tallis leaned down again to watch the scavenging women. The wind had caught their loose black clothing and it flapped about their bodies like bat wings as they worked. But it was what they were doing that made Tallis shudder. They were stripping and dismembering the dead. They stretched the corpses and removed jackets, belts, breeches and boots. One of them worked on the naked torsos with a knife that flashed dully whilst the oldest and most haglike used a long, curved blade and attended to the necks. When the women moved to another place the blind heads swayed and banged against the wood and the sad mouths gaped in silent protest.

The women's cart was heavy with the flesh of the dead. Two of them pushed it, now. There were three dead men in the middle of the hill and then—yes, Tallis was sure of it—then they would see Scathach below the oak.

She crawled back along the branch until the season changed. Her heart was thundering, her head heavy with confusion. What to do? *What* to do? She needed to know more. She knew how primitive these people were, therefore she could find appropriate defences—in time! And she could make time. She could sustain Scathach's life simply by not watching him. But that was not possible. She was too concerned. What if the cessation of time in his world did not continue? What if, *even now*, the hags were closing in on him to pick over his body, crowing as they trundled their rattling cart towards the succulent prey?

She scrambled back to winter. She could hear the laughter of the women before she even parted the leaves to see better. Metal rattled, wheels creaked, and the storm wind brought ancient smells of blood and smoke from the darkening field where the battle had been.

It was cold in that place. The distant trees swayed as the winter began to strip their branches. The smoke from the fires streamed chaotically in the glowering heavens. And Tallis realised that the hags had seen Scathach.

They ignored the bloody corpses in the middle of the field and dragged their squeaking cart towards the oak. The wind made their hoods billow and Tallis saw their ash-grey faces, the tight skin on the bones, the open mouths just black hollows from which emerged their predatory cries.

They stopped. They had seen the stone heads—Leaf Man and Leaf Mother—hanging above the body which they had come to loot. Perhaps they could see how the heads dangled from thin air. The creaking of the wheels ceased. The grim heads lolled as the cart's handles were dropped and the women came cautiously forward.

They looked at the stones. They looked at Scathach. Then the oldest brandished her butchering blade and stepped forward.

"*No!*" screamed Tallis from the branches of Strong against the Storm. "Get away!"

The old women were stunned. They looked up, backed off, then stopped. Then the oldest took two steps towards the oak.

"Go back!" screeched Tallis. "Leave him! He's mine. He's mine!"

This oldest woman seemed to look right at Tallis, but the focus in her pale, watery eyes never hardened. She looked through Tallis, and to the side, and above her . . .

"He's mine! Go away!" the girl screamed.

And the situation dawned on the women at last. There was no-one in the tree, no *human*. They cried out, backing quickly away, arms crossed in front of their faces, the fingers of the right hands shaped into horns, those on the left indicating the Eye. They spoke a confusion of words, then picked up the cart and swung it round, hauling it away across the field towards the storm and the forest where the fires burned.

Tallis laughed to see them go. Her laughter haunted the old women who began to run faster. She had won! She had driven them away! Scathach would be safe with her now.

But her triumph was short-lived.

She lay contentedly on the branch for a few minutes, watching the storm encroach, feeling the wind rise, seeing the hill become shadowy and grey. Still Scathach lay without moving, but she let him sleep. In the morning he would wake with the winter sun, she was sure of that. The crows would not get him now.

It was dusk, and from the direction of the woods light flickered. As she stared in that direction she saw several torches. Her heart jumped. Dark shapes were crossing the river. The torches flared more brightly. She could hear voices.

It was the women again. They still hauled their cart, but now it was piled high with what looked like wood . . . and a long stone. Behind them came a man. He was swathed in a long grey cloak, made of fur. He carried a tall staff. As he came closer, Tallis could see that his moustache was long, as was his grey hair, but he had no

beard. His feet were bare. And there were not four women this
time, but five. The newcomer wore an odd and frightening black
veil across her face, but was otherwise as raggedly dressed as her
companions.

"Go away . . ." Tallis whispered, feeling first despair, then
anger surface again. "Go away!" she commanded more loudly, and
the sombre procession slowed for a moment before continuing to
advance.

Before they had reached the area of the haunted oak, Tallis
stopped time again. She gathered several of the painted stones,
selecting only those with eyes and circles on them.

In Scathach's world again, the fire from the torches streamed
violently in the wind. The dark storm-clouds moved swiftly across
the field and Tallis could smell rain in the air. She could hear
thunder.

The women rammed the torches into the ground, forming a half
circle around the oak. They stood there, ragged clothes whipping
about their angry bodies. They screeched in a single voice, the
sound an eerie and terrifying ululation. They watched the oak
branch where Tallis crouched and they made magic signs with
their hands and arms. The woman with the veiled face whispered
to the man, then stepped back a little. The old man stepped
forward. He raised his staff and struck at the Leaf heads above
Scathach's body. The action was sudden and violent and Tallis
responded with a scream of her own and a stone thrown viciously
at his head. The stone struck him on the shoulder. He roared
words of pain and anger into the tree, then stooped to pick up the
talisman. Almost immediately he dropped it, frightened by it, but
the veiled woman scurried forward to claim it, turning it over in
her fingers; Tallis thought she heard the woman laugh, and this
frightened her.

So she screeched, "He's mine!" And threw a second stone at
one of the torches. The women continued to wail, the oldest
brandishing her long, dull knife. "Leave him alone!" Tallis
screamed. "Don't cut him. Don't hurt him!"

The old man was furious. He waved his staff and made strange
patterns in the air with his left hand. He pointed to the sleeping
form of Scathach then slapped his chest. He said something; the
words were simple, urgent.

Tallis threw an eye-stone at him and it struck him on the brow, sending him staggering back. When he had recovered from the blow he unloaded other torches from the cart and lit each one, ramming them into the soft ground to increase the circle of fire around the tree. Tallis watched. The darkness grew deeper; the flames made the pale faces of the hags glow.

When Tallis scrambled down from the tree for more eye and circle stones she realised that dusk was approaching in her own world. She carried more stones from the base of Strong against the Storm, into its heart.

She passed again from peaceful dusk to storm-blown night. The crackle of the torches was loud and the screeching of the hags sounded like wild animals howling with pain. When she looked down into the forbidding world she could see that the old man and two of the women were pushing the tall, grey stone from the cart. They could hardly manage it. They succeeded in getting it upright, where it balanced, held by the women. The veiled woman placed her hands upon it for a second, then said something to the old man, who struck it with his staff then walked around it, crying out in his strange tongue. Each time he passed between Tallis and the stone he struck the smooth grey surface.

At last the strange ritual was over. Tallis watched as he took a knife and scratched the stone in a line from top to bottom, then used the blade to strike it powerfully along its edges . . .

The blows didn't seem strong enough to have made the deep marks of ogham, but Tallis watched intrigued. Were they carving Scathach's name? Was this the strongest spell they knew with which to steal the warrior?

Suddenly it was done. The stone fell heavily to the ground. (There was no Stretley Man in that position in Tallis's own time.) The women ran at the sleeping form of Scathach and were met by a hail of stones from the tree. The attack drove them off, bloody and screaming. Only black veil was unaffected, standing a little way back, watching the tree.

"You won't take him. You won't take him!" Tallis screamed. "He's mine. He belongs to me . . ."

She was out of stones again. She slipped quickly back to the heart of the oak to gather more. Thunder struck loudly and she was rocked in her precarious perch by the gusting, powerful wind. As she filled her arms she suddenly froze.

Where was the dusk? What was the storm doing *here*?

"Scathach!" she screamed. "Oh no. Oh no!"

She fled back along the branch, almost losing her grip. She flopped down at her vantage point and stared into the field, between the fires.

Scathach was gone. She could hear the cart creaking and she leaned down to watch it go. Scathach was flopped in it, his legs trailing over the edge. The old man was walking beside it, his staff across the body. The old women wailed and hauled their prey to some quiet place, to strip it in peace. The black veil had been tied around the standing stone, the hag's triumph blowing in the storm.

"*Scathach!*" Tallis cried, repeating the name endlessly as the tears and the grief came.

She had failed. She had failed to protect him. She had failed the Hollower's task for her. Anguish was a cold, twisting knife, cutting her bones, her flesh, her spirit.

Fire was spreading up the oak from two torches which had been flung to its base. Tallis sobbed, watching the flames. She had tried so hard to save her lovely warrior, and she had not been old enough to do it, her spells had not been strong enough. The Hollower had whispered the way of vision-making, and she had controlled time in the vision until she had *doubted* herself: she could remember the exact moment when she had lost control of the Hollowing, when she had become afraid that her simple presence in the tree would not be enough to dictate the flow of Scathach's life . . .

And she had paid the price; Scathach had paid the price. She had failed to save him. Her doubt had been an interference, and by interfering she had *changed* Scathach's story.

> *I blunt iron*
> *A shadow through Time I cast*
> *I am unshaped Earth. I stand alone.*
> *I am the second of the three. I am Stone.*

Or *had* she changed the story?

It was only as her desperation and despondency eased that she was able to review the events of the last few hours and finally see the actions that gave the lie to her belief in Scathach's gruesome fate.

It was with a sense of shock that she realised that the wailing of the women had not been a cry of triumph, but the keening of despair, of sadness; if there was triumph it was for the rescuing, not the stealing of the warrior's corpse.

Everything she remembered, now, increased her awareness that she had mistaken the plangency of their voices for the crowing of carrion birds, alone with their prey. The image of that old man, pointing to Scathach, pointing to himself . . . Had he been saying that he belonged with them? Is that why the hags had abandoned the bodies in the middle of the field, because they had seen one of their own princes?

It all came horribly clear to her. The hags had been of *his* people, and they had seen him below the tree, and seen the tree spirit which guarded him, and assumed that the spirit was trying to *steal* him. They had tried to *save* Scathach from the tree spirit. How badly they had misunderstood what she had been doing. She had been protecting him from slaughter. Now it seemed she had been protecting him from his own kind, his own clan.

Perhaps she could bring him back by calling more gently. Yes, that would be good. They had not yet reached the river and they had heard her shout once before. She would climb into the arms of Strong against the Storm for one last time and call to them, to reassure them, and tell them her name so that when Scathach was recovered fully from his wounds he would always remember her fondly.

Her time with him was not now; it would be later, when she was older.

For the moment she was just a tree spirit, but not one of whom they needed to be afraid.

She ran three times around each of the fallen stones, the Stretley Men, not knowing which of them was Scathach's stone, then she returned to the tree and climbed it swiftly, crawling along the branch to where the storm was raging and a torch-lit night stood as the first marker of the dead of the lost and ancient battle.

She had expected to see the cart and the rag-robed women and it was with a final, sickening shock that she realised that time had eluded her again. Now, by the river, a great pyre burned, its flame a silent dance against the wall of the forest behind.

A man lay on that pyre. It was Scathach, of course. Tallis could tell that—and she could see, too, that already the fire was claiming him for ash.

Below her the oak tree was burned and blackened, the fire gone, its ghost residing in the smouldering trunk; but Tallis was hardly aware of this. She cried for Scathach, watching as the flames began to consume him, bright life rising into the storm sky.

And the last thing she saw was a horse and rider gallop from the forest and pass around the blaze, black cloak and dark mane streaming. Why she thought it was a woman Tallis couldn't tell, but she saw the rider pass around the pyre from right to left, once, twice, and then again, the flame bright on her white, clay-stiffened hair, the gaunt black lines on her face, the red streaking of her naked limbs. Her cries of sorrow were like the fleeting cries of the dawn birds, banished from this forbidden place of winter, this Bird Spirit Land.

[SKOGEN]

Shadow of the Wood

(i)

She was still distressed a week later—it was early August, now—and had not become involved in any way with the preparation in Shadoxhurst for the annual festival of singing and dancing. She didn't have much to say to anyone and her parents left her to her sullen contemplation of the land. When her mother spoke to her about the manifest concern that her daughter was feeling, Tallis simply said, "I have to make it up to him. I misunderstood. It will have hurt him. I *have* to make it up to him. Until I do that I can't start looking for Harry again. Or the Hunter."

This was not especially illuminating for Margaret Keeton and she left Tallis to her own devices.

But what devices?

Tallis had made a grotesque mistake. The Hollower had helped her to open the first gate *clearly* to the forbidden world, to the otherworld, to the ancient realm whose real name still eluded her, though she had struggled several times to "hear" the name in her mind. The Hollower had trained her and she had ruined the training. Instead of witnessing the sad death and wonderful spiritual release of Scathach, she had *interfered* with a process which should only have been *watched*. She had changed something. She had done something very wrong. The Hollower, the masked woman from the wood, was very agitated. She followed Tallis, now, but withdrew into the shadows whenever the girl tried to approach.

Tallis had *changed* the vision. She had interfered. She had acted wrongly.

She felt an urgent need to make amends with Scathach. But she had no idea how to break the spell of change. She had no idea what magic to use to send his spirit on its way, to release him from the image in her own tormented mind, an image which, she was quite convinced, was trapping him in Bird Spirit Land.

She was holding him between worlds. In limbo. She had to find the charm to release him to his journey. Then, too, she would be released to pick up her own journey, in pursuit of Harry, in search of the way into Ryhope Wood.

On the day of the festival Tallis woke before dawn. She dressed quickly and tiptoed out of the house, running across the nearer fields until she came to Stretley Stones. There she stood by Strong against the Storm and watched its summer branches, listening in the silence for any hint of a winter storm. She heard nothing. The faces of the crows, scratched there a few days before, had faded. Already the great tree was absorbing her magic, healing its wound. In the days since the hollowing had ended no birds had entered the meadow, Tallis had clearly noticed that.

She felt an urge to enter Bird Spirit Land and sit on the stone she imagined to be Scathach's, but she resisted that urge because of what had happened. For some reason she imagined that the meadow, and his grave, were forbidden to her. So she skirted the field and went on to Hunter's Brook, crouching down and watching the nameless field and the dark stand of woodland by the damp, cool light of the new day.

It was the same wood that she had seen in her vision, and a clay-painted rider had come from it, crying out, grieving for the dead man . . .

I *must* cross the field, Tallis thought angrily. I *must* find its name so that I can cross safely to look for Harry. But it has no marks, no stones, no hillocks, no trees, no scars, no ditches. What are you called? *What are you called?*

She heard the sound of someone whistling. It was a jaunty melody. It reminded her of songs she had heard throughout her life; Gaunt was always whistling to himself. It was the sort of tune that would soon fill the air at Shadoxhurst, as the dancing and the playing got underway. Only this tune wasn't coming from a flower-hatted Morris dancer, or gaily-skirted local girl in clogs and bonnet.

Tallis watched the old man carefully. He seemed to have emerged from Ryhope Wood. As she concentrated on the figure the edge of her vision was alive with hovering, darting shapes. He was a mythago, then; she had called him from her own mind, like the Hollower, like Gaberlungi . . .

The old man walked along the edge of Ryhope Wood, through the long grass and dense bush. Soon the marshy ground began to suck at him. His whistling stopped and his voice grumbled with irritation. He waded out of the undergrowth and came across the dry field, towards Hunter's Brook. He was limping and used a stick to help in his movement. He saw Tallis crouching on the other side of the water and, as he raised his stick in greeting, so she straightened up.

The stranger was very tall and very robust. He was wearing green trousers and heavy boots and some sort of showerproof jacket that hung on his shoulders like a baggy cloak. His hair was very short and very white and parted precisely, high on one side of his head. His face was pale, quite heavy, but he had a warm and kindly look about him. He smiled at the girl, then pursed his lips and whistled again, arriving at the edge of the stream and easing down to pull off his boots.

"Not thinking what I was doing," the big man called to Tallis. "Walking along, enjoying the early morning: straight into a bog. Could have been twenty feet down by now."

There *are* bogs in the fields, Tallis thought, but not where you were walking.

She remained silent, nervous of the creature . . . increasingly uncertain that he *was* a mythago. The stranger was glancing at her uncomfortably.

"You're out early too," he called.

Tallis nodded. The man smiled. "Cat got your tongue?"

She protruded her tongue, cheerfully, to demonstrate that the cat had not been near her.

He had completed the removal of his boots. His socks were quite wet and he stretched his legs out so that the new sun could dry them. He leaned back on the grass, resting and relaxed. "I stayed the night at the Manor House. A very nice place indeed. A very good supper. Henry the Eighth used to hunt here, you know." He propped himself up on his elbows. "I'm here for the festival. Are you going to the festival?"

Of course, Tallis thought. Everyone goes to the Shadoxhurst folk festival.

"If you are, then no doubt I'll see you there. I shan't be doing any dancing, though." He chuckled, looking around at the quiet landscape. "Mind you," he added, "that said, I used to be a very keen dancer. I came here when I was a very much younger man. I was collecting songs. Old songs. Country songs. The festival in the village was *very* exciting for someone like me, newly down from London. The place has a certain charm. A certain *magic*. I can't explain it. Can you explain it? All I know is, it has drawn me back after many years and I feel as excited as a child given his first train-set." He looked at Tallis quizzically again. "Are you frightened of me? Told not to talk to strangers?"

Of course not, she thought. Not frightened of you.

"Of course not," she said aloud.

"Ah! It speaks after all. Is there a name which goes with your caution?"

"Tallis," Tallis said.

The stranger looked impressed. "That's an unusual and a lovely name. It's *well* named, too. A very fine man had that name once. A few hundred years ago. He wrote music for the church. Very good music indeed."

He felt the bottoms of his feet, then tugged on his boots and stood up. "It all begins at mid-day, doesn't it?" And added, "I thought so," as Tallis silently affirmed. "Well, there's just time for a bite of breakfast. By the way, do *you* know any songs?"

Man and girl faced each other across the running brook. Tallis smiled, then gave loud voice to *Baa Baa Black Sheep*. The man laughed and rolled his eyes. "Yes. Well. I think that one's a little too familiar to bother collecting."

"Do you collect songs?" Tallis asked.

"Didn't I tell you? Music is still my business. I've heard a thousand songs sung in a thousand ways, and many of them are truly beautiful and very old indeed. But I do wonder, sometimes, how many songs I've missed. And there's certainly *one* that I've missed. I heard it when I was a young man, and it slipped out of my head before I could write it down." He smiled at Tallis. "It would be nice to find it. So if you hear it, perhaps you could come a-calling. A new song can work magic."

Tallis nodded solemnly. She raised a hand as the big man walked away. Then she called, "Is there a name which goes with your search?"

He turned, raised his stick and laughed. "Williams," he called. "Very ordinary. Very plain. But Tallis is a *lovely* name. Very lovely. See you at the festival!"

And he turned and strode back towards the wood, walking awkwardly but with great purpose.

Tallis had no sooner seen the old man out of sight, past the woods which haunted her, when his words made an impact upon her as powerful as an unexpected and mocking echo.

There is magic in a new song.

Yes! Of course! That was the answer. A song. A new song.

At last. So easy. So obvious! She would *sing* to the memory of Scathach. A silent song, woven about his stone, repeated and enriched from those unknown regions which were her own passions, from the pleasures and visions that were all her own. A song: until the spell was broken.

A song for Scathach.

She ran towards Stretley Stones meadow. Already she knew how the song would begin, although the words, in her mind, had an eerie chanting quality about them, a cold quality despite the image of the words . . . no melody as yet:

> *A fire is burning in Bird Spirit Land,*
> *In Bird Spirit Land lies my young love . . .*
> *I will scatter the black carrion birds . . .*

Gaunt often sang songs. Sometimes he sang while he worked, sometimes while he sat drinking cider, sometimes when he was waking from a doze, in his chair by the apple shed. Tallis could never understand the words, droned out as they were in a rich dialect and with a melodic but deep tune. But he had said one thing to her a year or so back, which she remembered now.

She had asked him, "How do you manage to remember so *many* different tunes?"

"Tunes is easy," he said. "It's the words that are important. Once you've got the new words clear in the heart, the tunes come according to how you feel. There's always a tune."

"But your tunes are very pretty."

"You like my singing, do you?"

"No," Tallis admitted. "Not your *singing*. Just *what* you sing. The tunes are nice."

Gaunt chuckled at that. "Well. It's because I don't think too hard about them. So they sort of come from where they live, not prettied up in any way. My father sang them before me, his before him. Gaunts have been singing them since, oh, I don't rightly know. Since before the Almighty saw fit to teach them to Adam, probably."

Now Tallis went to the field where the stones lay and, acting quite impulsively, jumped on to the fallen monolith which she believed might have been named for Scathach. There was a flurry of disturbance in the branches of the trees around the meadow. Birds, of course. They lurked in the oaks and in the hedges, watching the rich pasture, but unable to fly across the field.

She began to sing the silent song, not thinking about any tune, just letting the words flow through her mind. The notes rose and fell, the rhythms changed. As she sang to herself so she stood down from the stone and stepped slowly around it, dancing to the metre that she imposed upon her awkward words, letting the words change as they wanted, letting everything come from where it lived.

She was singing out loud before she had fully realised it. The branches rustled nervously. The wind flowed through the tall grass. Her voice rose high into the air, a sweet sound, carrying Tallis's Promise away from the sanctuary.

> *A fire is burning in Bird Spirit Land,*
> *In Bird Spirit Land lies my young love.*
> *A storm is raging in Bird Spirit Land,*
> *I will scatter the black carrion birds.*
> *I will watch over the kissing clay of my young love,*
> *I will be with him in Bird Spirit Land.*
> *A fire is burning in Bird Spirit Land.*
> *My bones smoulder.*
> *I must journey there.*

With the charm broken, the singing stopped. Tallis felt a moment's intense sadness and allowed tears to roll down her face. She stared at the stone, then at Strong against the Storm.

All of this had been for a purpose. Somewhere, a thousand years away, her song had sent Scathach to a place where the hunting would never end, where every man could sing well and where the loving was as fierce in the winter as it was in the spring. To that many coloured land. To that other world. To that bright side of the forbidden place . . .

There was nothing more she could do here, now. The meadow was just a meadow and the grey stone was cold again, the spirit gone from it.

She would have rejoiced to see the Hollower at that moment, but the shadows in the wood were empty.

(ii)

Throughout the afternoon Tallis wandered through the crowded village of Shadoxhurst, looking for the old man, Mr Williams, whom she had met by Hunter's Brook. She wanted to tell him how much he had helped her, and to sing him the new song she had composed for Scathach. But she couldn't see him at all and this confused and worried her.

So she sat with Simon, and several other local children, on the stone wall around the church, watching the crowds and the dancing, and the strange puppet show known as the Folly Play, and of course the driving of the cattle on the village green. Tallis liked the driving of the cattle. Every so often, as one of the docile animals was being urged between the two bonfires, it would go mad, leaping about among the spectators, causing havoc. Such moments of excitement and danger were what made the festival fun, but they rarely happened.

The afternoon began to seem endless. The half-ox burned black on its charcoal fire and was eventually sliced down to its pink bones. Races and contests alternated with the dancing, but Tallis remained on the wall, a passive observer. Only when the Shadox men came to dance did she leave the uncomfortable perch at the church's boundary and go and watch from closer to. Simon went with her.

"I'm going to be a Shadoxman when I'm older," he said. There was a glow in his eyes as he watched the local Morris team. "I'm going to be Iron!" He was eyeing the silvery blade stitched to the dancer's chest.

Each of the ten dancers wore a different emblem, and was known by its name. Tallis knew them off by heart: feather, iron, bell, owl—who wore a stuffed owl's head round his neck—oak, thorn, ivy, stone, bone and the leader, fire. The leader carried a tarred torch which would be lit at nine o'clock and used in the most important of the ceremonies. Bone, the tallest and most robust of the dancing group, carried a great bone horn at his waist.

"If you're going to be Iron," Tallis said to her cousin softly, "then you won't be my friend." Simon glanced at her, frowning, but she ignored him.

The Shadoxmen performed four dances before giving way to one of the guest teams. All were quite routine. The men danced in two lines of five. They fought mock dancing battles with hazel rods and small sleeve-shields and finally stripped the shields from their arms and flung them into the crowds. The person who caught the "fire" shield was chased through the dancers to the increasingly rapid chant of "*Into* the wood and *out* of the wood and *into* the wood and *out* of the wood . . ." before being hoisted up with a cry of "Ropeburned and daggered, she'd die if she could!"

The fire shield was always thrown to a young woman and Tallis was not unaware of the sinister connotation of that piece of folk fancy.

At dusk her parents came looking for her. They had been helping out on several of the side-shows during the afternoon and were now going for supper. Tallis decided to stay in the village and was told not to part company from Simon. She agreed. But the moment the Keetons had disappeared from the village square, Simon ran off, leaving Tallis alone again.

Now, though, as she watched the surging crowds of adults, she caught sight of the big man from Hunter's Brook, noticing his white hair as he walked along the road on the far side of the common. He was mobbed by people and moving slowly to a place on the far side of the road, facing the green. This was where, later, the final dance—the Shadow dance—would be performed.

It was nine o'clock and the real ceremonies were about to begin. The sky was still quite light but already the sparks from the dying

embers of the ox-fire appeared brighter in the air, and the two
floodlights had been turned on to illuminate the grey face of the
church with its dark windows. A noticeable change in the
atmosphere of the village occurred, the people becoming more
subdued, the air more vibrant as excitement grew.

Tallis squeezed and shuffled her way through the bodies until
she came to the place, on the road, where she had just seen Mr
Williams. She found him, seated on a canvas chair between two
old men of the village and surrounded by four more. They were all
of a kind, Tallis thought about the farmers, from their muddy
boots and baggy grey flannel trousers to the loose tweed jackets
that hung from their shoulders. They wore caps on hair that was
cut high over the ears, so that skin gleamed white between dark
hat and tanned face. She knew some of them by name—Pott'nfer,
Chisby, Madders. Pipes smouldered and thin cigarettes smoked
between hard, yellowed fingers. They talked slowly, but in
Gaunt's thick dialect, and Tallis had trouble following what they
were saying, even though she was a local girl herself. But Mr
Williams, who laughed loudly and talked in his own low murmur,
seemed to understand everything that was being said.

They were all facing the street, where already the unlit torches
were being lined up ready for the "running of the fire". The leader
of the Shadoxmen would start the relay, lighting his torch from
the embers of the bonfires on the green. He would then run around
the square, around the village outskirts, lighting each of the fifty
torches. Eventually the whole community would be surrounded by
a double wall of fire.

If all the torches still burned when the leader arrived back at the
great oak on the green, the village would be safe from Grim
himself!

Tallis stood behind the broad shoulders of Mr Williams, wrinkling her nose at the heavy odour of the tobacco from his nearest
companion's pipe.

"He runs faster every year," growled this local man.

"We get older," Mr Williams observed. "They just seem to run
faster."

"But in days gone, torches often faded before the circle was
run . . ." muttered the pipe-smoker. "Bad luck struck'en then."

"Better quality torches always help," Mr Williams said with a
wry chuckle, and all the farmers laughed.

Behind him, Tallis said softly, "But there's *magic* in an old torch."

Mr Williams turned sharply in his chair, frowning. He was breathing quite heavily and a smell of smoke and beer hung on his clothes, though he himself held no cigarette or glass. His face was very pale, Tallis thought, but his eyes twinkled with humour and delight as he recognised the child.

"Is there indeed? And a new torch? No magic in that?"

"Only a new song," Tallis said. "You told me that. This morning."

"Yes," he said, pleased. "I know I did."

"Any luck?"

He pulled a face. "If you mean have I heard a new song . . ." He looked crestfallen, shaking his head. "Some good versions of old songs. Nothing from the unknown archives."

"Not that lost song either?"

"No. Sadly."

"I've got one for you," she said brightly.

"Have you indeed?"

A great cheer went up from the crowds. The leading Shadox-man, brandishing his torch, had stuck it into the dying fire and it burned fiercely in the gathering gloom. He crossed the green to the church gate and the second torch was struck. The young man raced around the village centre. Each torch became a flare of light. One flare streamed as it moved. Someone raced past the group of old men on their chairs, flame trailing in the still air, scenting the night with the odour of tar. Children pursued; two dogs followed the children. The ruckus passed from the village centre to the perimeter, where the demons lurked.

For a few minutes there was peace, although the local dancers were clapping their hands and singing a simple chant (it was called "run torch run"). Mr Williams turned round again, leaning on the back of his chair and watching the girl.

All the old men stared at her, one or two of them smiling. Tallis felt slightly daunted by their amused, benign, but intense gazes.

"Well, we're waiting," said Mr Williams.

Tallis drew a deep breath. Then, in her best voice, she sang the song to Scathach.

> *"A fire is burning in Bird Spirit Land*
> *In Bird Spirit Land lies my young love . . ."*

It was a melancholy sound and tears came immediately as both memory and the haunting qualities of her own song roused the passions in the girl's young heart.

One of the farmers said, "That's *The Captain's Apprentice* . . ."

"Ssh!" said Mr Williams.

Tallis, who had hesitated at the interruption, continued singing.

> "*A storm is raging in Bird Spirit Land,*
> *I will scatter the black carrion birds . . .*"

She finished the song but it had not gone right. The words had changed and the tune had changed. It had been *perfect* this morning, but now, under different circumstances, she felt she had distorted it.

She watched Mr Williams, who took a moment to realise that the song had finished.

"That's very nice," he said. "And you have a nice voice. Very nice."

"Is it a new song?" Tallis asked anxiously. "Does it have magic?"

Mr Williams hesitated awkwardly before saying, "It's a truly *lovely* song. The strangest words I've ever heard. Truly lovely. I would like to write it down, with your permission."

"But is it a *new* song?"

"Um . . ."

She stared at him. His face told it all. She said sadly, "An old song?"

"An old song," he agreed sympathetically.

"But I only made it up this morning."

He leaned towards her. He was impressed, she thought. "Then it is still a remarkable achievement."

She was confused, sad, slightly irritated. "I don't understand . . . I made up the words! I really did!"

Mr Williams watched her thoughtfully. "Such strange words . . ." he whispered. "Such a strange mind . . ." He drew breath and sighed. "But alas . . . the tune you used is just . . . well, how shall I put it? Is just a little reminiscent of something else."

"*Same* bloody tune," said one of the men, and the others laughed.

Mr Williams ignored them, letting Tallis share his own con-
tempt with the merest hint of a smile at her. "It's called—in one
form, at least—it's called *The Captain's Apprentice*. I used it once
myself, in a piece of music. My music wasn't as nice as yours. Too
many violins. But it's quite an old tune."

"I heard it in Sad Song Meadow," Tallis said. "There was
nobody there, so I thought I could use it. I didn't mean to steal
it."

Mr Williams stared at her. "You first heard it . . . *where* did you
first hear it?"

"In Sad Song Meadow. It's near my farm. It's really called The
Stumps. But when I was nine I began to hear the singing. I'm not
afraid. My grandfather told me not to be, so I'm not." She
frowned. "I really *didn't* mean to steal it."

Mr Williams shook his head. He scratched at his chin nervously. "Why not? That's what they're there for. Tunes belong to
everybody. So do stories."

"I didn't steal the words," the girl said quietly.

"I know you didn't. Words are always private, even if they're as
strange as the words you used!" He smiled. "Your 'young love' in
this 'bird spirit land' is a lucky young man indeed. Does he go to
the same school as you?"

The old men laughed again. Tallis looked up at them, not liking
the feeling that they were mocking her. Mr Williams looked
contrite, but he said nothing. Tallis decided to forgive him. "His
name is Scathach."

"The song was very sad," Mr Williams said. "Any reason for
that?"

For a moment Tallis was inclined to say nothing about the
events in Stretley Stones meadow. But the kindly look in her
friend's eyes, and his slight frown of concern, finally overwhelmed
her caution. Although she had sung to Scathach, she had not yet
shared the burden of her grief with anyone and now, fighting back
the tears, she let the feelings and the words flow from her.

"He's gone away from me," she said. "I don't know for how
long. I saw him at the bottom of the oak. It's a *hollowing*. The oak
tree, I mean. A place of vision. You know, somewhere where you
can see into the Otherworld? So of course he doesn't belong to our
world at all. He'd been very badly wounded. He must have lived
hundreds of years ago. The crows were trying to get him, but I

drove them off. I made the place into Bird Spirit Land and that
will have made them angry. Then the hags came, though. I don't
think they're the hooded and masked figures that haunt the wood.
They're mythagos. These hags were part of the vision. They came
and dragged him away, on a horrible cart with all heads and limbs
tied to it. I thought they were going to cut him up, but they were
his friends after all. They burned his body on a pyre. Not his spirit
of course. That will have gone through its own hollowing and I
can fetch it back. But then . . . but then a woman came. She came
out of the wood, all chalk-streaked and screeching. She rode
around the flames. She was very upset and it was probably his
lover, in which case, who am I? And what am I? He can't have *two*
lovers. That wouldn't be right. And I was too busy thinking about
it and the hollowing slipped away. So it's just a tree again. But I
felt I had to sing the song to him, just to let him know that I really
do want to love him one day, but I'm not old enough to follow him
yet. And in any case, my brother Harry is in the wood, and I've
promised to look for him too. But I can't look for them both, so I
really don't know which way to turn . . ."

She wiped her eyes and took a deep breath, watching Mr
Williams as he sat in absolute, blank-faced silence. The farmers
around him were staring at her in astonishment.

At last, with the merest raise of his eyebrows, Mr Williams drew
in his breath and said very quietly, "Well, yes. That certainly
explains everything . . ."

A great cheer went up from the festival crowds. Shadox Fire ran
back into the central green and crossed to the oak, where the first
torch still burned, held by Shadox Thorn. The two Morrismen
pushed the brands together above their heads and dull flame
became briefly alive, so that the renewal, the protection, was
complete.

When the applause and cheering had died down Mr Williams
winked at Tallis, who had recovered her composure, then slapped
his hands on his knees and said, "Well then. There we are. Safe
from the Devil for another year."

Tallis smiled. Several of the old men chuckled, but Judd
Pott'nfer just shrugged. "Better safe than sorry," he said, and
Tallis noticed how Mr Williams was suddenly humbled, thinking
hard about that simple statement.

"Best is yet to come, though," the sour-faced Mr Pott'nfer went on. "Shadow Dance, now. We've been dancing the Shadow Dance from before the name of the town."

Tallis stared at him. What he had said simply could *not* be true.

"But Shadox *is* the town's oldest name," she said. "Nothing is older than Shadox . . ."

Without looking at her, Pott'nfer said, "This dance is the oldest dance in the area. Older than Stretley Men. Older than anything."

"Then it's older than history," Tallis murmured, staring at the white band of newly-shaved skin below the farmer's dark, peaked cap.

"No arguing with that," Pott'nfer said, and his friends laughed, a private joke that neither Tallis nor Mr Williams understood. Mr Williams glanced at her and asked, "How do you know about the village's name?"

"I've got a book on it," Tallis said. "Place names. And our gardener, Mr Gaunt, he knew anyway. Shadox means *shadows*, but not like a sun's shadow. It means a shadowy place. A ghostly place. A *moonshadow* . . ."

Mr Williams looked fascinated. "It seems to me that this village has more than its fair share of ghostly associations."

Before Tallis could reply, Pott'nfer said gruffly, "This dance is older than words. So why don't you just be quiet, young miss, and watch the fun?"

Mr Williams raised his eyebrows as if to say to Tallis, Well, then. That puts paid to that. He whispered, "Meet you in that field? Tomorrow? Before breakfast?"

Tallis nodded enthusiastically and the man turned back to watch the dancers form up in their lines, ready for the Shadoxhurst Shadow Dance.

It was well past dusk, now, and night was gathering. The church was floodlit and the moon was up. The torches still burned around the green, those from outside the village having been brought in. They were expiring slowly, but there would be firelight enough to see the dance through.

"I *love* this dance," Mr Williams whispered.

"It frightens me," Tallis contended. "It's not like the others."

"That's why I find it so fascinating. The Abbot's Bromley Horn Dance, and this Shadow Dance, come from a *very* ancient tradition. No 'happy rustics frolicking'. Except perhaps for the wild jig at the end."

Tallis shivered with apprehension as she thought of it.

On the green, close to the solitary oak, the Shadoxmen had lined up in two rows, facing each other. Between them was a tall, weird-looking woman, dressed in black rags down to her feet and covered with a crudely-stitched cloak of hide and wool. Her face was whitened into featurelessness. On her head she wore a "crown" of feathers, straw and strands of twigs. In one hand she held an L-shaped fragment of deer antler—the beam and the crown point—in the other a flaxen noose. She remained quite motionless.

To the single, simple sound of a violin, a melancholy yet lively tune, the dancers approached each other and parted, then slowly skipped around the solitary female figure in their centre. The tune abruptly changed to a leaping jig and the ten burly locals obliged, striking at each other as they leapt vertically into the air. Accompanying this terrific leap, the words, shouted as one voice: "One of us must go but it won't be me!"

As they crashed back to the earth, so one of the Shadoxmen split off from the group and ran into the crowds, leaving only nine men, then eight, and so on until only one of the Shadoxmen remained, circling around the central female figure.

"This is the bit I *really* like the best," Mr Williams whispered.

Tallis, aware of what would happen at the end of the dance, was looking apprehensively around among the crowds. Where were the dancers who had quit the field? Where were the guest dancers, the Pikermen, the Thackermen, the Leicester Hubbyhousers and the rest? They would be sneaking through the audience, selecting their targets for the wild jig. Tallis secretly wanted to be pulled on to the green to dance, but was less than secretly embarrassed and afraid at the thought of it.

She could see no movement behind her.

On the green, the last of the Shadoxmen to remain—Shadox Bone—drew the bone horn from his belt and began to sound it, only inches away from the stationary woman's face, as if challenging her . . . or calling to her. This deep and eerie summoning lasted for all of sixty seconds, and the audience watched in breathless silence.

And suddenly the female shape shuddered. From beneath its

skirts darted a girl in a green and red tunic, with her face painted featureless green. The crowd cheered and the blowing of the horn ceased. The girl took the antler pickaxe and the noose from the hands of the mannequin. She "struck" at the Shadoxman, then "hanged" him. Each action was accompanied by a great roar of approval from the watchers, and then the accordion started up a sprightly and rhythmic wild jig.

The crowds parted and eight of the nine dancers who had been "lost", plus all the guest dancers, came racing back on to the green, each with a struggling, twitching "victim", some of them children, most adults, men and women both.

Tallis started to laugh with glee at the vision of the protesting audience, but the laughter turned to a scream as two firm hands lifted her from her feet and whisked her through the old men and on to the dancing square.

"No!" Tallis shrieked. "Mr Williams!"

But all she could hear was Mr Williams's loud, cheering laughter.

Who had got her? Which of the Shadoxmen had taken her? She had to know! She had to know!

She was swung around dizzyingly, pulled forward into the dancing mass then back again. The man who held her seemed to spin before her face, a blur of white and colour, a brief scent of the flowers that laced his belt, a sudden jingle of the bells that were tied to his wrists. She tried to see his face but could see only the orange of his beard. She looked for the symbol that he carried . . .

Owl? Stone? Iron? Feather? Which one? Which one?

She saw it at last. A spray of twig, with its five red berries, stitched to his breast.

He was Thorn, then. Thorn.

A friend.

Oak passed in front of her, grinning down at her, a thickly bearded man, strong like the tree. Bell swung her round, the bronze bell on his chest ringing out in its different, duller tone. She held hands with others and skipped in the spiral line, through arches of arms, through tunnels of bodies bent at the waist, in and out of the leaping figures of the Morrismen.

Arms up, arms down, a rousing cry of nonsense words (*riggery, jiggery, hoggery, huggery*) and around again, trapped in the swirl of bodies. She looked up and saw the pale face of the clock on the church. The night sky was full of sparks from the fires which had been kicked into new life by the wild dancing.

She came close to the split oak on the green and as she was whirled past thought she saw white birds emerging from the hollow trunk. It was a moment of alarm. Something beat around her head, a whirr of wings. She looked back—

The oak shivered and leaned towards her . . .

Something was rising within it . . . ghostly . . .

Tallis was whipped up into the air by strong arms, then placed down, tugged and twirled by the raucous dancers. She laughed, then stumbled.

She fell on the cold earth, her hand getting muddy where the turf had been churned to the soil. A strong arm wrenched her up to her feet again. She looked up and felt a moment's panic as she saw the owl's head on the man's chest. A second figure grabbed at her and sent her flying and she saw the pale features of Feather, the bird's wings bristling on his hat. The music faded, the swirl of bodies, the cries of the festival folk, became distant, even though they flung themselves around her. All she could hear was the cry of birds, voices raised, the screeching, howling, chattering sounds of all the birds in the world, and she could feel their wings and the air stirring and the night sky darkened as they circled above her.

Owl grabbed her, flung her to Feather. Iron stepped between them, grim face grey, iron blade flashing in the torchlight.

His hand lashed out, a stinging blow to her face, sending her reeling. Another hand, another blow. She was in a dream. The dancing circle had become shadows, dark against the bright wall of fire, torches burning too hard, too high, too fiercely for them to be real.

The birds taunted her. The slapping blows, wing blows, finger blows, blinded her with tears.

"Help me!" she shrieked. "Let me go!"

Bird heads pecked at her. The white robed man was taller, somehow. His face stretched into a beak, his eyes glittered brightly. There were more of them, now—all birds, their bodies cloaked in feathers, hair bristling and on end, their dancing movements the short, jerky movements of crows.

Among them stalked a tall thing, horrible to see, terrifying to hear as it opened its long bill and uttered its cry of anger. It was like a creature on tall stilts, a thin body, thin legs, impossibly high, twice the height of a tall man. Its beak was an arm's length from face to point. The long-feathered crown tumbled about its neck as it stalked around the circle, watching Tallis all the time. It suddenly flung itself at the girl, bending low, jabbing its beak towards her but pulling short as Tallis screamed. The glittering eyes that watched her were human, though the rest of the features were those of a heron.

It went up, then, up into the night, graceful, motionless, wings extended and carried out of sight into the darkness by some wind that Tallis could not feel. The music blared, the dancers laughed, people collapsed exhausted on to the grass, the jig finished.

Tallis stood there, shaking, watching the Shadoxmen, seeing how the Owl and the Feather were just ordinary men, laughing with the others, undoing their tight shoulder harnesses to give some relief to the tired muscles below. Tallis stared above her head, where a few stars gleamed. There was nothing flying there.

A dream? A vision? Had she alone seen the stalking bird? Had no-one seen Feather striking her round the face?

A vision. A crude after-echo of the hollowing of a few days ago. That was the only explanation.

She saw the piece of antler lying on the ground, where it had been dropped during the frenzy. She bent to take it but a hand snatched at it first. She looked up to see the green-painted girl holding the bone to her chest and backing away, a silly smile on her face. The girl turned and ran, vanishing among the departing crowds.

Tallis walked home in a very grim mood indeed.

[CUNHAVAL]

The Bone Forest

For most of the following morning a summer rainstorm kept Tallis sitting miserably in her room, watching the sweeping darkness on the land. But in that time she saw two horsemen canter across a distant field and up the slope to Morndun Ridge. She could see no further detail. Also, her mind was active. She relived the frightening event of the evening before and suddenly understood what had happened. She had created a hollowing, albeit unwittingly. Through it, the vengeful spirits of birds had come and briefly possessed the dancing. Tallis felt at once both relieved and regretful. She longed to return to the green in Shadoxhurst.

When the rain stopped she pulled on her coat and told her parents what she was doing. Normally she would have entered Shadoxhurst along the bridleway that crossed the Keetons' farm; such a journey would have been her own business. But the bridleway was a rough track and would be filthy with mud, now. She would have to walk along the road. James Keeton had insisted that she always tell them when she was going to walk on the country roads.

She was at the village ten minutes later. She went straight up to the split oak and stood on its most prominently exposed root.

"You're an old tree, I know that," she said to it. "But you're *oak*. I thought all oaks were my friends. Like Strong against the Storm, who helped me see Scathach. I thought all oaks were on my side.

So I was angry last night, when I thought you had helped the bird spirits." She leaned forward and ran her fingers over the ridged bark, pressing her hand flat against the tree so that her heat could penetrate its wood. "But it wasn't your fault! I understand that. I learned it this morning. They used you, that's all. It wasn't your fault. You're part of the wood. Even so far away, you're still part of the wood. I know your name, now. You're the One Alone. They used you and I shouldn't have been angry with you . . ."

From the corner of her eye she noticed the priest, in his shirtsleeves, standing in the open door to the church, watching her suspiciously. She waved to him, stepped away from the tree and walked along the massive, exposed root that pointed towards her own farm, and Ryhope Wood beyond.

She was almost certainly right. The life of the tree reached all the way to the old, dark forest. She could imagine the root as it probed across the mile or so of land to link with the edgewoods of the estate; perhaps it had always been there, the tenuous contact between a solitary adventurer into the brick and tarmac realm of the world and the moist and gloomy world of its birth.

A car pulled up by the roadside and sounded its horn twice, breaking Tallis's contemplative mood. Mr Williams stepped out from the back of the car, on to the green. Tallis slapped a hand to her mouth, feeling at once very guilty and very embarrassed. He smiled at her briefly, then plodded over, buttoning up his jacket against the cool summer's afternoon.

"It's just as well that I forgot," he said as he came up to her. There was an edge in his voice, Tallis thought.

"You forgot?" she said.

"That we were supposed to meet."

"I forgot too. But at least we didn't get soaked."

A flash of irritation touched the man's features. He seemed about to say something, but then changed his mind, smiled and said, "No. We didn't get soaked, did we? Ah well." And brightening: "Did you enjoy the dancing?"

"Not much."

"You seemed to be having a good time, being whirled around by those burly youngsters. I felt tired; I wanted to think about your strange song; so I went back to the Manor." He looked around at the green with its churned up turf and the scatter of litter. Then he looked at the tree, and at Tallis.

"You've got a certain look in your eyes," he said, frowning. "One of *those* looks. Something's up. Something has happened. Can you tell me about it?"

"Old Forbidden Place," Tallis said.

"I beg your pardon?"

"Old Forbidden Place," she repeated. "I don't know its true name yet. It's a place in another world. My brother Harry is lost there, I'm certain of that. I've had glimpses of it. And someone —not Harry—has come from that forbidden place to the edge of the wood. Last night I worked out some more of the story, but I still don't understand the whole thing. And I still don't know where Harry fits in . . ."

Mr Williams smiled and shook his head. "I can't understand a word of what you say," he said after a moment. "But I like the *sound* of what you say: Old Forbidden Place. Yes, it has a ring about it. It sounds mysterious. Unknown."

"It is. Very unknown."

He leaned towards her and spoke quite softly. "Darest thou now O soul, walk out with me toward the unknown region. All is a blank before us, all waits undream'd of in that region, that inaccessible land."

"Yes," Tallis said, shivering. "Yes. I do."

Mr Williams seemed taken aback for a moment. Then he chuckled. "It's part of a poem. By Walt Whitman. Your strange name reminded me of it."

"Oh."

"Your place, your forbidden place . . . it must have existed long ago. A very long time ago."

"Longer ago than memory," Tallis said. "But you mustn't say the name again. Not until we know its *true* name. I've already said it twice, you once."

Mr Williams nodded amused agreement, then looked at the oak tree, the One Alone. "This is a fine old specimen. Three hundred years if it's a day. Do you think it reaches right down into the earth? Even as far as your forbidden, secret place?"

Tallis said, "This is the One Alone. Its name has just come to me and I've realised what it is. It's not a lonely tree at all. It's part of the wood."

"Part of the wood? Which wood?"

"Ryhope Wood," the girl said, and added, "where you were walking yesterday."

"That's a mile or more away—"

"But this tree is a part of it, and probably always has been. Its root tells you that . . ."

Mr Williams followed her fleeting gesture across the common to the road where the root could be seen to rise above the level of the turf. Tallis went on, "If I stand round here—" she went round to the far side of the tree—"I'm outside the wood. But when I come round . . . like this . . . I'm coming into it. The edge of the wood is the *farthest* tree, no matter how far that is from the main forest. That's how the bird spirits came to me, last night."

"Bird spirits?" Mr Williams asked weakly.

"Mythagos. They attacked me. I created the gate they came through. I don't know if I created *them* or not. But they're definitely mythagos."

"Mythagos?"

"They attacked me. I thought the tree was my enemy, but trees can't help the way they're used and mythagos always come from the trees. The birds came to punish me for driving them off from Scathach. Like I told you yesterday. I made the field, where he lay wounded, into a magic place, a secret place. No birds could get into it except as spirits. Bird spirits. For some reason that has caused *anger*. They're very angry with me."

After a time of contemplative silence, the old man laughed. "This is a game, is it?"

"No," Tallis said, amazed. "No. It's not."

Frowning: "Then you can really work magic?"

"Simple magic. Simple enough to drive the birds off."

"Will you tell me more about it? About Old Forbidden Place?"

She raised a finger to her lips. "Don't say the name again. It's unlucky."

"But will you?"

"I don't know the whole story. I can only tell you part of it."

"That will do."

Tallis thought hard. "Tomorrow," she said. She looked up at the One Alone. "I'm still learning about it. Tomorrow I might know a little more."

"Tomorrow . . ." Mr Williams repeated. He came to a decision, then, and returned to the car, speaking briefly with the driver. The car drove off. When he returned to Tallis he was smiling. "I've decided to stay. Your story is something that I would very much like to hear. I am about to begin final work on a piece of music and I need some inspiration. If I can't find original songs—" he beamed down at the fair-haired girl—"perhaps I will hear an original story."

"I know lots of stories," Tallis said. "Would you like to hear the whole story of Bird Spirit Land?"

The old man nodded thoughtfully. "But I'd rather hear about you, first. Tell me as we walk. And then we'll find somewhere to have a cup of tea . . ."

A while later they were in Stretley Stones meadow, wading through the damp grass to the fallen stones. The sun was out, it was warm again. Tallis showed Mr Williams the ogham markings and explained what she believed them to say; she let him stand beneath the oak where Scathach had lain so helplessly; he closed his eyes and tried to imagine the scene.

When they sat on Scathach's stone Tallis felt sad for a while and Mr Williams, seeing this, remained thoughtfully, respectfully quiet. When the sadness had passed Tallis told him the story. He sat rapt and silent throughout, and when she had finished he remained staring at her, his head slowly shaking.

"That's a good story."

"It's a real story," Tallis said. "It happened here. It happened to me."

"What a dark and gloomy world you paint. Bird Spirit Land sounds like a frightening place; do you believe it really existed?"

"It exists now," Tallis said. "I made it. Or at least, I *saw* it. This is it. We're sitting in it. This meadow. Wherever Scathach is, it exists there too."

"In the 'long ago', perhaps? The long past."

"In the long past," Tallis agreed. "I was shown a vision of the place, but I interfered with what I saw. I opened the *hollowing* to Scathach's world; I used my own mind to do that; but then I attacked the carrion birds, drove them off. That's why the bird spirits attacked me yesterday. They came to the edge of the wood to try and kill me, but I danced too fast for them . . ."

It wasn't true. She shuddered as she caught herself in the lie. She had been helpless in their grip, thrown between them like a

rag doll. For whatever reason, they had let her live, leaving her to
stumble in the mud and reach for the antler . . only to see it
snatched away by the green girl, the spirit of the earth from the
Shadow Dance.

She realised that her friend was speaking to her. He was saying,
"Is this the only strange world that you've created? The only place
of visions? You said something about Old Forbidden Place."

"Old Forbidden Place is everywhere," Tallis said quietly,
staring at the oak tree ahead of her. "All the hollowings are just a
part of it."

"Hollowings?"

"Visions. More than visions . . . contacts. But I can't make any
sense of them, or of the forbidden place. Not until I know its true
name."

"This business of names," Mr Williams said, "is slightly
confusing. Who exactly *knows* its true name?"

"People who have been there and come back. If they didn't
know its name they wouldn't have been able to *get* back."

"You seem to know all the rules . . ."

Tallis shook her head. "I don't, though. And I don't know all
the names, either."

"It sounds a very grim place indeed. Is it like the Underworld,
do you think?"

"I suppose it is. But a living world, not a world of the dead."

"Like Avalon?"

Tallis, perhaps to his surprise, turned wide eyes upon him. She
seemed startled. Then she frowned as she whispered, "Yes . . . yes
it is . . . that's something like it. That name. It's an old name.
Avalon . . . something like Avalon . . ."

"Avalin?" Mr Williams ventured. "Ovilon? Uvalain . . . ?"

Tallis waved him silent. "I'll hear it soon. I'm sure I will."

"Iviluna? Avonesse?"

"Ssh!" Tallis said, alarmed. Her head was full of echoing
sounds, like a voice in a valley, shouting at her, half lost on the
wind. The sounds came and went, a name, so close . . . so
close . . .

But it drifted away again and she was left with the smell of damp
air and the touch of heat on her cheeks as the sun began to burn
fiercely from between the clouds.

Mr Williams watched the girl anxiously as the minutes passed and she remained quite still, as if in a daze, staring dreamily at him. She seemed to be listening to something a long way off. Indeed, there was a sudden movement in the hedge and when Mr Williams glanced there he realised that they were being watched. He caught a glimpse of a dark cowl, and the hint of white below it. Almost at once the figure withdrew into shadow, but Tallis had gone pale, her face almost rigid, almost old . . .

"Are you all right?"

Tallis said, "A name is like a call. When you name something you call it. Now I begin to understand . . ."

"What do you understand?"

Tallis's whole demeanour had changed. She was shivering, despite the heat. Her wretchedly pale face became even gaunter and the fair hair that hung so lank around her shoulders seemed to shiver and glitter with the shaking of the girl's body. Mr Williams felt a slight breeze around him and glanced back to where that enigmatic figure had been standing, just seconds ago.

A white face . . . a movement . . . then just shadow.

Tallis smiled at him suddenly, disarmingly. "The Bone Forest," she said. "Yes . . . of course . . . now I have it . . ."

"Speak to me," Mr Williams urged, concerned for the girl's well-being. "What's going through your mind?"

"A story," she whispered. "I've been thinking of it on and off for several days. Now it's been told to me completely. Have you had enough stories yet?"

"No. Not yet. The more the merrier."

"Then I'll tell you the Tale of the Bone Forest."

"Another good title."

"It's an old tale, but not as old as some, and not the oldest version of it, either."

Reaching out to take her hand, Mr Williams said, "Someone told you this story?"

"Yes."

"When?"

"Just now. Just a moment ago. Do you want to hear it?"

Mr Williams felt frightened, he didn't know why. He let Tallis's hand drop and sat up straighter. "Yes please."

She was strange, very tense. Her voice was the same, but the words seemed wrong for her. Although her eyes glittered as she spoke, and her lips moved, and her tongue licked her lips, and she breathed between sentences . . . the old man had the distinct sensation that someone was speaking *through* the girl.

And yet . . .

It was a disturbing moment, but he had little time to think about it because Tallis had raised both of her hands for silence, had closed her eyes and re-opened them, exposing a watery, vacant gaze, focused in the middle of nowhere.

"This is the story of The Bone Forest," she said softly. "When you summon good, you always summon evil . . ."

The Bone Forest

The young woman had not been born in the village, and so she was forced to make her camp outside its walls. She had arrived at the edge of the forest one spring day, and she was a very sorry sight indeed. Her skirts were long but ragged, as if stitched together from bits and pieces of the cloth that is used to dry the sweat off a horse. Her blouse was stained with the juice of berries. Her hair, which was very tangled, was so dirty that it took a sharp pair of eyes to catch the fine fire of its hidden colour. She was pretty, though, even if two of her teeth were missing. And she carried—apart from a cloth sack with her simple tent and utensils—two leather pouches.

There was a young man in the village who had been named Cuwyn, because he had once been hound-footed and fast on the hunt, but was now lame. He was the youngest of three and his brothers had fought in battle, died honourably, and been given burial beneath fine mounds of chalk and earth. He watched the young woman from the village wall and after a year he decided to go out and ask her three things. So he dressed in his hunting green, and strapped a paunching knife to his belt. He sharpened two spears and mended a net.

In the village he was laughed at. Cuwyn "fleetfoot" was going on the hunt. A lame stag is living in the north, they told him; then laughed. A fish without fins has been seen swimming in the slow brook!

Cuwyn ignored them all. He was an outcast in his own village.

He was the warrior who had not died and been buried with his brothers.

He recognised a fellow traveller.

So he polished his teeth with a piece of stripped hazel and went out to the woman's camp, where she was prodding at a small fire. She looked very thin and very hungry.

"I have three questions for you," he said to her.

"Ask them," the woman said.

"The first question is, what is your name?"

"I have been here a year, ignored and abused, and no-one has asked me my name. So make any name you like."

"I shall call you Ash, since I see that you have an ash twig in your right hand and in all likelihood it is to ash that you will return when you are dead."

She smiled but said nothing.

He asked his second question. "What have you been eating for the year?"

"My own heart," said Ash. "I came here to bring luck to you all, and you have left me out here with only lame wolves, stinking boars and carrion birds for company. Fortunately I have a big heart and it has kept me going."

"Well, I'm glad to hear it," said Cuwyn. "This is my third question. What have you got in those two sacks?"

Now Ash looked up at him and smiled. "Prophecy," she said. "I thought you would never ask."

"Prophecy, is it?" the young man murmured, scratching at his cheek and thinking hard. "There is one thing in the way of prophecy which this village could benefit from . . ."

"And what is that?"

"A knowledge of the forest. Too many times we hunt without success. The wood is deep, dark and dense. You could be standing next to a brown bear and both of you miss the other."

"Are you a hunter then?" Ash asked.

"I am," lied Cuwyn, glancing away.

"Then I can help you," said Ash. "But only you. In return for a small cut of the meat I shall make you into the Hunter himself. Your hunting will be wilder than the Devil's. The beasts you bring home will feed whole armies."

So Cuwyn sat down by the young woman's fire and watched her strange way of prophecy.

In the first leather bag she had twigs from every tree that grew in the wood. She had gathered them over the years and there was not a tree in the land which was not in the bag in the form of a short, trimmed stick.

"This is my forest," Ash said, as she held the twigs towards him.

"Every forest is here, even from before the Ice, and until the next Ice, which a few women have seen by looking into the fire which melts copper. All the woods from every age, here, in my hand. If I break a twig, like this—"

And she broke the ash twig that she had earlier been holding—

"—I have destroyed a forest in a far off place and a far off time. Can you hear the howling of the fire? The screaming of the men who run before its flames?"

"No," said Cuwyn.

Ash smiled. "Because you have no true hearing."

She rattled the second leather bag.

"In here I have the bones of many beasts, small fragments that I have gathered on my journeys. Not everything is here. But Man is. And for food there are pigs, and hares and deer and horses. There are plumed birds and fat fish. More than enough to keep a sallow youth like you from going hungry."

He looked at the shards of brown bone, which Ash had tipped into the palm of her hand.

"They mean nothing. They are bits of dulled ivory. How can you tell which is which?"

"I can't," she said. "Not until they are thrown."

So she closed her eyes and cast the twigs and the bones. Eyes still shut she reached into the pile of wood and drew out two of the sticks. She placed them in a cross before her. Still blind she took a piece of bone and placed it on the top of the twigs. When she finally looked at them she hesitated, then said, "In a forest of oak and hazel, a giant pig is running on a northward track."

Cuwyn needed no second prompting. He gathered up his spears, nets and snares and ran twelve miles around the forest until he saw a place where oak and hazel crowded to the light. As he entered the wood the sky changed and everything became silent. He was unnerved at first, but his vision had changed too and he seemed to see right through the trees. He noticed how a giant pig, its back raised into lethal spines, was running on a northward track. He hunted it and caught it, and although the tussle was a long one, he cut off its life and dragged its carcase home, cutting off a slice of the meat and leaving it with Ash.

The second week he visited her he felt stronger. He carried two spears and two knives, but he had dispensed with the net and the snares. He crouched before Ash and she shook the bags out on to the ground, blindly selecting the two twigs and the gleaming piece of bone.

"There is a forest where hornbeam grows in tangles with thorn. In it you will find a deer taller at the shoulder than a tall man."

Cuwyn stared at her. "In all of this land there is no forest of hornbeam and thorn."

"Call to it and it will come," Ash said. "It is there to be found. I did not say that you were hunting in this land alone."

Puzzled by that, Cuwyn began to run around the edge of the forest. After a while he grew tired and entered the dense wood to find shade and a few nuts. He scratched his hand on a thorn and followed deeper into the wood, and soon the silvery trunks of hornbeam began to gleam and beckon. He battled through the thorny tangle, listening to the silence and watching the eerie sky, for it had grown dark, but not in the way of night. It was cold, too, as if there was ice on the land around. There was a deer caught in a thicket and he struck it quickly in the neck, warming himself on the paunched carcase before dragging it back to his own land.

"Did you find your forest of hornbeam and thorn?" Ash asked on his return.

"Yes," the young man said, giving her a cut of the meat. "But I swear it was not there a year ago."

"It is not there now," the woman said. "But it existed once, when the land was younger."

"Cook your flesh," Cuwyn said. "Your words frighten me."

And so it went on:

In a forest of alder and willow two wild horses were lapping at a pool.

In a wood of oak and lime, hares as fat as hogs were bounding on a southward track.

In a woody scrub of beech and juniper, game birds, too heavy with feeding, were ripe for the kill.

For nine weeks Cuwyn ran the forest edge and found these strange woods, and in each he found the hunting that could sustain the village. His confidence grew. The wound in his leg troubled him less. He became fleetfooted. The village no longer laughed at him. He laughed at them. He felt great courage.

On the tenth visit to Ash he carried only a single spear, and one gutting knife.

She cast the twigs and picked the bone, placing it on top of the cross and opening her eyes. But she said nothing. Beneath the grime on her face her skin went white. As she made to cover the charm, Cuwyn reached out and stopped her.

"The village is hungry. Tell me where the hunting is."

"It is in a forest of birchwood and thorn," Ash said.

"But what is there to hunt?"

"No beast known to mortal man," she said softly. "I do not recognise this piece of bone at all."

"Then I must take the chance that it will be good to eat."

"You will take more of a chance than that. What is stalking in the wood is more ferocious than anything you have ever hunted. And it is not running, it is looking for you. It is, itself, a hunter. Wait a week, Cuwyn, and I will throw again for you."

"I cannot wait. The village cannot wait. I am the only hunter now."

Ash stared at the bone forest. "This wood is an evil place. Even the land rejects it." She broke the pattern of twig and bone. "What walks there is a mad thing, made from a mad mind. It has stepped out of darkness to stop you. You have taken too much. You have repaid nothing. It is my fault too. My charms, and your good hunting, have summoned an older force into being."

"It will have to reckon with me," Cuwyn said. "I will bring you a cut of its meat before duskfall."

"You will be dead before noon."

"I will survive longer than that."

"I believe that you will," Ash said, "but not in this world."

He went, then, running along the forest edge.

Ash thought about his words. At noon she cast the twigs and the bone, but they said nothing to her. She smiled and was pleased.

He had been right, then, right in that one thing.

But an hour later she cast the twigs and the bone and shook her head sadly as she looked at the forest of birch and thorn, and the splinter of human ivory that lay upon it.

In a forest of birch and thorn, a man is running from a shadow . . .

When she picked up the bone she could feel the scream and the warmth of the blood.

A few minutes later her body was racked with pain, and the stone became cold in her grip.

Ash gathered up her things and prepared to leave the outskirts of the village. She picked up the broken ash twig and a handful of ash from the fire, stared at them and smiled to herself.

"That was a good name," she said aloud. "You almost understood. I have been named many things, but this name came closest. When I am named so am I called, and when I am called I must serve in the way of the name. But this name came closest to what I truly am. You have almost understood my nature, and that part of me which is unnatural. Cuwyn, you were both hunter and hunted; the shadow of your thoughts was the beast which killed you. But for the kindness of my name, you shall ride the wide land without pain."

In the woodland the beast was coming. It had left the old place, after being summoned by Ash, and was coming to the village, to feed upon the flesh of those who lived there. Her job was done here. The Hunter would finish the work. Times, for the village, would now change. And now she faced a long journey, before finding the time and place next to call her master into the world.

But before she left she scattered the ash on to a small mound of fresh earth and chalk, and wrote Cuwyn's name on the broken twig, burying it there with the fragment of her dead son's bone.

When she had finished the story Mr Williams thought hard about what he had heard. "I don't understand," he confessed at last.

The colour had returned to Tallis's skin. She brushed a hand through her hair and took a deep breath, as if recovering from a great exertion. Curiously, she watched him. "What don't you understand?"

"Did the woman—Ash—summon the devil deliberately?"

"It wasn't the devil. It was the Hunter."

"But she called it to destroy the village, and young Cuwyn as well. Why kill the young man?"

Tallis shrugged. "I don't think she wanted him dead. It was her job. Her function. She called the Hunter to the land."

"But why?"

Frustrated at the questions Tallis said, "I don't *know*. Ask her! Because she had no real power of her own, I suppose. Her power of prophecy came from the Hunter, and so whatever good she could do she would do willingly, but always she would end by summoning the storm."

Mr Williams watched her. "Bringing him into the land. To destroy."

Tallis raised her hands, palms upwards. "I suppose so. The village had had nine successful hunts. But they gave nothing back."

"But your story seemed to suggest that Cuwyn and the Hunter were one and the same."

"Of course," Tallis said. "Cuwyn had taken from the wood. The wood took from him, it took a dark side, it made the Hunter *from* him. That is what Ash had said she would do. Her words were ambiguous."

"I'm still confused," Mr Williams admitted. "At the end, whose *bone* was it? Was Cuwyn her son?"

"It's just a story," Tallis sighed. "It really happened, once, a long time ago, but this is a very recent version."

"How recent?" Mr Williams asked curiously. Her answer clearly astonished him.

"A few hundred years, perhaps. A little longer . . ."

"A few hundred years. How could you possibly know that?"

"I'm inspired," Tallis said mischievously.

"You certainly are. But if I were you, I'd work out a better ending."

Tallis shook her head, confused at the suggestion. "If I did that then I'd change the story."

"Indeed you would. For the better."

"But you can't change something that *is*," she said in exasperation. "The story exists. It's the way it is. It's real. If I change it, if I invent something, then it becomes unreal."

"Or improved."

"But that's not the point. It's not a *fairy* story. It's not Enid Blyton! It's *real*. Why can't you understand that? If you think of a tune, and it's beautiful, you write it down as it is . . ."

"Of course."

"You don't change it later."

"Yes I do."

She was taken aback. "Then the original vision is weakened, isn't it?"

"Original vision," Mr Williams shook his head in silent amazement. "From the mouth of a thirteen year old . . ."

Tallis looked annoyed, sitting straight up on the stone and turning away from him. "Don't tease," she said stiffly.

"Sorry. But the point remains. A story, or a tune, comes as a piece of magic—"

"Yes. I know."

"But they belong to you. You can do what you like with them. Change what you like. Make it personal."

"Make it unreal. Things change in life when you change them in stories."

"I assure you that they don't."

"I assure you that they do," she retorted sharply.

"So are you telling me . . ." he composed his thoughts. "Are you telling me that if you told the last story again, and changed the young woman to a young man, then somewhere in history that same young woman would suddenly grow a beard?"

Tallis laughed at the image. "I don't know," she said. "I suppose so."

"Ridiculous."

"But stories are fragile. Like people's lives. It only takes a word out of place to change them forever. If you hear a lovely tune, and then you change it, the new tune might be lovely too, but you've lost the first one."

"But if I stick to the *first* tune, then I've lost the second."

"But someone else might discover it. It's still there to be born."

"And the first tune isn't?"

"No," Tallis insisted, although she was confused now. "It has already come into your mind. It's lost forever."

"Nothing is lost forever," Mr Williams said quietly. "Everything I've known I *still* know, only sometimes I don't *know* that I know it."

All things are known, but most things are forgotten. It takes a special magic to remember them.

"My grandfather said something like that to me," Tallis whispered.

"Well there you are. Wise Old Men, one and all . . ."

"But you've lost your childhood," Tallis said. "That can never come back."

Mr Williams stood and walked around the fallen stones, using his foot to push aside the grass and expose the ogham script. "I don't believe that," he said. "That it's lost, I mean. It's hard to remember the *events* of childhood, sometimes. Certainly it is. But the child still lives in the man, even when you're as old as me." He winked at Tallis. "It's always there, walking and running in the shadows of taller, newer spirits. Wiser spirits."

"Can you feel it?"

"Certainly I can feel it."

Tallis stared up into the sky, thinking of one of her masks: Sinisalo, *to see the child in the land.* She had wondered about that mask when she had made it. What child would she be seeing?

She began to understand. The land was old; the land remembered; the land had been young once, and that innocence was still there to be seen. Yes: Sinisalo would help her see the shadow of the child, and that meant the shadow of herself as she grew older.

All too quickly the day began to fade and the church at Shadoxhurst began to toll its bell, calling for evensong. Tallis returned home and Mr Williams began the long walk to the Manor house.

His last words to the girl were, "Tomorrow I want to hear the *real* story. You've made me a promise, now. So don't forget."

Tallis stared fondly after the big man. *Tomorrow, I'll do more than tell you the story. I'll show you where Harry is adventuring. You'll understand. I know you will.*

As good as her silent promise, the following day Tallis led Mr Williams into the narrow alley between the machine sheds. He edged warily through the nettles, his body turned slightly, his eyes showing the slight alarm he was experiencing at this odd journey. At the cleared space by the greenhouse window he crouched down among the dolls and coloured chalk marks, feasting his gaze on the weird symbols and hideous idols.

"All your own work?" he asked Tallis. The girl nodded, eyes sparkling.

They sat there for about half an hour. Mr Williams grew slightly edgy and Tallis, too, began to wonder if perhaps it was just her *solitary* presence that summoned the gateway to the winter world.

Just as she was about to abandon the vigil, however, a snowflake touched her cheek and the air around her frosted and grew bitter.

"It's here," she said quietly and wriggled round, on to her knees, facing the grimy glass.

Soon she began to hear the wind in Old Forbidden Place. There was a storm there, and the chill air gusted along the mountain path. She could hear the usual clatter of stones as something or someone moved, and the flap and crack of canvas, the tents of the people who were visiting that particular part of the hidden world.

"Can you hear me?" she called. More icy touches came on to her skin and she brushed at them, rubbing the wetness between her fingers. Mr Williams watched her, frowning. She leaned closer to the slit between the worlds, peered through at the grey, swirling snow beyond. A horse whinnied and struggled against its tether, its saddle harness rattling. A woman was chanting in an unknown language and something knocked regularly against wood, a high-pitched drum beat.

"Can you hear me?" Tallis called again.

And she remembered Harry calling to her. *I've lost you. Now I've lost everything* . . .

"Harry?" she shouted, startling Mr Williams. But her call was a vain hope, and she had not really expected to hear Harry's voice again.

Someone slithered to the gap, however, and came close to where Tallis was peering into the grey storm. She saw movement, smelled sweat. A dark shadow. The person on the other side peered closely into Tallis's summer world. "Who are you?" Tallis whispered.

The voice rattled off words. Tallis realised it was a child. A moment later the shadow vanished, the sound of its wailing cry muffled by the snow.

Tallis leaned back on her haunches, then turned to Mr Williams and smiled.

The man looked at her, then at the greenhouse. "Who were you talking to?"

Tallis was alarmed. She realised that he was not sharing her experience. "Didn't you hear the child?"

He frowned, then shook his head. Tallis pointed to the fading split in the air. "Can't you see that? Can't you see the way through?"

Mr Williams followed the girl's finger, but confessed that he saw nothing but glass. Tallis felt something like panic. Gaunt had smelled the woodsmoke on that day, many years ago, so the experience wasn't *completely* solitary. Could it simply be that Mr Williams, unlike Gaunt, was not of this part of the land? There were no ashes of the Williamses joining with the ashes of the Gaunts below the greensward?

A snowflake touched her hand. She held it up to the old man. "Snow," she said, and Mr Williams touched the damp spot with a finger and looked surprised. "Good Lord. I thought I felt a touch of winter in the air."

"That was it!" Tallis said, pleased. "You *did* feel it . . . you felt the underworld. That's where Harry is, trapped there. He called to me once. I'm going to go after him, to help him."

"How are you going to do that?"

"Through Ryhope Wood. There's something about that wood which isn't natural. Just as soon as I can find the right way to enter it, to explore it . . ."

Tallis led the way from the alley. They entered the fields and walked slowly towards Hunter's Brook, in the distance.

"Snowflakes," Mr Williams whispered and Tallis stared at her hand, still cold from that silent touch.

"From a terrible place . . ." she said, and the man glanced at her.

"So you still don't know its secret name?"

"Not yet," Tallis said. "And perhaps not ever. Secret names are very hard to find out."

They crossed the stile, walked on across bright meadows. "And you don't even know the *common* name of the place."

"Not even that," Tallis repeated. "Common names can be difficult too. I need to find someone who has been there, or heard of it."

"So . . ." said the old man, "If I understand correctly . . . what you are left with to describe the strange world is only your *own* name for it."

"Only my private name," Tallis agreed.

"Old Forbidden Place," Mr Williams murmured, and Tallis rounded on him, silencing him.

It was bad luck (he learned) to say such a name more than three
times in a day, and in their conversation in the alley they had used
up the quota. Mr Williams was certainly confused by the "naming
rules". Some things had three names, some only two. Sometimes
Tallis's own names were the common ones, very repeatable.
Sometimes they were more private and subjected to voice-taboo.
All in all, the man reflected ironically, the rules of the name-game
don't seem very well worked out.

He said nothing, of course. It wasn't his place to question the
secret world of the child . . .

Child? He smiled to himself as he glanced at the sophisticated
young girl, her body so bony and gangly, childlike, but her face,
her mental bearing so grown up. There was a look in her eyes that
reminded him not of a child but of an old, old woman. He could
see the adult in her as easily as he could see the straw-coloured hair
on her head. He felt, with a shiver, that he could see the corpse in
the child when she went so pale on telling a story. The bones of
her cheeks protruded, and her lips thinned. It was a terrible and
frightening sight, and that it was possession was something he did
not, now, doubt.

A spirit? An angel? A demon? What did these things really
mean? As he followed Tallis across the field he remembered only
her words from yesterday: *someone told me the story . . . just now
. . . just a moment ago.*

Someone in her mind? A silent voice in her head . . . herself,
of course, some form of unconscious communication within the
confines of her youthful skull. But the effect was dramatic.

There was more in the girl's head than just Tallis Keeton.

He stood in the baking sun, now, and was informed by Tallis
that he was standing in a cave. The girl, highly amused by his
puzzled look, was quite insistent that *she* could feel a deep, dank
cave, leading into an invisible hill. There was nothing he could do
or say at this juncture and he saw the disappointment in her eyes.
She was desperately trying to show him something of her own
experience, and failing. Perhaps he was not close enough to the
land here.

Don't try so hard, child, he thought to himself. Your stories are
the things that make me believe you.

She had created her own fantasy world in the streams, fields,
hills and woods around the farm. Now, something ancestral spoke

to her, peopled those woods, journeyed across those fields. And the fallen ogham stones, upon which they had sat the previous day, showed clearly that this place went back a long way. There had been people here for thousands of years. Tallis was their spiritual descendant, if not their blood one. Perhaps they *were* speaking through her.

Music filled his head as he walked. The images of the past, the sense of a dark and storm-laden landscape, of riders by night, of surging rivers . . . they were music, and he could hear the voice-music of a lament, and the stirring of wind, and the chanting of people huddled in tents. It was eerie music and he wished he had his notebook with him to sketch down the essential themes, to note the link between the sounds of nature and the sound of voices.

He wondered if in this way, creating his own story, he might have been coming closer to Tallis's vision of the strange world than he realised.

To each his entrance to the realm. To each his gate.

There was a memory in the land. It was all around him. He was walking through it. It whispered to him as he walked, as it whispered to Tallis, but speaking a different language, engaging a different passion . . .

Something happened here . . .

These thoughts remained unspoken. Soon they had reached a tree called Old Friend. Its trunk had been split by lightning, forming an uncomfortable seat which he tried to occupy.

"Are you sitting comfortably?" Tallis asked.

"No," he said loudly, and was amused when the girl said, "Good. Then I'll begin."

When she began the tale she used the oldest opening to a story imaginable. He teased her about it, interrupting her and taking a mischievous pleasure in her growing irritation. He felt the stirring of a woodland breeze on his skin. Behind him, in the dense undergrowth, there was a heavy, almost tangible silence. Tallis was facing the forest, but for a while she seemed unaware of it, berating her companion for failing to take her story seriously.

And then it happened.

It was as if something stepped past him, a terrible shivering presence. Tallis's whole bearing changed and her face grew gaunt.

Now, for the first time, he silenced himself and leaned forward, watching the possession.

The girl's language changed. He had read the *Mabinogion*, those half remembered tales from the surviving fragments of Celtic story-cycles. He noted how close her language came to the style of those stories. She spoke quickly; dialogue ran into dialogue; she used a formal, almost awkward construction of phrases, a sort of archaic style, much as modern writers used when they were trying to evoke a sense of the past, all inversions and tumbled adjectives.

But it had power, he thought. By Heaven, it had power, and he sat entranced, her words creating a world in his mind:

A world in which a King had decided to bury himself in his own Castle, filling the rooms with earth, an enormous burial mound, the ruins below.

A world in which a Queen used magic to haunt her dead husband in the Otherworld, all the Otherworlds, all the different realms of death to which her husband's spirit ran: the Bright Plain, the Many Coloured Land, the Isles of Youth.

A world in which three brothers strutted and stalked for supremacy. The youngest was called Scathach, the name Tallis had given to the ghost in Stretley Stones meadow. Denied his birthright of a Castle in the land, Scathach passed into the Otherworld itself, into Old Forbidden Place, and there found a fortress made of ur-stone, stone which was *not* stone, some magic substance. He had performed that deed which must have excited the minds of the ordinary folk of old: he had ridden, whilst still alive, into the realm of the dead. He had shut himself off from the dead, and from the living, a place with no name, with no warmth, with no heart. A dead place, a prison, hidden from the eyes of both real world and afterworld.

And he wanted to come home.

And his sister loved him . . .

And mad things ran from the crevices of his mad mind.

It was an odd feeling for the man who listened. All of the ingredients of the story were familiar to him, and yet the story was unfamiliar. It was unlike anything he had ever heard, and this was perhaps as much to do with the manner and nature of its presentation. At its heart it was just a fairy tale; but Tallis had invested it with something from herself which was so intriguing that it marked the journey as something quite different. There was

so much that was implied by the story. Whole years, whole
sequences of action had been covered by the girl's mysterious
words: *Many years passed. Years without vision.*

And Mr Williams knew the child well enough, now, to understand that she was waiting for those visions to come, to fill in the
gaps . . . to show her where Harry might be hiding, and how she
might find him.

She had cut the story short. It was not by her own choice but
rather as if a shutter had come down, cutting off the flow of words.
So that it was a lie when she answered "no" to Mr Williams's
question about the completeness of the tale.

It took Tallis some moments to recover from the intensity of the
images that had packed her mind, from the smells and sounds, and
from the heat of that fire. She could still see the fire in the hall of
the great Castle. It burned fiercely before her eyes, an enormous
flame, reaching high above the feasting tables and the cold floor.
She could still see the harsh glare, and the dark shadows that it
formed, on the pale, angry faces of the young men who stood
before her. They were disgraced and on the fire-side of the table,
their hair like burnished copper, their clothes brightly coloured,
but their faces like grim death.

It was an image which was so vivid that she knew it must have
happened exactly like this. She was frightened to think of herself
so close to the real events in Scathach's life. Scathach, too,
frightened her because in her mind's eye he was much harder than
the vision of him in the meadow. His scars were terrible. His hair
was lank, his fists dark with bruises and healed wounds. Of all the
brothers he glowered the most, and each cut of his dagger on the
plate before him was a stab at his father's heart and a stab, too, at
Tallis, who seemed to sit beside the father, staring across the table
at the angry sons.

Who *was* she in this story? Why did Scathach look at her so
fiercely?

The Queen was there, on the other side of her. She smelled of
damp linen and a sweet, sickly perfume. Her hands were like birds,
hovering over the table, long pale fingers picking like beaks at the
bread and the cheese. The worst smell coming from her was the
smell of death. Alive in body, she was already close to the Bright
Plain, where her screaming shade would haunt the cruel King.

Most vivid and disturbing of all: the view of the place that haunted Tallis herself, the realm across the wide, deep gorge. When she told the story she almost toppled, so dizzying was her height above the river. The wind caught her and threatened to throw her into the gorge. The river below was a silver thread, and yet she knew that it rushed and roared across the rocks, a terrible flow. How Scathach had ever crossed that chasm she didn't know. She looked into the distance, to the mists of the world that was Old Forbidden Place, to its icy edge. The forest seethed and grasped the land, roots like giant claws, an immense and stifling cloak of death and confusion. Rising from its tangled grip, the ruins of a grey and ancient castle . . .

All of this she saw without wishing it. She felt her tongue move, felt power to speak, but felt controlled by whoever had reached for her, to communicate the tale. And she had cut the story short; Tallis was fleetingly puzzled by that. There had been an image of Scathach, and a girl glimpsed by moonlight. And an odd thought: *he took the name of the tree.*

It did not fit with the story she had told to Mr Williams.

When the spirit left Tallis she felt as if a great weight had been lifted from her lungs. Her body almost floated. Mr Williams asked his questions and she answered them impatiently and sadly, because she knew he would soon be going.

At least they walked back towards the bridleway to Shadoxhurst, away from the unnamed field that guarded Ryhope.

"Do you *have* to go?"

"I have to go. I'm sorry. I have music to write. I don't have much time. It's the blight of growing old."

"I shall miss you," Tallis said.

"I shall miss you also," he said to her. "But I'll come back next year, if I can. To this very place on this very day. And that's a promise."

"And a promise made," she reminded him, "is a debt to be paid."

"Indeed it is."

He walked off along the bridleway towards the village where, no doubt, he was to be met by the car.

Tallis called to him, "Write some good songs."

"I shall! Tell some good stories."

"I shall."

"And by the way," he called.

"What?"

"That field around the wood. I think I know its name. It's Find Me Again Field. Try it. Then you can visit your glade without fear."

He had gone, but Tallis didn't notice. She was staring at the distant wood, and her eyes were wide with astonishment and excitement.

Find Me Again Field.

Geistzones

(i)

That evening she fashioned Find Me Again Doll. She used a piece of hawthorn, the wood of the first doll she had ever made. The name made her think of returning to first friends, or first visions. The doll itself would be buried at the edge of Find Me Again Field, close to Hunter's Brook.

During the night she went to the alley between the sheds and knelt there, masked by the Hollower. She felt the immediate closeness of Old Forbidden Place and watched without alarm as space opened between the worlds, the thin strip reaching from the ground to a point above her head. Snow swirled from the gateway and wind gusted and tugged at her hair. The lamenting woman was there, the struggling horse, the noisy child. The drum that sometimes sounded began to beat all at once, its odd tattoo becoming more menacing as the minutes went by.

When Tallis sang the song, echoing the woman's lament, she felt the power of the music and sensed the awesome effect her own voice was having in that frozen, that other, place. She knew, now, that her journey would take her to the same remote mountainside. It had to. She had dreamed of that place. She had told stories of it. Her brother Harry was wandering there. Perhaps Mr Williams's forgotten song was being sung there too. It was the place where lives ended and lost things could be found. It was a place forbidden to ordinary folk, but Tallis Keeton was not ordinary. Thinking this was as natural to her as thinking that before too long she would need to relieve herself of the evening's burden of cherryade. That was a comfort in just knowing, in just accepting. She was aware of how close the mask-makers were, but also of the fact that their job was done . . . Gaunt had said it to her a long time ago: *someone was showing her how to make the dolls.* And today, Mr Williams had said it too, when he had questioned her about the story she had told, and she had said that someone had just told it to her, someone alive yet not alive.

"What do you want from me?" she whispered to the ghosts in Old Forbidden Place. "What can I do? I couldn't even save Scathach. I got it all wrong. I tried to save him from you. He almost didn't get to his funeral because of me. What can you possibly want *me* for?"

As she whispered the words, an image of Scathach in the castle came to mind, the fierce, scarred-faced young man, stabbing his dagger into the wooden platter on the table, each blow a meaningful strike of anger, his gaze torn between his father, whom he hated, and Tallis . . . Tallis sitting next to the King . . . Tallis at the high table in the castle . . . but who was she? What role did she play there? Who was it, in her story of the King and Old Forbidden Place, whom she could not see, but whose consciousness she shared?

"Mr Williams was wrong," she said softly. "It all belongs to me, yes. But it has been passed *on* to me by someone. It's a small inheritance. Someone else owned the stories first. I mustn't try to tamper with them. They're only partly mine, and in any case they are only mine for a while. But who am I? Who *am* I?"

Sitting by the King . . . sitting close to the Queen . . . Watching the three angry brothers . . . Watching the fire . . .

"I'm the daughter, then. I must be. That's all I can be. The King's daughter. The Queen's daughter. Then why do I feel so old? And why do I feel so *cold* in the dream story?"

She remembered Mr Williams's teasing words to her, as she had tried to tell the story:

But at least we know there was a sister . . . and her brothers loved her in different ways . . . her story is a different story than this one . . . loved in different ways . . .

The gateway to the winter world had long since faded. Tallis, staring at a glimmer of light on the dingy glass of the greenhouse, realised that it was a sign of the new day. She began to hear activity everywhere. It was as if she were coming out of a dream. The sounds of dawn intruded into her conscious mind and at once made her feel cold.

She picked up her new doll and went into the garden, scudding her feet through the dewy grass to make patterns in the moisture. The dog was prowling in the garden, sniffing out the signs of night's visitors. Distantly, rooks called and flapped restlessly in their high nests.

There was another sound, though, and this one set her pulse racing. It was like a low roar, very animal, very weird. She ran to the gate and stared into the distance. A heavy mist hung over the stream at the bottom of the field. But as she watched she heard the sound again and saw the furtive yet confident movement of a tall animal in the hollow.

Its antlers pierced the surface of the fog, moving like hard fingers in the clearer day.

Suddenly the beast broke cover. It was on the far side of the water and after a glimpse of its broad body, Tallis lost sight of Broken Boy among the oak and elm hedge that lined Sad Song Meadow.

"Wait for me!" she shouted and clambered over the gate. The dog chased after her, barking loudly. It didn't jump the gate and by the time Tallis was at the stile it had become silent again. The girl entered the mist by the stream, picked her way across the stepping stones and emerged on the stag's spoor, tracking it precisely along the hedge.

After a few minutes she arrived, breathless, at Hunter's Brook.

Without ceremony, but moving very carefully, she took four steps into Find Me Again Field. She was being watched from the far wood, but when she looked there she could see no movement, nor guess where the watcher was hiding. It was Broken Boy, though, she was sure of that. He had waited for her all these years. He had been thought dead, killed by poachers, and perhaps, indeed, he had suffered just that fate. But there was far more to Broken Boy than just old meat on tall bones.

And he wanted Tallis!

She bent down, now, and pushed the hawthorn doll into the

hard ground, working it vigorously to break the sun-dried turf,
then twisting it into the clay earth beneath. When the head was
below the grass she closed the wound with her fingers, spat on the
cut and placed her hand upon it. "I know you now," she said
aloud. "I know your name. You can't trap me."

A few minutes later she reached the broken road which had
once led to the lodge. She stood in the high grass, listening to the
sounds of movement in the dense woodland. Then she
approached the fence, with its faded notice, and quickly clambered over the loose wire. Immediately she could see the yellow
light of the glade by the ruined house.

She picked her way carefully along the hard path underfoot and
came, for only the second time in her life, into the garden of the
place which the wood had claimed. She was shocked by what she
saw.

The great black totem had fallen, split along its length and now
a mass of beetles crawled in the hollowed-out inside; it was sinking
into the clinging grass that had once been a lawn. Its leering smile
was turned into the earth. Draped on the trees around the clearing
were skins and fragments of hide; deer, fox, and rabbit. The deep
pit in the lawn, which a few years ago had been dry and dead, was
smouldering now. Tallis approached it cautiously, glancing fre-
quently at the crowding trees with their rotting rags of animal
skin.

The pit was filled with charred bone. She kicked at the fire's
remains and a fine ash floated into the dancing light.

Nervously she called out. The heavy trunks of oak absorbed her
words, deadening the sound, and replied only with the rustle of
bird life in their branches. Tallis patrolled the small garden area,
observing everything: here the remains of a wire fence, there,
impaled by roots, several slats of wood which might have come
from a chicken coop, or kennel.

With a start she suddenly saw the crawling carcass of a sheep; it
had been thrown into the undergrowth and its bloody face,
stripped of flesh, seemed to be watching her. Now, as she listened,
she heard the buzz of flies; and when she leaned close she caught
the first smells of the process of decay.

Who had been here?

She crouched by the warm ash and picked out five or six
fragments of bone. They were small, from some small animal . . .

a rabbit perhaps, or a small pig. When she closed her fingers around them no images came into her mind and she smiled to herself, remembering her own story of the Bone Forest.

"No talent for prophecy," she murmured aloud.

She gathered more of the bone and filled one of her pockets. She searched the ground for footprints, but found only traces of a horse. Following these she found the track which led into the deeper wood, through the dry fern and nettle that constantly grew to block such paths.

And she thought of the young man wearing the skin of a stag, the sun making his pale body seem smooth, his movements lithe, like an animal's, his actions, by the stream, so swift, so savage . . .

"So this is where you've been hiding . . ."

Was he watching her? Was he here now? She looked slowly round, but sensed no danger.

And she was here for a different purpose, in any case. She walked through the saplings that crushed against the house, stepped carefully through their guarding ranks and pushed at the broken windows of the study, moving them in, then tugging them out again to make a gap through which she could squeeze her body. It was quite bright in the room, the roof being open in several places to the elements.

Broken-backed and rotted books lay everywhere. Tallis walked among them, kicking them aside, and stepped round the central feature of the study, a great oak, forked at its base to form an awkward seat. Its double trunk reached through the crumbling plaster ceiling, into the light. Like everything else in the room it was laced with ivy.

Some of the display cases still had their glass fronts intact, but they were upturned and their contents scattered. Tallis picked through a pile of broken pottery, touching the shards and moving them aside almost gently to expose metal spearheads, flint artefacts and all manner of strange coinage and bone statuary.

But it was not for these mementoes of history that she had come and she moved back around the central tree to the ivy-covered desk which she had seen on her previous visit.

As she began to strip the ivy from the drawers she realised with a shock that someone else had been here recently; the ivy was already torn, though replaced to cover the desk like a leafy tablecloth. When she pulled at the top drawer it slid out easily, and the sodden, rotting mass that was contained within was revealed in all its stinking glory: sheets of paper and envelopes compacted into a single, yellow mass; photographs and exercise books; a bible and a dictionary; a pair of woollen gloves; a seething mass of beetle larvae.

Tallis closed the drawer and drew in a deep breath, wrinkling her nose at the terrible odour. But in the second drawer she found what she wanted, the journal she had known was here; her grandfather's letter had referred to it and she had dreamed of an old man writing at this very desk, an image of the man who had studied Ryhope Wood's "mythagos".

The journal, too, was water-sodden and mouldy, despite its thick leather binding and the oilskin sheet which was wrapped around it. Over the years just too much water had poured from the gaping hole above the desk, and seeped into the precious pages.

But again she saw . . . someone else had already opened the journal. When she eased the pages apart they opened naturally towards the end, and a green leaf had been placed between two sheets. She turned the pages carefully and could make out words, though much of the ink had run, and in places an orange mould had eaten through the paper. When she came to a page where the precise, rounded handwriting could be easily interpreted she bent forward and began to read.

> . . . *The forms of the mythagos cluster in my peripheral vision, still. Why never in fore-vision? These unreal images are mere reflections, after all. The form of Hood was subtly different—more brown than green, the face less friendly, more haunted, drawn* . . .

Tallis was confused. Hood? Robin Hood? She turned to the front cover of the journal, easing it open. She found that her hands were shaking. She was trying not to damage the book any more than years of rain and rot had done. There were words written on the frontispiece and she stared at them long and hard:

> George Huxley. *Account and Observations of Woodland Phenomena, 1923–1945.*

After a minute of silent contemplation, Tallis flipped carefully back into the body of the journal:

> . . . *mythagos grow from the power of hate, and fear, and form in the natural woodlands from which they can either emerge—such as the*

Arthur, or Artorius form, the bear-like man with his charismatic leadership—or remain in the natural landscape, establishing a hidden focus of hope—the Robin Hood form, perhaps Hereward, and of course the hero-form I call the Twigling . . .

. . . Wynne-Jones suggests we go back into the woods and call the Twigling deep, perhaps to the hogback glade where he might remain in the strong oak-vortex and eventually fade. But I know that penetrating into deep woodland will involve more than a week's absence, and poor Jennifer is already deeply depressed by my behaviour . . .

Tallis continued to turn the pages, and at last came back to the page marked out by a leaf. The writing was blurred, the ink smeared, and almost at once she came upon a word that made no sense to her at all. But as her gaze drifted down the lines one passage sprang out at her:

. . . As he recovered he repeated the phrase "forbidden places" as if this were some desperate secret, needing communication. Later I learned this: that he has been further into the wood than . . .

After that, in an infuriating parallel with her grandfather's letter to her, the words became obscure.

She stared at the page and came to a decision. She would have to ask her father to help her understand the words. So she wrapped the journal in its oilskin, tucked it under her arm, and eased the desk drawer shut. She felt as if she was disturbing the dead, but she knew she would bring the document back.

She turned to the French windows, intending to leave the lodge and return to her own house, but a sound outside made her start with fright. It was a rustling movement in the undergrowth. Almost immediately she thought "Broken Boy"!

She ran quickly to the windows, and started to push them open, hoping to see the stag waiting for her in the clearing . . . but she froze, then took two quick steps back into the room, as she saw, coming towards her through the saplings the tallest, strangest-looking man she had ever seen. He was encased in fur, from the hood around his head to the thick boots on his feet. The fur was black and silver and seemed wet; it was tied around his arms and waist and legs with wide strips of leather, from which hung gleaming shards of white bone and stone and the shrivelled carcasses of tiny birds, still in their dark feathers. From beneath the hood the face that peered so intently at the house seemed very dark, but whether with dirt or a beard Tallis was not at first sure.

A second after Tallis had reached her hiding place—behind the V-shaped bole of the oak in the room—the light from the French windows was blocked by the man's shape. He was so tall that he had to stoop to enter the study. Strangely, on this hot summer's day, there was a smell of snow about him, and of wet. Tallis, her heart thundering, crouched low against the cool, hard wood, clutching Huxley's journal to her chest. As the man picked his way carefully through the rubble, kicking at the shards of wood and glass, Tallis edged around to keep the tree between herself and the stranger.

His breathing was slow and he was whispering to himself, the words sometimes emerging as a growl.

Then from elsewhere in the house came the noise of wood cracking. A voice shouted, the words incomprehensible, the tones clearly female. The man in the study shouted back. Tallis risked a glance from behind the oak and saw that he had pushed back his hood and was tugging at the door from study to hall. His hair was thick and black and tied into a topknot, with two long pigtails on each temple. It looked greasy. Two stripes of red had been painted above each pigtail. The leather binding of the topknot was slung with the skull of a blackbird, the yellow beak tucked into the tight hair at the back of the man's head.

When the door shattered before his strength, the man stepped through. Tallis immediately darted for the outside, holding on grimly to the heavy journal. She heard a cry from behind her and the fur-clad figure came crashing through the study. Tallis yelled and slammed shut the French windows. She raced through the saplings and reached the track which led to safety. But she hesitated, catching sight of something from the corner of her eye.

A boy was watching her from the undergrowth. He stepped out into full view. He was almost as tall as her and swathed in the same black and silver fur as the man. His hair, too, was tied into a spiky bunch on the top of his head, but it was short; he wore a white strap around his hair from which hung several tiny mammals' feet. His cheeks were smeared with green and white paint. He watched through wide, coal-black eyes. Tallis noticed that in one hand he held a small wooden figure.

This was all she observed before the boy began to screech at the top of his voice, pointing at her. What he yelled was one word, and Tallis remembered it as she ran from the lumbering man who now pursued her.

"Rajathuk! Rajathuk!"

She fled through the dark wood, veering into the undergrowth as again she sensed a man standing close to her, although when she looked back she could see nothing. She could hear the tall figure from the study grunting and battling with the thorns that had snared him. Tallis reached daylight and climbed the wire fence.

Outside, looking in: she backed away from the trees, stepping through the long grass carefully. The breeze shifted the wire, rustled the leaves. A face slowly formed in the gloom, a man's face, shrouded in green. It peered at her, then frowned. She stood quite still, wondering whether the man would leave the wood and give chase, but after a while the face withdrew.

It had not been painted. It had not been bearded.

As she walked home she had the uncanny feeling that someone was keeping pace with her, just out of sight among the underbrush.

She read all afternoon and into the early evening, and began to make a little sense of the sprawling journal entries, although most of what was legible was beyond her comprehension. When her eyes began to water with the strain of deciphering she closed the book and carried it downstairs. Her father was in the sitting room, working at the round table, a cigarette smoking between his fingers. He looked up as Tallis quietly entered the room and stubbed the cigarette into a glass ashtray.

From the music room came the sound of scales as Margaret Keeton loosened up her fingers for an hour or so of practice. As Tallis placed the journal on the table so the sound of a sonata replaced the scales and Tallis felt relaxed, enjoying the familiarity and the delicacy of her mother's playing.

Her father sniffed the air, then peered hard at the damp book. "What have you got there? It stinks. Where did you dig it up?"

"In Ryhope Wood," Tallis said. Her father glanced at her, a touch of exasperation in his expression. His grey hair was damp from being washed—the Keetons were going to a dinner that evening—and he smelled faintly of after-shave.

"More fantasies?" he murmured, closing the file on which he had been working.

"No," Tallis stated flatly. "It was in a desk in the ruined house at the edge of the wood. Oak Lodge. I went exploring."

Her father stared at her, then smiled. "Did you see any ghosts? Any sign of Harry?"

With a shake of her head, Tallis said, "No ghosts. No Harry. But I saw a mythago."

"A *mythago*?" A brief moment's thought. "That's one of your grandfather's gobbledegook words. What is it, anyway? What does it mean?"

Tallis brought the journal round to where her father sat. She opened the book at one of the easier pages, where the water had not stained the sheet with ink; where Huxley's writing was less cryptic than so often during his frantic entries. She said, "I've tried to read bits of the writing, but I can't manage very much. This page is obvious, though . . ."

Keeton stared at the words, then read softly: "*Have detected clear mythopoetic energy flows in the cortex: the mythago form comes from the right brain and its reality from the left hemisphere. But where is the pre-mythago genesis zone? WJ believes deep in the brain stem, the most primitive part of the neuromythogenetic structure. But there is activity in the cerebellum whenever he is inducing mythogenesis in the wood. Our equipment is too crude. We may be measuring the wrong psychic energy* . . . This is all nonsense. It doesn't make any sense. It sounds scientific, but it's just gobbledegook . . ." He turned a page. "*The Hood form is back, in a very aggressive form. No merry men for this particular Robin, just prehistoric wood-demon . . .*"

He looked up, frowning at his daughter. "Robin Hood? *The* Robin Hood?"

Tallis nodded vigorously. "And Green Jack. And Arthur. And Sir Galahad the noble knight. And the Twigling . . ."

"The Twigling? What in Heaven's name is that?"

"I don't know. It's a hero of some sort. From before the Romans. There are heroines too, some of them very strange. All in the wood . . ."

James Keeton frowned deeply again, struggling to understand. "What are you saying? That these people still *live* in the wood? But that's silly . . ."

"They're there! Daddy, I've *seen* some of them. Hooded women. Grandad knew about them too. They come out of the wood sometimes and whisper to me."

"Whisper to you? What do they whisper?"

Violent chords sounded from the music room and Tallis glanced at the intervening wall, then turned back to her father. "How to make things. Like dolls, and masks. How to name things. How to remember things, the stories . . . how to *see* things . . . the hollowings . . ."

Keeton shook his head. He reached for another cigarette but toyed with it in his fingers rather than lighting it. "You've lost me. This is one of your games, isn't it? One of your fantasies?"

That made Tallis angry. She pushed back her hair and gave her father a grim, cold stare. "I knew you'd say that. It's your answer for everything . . ."

"Steady on," the man warned, wagging a finger briefly. "Remember the pecking order in this house . . ."

Unabashed, Tallis tried again. "I've *seen* them. I really have. The stag. My Broken Boy. Everybody knows he should have died years ago. But he's still out there—"

"*I've* never seen him."

"But you have! You saw him when I was born, and you *know* that he has been seen near the wood since you were a boy yourself. *Everybody* knows about it. He's a legend. He's real, but he came from *here!*" Tallis tapped her head as she said this. "And *here* . . ." Tapping her father's skull. "It's all in the book."

Keeton touched the open page, fingered it, then turned it; he was silent for a long time. The cigarette broke in his fingers and he let it drop. Perhaps he was torn between the two conflicting beliefs: that his daughter was slightly crazy; and that he had before him the journal of a scientific man, and that journal contained statements as strange as his daughter's visions . . .

And he *had* seen Broken Boy, and could not deny that the stag was an oddity.

He leaned forward again and flipped the dank pages of the book. "Mythogenetic zones," he read, scanning down the writing. When he spoke his tone was disbelieving, then incredulous; he articulated the words as if to say: this is astonishing, this is simply unbelievable. "Oak vortices! Ash-oak zones . . . reticular memory . . . pre-mythago vortices of generative power . . . *ley matrices*, for God's sake. Elemental image forms . . ."

He slammed the book shut. "What does it all mean?" He stared

at Tallis darkly, but was a confused rather than an angry man.
"What does it mean? It's all just so much—"

"*Gobbledegook!*" she finished for him, knowing the word he
would use, using it sneeringly. "But it *isn't* gobbledegook. You
have dreams. Everybody has dreams. People have always dreamed.
It's as if those dreams were becoming real. All the heroes and
heroines from the story-books, all the exciting things that we
remember from being young—"

"Hark at the girl. Hark at the way she speaks. She's
possessed . . ."

Ignoring his astonishment, Tallis said, "All of those things,
they somehow come *real* in Ryhope Wood. It's a dream
place . . ."

She sighed and shook her fair head. "Grandad must have
understood it better than me. He talked to the man who wrote this
journal. Then he wrote to me in my folklore book."

"I read the letter," Keeton murmured. "Rambling. Silly. An old
man going senile." Wistfully, he added, "An old man dying."

Tallis grimaced, then bit her lip. "I know he was dying, but he
wasn't losing his mind. He just didn't understand *everything*. Same
as you. Same as me. But he said something in the letter that I *am*
beginning to understand now. And in this journal—" she quickly
turned to the leaf-marked page, where the ink had run so much
—"this page is important, but I can't read it. I thought—I thought
you might read it to me. You see? Here, where it says 'Forbidden
places . . .' I can read that sentence all right, but nothing
else."

Her father stared at the blurred page for a long while, nibbling
at his lower lip, then rubbing his lined forehead, then sighing,
then bending closer to scrutinise the writing. And at last he
straightened up.

"Yes," he said. "I can make sense of it. Of the words,
anyway . . ."

WJ has returned from the wood. He has been gone four days. He
is very excited, also very ill. He is suffering from exposure, two
fingers quite badly frostbitten. He has experienced a climate far
more severe than this cold, wet autumnal England: he has been
in a winter land. He took nearly two hours to "thaw", his fingers
bandaged. Drank soup as if there was no tomorrow. As he

recovered he repeated the phrase "forbidden places" as if this were some desperate secret, needing communication.

Later I learned this: that he has been further into the wood than either of us. Subjective time for WJ is two weeks, a frightening thought. This simple relativistic effect seems confined to certain woodland zones. There may be others where the effect of time on the human body is the opposite, the traditional time of the fairy world, where a traveller will return after a journey of a year to find a hundred years have passed.

WJ says he has proof of this, but he is more excited about what he calls his "geistzones", and I must record as best I can his rambling, difficult description of his recent experience.

He has come to believe that the mythogenetic effect works not only to create the untouchable, mysterious figure of lore and legend, the hero figure, it also creates the forbidden *places* of the mythic past. This would seem obvious enough. The legendary clans and armies—such as the ancient *shamiga* who guard their river crossings—are also associated with *place*. And the ruined castles and earthworks, too, would fit into this category. But WJ has glimpsed these realms he calls *geistzones*, archetypal landscapes generated by the primordial energies of the inherited unconscious, lost in the lower brain. He has found a mythago which he designates "oolering man" after the chanting cry that the figure emits before it steps from the woodland through the entrance to the *geistzone* which it has created, or made to appear.

The *geistzone* is a logical archetype, logically generated by the mind. It can be both the desired realm, or the most feared realm; the beginning place or the final place; the place of life before birth, or life after death; the place of no hardship, or the place where life is tested and transition from one state of being to another accomplished. Such a realm would appear to exist in the heartwoods. There are clues enough to this fact in the mythic ruins that abound in the outer zones of the wood.

WJ sees the "oolering man" as a guardian of the *way* to that land. It is a shaman figure, that much is clear. Its attributes are a face painted white but with the eyes and mouth striped with red; a body clothed in ragged strips of uncured hide and skin, some blackened with age, some fresh and still bloody; a necklet of severed birds' heads, long-beaked birds such as herons, storks and cranes being central, and the coloured bills of smaller birds taking up the back; various rattles and whistles to simulate bird-song; and a dancing movement that imitates a wading bird, pecking through the water to the mud below.

WJ will try to relate this to the myths of birds as messengers of the dead, bringers of omens, and transformation into human form. (From the eyepoint of a bird, all the *extremes of the land* are visible, and the shaman emulates this far-seeingness by adopting the trappings of flight.) But the "oolering man", with its function at the entrance of heaven, or hell, is of more interest than this simple shamanism. It seems to be able to *create* these gateways. Belief in such a thing must once have been very strong. The *geistzone* that WJ witnessed was a winter land, and a freezing and hellish wind blew from it for three days, while the "oolering man" sat before it, facing the unwelcome visitor, almost defying him to approach. WJ has suffered from this, though the "oolering man" seemed to come to no harm. Eventually he rose, stepped through the entrance to his *geistzone* and folded space around him.

When James Keeton looked up from the smudged text he saw his daughter standing by the window, watching him through the crudely gouged eyes of the white and red mask which she held to her face.

"Oolering man?" he said. "Geistzones? Shamiga? Do you understand *any* of what this means?"

Tallis lowered the mask. Her dark eyes were bright, her pale skin vibrant. She stared at her father, but at the same time was looking through him. "Hollowers . . ." she whispered. "*Oolering man . . . hollower . . .* the same. Guardians. Creators of the path. Creators of the ghost realms. The story is coming clearer . . ."

He was confused. "Story? Which story?" He rose to his feet as he spoke, adjusting his braces, pacing round the sitting room. The smell of rotting wood and earth was strong.

Tallis said, "The story of Old Forbidden Place. The journey to Old Forbidden Place. Harry's geistzone. So near yet so far . . ." She suddenly became excited. "It's what Harry said to me. Do you remember me telling you?"

"Remind me."

"He said that he was going somewhere very strange. Somewhere very close. He would do his best to keep in touch." Tallis walked over and took her father's hand, and Keeton closed his two hands around the small, cold fingers. Tallis went on, "He went into the wood. But he went further. He went into a geistzone, through a hollowing. I thought they were just visions, but they're gates. He's here, Daddy. He's all around us. He's somewhere close, perhaps trying to get home right now. He might be in this very room, but to him . . . the room is somewhere else: a wood, a cave, a castle. An unknown region."

She raised the mask to her face again. The sinister features stared at Keeton from another age. Tallis, from behind the wood, whispered, "But he's in the wrong part of the Otherworld. I'm sure of it, now. He's in hell. That's why he called to me. He's lost in hell and he needs me to go to him." Lowering the mask, looking confused. "I've opened three gates. I've *hollowed* three times. But I only opened them to the senses. I could only see things and hear things and smell things . . . no . . . in Stretley Stones meadow I threw stones into the other world. But I don't know how to travel yet. I don't know how to open the space and close it again, like the 'oolering man'."

Her father looked alarmed. "You're not planning to run away, now, are you? To hell? I'll have to put my foot down about that. When you're twenty-one, you can do as you please."

Tallis smiled and stared out of the windows, across the lawn and the fence to Morndun Ridge.

How to *journey*? That was the question.

What was it her grandfather had written to her? *I have made my mark upon that ragged tree. When you have done the same it will mean you are ready for the riders.*

All her life she had heard the sound of riders where there were no riders to be seen. The same ghosts seem to have haunted Grandfather Owen. He had known more than he had written in the folklore book . . .

"I must find Broken Boy," she said from the window. "The ragged hart. I must mark him."

"You persist in believing in this ghost . . ." her father said gently.

"I do. So should you, Daddy. When I find Broken Boy, and mark him—"

"How will you do that?"

"I'm not sure yet. But when I do I'll be able to take the first step into the wood. I'll bring Harry home to us. I promise. It's in the story. I'm sure of it. It's in the story. If I just knew the *ending* of the story . . ."

In the story!

Her grandfather had at least known of the Bone Forest: he had referred to "Ash", in his letter. Had he known of the other tales, and of Old Forbidden Place?

They will tell you *all* the stories, he had written. All her life she had thought up gentle stories, and epic quest adventures, and sad tales of lost knights, and funny stories of people who lived in the woods. Perhaps she had them all, then; perhaps they had all been told to her by White Mask. She suspected not. There were more to come, more tales, more fragments of the oldest story of all, the epic vision that filled her head, with its deep gorge, its impossible creatures, its gigantic trees, and the castle of stone which was not stone . . .

Somewhere in that story were the clues to finding Harry. She had an absolute conviction, now, that Harry and the story were linked. To bring him back she simply had to wait to hear how Old Forbidden Place would end.

Her father was leafing through the journal again, distractedly now, perhaps overwhelmed by what he had been hearing, exhausted by his daughter's strangeness, and her strange alertness. "WJ," he said. "Who was he, I wonder?" He closed the book. The sound of the piano stopped. Outside, a bicycle bell rang and Tallis's cousin Simon appeared, walking across the lawn, hands in his pockets. He was to be a companion for Tallis for the evening while her parents were out.

James Keeton said, "I'm beginning to be frightened by you. By what you say."

"Don't be. There's nothing to be frightened about."

Her father gave her a tired, sardonic smile. "There isn't? Harry is wandering around some bleak and snowy *geistzone*, below the earth on the borders of hell, guarded by these ooling people—"

"Oolering man. Shaman."

Keeton laughed and ran a hand through his damp hair; the laugh was a desperate sound. "Good Lord, child. I don't even know what a shaman is! I can only think of witch doctors!"

Tallis said, "They're keepers and teachers of knowledge.

Knowledge of the animal in the earth. In vision, in story, in the finding of paths."

"Where did you read that?"

She shrugged. "I just know it. I expect one of the masked women told me."

"Whispered to you . . ."

"Yes."

"Psychic powers? Is that what you think?"

"The whisperers *belong* to me," Tallis said. "I made them. In one way, what they know is what I know."

"Mythagos," Keeton breathed. "Images of myth. And we all carry them in our minds. Is that right?" Tallis nodded. Her father went on, "But we can't see them or hear them or know them until they become *real*. They are brought into existence, in the woods, and then we can talk to them . . ."

"Yes."

"Like talking to ourselves."

"Our old selves. Our dead selves. Ourselves of *thousands* of years ago."

"Why haven't *I* made any of these things?"

With a mischievous laugh, Tallis said, "Perhaps you're too old."

"But Grandad seems to have managed it."

"He had the right feelings," Tallis murmured.

"That makes a difference, of course," her father said with a smile. He leaned forward and kissed the top of her head. "I'll make a deal with you. Don't do anything rash, like adventuring into the underworld, until we get back from dinner tonight. Tomorrow evening, when I get home from work, I'll go with you to the house in the woods. We'll stay there until we see a mythago. I'll listen and learn."

Tallis was delighted, as much from the relief that his words brought to her, the sign that he was beginning to believe her, as from his offer to accompany her back to Oak Lodge.

"Do you sincerely believe that Harry is still alive?" she asked him.

Keeton stooped, placed hands on her shoulders and nodded solemnly. "Yes!" he said emphatically. "Yes I do. I don't understand how or why. But I'm willing to learn. Tomorrow. Lessons begin tomorrow. For both me *and* your mother. We must both receive the education."

Tallis squeezed her father round the waist. "I knew you'd believe me one day."

He was sad, yet he smiled. There were tears in his eyes. "I don't want to lose you," he whispered. "You must try to understand how sad this house has been. I love you very much, even though you're as weird as they come. You're most of what I have left, now. Losing Harry was a terrible blow—"

"Not lost forever!"

A touch of large finger to small nose. "I *know*. But he's not with us *now*. Things between your mother and me . . ." He broke off, looking uncomfortable. "It happens sometimes that two people grow more distant from each other. Margaret loves you as much as do I. We'd both be lost without you. She doesn't show affection as easily as some people. But you mustn't ever think she *doesn't* love you."

"I don't think that," Tallis said quietly, frowning slightly. "She just gets very angry with me."

"Part and parcel . . ." her father said pointedly. "Now go and say hello to Simon."

(ii)

She needed to think; the day had been an eventful one, to say the least. Images and information crowded her young mind. She needed time and a peaceful environment in which to let the things she had seen, and the facts she had learned, take a fuller shape.

Something was making her uneasy. Something about what she had seen, or perhaps read, was trying to draw attention to itself. She felt overwhelmed and at the same time determined. A thought needed to crystallise, and that meant she would have to go to one of her secret places.

From her bedroom window she could see cows moving in small numbers along the edge of Stretley Stones meadow. The dark line of trees that was Ryhope Wood was also obvious. The alley between the machine sheds was empty and silent. But on Morn-dun Ridge, close to the ancient, wooded earthworks, there were the silhouettes of human figures. As Tallis watched, so they seemed to dissolve into the late afternoon shadows and the girl immediately felt called.

With her cousin Simon in tow, Tallis left the house and went up the hill to the old fortifications. The boy stalked off among the trees that grew from the earthen banks, walking around these battlements, perhaps fantasising about the knights who had once lived here.

Tallis stood in the entrance to the ring of earth. Once, perhaps, this gate had been marked by great stones, or the tall trunks of trees. The banks had been steep and high. Inside, where sheep now grazed . . . what had there been? The great castle she had always imagined? Or just a village? Or even a shrine? Tallis didn't know, although when she looked back into the enclosure she felt a shiver: someone walking over her grave, she thought. For a second she smelled smoke, and something else, something rotten, like a dead animal. The evening wind stung her eyes and she turned away again, looking back towards her house, across the slope of the fields. Her home was in shadow, a dark shape. Above her the skies were becoming overcast, dark clouds swirling towards the east, forming strange patterns in the heavens over the fields behind the Keeton farm. There was a hint of rain in the air, even though the early evening was still warm.

Darkness was gathering. There was movement on the fields, mimicking the movement above the ridge. The earth vibrated slightly beneath her feet, but the eerie sensation passed swiftly away.

Winter.

Everything that she was witnessing, everything that seemed to obsess her, was connected with winter. Her grandfather had written to her on a winter's night, then walked out into Stretley Stones meadow, there to sit upon a stone and die quietly, perhaps seeing a vision that delighted him in that last, frozen moment of his life. The stories she told were most vivid in her mind when she thought of the winter sequences. It had been winter in the land where she had seen Scathach. The camp in the alley, the hollowing that she was able to conjure there, sent the strongest and most potent scents of that dead and icy time of year.

And the man in his furs today!

Of course. *That* is what had been nagging at her consciousness! The cold, wet animal skins that had clad the intruder to the ruined house; he had come from a biting winter. He would have been boiled alive in the summer heat, and even as she had watched the man in the room so he had begun to divest himself of his thick, protective layers.

Excitedly, Tallis relived the movement and the sounds of the visitation. He had come from the deep wood, and the ice had still been on him. The last time she had been in the glade she had dreamed a similar apparition . . .

An "Oolering man", according to the Huxley journal, guarded the gateway to a terrible winter, to a fearsome geistzone.

It was possible, then, that the visitors had come to Oak Lodge *through* such a gateway. Yes! There was a hollowing in the wood, a way to pass into the cold world. And it could be Tallis's way too, into the realm where her brother was a lost and frightened soul.

Simon had been prowling through the dense wood on the north side of the earthworks. At the sound of Tallis's cry he reappeared in the field. "What's up?" he called.

She ran over to him, breathless and bubbling with delight. "There's a gateway in the wood. Close to the old house. There *must* be. The fur-clothed people came *through* it today. That's why they were still icy."

"Who were still icy?"

"The ancient folk. Two of them. A man and a woman. There was a boy with them too. He called me *rajathuk.*"

"I call you looney," Simon said after a moment, but Tallis ignored the comment.

A hollowing to the winter world, close to the house. All she had to do was find it. That, she imagined, is how Harry first entered the Otherworld. A place close by, yes, but far away.

He must have found the way to make his mark upon the stag, if mark it he had done. And perhaps . . . perhaps he was lost because he had *not* marked the stag.

What did the ritual involve? What did it mean?

Simon was waving a hand in front of her face. "Tallis? Wake up Tallis! The men in the white coats are coming . . ."

She stood there, her back to the trees, dusk casting shadows on her face. Simon was holding a long stick and he walked away from her, beating at the turf. He moved towards the animal shelter, staring away through the gate, towards the farm-house.

Tallis was about to follow him when a hand reached out from the darkness behind her and touched her shoulder.

She stood quite still, her heart racing. She was terrified. A second hand touched the top of her head and ran its fingers gently over her hair. She felt dizzy with fear. She had not heard anyone approaching, but they were right behind her and she could sense gentle breath on her neck.

"Simon . . ." she called in a tiny voice. "Simon . . ."

The boy turned. He looked suddenly shocked. His mouth gaped slightly and the stick fell from his fingers. But he remained quite motionless, staring at Tallis and at whoever it was who had hold of her.

A blast of cold wind made her wince. Her eyes stung. The unexpected brightness of snow made her blink. What was happening? What had happened to summer? The air was heavy with the smell of burning. Several figures walked across the enclosure; they were clad in dark clothes. They were moving from the entrance gate towards a strange-looking hut from which the smoke was billowing. The entrance was guarded by two enormous trees, their branches severed, their trunks sheer and thick. A high wooden fence surmounted the steep earth walls. Coloured rags fluttered from the points. One of the figures carried a pole with the enormous antlers of an elk strapped to the top. White rags fluttered from the blades.

The vision was brief, a fleeting glimpse of a world beyond her own. Then real-sight returned, and Simon was standing before her, a few yards away. It had grown even darker. The hands ran their old, cold fingers over the skin of her neck, then her cheek. The fingers smelled of earth. The nails were broken, grimy. When they touched her lips she didn't flinch. She tasted salt.

The hands were removed. Her head filled with whispers. Trees creaked and groaned before a hard wind; horses whickered and struggled through snow. Riders shouted, leather straps whipped against taut hide. Harnessing jangled. Women shouted. Children wailed and were hushed. A drum beat a sharp, slow rhythm. She could hear the sound of pipes, imitating bird-song.

Slowly, Tallis turned; the sudden sounds in her mind faded again. One of the hooded women stood behind her, the dark robe stinking of sweat and woodland. The old hands, pale-fleshed and gaunt, hovered before her face, the fingers flexing slightly and occasionally touching her skin. The white mask regarded her expressionlessly through its slanted eyes. The unsmiling mouth seemed to have saddened slightly.

Tallis reached up and took the mask, lifting it gently away from the face beneath. Dark eyes, old eyes, watched her from deep folds of sagging flesh. The mouth smiled but the lips stayed pressed together. The broad nostrils widened as gentle breath was sucked from the summer air. Wisps of white hair blew from beneath the cowl.

"You're the one who tells me the stories," Tallis whispered. "What do I call you?"

There was no response. The ancient gaze remained, studying the child's face with great curiosity. Then the bony fingers plucked the mask from Tallis's grip and the lips twitched again in the slightest of smiles.

Which faded almost immediately. The ground shook slightly. The old woman glanced to the west, alarmed. There was a sudden, frightened movement among the trees and Tallis saw White Mask's two companions, heard their anxious cries.

The earth vibrated.

Tallis frowned and the frown deepened as White Mask stared at her, more in fear than friendship. The sparkling eyes widened slightly in their nests of wrinkles. Her right hand reached out and pushed Tallis gently on the shoulder.

"Oolerinnen," said the woman, her voice an odd whisper.

"Oolering?" Tallis repeated.

"Oolerinnen!" White Mask said urgently and tapped Tallis's head before pointing to the Keeton house on its far hill. Then she was running swiftly back into the concealing trees, scrambling up the earth bank and moving to the place where the field hedges led to Ryhope Wood.

When Simon spoke to her Tallis jumped with fright. She had not noticed the boy coming up to her, standing right by her. She had been lost in her own mind, an intense image, this time, of walking stiffly and carefully along the edge of a great cliff, of a feeling of terrible despair wrenching at her heart . . .

"Who *were* they?" Simon asked again. His face had lost all its character. It was round and pale, frightened.

"My teachers," Tallis murmured. "But something has frightened them." She walked quickly to the low gap in the earth banks and stared at her house, not just a dark, angular shape on the skyline. "They said . . . they said I was hollowing . . . but how can I be? I don't understand. What were they trying to say?"

Simon was unnerved. He had retrieved his stick and now carried it like a spear, raised above his shoulder. "I'm going home," he said. The sunset was an orange glow, streaked with black clouds. It reminded Tallis of fire, over beyond the wood, beyond the dark land.

"Wait . . ." she called and after a moment's hesitation the boy came back.

"I'm scared," he whispered. "Those people were gypsies."

"They weren't gypsies. They were my friends."

Simon glanced in the direction of the wooded slope. "Your friends?"

"Really! And one of them told me a part of a story. I need to tell it to you, to settle it. To make it real . . ."

"Tell me at your house."

"I want to tell you now. Here. In the tomb place."

Again, Simon was puzzled. He looked around. "The tomb place? This is an old fort. You know it is. Brave warriors rode out from here, blades gleaming, shields rattling."

"Dead men were burned here," Tallis contradicted. "Bones smouldered. Now be quiet."

He had fought against his father and been banished to a place where there was no true stone. He was alone in the strange land except for the hunting. He hunted with weapons of bone and ash and polished obsidian. He rode wild horses. He ran with hounds that were as tall at the neck as a horse. His bone-tipped spears impaled salmon whose scales were fashioned from silver. To travel far, in this world of mad creation, he was carried in the talons of an owl.

His need to return to the place of his birth became overwhelming. But there was no way back for him, and though he rode north and south along the great gorge, and found caves and ancient tombs through which a strange wind blew, he could not escape the dream. His world lay out of reach.

He tied his white standard to the antlers of an elk and rode on the beast's back, but when it reached the high mountains it shook him off.

He made a bark canoe and let the river take him, but he slept during the night and when he woke he was beached again, close to the steep track up to the castle gates.

He tried magic and entered a strange forest. Here he found
the image of a woman carved in wood; in moonlight she came
alive and he fell in love with her, and he lingered here and was
lost again for many years.

But out of the night, out of the dream, his mother came to
him. She took his hand and led him to the waters of the gorge.
She placed him in her barge, where he lay with his head in a
pillow made of her robes. She summoned the spirit of her father,
which appeared in the form of an animal. She tricked the magic
from him and launched the barge, which drifted with the current and this time crossed the river. His mother watched it go.

His journey home had begun at last.

"Have you finished?" Simon asked at length. He looked apprehensive. Tallis was aware of him, but her thoughts were elsewhere.
She stared hard at the place where she had met the cowled
women, where they had finally made physical contact with her.
Why had they suddenly been so frightened?

"We *should* get back," she said distractedly. "There's something
happening . . . I'm not sure what exactly. But I'm frightened."

Simon needed no second prompting. He was off and away.
"I don't want to end up on a roasting spit . . ." he shouted
dramatically.

Tallis was irritated by her cousin's cowardice. As she ran after
him, through the earthwork's gate, she shouted, "You're old
enough to know the gypsy stories are just to stop us falling into
ponds."

"That's what I thought until those old crones followed us here,"
Simon argued. He was already at the bottom of the hill.

"Simon. Wait! There's something wrong . . ."

Half way down the hill she stopped. There was movement on
the darkening land, a shifting of earth features that was wrong.
Behind her the trees shuddered. The hill seemed to tremble, to
shiver. The wind, a warm summer breeze, began to swirl; it carried
the scent of snow.

"Simon! Come back . . ."

"See you at the house!"

It was so dark. It was wrong. It had been twilight a few moments
before, now it was night, even though the sky to the west was still a
broad strip of brilliant orange.

At the bottom of Barrow Hill she crouched down, aware that the whole world was trembling. The surface of Hunter's Brook broke into violent ripples. The alders almost hissed as they shivered. Above her, night's clouds formed a vortex, a great storm pattern centred over the earthworks.

She imagined White Mask tapping her head again . . . saying the word . . . oolerinnen . . . oolering . . . hollowing . . .

"I'm hollowing," Tallis said aloud. "It's happening *through* me. I'm making a gate. It'll trap Simon. *Simon!*"

As she screamed, so she stood. Simon was a distant silhouette, still running. The earth around him writhed, snake-like. Something thrashed into the air, scattering dark matter as it moved. The boy's shape vanished.

"*Simon!*"

She started to run. With a great crack and an exhalation of foetid air, the earth before her opened and a stone slid into the world, rising into the night, scattering mud and turf. The dirt rained down. The stone screeched like an animal as it twisted upwards, twice her height, then three times. It began to lean . . .

Tallis backed away, stunned, astonished. The great monolith shuddered, then began to fall, smashing into tree and land, hitting with a primal sound that made the girl's stomach knot with fear.

I can't be doing this . . .

She crossed the violent stream. Ahead of her, where the field began to rise, a pillar of wood twisted into view, its gnarled trunk warped and wrenched by hidden forces. It cracked, like a tree broken in a storm; where the broken section fell to the ground it formed a clumsy arch and a brilliant winter light shone into the evening; a blast of snow curled through and stung Tallis's skin.

A shape moved there, a man on horseback, twisting the mount around and around to keep it on the spot, to stop it surging through the gate. Light shone on polished helm, on the iron trappings of the bit and bridle. There was a flash of colour. Metal jangled.

Tallis veered to the right as she ran, avoiding the broken tree. Tree roots looped terrifyingly into the air, thrashed and whipped at her, formed loops and arches through which chill winds blew from hidden worlds. The sound of riders was loud; men cried out, calling to her.

"I'm not ready!" she shouted. "Don't take me now! I'm not ready!"

Where was Simon? What had happened to him?

"Tallis!"

The slow cry was loud, but in a voice she didn't recognise. It almost taunted her. She stumbled away from the sound, tripping over squirming roots, screaming as they wrapped around her legs. She tugged and kicked, pulled at the earth to free herself . . .

The ground thundered. It opened, sending her reeling back as a great grey stone thrust up from the earth, and beside it a second, forming a weatherworn gate through which the eerie light of the Otherworld glowed.

She fought against the raging winter wind, head low, hands reaching out to force herself away from the freezing rock. All around her, monolithic stones and scarred trunks of wood were rising into the night world. The dead returning. The past coming back, to trap her, to trip her, to summon her to the forest.

She reached Windy Cave Meadow. She almost stumbled into a henge, not seeing the glitter of alien starlight in the space between the ortholiths until she was almost upon it. She twisted to one side, tripped over a thick root which was squirming from the earth, then picked herself up and reached the gate to her garden.

She couldn't find the latch. She flung her body over the gate, pulling herself home, falling heavily on to the lawn on the other side.

An odd silence seemed to fall. She stood at the fence staring out across the tortured fields, seeing the black shapes of tree and stone against the fainter grey of the sky. A man called to her again. The way in which he shouted her name was curious, quite frightening. She looked to the sound and saw three human shapes, running towards the house.

For a third time her name was called. The men were coming up the hill from the brook, one leading several horses. Behind them four torches burned on the land and a white, man-like shape was moving in a strange, erratic way, as if dancing. Birds flew overhead. The sound of their wings told Tallis that they were circling. She watched them for a moment before another sound drew her attention to the woodsheds.

For a second she thought she was looking at a tree. Then she saw it was a man. As he stepped out of night's shadows she could see that he wore long, thin twigs of thorn, stitched to a dark hood which covered half his face.

"Thorn . . ." Tallis whispered, appalled. "I thought you were my friend . . ."

She fled to the house, slamming shut the door and bolting it. She stood in the kitchen, watching the handle. When it was tentatively tried she screamed and went through into the sitting room. She closed the curtains just as a bird banged against the glass, its black body fluttering for a moment before it recovered its wits and sped back into the night.

The front door was open. She rammed it shut, bolted it, then noticed Simon's stick on the hall floor. He had run well. He was safe.

On the landing she jumped up to the window and peered out towards the earthworks.

Fires still burned on the fields between the house and the wood of the mythagos. Shapes moved.

"I'm not ready," she whispered. "Harry! . . . I'm not ready to go yet! I haven't marked Broken Boy . . ."

White rag on the beam of the antler. The image from her vision was powerful. *Her birth gown, a strip of white, tied to the broken tine of the stag. It was what she needed to do. First! Before going!*

She crept back to her room.

Closing the door carefully behind her, she listened for a moment, then turned to the window intending to see who or what might have been in the garden.

A man was standing there and she screamed. At once the man moved across the room towards her. The strands of thorn bound to his hair rustled slightly. He raised a hand and held an object towards the terrified girl.

When he stopped in the middle of the room Tallis calmed down. By the faint light from outside she could see that the window behind him was open and that he was the figure from the garden.

He was holding Find Me Again Doll.

"I buried that in a field," Tallis whispered.

His broad hand took hers, pressed the earth-spattered piece of wood into her fingers. He was not a tall man. His body had the smell of leaves about it. The mask on his face was made from soft skin, an animal's, dark-furred . . .

"You're Thorn," Tallis said softly. "I thought you were my friend."

Thorn shook his head. His wide lips, visible below the flap of the mask, stretched into an odd smile. There was something familiar about him . . . Then he reached up and removed the thorny branches from the leather band tied around his head. "Dressed up to look like Thorn," he said softly. "But *still* a friend."

His voice . . . it echoed in Tallis's mind, a haunting sound . . . so familiar . . .

He hesitated, then added, "It's a good defence against the carrion eaters."

Tallis was startled. Not just the sound of his voice but the fact that he was speaking English. She had come to expect only alien sounds from the woodland creatures, the mythagos. This awkward but understandable speech was a surprise to her.

"You speak English," she said unnecessarily.

"Of course. It's my father's language."

Tallis frowned at that. "What language does your mother speak?"

Not-Thorn said, "The language of the *Amborioscantii*."

Tallis swallowed hard. "I've never heard of it."

"Hardly surprising," Not-Thorn said. "It hasn't been spoken in this land for generations. The *Amborioscantii* are the *shadows-in-the-stone* people. They built a great spirit place of stone; the faces of the dead look out from each grey rock. My mother was the fabled daughter of their greatest leader. Her name was Elethandian. Stories about her probably still exist in your world, but my father was unsure. Nevertheless her story is a terrible one, and has a terrible end. My father knew her for only a very short time, a few years, before the heartwood called to her again and she vanished. I have only the faintest of memories of her . . ."

"That's sad . . ." Tallis whispered. Her eyes were well accustomed to the darkness, now, and she realised that this young man was the Stag Youth from the year before, after whom she had named Hunter's Brook. Now, though, he was dressed more fully, a baggy shirt which might have been wool, and trousers that appeared to have been stitched together from ragged strips of leather and linen, an odd and ungainly apparel.

And yet his voice . . . it still murmured at her. She had heard it before. She knew this man from another place, and perhaps even now she knew where that place had been, but was unprepared to confront it . . .

"The last time I saw you," she said, "you were naked. Nothing on but that mask and your boots."

Stag Youth laughed. "I didn't know you then. I had only been in the forbidden world for a few days. I was starving and that young deer saved my life."

"But why were you so bare?"

"Why? Because the animal on my head, the mask, helps me think like the beast. The animal on my feet helps me stalk like the beast. The earth smeared on my body helps me hide against the land. It's the only way to kill a deer."

"Are you hunting now?" Tallis asked boldly. "Why are you wearing the mask?"

He reached up and removed it. In the faint light his green eyes gleamed. He seemed anxious as he watched the girl, saw her surprise, then a half-smile touched his lips.

"You know me, then . . ."

Tallis was stunned. She was staring at the man, she realised, her eyes wide, almost frightened.

What should she say? What *could* she say? That only a few days before, she had seen this man lying half-dead in a field, at the base of an oak tree? That she had sensed the passing of his life even as she had watched him?

Stag Youth was Scathach. The voice had told her, and now, by starlight, she could see the same proud features, the same gentle face, the same strength, the same fire in the eyes.

What should she say?

"*Do* you know me?" he asked again.

Tallis began to feel light headed. She had seen this man's death and now he had returned from death to find her. Or perhaps not even that: she created visions; it was a new talent. So perhaps she had seen a vision of the future. Here was Scathach, unaware as he stood so quietly before her, that she was the sole possessor of the knowledge of his burning . . .

"Scathach . . ." she whispered, and her eyes filled with tears. The man before her was startled.

But before he could speak, a man called from outside. He went over to the window, peered out, then shouted something in a strange tongue. Tallis heard a horse whinny nervously. Another shout, more urgent this time.

Scathach seemed frightened. "There is very little time," he

said, turning back to the girl. "Something has happened . . .
you've done something . . . it has made our stay in the forbidden
world too dangerous . . ."

That expression again. Forbidden world.

Scathach was saying, "We must go. And I need you to help
me . . ."

But Tallis said, "Which is the forbidden world?"

Scathach frowned again, perplexed by the question. "This one.
Which other?"

False understanding blossomed in the girl's mind. "Of course!
You're a mythago. I *made* you. My *dreams* made you. Like the
journal said . . ."

The young man shook his head. "Am I mythago? I wish I knew.
But whatever I am, *you* didn't make me. I have come a long way to
this place. It has taken me many years. And I have spent a full year
here, camping near to the shrine, exploring the land, watching
you."

"You've been watching *me*?"

He nodded. "It took me a while, but at last I realise who you are.
I saw the *gaberlungi*, the masked women. *They're* your mythagos. I
saw them follow you. I saw the way they helped you create the
oolerins, the gates, some of them simple some of them wild . . .
dangerous . . . that's why I opened the Book for you."

Opened the Book? Then Tallis understood. He was referring to
the journal, to the way it had been marked for her.

"That was you? You opened it at that page?"

"Yes," Scathach murmured. Outside, the shouting had not
stopped. It distracted Scathach for a moment, and when he turned
back to Tallis there was renewed urgency in his voice. "But you
should not have taken the Book from the shrine. It must never be
removed. It is there for the journeyers, for the travellers, like me.
It has taken me a long time searching for it, discovering it. It is a
book of great power. It should not have been removed from the
shrine."

Puzzled for a second, she began to comprehend. "The ruined
house?" she asked. "Do you mean the old house in the woods?
That's the shrine?"

Scathach nodded slowly. "It is a place that is talked about in
legend . . ."

"It's just an old ruin."

"It is the first Lodge, the place of first wisdom, of the first *seeing*. The man who wrote the words of the Book had been born from the mud bank of a river, out of its union with the roots of the willows which grew there. His was the eye that saw and the ear which heard; his was the voice that sang the first histories, and the hand that wrote the words. From his dreams came the wood; from the wood came his prophesies."

"He was a doddery old man, according to Gaunt . . ."

"You should not have taken the Book," Scathach insisted. "It belongs in the shadow lodge, in the ivy box."

Tallis was stunned by this odd tale. The "Book" was a simple journal, written by a scientist (by all accounts an eccentric man) and left to rot in the ruins of his house. But to Scathach that journal was already an icon; a Grail; an object imbued with deep, mystic power.

"I'll give it to you," she said. "You can take it back yourself."

"*You* must bring it," he said sharply. "You took it. Replace it in the ivy box, just as it was. In later years there will be others who will come to find what is written on the pages."

"And what about you?" Tallis asked hesitantly. "Have *you* found what you wanted?"

Scathach was silent. In the faint light Tallis saw his eyes sparkle as they watched her. "No," he said. "I don't think I have. My reasons for searching out the shrine are strange ones, personal ones. I came here to find something, but even now I'm unsure . . . do I belong here? Or is it truly a forbidden place to me? I can't answer the question. But I do know that I'm frightened, and I *do* know that I was meant to find you. Finding you has turned out to be the most important thing of all."

"Me?" Tallis said. "Why me?"

Again, from beyond the window came the urgent cry of a man.

"The Jaguthin are getting impatient," Scathach murmured, and turned again to peer out at the night. Tallis followed him.

"The Jaguthin . . ." she said, staring at the three men on horseback; one of them held the dark horse that belonged to Scathach.

"My rider friends . . . straight out of the heart of the wood. There were twelve of them once . . . they have been good company . . ."

Then he made a sound, of surprise, of horror. He was looking beyond the riders, towards the dark land where Hunter's Brook flowed. The white shape hovered there, taller than the trees. It was the first time he had seen it.

"Time is running out," he whispered. "You have *certainly* done something to allow that thing through to the land." He turned on Tallis quickly, grasping her by the shoulders. "What is your *gurla*? How do you summon it?"

"My what?"

"Your animal strength! Your guide!" Scathach's look became one of horror; then he made a sound of exasperation, as if he had finally understood something.

Confused, Tallis stepped back into the darkness of the room. She was thinking of Bird Spirit Land. Had her simple actions —driving away the carrion birds from the body of a prince —somehow summoned creatures of great malevolence?

She asked, simply, "Why is it important to have found me?"

"You have the talent of the oolering man. There is something of the shaman in you. You can open gates. But without a *gurla* I doubt if you can journey through them. I am trapped in this world. I had hoped to use you to re-enter the realm. Though this place is certainly the world of my first flesh, I don't belong here as my father did. The Jaguthin can return to the heartwoods, and they are impatient to do so. But not me. I don't belong *here*, Tallis. But I don't belong in the wood either. I cannot penetrate beyond a place in the edgewood which my father mentioned: a horse shrine. The wood turns me back. I no longer belong, and yet I need to return to my father's lodge . . ."

Tallis was aware of the sadness in the man's voice. Scathach hesitated, then murmured, "I have a very great need to see him again, just once more, before the heartwood calls for him. Before he rides the spirit wind to Lavondyss and beyond . . ."

Lavondyss!

The word screamed at Tallis. Her heart surged. Her mind soared. Scathach's words, his concern, faded. His sadness was forgotten in the ecstasy of discovery.

Lavondyss!

She had found the secret name at last. It had taunted her and eluded her for years. She had come close. She had *felt* the name; she had *smelled* the name; but it had haunted her, a shadow, just out of reach.

Now she had it! A name, as Mr Williams had said, very like Avalon. Very like Lyonesse. And in those more familiar names was the echo of the first name, the memory in folklore and legend of the name that had *first* been articulated to describe the warm place, the magic place, the forbidden place . . . the place of peace; a name used when the great winter had stretched across the world, when the cold and the ice had driven the hunters south and had eaten at their bones, and snagged their hair, and they had run from the frozen spirit of the land . . . dreaming of safety.

And a place, too, of the dead, where the dead returned to life. The place of waiting. The place of the endless hunt and the constant feast. The place of youth, the land of women, the realm of song and sea. Old Forbidden Place. The underworld.

"Lavondyss . . ." she breathed, sounding the word in her mouth, savouring the syllables, letting the word make images in her mind, letting the sound send its spirit wind coursing through her . . .

"Lavondyss . . ."

(iii)

She had been conscious of Scathach moving past her as she dreamed, but had not responded. Now she realised he had gone. She went quickly to the open window and saw him, crouched on the outhouse roof a few feet below her, ready to spring to the ground.

"Don't go!" she shouted. "I need to talk to you. I need to know about Lavondyss!"

"Hurry, then!" he hissed back. "If you want to come, then come now!"

Even as she spoke, again she saw the distant shape that seemed to have frightened the riders. She frowned as she stared at the dark trees by Hunter's Brook. Her eyes filled with the eerie vision that moved there: immense; white; like a bird yet like a man, towering above the trees but not flying, just stalking along the stream, watching the night-land towards the house.

"What is it?" she whispered.

Detail was obscure. She could see the beak, she could see light shimmering in its body. And around and above it there was a dark cloud, like a flight of bats wheeling against the night sky. The flying shapes were emerging from the brightness of the body and circling slowly above Windy Cave Meadow . . .

"No time!" Scathach called to her. "We must go. *Now!* It's too dangerous to stay."

"I'm coming with you," Tallis said urgently, her eyes fixed on the terrifying bird-shape that seemed to guard the way to Ryhope Wood. "But I must fetch something . . . to mark Broken Boy . . ."

"Hurry!" Scathach urged. By the fence the three riders were already calling for their leader, their horses turning nervously on the spot, torches flickering in the night air.

The sky was alive with wings.

Tallis ran quickly to her parents' bedroom, flung open the treasure chest where their precious accumulations of photographs, clothes and locks of hair were kept, and searched down among the junk for the fragment of antler which Broken Boy had given her. She found it. It was bigger than she had expected, a curved tine several inches long. It was encased in the strip of yellowing christening robe, tied with two pieces of blue ribbon. She slipped the antler from the silk and replaced the horn in the chest, tucking the fragment of material into her belt.

In her own room she looped a piece of string through the eyeholes of her masks, knotted the cord and slung them over her neck. They were heavy; they made her unwieldy as she moved to the bed where the secret journal lay. She closed the book and stepped quickly to the window. Scathach was already on his horse, beyond the fence. He saw Tallis and shouted almost angrily.

"If you're coming, *come!*"

One of his companions was riding towards the bird figure, lance held high. He weaved between the stones and trees, cantered across the hollowed land.

Tallis picked up the journal and clambered through the window on to the outhouse roof. When she jumped to the lawn she fell heavily. Scathach came to meet her at the gate, dragging her by the scruff of her shirt up on to the hindquarters of his horse. She clung on to his wool shirt with her right hand, the book held firmly in her left. Her masks clattered by her side as the steed was given its head and Scathach and the other two riders began to gallop through the chaos in the field.

"What *is* it?" Tallis shouted against the deafening sound of wings.

"Oyzin," Scathach shouted back. "I felt it was coming. I thought we would get away before it came through . . ."

Tallis held on desperately to the young rider's body. Her legs were bruised, her vision blurred with the jolting action of the horse below her. She felt sick and frightened. But she could not take her eyes from the strange creature by Hunter's Brook.

"It's not real . . ." she whispered.

"It's real," Scathach muttered darkly. "But Gyonval will go . . . Go now!" he shouted suddenly, and Gyonval, with the lance, kicked his horse into a gallop, riding at the bird thing.

As Scathach galloped closer Tallis could see how the swirl of birds around the Oyzin were flying *through* its elongated body. They spiralled from the winter brightness of a world glimpsed through the feathers, then circled into the dark storm sky of the real world before flowing like a tide back into the winter. Giant wings rose and fell. A cry like the screeching of a crane cut the night air and the wind around Tallis's clutching figure gusted violently.

Gyonval's horse reared and bucked, a final protest before the strange knight plunged into the shuddering form of the mythago. At the last moment the horse rose in the air as if flying. The lance flashed, buried itself in the downy flesh of the creature's neck. Then horse and rider had passed out of sight, through the body of the beast, lost in the swirl of wings and snow.

The Oyzin exploded, bursting in a silent spray of snow and ice, of birds and feathers. Tallis ducked down. Wings struck her hair, beaks pecked her back. Scathach brushed with his hands at the frantic flock, kicked his horse so that the animal leapt the stream, stumbled, straightened and galloped for its life towards the shelter of the wood.

The surviving Jaguthin followed. Of Gyonval there was no sign. Tallis glanced back and saw a vortex of brightness drifting up into the night, dense flights of birds flowing with it as it faded.

Scathach led Tallis along a winding track, through briar-filled hollows and over mossy rocks, until at last they came into the glade before the house, the old garden. She was clutching Huxley's journal to her chest. She was cold; the book gave her a last warmth. For a moment they kept to the edge of the wood, watching the dead house, the silent starlit clearing with its fallen totem, its rags, its ghosts. When Scathach was sure it was safe he led the way through the darkness to the French windows, then stood guard outside while Tallis returned the book to its shrine, pushing shut the drawer, reaching in the blackness to tug back the ivy, covering the secret place.

When it was done she said a silent "thank you" to the man whose wisdom had created this icon of belief and quest, then slipped out to rejoin her stag-youth.

"It's done," she said.

"As is my time here," Scathach whispered. "Come on. If the Oyzin formed then the carrion eaters can't be far away . . ."

"Carrion eaters?"

"You saw them today. Here. Head-hunters; eaters of human flesh. There is very little time and I still don't know what magic you used to bring them through."

"Bird Spirit Land," Tallis said quietly, and she felt the sudden fright in Scathach's body as he ran. He stopped, stared at her hard. He knew the name.

"Bird Spirit Land," he whispered, his head shaking as if he could not believe the words he was hearing. "What have you done? What *have* you done?"

Nervously, Tallis reached out to touch his arm. "I'll show you," she said. "It's a meadow. Stretley Stones meadow. Close to the stream . . ."

"Quickly, then . . ."

She led him from the wood to the place where the old sign still rattled on its wire fence. Skirting Ryhope, keeping to the shadows, to the marshy edge, they came back to Stretley Stones. There was no sign of the Oyzin. The sky, cloud-streaked and bright, now, seemed empty of birds. But there was a sharp, unpleasant smell in the air, like bleach.

Tallis led the way to Strong against the Storm. The other tall oaks round Stretley Stones meadow seemed to shake as she came close. Tallis showed Scathach the mask of the bird which she had carved on the oak. The man ran his finger lightly over the shallow scar in the bark, feeling it rather than seeing it.

"When did you do this?" he asked.

"At the start of the summer," Tallis said. "A couple of months ago."

He laughed, banged the tree with his hand. "That was when I felt called *back* to the wood. Someone wanted us together . . .

It was two months ago that I first realised who and what you were . . ."

"There are more," Tallis said. And she showed him how the whole field had been ringed by her protective symbols. She indicated where she had buried the bones of blackbirds, crows and sparrows. She hinted at the knots of feathers tied to the thorn between the oaks. She remembered the circle of bird blood and urine that she had painted round the field. "Bird Spirit Land," she said, watching Scathach carefully, frightened to think of what she knew and what she should tell him. "And all to stop the birds from coming and pecking at a friend."

Now he stared at her through his pale, sad eyes. She could smell the concern in him; she *knew* he knew. But he asked, "What friend?"

What should she say? What would be right? If she told him what she had seen perhaps he would flee in panic, back into the wood. Perhaps he would leave her, and she needed him, now. He knew the wood. He knew about the realm beyond the wood, where Harry was held prisoner. She had made a pledge to her parents to bring Harry home, and since meeting Scathach for the first time she began to feel that she could achieve that difficult task. She needed her Stag Youth as much as he seemed to need her. She needed him to help her understand. She needed his wiles and ways of the wood. She needed the reassurance of his company. And in any case, she had declared her love for him. He was strong, and he was fine looking. She knew she was supposed to *feel* things for him, in her heart, in her chest, but that would come. That would come.

Selfish! Selfish! she said to herself, but still she took the coward's way again, shivering as she told the lie. "It was a vision. The vision of a battle. One of the hooded women taught me the way of vision . . ."

"Go on . . ."

"I saw the battle that once occurred here. There were dead men everywhere. It was dusk, in early winter, and a storm was coming. There were fires in the distance. Old women were moving through the field of the dead. They were hacking the heads from the bodies, and stripping the armour . . ."

"Bavduin," Scathach said, his voice trembling as if some terrible truth were being revealed. Tallis watched him by darkness, remembering that name—*Bavduin*—from her tale of Old

Forbidden Place. "The lost battle . . ." Scathach said. "The forgotten army . . . Bavduin. You've seen it. You've had a vision of the place. And you say . . ." His hand reached out to her shoulder. "You say you saw a friend there?"

"There was a storm, and below the storm, birds, swirling like the birds that came from the Oyzin. It was a frightening sight, and I was frightened by it. One warrior was sprawled beneath the tree, this tree. I called to him. He was badly wounded. I told him my name and he called back the name by which I came to know him. I felt so sorry for him, and he was a heart-friend. I couldn't bear to see his body looted so I made a spell to stop the birds. I frightened the old women. They fled. But they returned with a man, a druid or someone like that. His power was greater than mine . . ."

"And what happened?"

Tallis shrugged. "They turned out to be his friends. They came and fetched him away and I was too late to stop them."

She could still see the flames on the pyre, by the wood at the bottom of the hill, and the woman rider, and her cry, and her hair, clay-painted and as bright as the flame. But she couldn't tell Scathach that it was him she had seen, his fate she had witnessed.

Scathach was ahead of her, however; perhaps she had betrayed the truth in every gesture, every moment of hesitation. "What was the friend's name?" he asked.

Tallis felt her heart race as she whispered. "Scathach. Your name . . ."

He nodded grimly. "My mother's name for me. In the language of the *Amborioscantii*, 'scathach' means 'he who hears the voice'. When I was born a prophecy was made about me, that I would become 'Dur scatha achen'. It is a common prophecy. It means 'the boy who will listen to the voice of the oak'. I had always supposed this meant I would grow up to be strong, like the tree. A warrio:. Strong against the storm," he added and Tallis glanced up at her old friend, the silent tree, the place of vision. Scathach went on, "But perhaps it has always meant something more. While I lay in a dream, your voice reached me from the oak tree. And you had a vision of that dream . . ."

What was he saying? That he believed their minds had touched through the spirit realm of dreams? He didn't seem to have grasped that it was his *death* she had seen. And yet . . . perhaps he was right.

He was saying, "Someone seems to have made sure of our meeting. But who connected us through the vision? Which lost soul, I wonder? Which 'fate'?"

"The gaberlungi?" Tallis hazarded.

Scathach wasn't sure. "They're mythagos. They have come from your own memories . . ."

"Or my grandfather's," Tallis said softly, thinking that the women had been known to the land from before her birth. "What about the carrion eaters? Could they have made the connection between us?"

"No," Scathach said. "They only came through today . . ." Of course! "And anyway, they're here because of this . . ." He slapped the hard bark of the oak. "When you made Bird Spirit Land in this world . . . you made it in another. Many others! Tallis, you are young and unformed in many ways, but you have a mind more powerful than I could have imagined. Your skills have reached beyond the wood, beyond the years. You have done something that I believed only certain shamans could do: you have manipulated forest in your world and created changes in the forests of many other ages. If used carefully it is a skill that gives access to many times, many ages, many hidden places. The Jaguthin, the questing band of knights, have been using those hollowings in legend since the first stories were told. Each is at the mercy of time and the dream, using the magic of people such as yourself to complete the cycle of their own legend. When you create a hollowing you call from past and future times, and the shaman should control the calling." He stroked the bird face on Strong against the Storm. "But you have called without control. You have released without safeguard."

Tallis realised that the young man was shaking. When she took his hand she felt how cold was his flesh, how he trembled.

And she was thinking of the story of the Bone Forest, and Ash, who could rub two twigs together and add bone and send the fleet-footed hunter to a strange wood, where the hunting was magic. *I am Ash*, she thought. *I am Ash.*

Scathach was saying, "I remember my father talking of Bird Spirit Land. A terrible place. A place of winter and slow dying, a place where a great battle was fought. A place that traps souls. The dark side of Lavondyss. When you create it, so it calls to the angry spirits of twenty thousand years. That's why the Oyzin came, and the carrion eaters. And more will be emerging from the wood. Bird Spirit Land is an *angry* place. Poor Gyonval . . . part of the cycle of tales of the Jaguthin contains their Seven Moon Rides; in one of them, a knight destroys a giant, who is disguised as a bird. I had not expected him to be summoned to his fate so fast. There are usually signs of the calling . . ."

He was suddenly nervous, glancing out across the night lands, then up into the sky, sniffing the air, listening to the murmur of the wind. "There is so little time," he said. "We *must* get back beyond the edge of the wood before dawn. We *must* find your animal guide . . ."

He took Tallis's hand again and ran with her, back towards the broken road that led into Ryhope Wood. Tallis, breathless, managed to gasp out, "Who *is* your father?"

"I'm afraid he's cold bones, now," Scathach said. "I've been gone a long time and the years run differently in the wood. But if he's still alive then he can tell us much. He can explain things to you far more clearly than I can. He has lived in the wood, at the very edge of Lavondyss, for many years. He understands the way of ghosts, the way of shaman, the way of the dream . . ."

"But who *is* he? He was from this world, you said."

"You read about him in the Book. He's my reason for being here. He sent me on an errand. But I'm afraid I've failed him . . ."

"WJ . . ." Tallis said. Scathach had stopped by the wood's edge, staring back to the place where Gyonval had destroyed the apparition of the Oyzin. He seemed tense, alert for movement.

"My father's great companion was Huxley. The man who inhabited the Shrine. Huxley died here, in this forbidden world, shot by an arrow that had been fired ten thousand years before. But my father entered the wood, came close to the heartwoods and became *Wyn-rajathuk*. He found peace, and magic . . ."

Wyn-rajathuk.

Tallis recognised part of the word from the encounter with the carrion eaters that morning. The child had shouted the strange syllables at her, as if in fear . . . or recognition. *Rajathuk.*

And Wyn?

Wynne-Jones, of course, Huxley's colleague, the little man who had helped Huxley work out the primal nature of the wood and the existence of the mythago life forms which inhabited it.

Wynne-Jones the scientist. And Scathach was this man's

half-human, half-mythago son, born of flesh and of wood, born of science and of legend: a woman, daughter of a fabled chieftain, who herself had been called away to fulfil the terms of her own forgotten story.

Tallis wanted to reach out and hug the young man, her Stag Youth. For no reason that she could fathom she felt sad and affectionate towards him. But he suddenly cried aloud, a sound of delight, and ran through the long grass to where a man was leading a limping horse up the rise of Find Me Again Field.

Gyonval had survived his encounter with the Oyzin.

(iv)

The Jaguthin were mythical hunters, Scathach whispered to Tallis, later during the night as they crouched around a small fire in a clearing. There were many mythago forms of the same legend, reaching back to a time which was quite unknown and unfamiliar to the people of Wynne-Jones's own world, England—Scathach's forbidden land. Those first forms of the Jaguthin had been seekers rather than warriors. They had been selected by lot among the clans of the first hunter-gatherers to trek across the winter land in the wake of what had been known as an 'Ice Age'. They had gone in search of valleys, plateaux, forests and game herds; their quests had been simple and practical, to help the clan families find peace and warmth and food in a world that seemed determined to obliterate them.

In his life in the wildwood, Scathach had encountered later forms of the twelve: there were always twelve, a number that contained a lost secret, or perhaps a lost significance. Twelve riders formed the Jaguthin, but though they rode together they were solitary souls, caught and tugged by the tidal wind of fate. Their summoning could come at any time, and the voice was the voice of the Earth, and the form of the calling was the form of a Woman. She was the Jagad. When she crooked her finger, one of the Jaguthin would venture through the ages. He would never return. He would become the forgotten stuff of legend.

The three riders who were Scathach's friends were all that remained of such an heroic band. Scathach was the 'outsider' who always featured strongly in the myth. Tonight it had seemed that Gyonval had been sacrificed as well, but the Jagad had not

summoned him and his deed of valiance had not taken him from
the time of his companions.

In later times there were other forms of the Jaguthin. Some of
these were wild and weird, tall, fur-clad men with horned heads,
or with tree branches to disguise their true nature. (One of these
was Thorn, the tree as which Scathach had disguised himself
while in this land of his "first flesh", and a tree, along with oak, for
which Tallis felt a special affinity.) Wynne-Jones had told stories
of Arthur, and a round table, of knights clad in a form of armour
that gleamed like the moon on water and which could resist the
swiftest of arrows. These were the last form of the Jaguthin, no
longer known by the ancient name. Scathach had glimpsed them
briefly in his life, but they were shadowy, insubstantial. For the
most part, when he encountered the band of questing hunters they
were of an earlier form, more savage, seeking places and totem
objects that were beyond his comprehension.

Nevertheless, they would be important to Tallis.

"If only I had listened to my father more . . ." Scathach
muttered darkly. "He had understood so much! But as I said, there
is one aspect of the Jaguthin cycle that always has an 'outsider', a
supernatural figure which has knowledge and skills beyond the
Jaguthin's own. Such entities in the wood leave their mark in the
fashioning and altering of legend. If Harry came into the wood,
then you may well find him involved with the Jaguthin in one of
their forms. He may have been real to you, Tallis . . . but to us he
would have been from a strange and wonderful 'Otherworld'."

In the firelight, Scathach's smile was very knowing, now.
"Whatever happens to me when we pass into the deep wood, that
is something you should do to find your brother: listen and watch
for stories of the Jaguthin."

His laugh was sudden, bitter. "You see? Already I am fulfilling
my role in the tale. I am the creature from the forbidden world who
has come back to his father's land and finds it has shut him out. I
belong in no realm at all. Gyonval is very moved by this.
Curundoloc thinks I should be sacrificed. Gwyllos has agreed to
accompany me to the place of my death. All of these reactions
from my rider friends are part of legend. You will find this out. You
will search on your own, but everything you do, and everything
people do with you, or for you, or to you, all is part of their myth.
They cannot help themselves. As my mother could not resist the

call to continue her legend. She spent time with an outsider, with a spirit from the forbidden world. She gave birth to that spirit's child. Then the Earth called to her, and she moved away . . ."

"To do what?"

"To do a terrible and wonderful thing," Scathach said sadly. "To bring to an end a cycle of tales that would leave you breathless to hear them."

"Tell me . . ."

"Another time," he said firmly. "First we have to find your animal guide. There must be one. There must have been an animal that seemed to be watching you—"

"Broken Boy," Tallis agreed. It had occurred to her almost immediately the subject of the *gurla* had been raised in her room, a few hours before. "The only thing is: it was here, in the land, for years before my birth."

"A horse?" Scathach asked.

"A stag."

"It was waiting for you," Scathach said confidently. "It was sent to wait. You probably sent it yourself."

"How can that be possible?"

"I've tried to explain," the man said. "The years, the months . . . in the wood they become meaningless. It was the one thing my father warned me of before I left. Different parts of the wood live their years at different speeds. A confusion of seasons."

"I must find a winter. Harry is there, and I just *know* that I can find him."

Scathach's smile was reassuring. "Of course. And I'll do all I can to help you."

"But I can't just leave my *home!*" Tallis said loudly, and she felt a sudden panic. Curundoloc stirred where he slept, below thick hides, then returned to slumber. Tallis was remembering her father's words. *We couldn't bear to lose you, not after losing Harry.*

She had spent years trying to get her parents to believe her, to understand her, and for the first time—this same night, before the land had given birth to stones and birds—they had agreed to come and see the things that were haunting her.

If she left now she would betray them.

If she left now, she would break their hearts . . .

Scathach watched her by the dimming light of the fire. He was gentle. "How long could you afford to be away?"

"I don't understand . . ."

"Could you come with me for a day?"

She didn't even think about it. "Of course."

"Two days?"

"Seven days," she said. "They would worry. But if I let them know that it would be a week only, they won't go mad in that time. If I'm back in a week . . ."

Scathach leaned forward and raised a finger. "At the edge of the wood, before it becomes too deep, you can have a *month* in the realm while only a week passes. My father was quite certain of this—"

Tallis remembered Huxley's journal, its references to Wynne-Jones's absences.

"One month to listen, to ask, to see, to hear," Scathach went on. "One month to get clues as to where Harry might be trapped. You'll go away for four weeks, back in only seven days. And you'll go in and come out using your own skills. The benefit to me is that I will be able to travel back to my home using those same skills. What do you say?"

"We'll need Broken Boy. I have to mark him . . ."

"He'll come," Scathach said with great confidence.

Tallis nodded, then smiled. "I agree," she said.

"Then get some sleep. Tomorrow's journey will be particularly difficult."

She had seen Broken Boy at dusk on several occasions, and at dawn on two, but never in the bright or dark hours between. So she took Scathach's advice and wrapped herself up in a coarse woollen blanket, curling up by the glowing embers of the fire and drifting off to sleep.

It was a welcome rest. She was exhausted and confused, and in her dreams she passed like a ghost through a dense forest and came to float at the edge of a wide gorge, staring at the strange castle which grew from the wooded cliffs a mile away, across the steep and terrifying drop. But when, in this dream, she turned to face the wood again the trees had somehow slipped away and a great driving wall of snow and ice was curling down towards her, a tidal wave of winter. Several human figures ran before it, escaping for their lives.

As they passed her she could smell the death upon them. There was a child among them, carrying a wooden totem, but it was a small statue not at all like the vast, rotting totem in the ruined house. He cried out *rajathuk!* The snow overwhelmed them. They floundered and screamed and Tallis screamed too, trying to rise above the swirling ice, grasping the cold, dead branches of the trees, clawing her way to the light as this liquid winter tried to drown her.

As she struggled against the running tide she saw a cave, and the cave mouth widened. A booming roar began to deafen her . . .

It was the roar of an animal, stepping closer . . .

It sounded again and she knew it, recognised it. It was a friend, shaking her as she drowned, shaking her half awake . . .

Wake up . . . wake up . . .

She opened her eyes, then, but a part of her slept on. The fire was glowing, its sweet smoke strong in the night air. From where she lay, wrapped in Scathach's blanket, Tallis could see the crouched woman. The images of dream tumbled; the fire flickered and changed. Awake, yet asleep . . . Tallis journeyed in a realm somewhere between the two states of mind, where the mythagos stalked her, where the gaberlungi women could reach her easily.

Hush, said White Mask. Old hand on young brow, stroking the soft skin in the summer night. Tallis's mind flowed like a swift and gleaming river, the water a torrent of words, the banks that slid behind her filled with the images of legend: creatures, and figures, and high places of stone, and strange lands . . .

Hush, said White Mask.

And as she slept, half awake, Tallis felt a story slip into her flowing mind, impressing itself upon her, impressing her with its simplicity, its starkness, its *age* . . . It was a story from the beginning, from the source; there was magic in the source. There was music there, in the wind, in the slap of loose hides against wooden frames, in the striking of stone against stone.

And music, too, in the cries of the hunters, as they faced death in this terrible age of ice and dimly glimpsed beasts, moving south over frozen rivers, seeking a place where there would be food again, and warmth . . .

There is old memory in snow.

The land remembers.

We came through the storm at the end of the failed hunt.

Asha was old, frozen, pitiful.

We placed her in the womb of the snow.
We blew our spirit breath upon her pale skin.
She sang of the hunts of her own life.
She sang of the fires in the great shelters.
She sang of the fires that had burned without end.
Young Arak held a bone knife.
He worked on a wooden eye for dying Asha.
Arak carved the face of Asha in living wood.
We placed old Asha's new eye upon her frozen flesh in the
snow's womb.
The new tree watched over Asha.
The storm divided us, clan from clan, kin from kin.
Wherever the earth was open we were as the young.
We embraced the dark and the safe.
Our fire was now a dim warmth.
Bear-savaged wolves ran before the snow.
Wolf-bitten bears died on their feet.
The proud elk was frozen.
In the elk's eyes were the memories of the herd, and of the
hunter.
The blood was cold in our bodies.
The water was ice in the black trees.
The trees were as stone, cold and lifeless.
The spirit of the sun had no comforting warmth.
The space in our bellies filled with cold.
The land was our enemy.
The creatures of the hunt followed the winter geese, away from
the ice rivers.
The kin were slow in their following.
The smell of fresh blood on the snow was sweet.
The coming of the wolf was swift.
Later the land gave birth to carrion birds.
A fire burned in Bird Spirit Land.
The bones of the kin smouldered and they journeyed there.
All of the kin cried to the wooden smile of Asha.
All of the kin listened to the voice from the oak.
Then young Arak journeyed to the unseen places of the earth.
Arak journeyed to the forbidden places of the earth.
But after he had been lost he was brought home again.
Walls of snow guarded him.

He was at home here.
There is old memory in snow.
The land remembers all things.
This is what I remember.

Wake up! Tallis! Wake up!
The beast roared. It towered over her. Its stink enveloped her.
"Tallis! Stop dreaming!"
She sat up quickly, confused and suddenly frightened by being
brought so swiftly back to consciousness. Then the fear dispersed,
and the chill too. She was wrapped in Scathach's horse blanket;
the fire was low. She was still in the clearing. The three Jaguthin
were standing, staring through the dark trees. Dawn light illuminated their dark faces, shards of gold on weatherworn skin, ragged
clothes. The ash from the fire drifted slowly upwards, caught in the
gentle breezes of the glade. The horses breathed softly, shaking
their heads, tugging gently at the tethers.
I've touched the source. That was a story from the beginning . . .
I've touched the source. I've come close to Harry. He's there, I'm
certain of it. I've touched the source. Harry is the source . . .
Scathach was watching her, but his attention was elsewhere.
And a moment later the sound came again, the unmistakable
roaring of a male deer.
"Broken Boy!" Tallis said.
"By the stream," Scathach agreed. "Beyond Bird Spirit
Land . . ."
Tallis watched the sudden confusion around her, standing by
the fire, the grey woollen blanket round her shoulders. The horses
were packed and led along the narrow track to the edge of the
wood. Scathach kicked over the fire, then slung his leather pack
across one shoulder. Tallis shouldered her masks, and fumbled in
her pocket to make sure the christening robe was safely there.
It was suddenly happening all too fast. She thought of her
house, her parents, perhaps still asleep. She had not told them she
was going, she had not said goodbye to them. They would be
worried about her, even if she was only gone for a few days. She
should have left a note for them.
In the new day she realised how misty, how damp the morning
was. She ran with the Jaguthin, skirting the wood, crossing the
marshy field and entering the thin trees that lined Hunter's Brook.

"The beast must be here somewhere," Scathach whispered. Curundoloc led the horses to the water to let them drink, crouching down by the cool stream, but watching nervously for any sign of the ragged hart. Tallis moved through the damp ferns, tugging at the blanket as it snagged on briar.

There was no sound, not even bird song. The dewy mist drifted gently through a wood that was as still as an animal catching its breath, watching for the furtive movement of a predator.

And through this silence came the sound of Tallis's name, called loudly, called by a man, called in a tone that showed not just anxiety but a terrible fear.

Scathach glanced up, pale eyes bright. But Tallis was staring up the field to the distant skyline where, the previous evening, strange trees and stones had formed; they had gone now, and the earth showed no sign of the power she had imposed upon it. There was a man's shape; he was running.

"Tallis!" her father called again. His voice signalled panic. It made Tallis shiver and her eyes sting. He was in his dressing gown. It flapped as he ran. He stumbled then picked himself up, a small, dark figure, still indistinct in the half light.

"Hurry . . ." Scathach murmured to the wood. The horses became restless. Gyonval murmured guttural words to them stroked one piebald face with his mail-clad hand.

"I must tell him I'm safe," Tallis said. "I must say goodbye . . ."

But Scathach tugged her down again as she rose. "No time," he said. "Look. There!"

Broken Boy walked forward, out of the fog, pacing stiffly through the water close to the uneasy horses. The Jaguthin drew back, letting the great beast pass them. Its antlers brushed the hanging branches of the alders by the stream. Its breath added mist to mist. Its dark eyes gleamed as they watched the girl. Its smell preceded it, drifting towards Ryhope Wood.

Scathach tugged the blanket from Tallis's shoulders, then nudged her forward.

"Quickly. Tie the rag. Mark it. The animal is your master, now. It will lead the way."

Tallis stumbled through the undergrowth, then splashed down into the stream. Her father was still calling to her. Crows rose from the trees around Bird Spirit Land and bird song began to chorus across the farmland.

Standing before the stag, Tallis felt overwhelmed again. She stared up at its huge form, then reached out and ran her fingers over the coarse hair of its muzzle. Slowly, Broken Boy lowered his head. In his eyes Tallis could see her face. It looked strangely dark, the eyes wide open, the mouth oddly formed, but her face without a doubt, and behind that image: winter snows, and dark shapes moving—three of them, then one, walking out of the beast into Tallis's consciousness.

Its smell encapsulated her. Its warmth spread around her. She could feel its breath on her neck, the weight of its body against hers. Her skin tingled, her body became excited in an unexpected and disconcerting way. It was so close to her. She looked beyond it, as if at blue sky. She felt the pressure of its movements, on and in her flesh . . .

The moment passed. Tallis, breathless, flushing, stretched up and tied the christening rag around the beam of the broken antler, knotted it twice, securing it well. As she did so, her fingers brushed three deep notches in the horn: Owen's mark, perhaps.

At once Broken Boy raised its head and roared, then pushed past the girl, brushing her so hard with its body that she sat heavily down in the water. As she grabbed at the necklet of heavy masks, the string broke. The masks scattered in the stream and she gathered them together, but one of them slipped from her hand again and she had no time to grasp it. Scathach was behind her, pushing her after the broad haunches of the stag, towards Bird Spirit Land and Ryhope Wood beyond. The Jaguthin were already mounted. Gwyllos was struggling to control his horse, which had reared up in panic and was pacing restlessly in a circle. He shouted at the animal and calmed it. Beyond him, on the land, Tallis's father had stopped for breath and was resting his hands on his knees, his face flushed, wet with tears.

"Daddy!" the girl shouted.

"Tallis!" he cried back. "Don't go! Don't go, child. Don't leave us."

"Daddy, I won't be gone long. Just one week!"

But her voice was lost against Scathach's angry cry. "Come *on*. No time . . . you've opened the best gate yet. Look!"

He reached for her and pulled her by one arm across the narrow back of the smallest horse. Around her the Jaguthin splashed quickly along the river, in pursuit of the stag. Tallis struggled into the saddle, clinging on to her masks with one arm, clutching for the reins with her free hand. Scathach whooped with excitement, a pagan cry, of delight, of triumph, and then cantered forward, slapping the animal on its hind-quarters so that Tallis was bucked in the saddle, then dragged through the drapery of branches.

Ahead of her she saw what Scathach meant by the 'gate'; she saw the hollowing that she had at last created with the help of her animal master. Here, in the world of her father, there was a hedge of tall trees and tight thorn. But in Tallis's world, now, the land dipped between high, overgrown banks, a real hollow, mysterious and woody, drooping down into the earth it seemed, though sunlight gleamed ahead of her, breaking through the dense roof of the overhanging foliage.

And in the far distance, a gleam of white, a shifting swirl that made her shiver as she watched it; the first sign of the winter that had haunted her from her birth . . .

The cold place. The Forbidden Place. Where Harry was wandering. Where Mr Williams's lost song might have been a gentle melody on ice-chilled winds.

The borderlands of Lavondyss . . .

Scathach kicked his horse forward and galloped on into the hollow, down into the underworld. The Jaguthin followed; only Gyonval turned and beckoned to Tallis, his face creased in a smile, a friend's smile. He shouted a word in his own language; unmistakably: *come on!*

Tallis felt her own horse start to canter, as if it, too, was anxious to return to the world from which it had been barred for so long. As it galloped forward, Tallis saw stones lining the holloway, and she thought of her grandfather, and the way he had been found, seated by grey rock, staring in just this direction; perhaps he had glimpsed the world that had not called him. There had been pleasure in that dying vision.

The last thing she heard as the sound of water began to grow in her ears was her father's voice, very distant now, the sound of her name more shrill than sad, as if he was already a mile away, a hundred years away.

When she looked back she could see him. He was standing in the stream, his dressing gown a ragged robe hanging on his shoulders, watching her, reaching for her. In the instant before distance and the underworld took her she saw him stoop to the water and pick up the mask she had dropped.

Part Two

In the Unknown Region

. . . all is a blank before us,
All waits undream'd of in that region, that inaccessible land.
                                                              Walt Whitman

[BIRD SPIRIT LAND]

The Mortuary House

There was new memory coming to the land; there was change. It had been present for weeks. It was affecting everything: the forest, the river, the spirit glades with their giant wooden statues, the mortuary house on the hill . . . It was even affecting the people, the *Tuthanach*, the neolithic clan which inhabited this part of the forest realm.

At first, the old man known to the clan as Wyn-rajathuk thought the changes must have been of his own doing, a last ripple of genesis from those primitive areas of his mind still tied to the primeval wood. But this was not possible, he soon realised. He was at peace, now, his unconscious long since emptied of its ancient dreams. He had been at peace for many years.

No; this subtle, eerie change was from another source.

He went into the spirit glades, walked among the giant idols and studied each grim face, listened to the voices. He followed a hunting trail through the choking woodland and eventually emerged on to the thorn-littered slope of a low hill. Through the dense scrub of red-berried trees he could just see the wall of chalky earth which had been erected about the hill's summit; a tight hedge of blackthorn had spread to cover this as well. He picked his way through the snagging underbrush, pushing aside the tearing branches, until he faced the crumbling entrance gate, whose wooden columns had slipped, letting down the earth and rubble.

He had to scramble into the grassy space of the enclosure.

Yesterday, the gate had been clear, the path through the thorns wide and easy.

He climbed the earth wall and turned to gaze to the north. The sun was low over the forest, everything in ruddy shadow, misty distance. The canopy was a dark sea, stretching endlessly to every horizon. The wind that blew from the heart-of-the-wood had turned chill; there was a smell of winter in the air, a blurring of the seasons.

Wyn returned to the bottom of the enclosure and walked around the semi-circle of tall, carved statues that guarded the way to the mortuary house itself. There were ten of them, and their faces were disturbing to look at; their ancient eyes followed him as he moved around the circle.

Eventually he stopped and smiled grimly. The face of one of the statues had changed, as had its shape. There were small branches growing from the dead wood. New life in the silent totem, bursting from the black rot of the bark.

He should have known. Of course! He should have realised. After all, he was not just Wyn-rajathuk: Wyn-*voice-from-the-earth*. He was the outsider. He was a scientist. He was the only man to have studied the living myth images of his own unconscious mind . . . here: in the wood, in the forest of the mythagos.

He entertained this moment of arrogance with ironic self-dismissal, because of course he had seen only a fragment of the magic that lived and hid and emerged, naked and stinking, from the leaf litter of this strange land.

Nevertheless, he should have understood the source of the change before now.

It was the Shadow-of-an-Unseen-Forest. It was Shaper-of-Hills. There was an ancient name for it, which he had discovered and which contained power when it was allowed to embed itself in the silent part of the mind: *skogen*.

A skogen was moving inwards, inwards to the heart-of-the-wood, and it was coming from *outside* the forest. It was coming from the realm which Wyn-rajathuk remembered only distantly.

Ahead of it, as it journeyed towards the land of the Tuthanach, all of the earth, all of the wood, was being squeezed by its madness.

"Wyn! Wyn-rajathuk!"

The girl's voice came to him from a great distance. It disturbed

his motionless, silent contemplation of the forest. He ignored her
for the moment. He realised that he had been sitting on the cold
turf for some hours; his seventy-year-old bones ached. The sun was
higher. The forest canopy extended into mist, in the direction of
the heartwood, but there was a bright quality to the light,
although the land was still haunted by shadows.

Wyn rose awkwardly to a crouch, brushing insects and dirt from
the patchy wolf-fur of his trousers, massaging his cramped muscles.
He noted the way the shadows of the totems crowded together,
one shadow, one voice. He turned and looked up at the great
semi-circle of broken, rotting wood: the rajathuks. They were all
different and they had stood here for years before he had come to
the land. Someone had passed this way before him, creating the
Tuthanach, their totems, their spirit glades. He was living in
another man's dream. But he knew the names of the totems, all of
them: Skogen (shadow of the forest), Falkenna (the flight of
birds), Oolerinna (the opening of the old track), Morndun (the
spirit that walks) . . . and all the rest, their names familiar, their
functions familiar, yet all of them strange, eerie.

And in his time here, among the Tuthanach, he had become
Wyn-rajathuk. These totems were his, now, and he had affected
them, shaped them in his own way. He controlled them. He
listened to the voices and learned what they spoke when they
spoke with *one* voice. They were his oracle. This is how they had
functioned in myth and because in this world magic *worked*, they
seemed to work for him. But the scientist behind the shaman had
long since recognised the unconscious *releasing* mechanism of each
of the patterned faces, symbols drawing on the primitive regions of
his mind; ten symbols, crowding together, effecting a powerful
release of insight and farsight.

His oracle.

Between these brooding, monolithic trunks he could glimpse
the structure they guarded. The mortuary house. *Cruig-morn* in
the language of the Tuthanach: the skin-cold-earth-place. He
always thought of it as the bone lodge.

As far as he had been able to determine, the Tuthanach were a
late neolithic clan from western Europe: they built mortuary
houses; carved shapes in stone and wood; hunted more than
farmed; were not violent; and had a sophisticated underworld
belief which involved taking small boats to great whirlpools, and

riding spirally into the earth, to the "sea-of-light". He had worked out the legend which imbued this particular clan with mytho-logical status. They were certainly the legendary first builders of the giant megalithic tombs that were scattered through Ireland, Britain and France. Their ruling deity was the spirit of the river.

The Tuthanach were mythagos, of course, although not of his own creation. Someone had passed this way before him, scattering the brooding forest with the living debris of his dreams. But there was certainly one child among them who had come from his own "primal echo", the exhausted neuro-mythological zones of his primitive unconscious. And that one child fascinated him. Fascinated him utterly. Terrified him.

Ten giant trees watched him, their faces patterned not so much with the representations of totem ancestors but with the weird symbology of the unconscious. Something hound-like, something moon-like, fish-like, owl-like, ghost-like . . . but these were only the totem manifestations of the deeper image, the powerful images which could combine to create *vision*.

How much he longed for the world of his birth—just to *discuss* the ideas with people. He had seen so much. He had found lost legend. He had understood the way of inheritance from the past. And there was no-one, not one soul, to talk to. He wrote it all down, on sheets of parchment either gleaned from the travelling forms of mythagos from future ages, or made by his own hand from clay and the fibre from the clothing which littered the wood: the tangible remains of mythagos which had faded and been resorbed by the forest.

"Wyn!"

The girl scrambled into view, coming over the earth bank between the thorns. She looked puzzled by the change, alarmed by it. She was holding a small, black object, a doll; her crudely-made bone necklace rattled about her chest as she slid down into the enclosure.

"What have you got there?" Wyn asked his daughter.

She stood before him, a chubby child, well wrapped in grey and brown furs, with deer-hide leggings and shoes. Her face was bright, the eyes deep brown and almost almond in shape. Moisture beaded her upper lip. Her black hair had been tied in tight plaits a few days before, and greased with animal fat to make them shine. They were coming undone now and bits of leaf littered the tangles.

"It's my first rajathuk," Morthen said, holding the doll up to her father. "I made it this morning."

Wyn took the doll and turned it in his fingers. She had blackened it in the fire. There was no recognisable face, but the circles she had scratched were representative enough. An instinct, born of years of experience, told him that the wood was blackthorn.

"How can it be a rajathuk?" he asked pointedly. Morthen looked blank. He said, "What part of the tree did you make it from?"

Sudden enlightenment! She grinned. "A branch—"

"So it's an . . . ?"

"Injathuk!" she said loudly. "Voice on the wind!"

"Exactly! The trunk brings the voice from the bones which live among the rocks of the earth; the branch spreads the voice on seeds, insects and the wings of birds. A very different function."

Morthen looked darkly up at the rajathuks, the ten enormous idols.

"Skogen is changing," she said with a frown. "He's different."

"Quite right . . ."

Wyn felt pleased with himself. He had predicted that Morthen —half human, half woodland creature, like her lost brother, poor adventuring Scathach—that she would have a human awareness of the change. The Tuthanach, mythagos, could not of course sense such things.

"Skogen is changing. What does that tell you?"

She fingered the bone necklace, finding reassurance in its cold, ivory smoothness. Her eyes engaged him totally; they shone; they were so beautiful; her mother had been beautiful too. Now that beauty had been reduced to bones, browning in the stale air of the mortuary house.

Morthen said, "A new voice is in the land."

"That's right. A voice from outside, from the ghost world which I've often told you about."

"England," she said, pronouncing the name perfectly.

"Yes. Someone from England. He is approaching us. He is causing change."

Wyn stood, reached for his daughter's hand. She took it gladly, holding her doll in the other. They walked slowly around the half circle of statues. There was a movement in the open entrance to the bone lodge.

"A jackal!" Morthen hissed, alarmed.

"Birds," her father said. "Birds are always allowed in and among the dead. Only birds, though."

The girl relaxed. They continued their slow walk. A dark cloud was gathering over the forest. There was the smell of snow in the air.

"Ten masks to see the trees," Morthen said, reciting the liturgy of her father's magic, "and ten trees to carry the voice . . ."

"And when they speak? What do they speak of?"

She had forgotten the answer. Wyn ruffled her hair and smiled. "They tell of what they saw!"

"Yes! Trees cast longer and older shadows than the Tuthanach. They see further than the people can see."

"Well done. We'll make Morthen-rajathuk of you yet!"

Again, there was movement in the mortuary house. Wyn frowned and held Morthen back. Since she was a child, she was not allowed beyond the guarding circle of wood.

"That's not a bird," Morthen said, her dark eyes wide. She clutched her doll to her chest, as if protecting it.

"I believe you're right."

Wyn-rajathuk walked unsteadily between the idols, brushing their massive columns with his shoulders. He thought the earth trembled slightly as he passed into the forbidden place. The narrow entrance to the mortuary house was empty, black. The smell of decomposition was strong; of ash, too, mixed with the rotting flesh. The grass on the turf roof was long; the earth had slipped, hiding the tops of the stones which formed the entrance. This sort of change was quite natural; but to have happened overnight meant that it was the work of the skogen. The wind caught the dull rags on the poles that lined the house, the clothes of the dead; they flapped in the wind while the silence of the bone-lodge swallowed the flesh they had once warmed.

Wyn-rajathuk stepped into the darkness that was his domain. The passage inside was long. Two rows of oak trunks supported the roof. Between the trunks were the urns of those who had been burned, and the hollowed stones where the grey stuff from their skulls had been placed for the birds to feast. Elsewhere were the bones of the childless. At the far end of the house crouched the shrivelled, stinking corpses of the two Tuthanach who had been recently drowned. They could not be burned until the water of the spirit had been squeezed from their bodies.

Jackals had certainly been here. Fleshy, chewed bone, littered on the stone floor, told the shaman this simple fact. And the carrion birds too had taken their fill, entering through the special gaps in the roof. Light penetrated dimly from those grassy windows. Two birds fluttered in the shadows.

And then . . .

The boy moved into dim light, crouched, apprehensive. He was holding the long bone of one of the child corpses.

"Put it back," Wyn-rajathuk said softly.

"I need it," Tig said.

"Put it back. You should have asked me first."

The boy darted behind one of the wooden pillars. Wyn stepped back into the daylight, standing before the entrance. A few minutes later Tig emerged, the child's femur still held to his chest. He crouched in the entrance to the bone lodge, a wild sight, an animal, ready for flight.

"Return the bone to cruig-morn, Tig."

"I need it. You mustn't make me."

"Why do you need it? What will you do with it?"

Tig shivered, glanced to his right, then looked up at the circle of guarding totems, their faces turned from him. He was afraid, yet defiant, and Wyn had been expecting this moment for some time. Recently, Tig's appearance had changed. He was still the same elfin-faced lad of eight, his features sharp, his eyes like a cat's, his hair tied back with a band of otter's fur; but the boyishness had been fading recently; he had begun to assume the appearance of a corpse; he could be drawn, pinched and deathly white. Wyn knew well enough that when he was in these states he was "journeying", flying . . . experiencing the detachment from his body which was a part of the growing shaman experience. This was a normal change and not the influence of the skogen. But the stress and physical abuse were taking their toll of his looks. He wore the same sort of trousered wolfskin clothing as Morthen, but he had pierced the hide with the bones of birds, sharp needles, hundreds of them; some of them had entered his flesh. The black blood stained the grey fur. He had scarred his face deliberately (but not deeply). He was becoming shaman, guardian of memory. And he had not even become rajathuk as yet.

"What will you do with the bone?" Wyn asked again.

"I will carve it. I will suck out what is left of its ghost."

Wyn shook his head. "The ghost of that child has been returned to the people, now. They have eaten its flesh. There is no ghost in the bone."

"There is always a ghost in the bone. When I suck it out I will have been well fed. I will become *white memory of life*. I will become *haunter of caves*. I will become bone itself. Bone always outlasts feather. My magic will be stronger than your bird magic."

"You are Tig. You are a boy. You have no magic. You are my son."

"*Not* your son . . ." Tig hissed angrily, shaking his head. The violence in the words startled Wyn, the anger silencing him. He watched Tig. Tig became uncertain, but there were no tears in his slanted eyes.

The boy had worked it out, then. An astonishing thing for a mythago to do. Wyn had always known that Tig would come to terms with the manner of his own creation. It was part of the myth-story that *was* Tig that he would do just such a thing. He had long since become aware that he had had no natural mother. And the Tuthanach, although they fed him and clothed him, were always wary of him. He lived with his father and his sister Morthen in Wyn's small, square hut, outside the enclosure of the village, but he was rarely to be found beneath the roof, spending far more time in the forest glades.

The Tuthanach were an embodiment of legend. But Tig was legend too. The two myths—Tuthanach and Tig—were overlapping. This strange accretion of two stories formed one of the earliest cycle of "outsider" tales: the boy with a strange talent coming among a people who are destined to greatness under his guiding light. In a few thousand years this myth would be replayed in more memorable form! But the story had been the same, in essence, four thousand years earlier. What Tig would do for this neolithic clan—whose story must have been strange for many centuries because of their life-ritual involving not *one* but *ten* totemic entities—what Tig would do would be to transform them with his magic, to affect their consciousness. Their story had long been lost from England by the time of Wyn's birth—a realm, a world, a whole past-life away—but it had once been of immense power; and naturally it had lingered in the shadows . . .

Wyn himself had no real role to play in this story of Tig and the megalith builders. His insight, his wisdom, his understanding of nature, his understanding of people, all of this had meant that it was inevitable he would become the clan's magic man, their shaman. He was from Oxford, after all! He had been accepted. He was clothed and fed. He had advised them on the matter of hunting tools. He had married into the clan and helped produce a child (he had been astonished at his potency).

Although he had once lived in the enclosure of the people he now kept apart. There was one thing which worried him, however: now that he had become shaman, had he inadvertently set himself up to play a minor, but very brief role in the Tig story?

"The land is changing," Wyn-rajathuk said to the boy. "Can you tell?"

Tig sniffed the air. "I smell new winter. New snow. I smell new memory. Yes. There is change."

"Do you understand the source of that change?"

Tig thought hard for a moment, then seemed to understand something. "A new ghost is in the land," he whispered. His voice became loud. "I shall fight against it. And for that I shall need the strength of the people!"

He shook the bone defiantly.

Behind Wyn, Morthen was restless, scraping her nails on one of the totems. Tig glanced at her, but ignored her. They were not true brother and sister, though occasionally they shared the same house and they had once both called Wyn "father". But in all the time together they had never spoken to each other. Indeed, Tig never seemed to *see* the girl.

Morthen's movement behind him distracted Wyn. Worried that his daughter would enter the forbidden ground he turned slightly, and in that moment of release Tig darted away from the mortuary house, scrambling over the earthworks and through the blackthorn.

"Damn!"

Wyn chased after him, but his bones were old, his flesh weak. By the time he had managed to climb the bank Tig was a long way off among the thorns. Soon he had vanished into the forest. Then Wyn caught the gleam of sun on a pale face as Tig stepped slightly out of his hiding place in the undergrowth; to watch his creator.

Morthen and her father went down the hill and entered the dense wood again, following a clear track between the huge, sprawling oaks. They skirted the cleared land where the village had been built, glancing only briefly at the palisade of stakes and hurdles, topped by the grim skulls of animals. They could hear a child laughing and a drum being roughly beaten.

Continuing on this track they eventually came to the wide river.

There was more light here; the canopy was thinner as it stretched across the water. The area was marked with feathered poles, each representing one of the dead of the clan who had been brought here to lie in the embrace of the spirit of the river, before being taken to the mortuary house, there to be left to rot, then dismembered, then burned.

Morthen hated this place, preferring the greener, more intense light of the hunting trails further down the river, where the water was deeper, the fish fatter, and there were strange ruins to explore and make camps within.

No Tuthanach would come to this river-spirit place, of course, unless they were carrying the decomposing dead, but Wyn had no such qualms and his daughter was partly of his less-superstitious flesh.

She parted from him now, though, and ran off along the bank to find a place to fish with her short spear, bone hooks and gut net. He heard her splashing through the shallow water, glimpsed her as a dark shape moving against the brilliant yellow green before merging again with shadows.

Wyn was left alone with the gentle rush of the river, the stirring of branches in the autumn wind, and the chatter and screech of birds.

He found his watching place, a deep nook in the stand of large, water-smoothed rocks at the woodland edge. Once, the river had been higher; it had scoured the limestone and formed a useful overhang for when it rained, a comfortable seat on which he could write, and gullies and crevices in which he could secrete the objects and totems of his *other* trade: his trade as *scientist*.

He curled up in the space between boulders, made himself

comfortable and watched the river, abandoning himself to thoughts of England again.

He spent hours of each day here, and sometimes all of the night. Morthen was aware of this, and was sometimes worried by it, but she never questioned her father's actions. He had told her that he was "journeying" into his spirit dreams when he came to this place. It was sufficient answer for the girl.

As daughter of the shaman she was well used to running his private lodge and helping with the gathering and preparation of food; her father had his own business to attend to: for the benefit of the clan.

The truth of the matter was that he came here to get *away* from the stone age! He wanted to think of his past and to indulge his never-ending fascination: the documenting of the movement of mythagos along the river.

In the last few months this traffic had increased dramatically, a fact which had made Wyn think with renewed interest about the river, and the vast expanse of marsh and lake from which this stretch of water flowed.

He was convinced that the whole waterway was an aspect of one of the small streams that crossed the Ryhope estate, where his colleague George Huxley had lived, and to which he, Wyn, had been a frequent visitor. The particular stream he was thinking of had entered Ryhope Wood just two hundred yards from the house; it emerged, on to the farmland beyond, no more than a quarter of a mile away.

And yet . . .

During its passage through the primal forest, that simple brook underwent a fantastic transmogrification, becoming at one point an immense sequence of rapids, boiling between sheer cliffs, and at another the silent marshes which Wyn had come to know and love in his years with the Tuthanach. The river flowed into the *heart* of the wood, into Lavondyss itself. Then it flowed on, back into the wildwood, back towards England . . .

The Tuthanach lived on the outward flow; Wyn's home was down-river. But the passage of the mythagos was in the opposite direction, to the north, to the heart of the realm . . .

The mythagos which passed this point most usually were on foot. A few rowed past in shallow boats, fighting the current; some of them rode on horseback. All passed warily by the rag-littered totemic poles, aware that they should not linger in so haunted a place.

In the years that he had sat here, studying the products of his own and other men's dreams, he had seen fifty or more of the legendary creatures. He had seen Arthur, Robin and Jack-in-the-Green in so many of their manifestations that he felt he had seen them all. He had seen Norse Berserks, Cavaliers, British soldiers, armoured knights, Romans, Greeks, creatures with much about them that was animal, animals that seemed to have a human awareness, and an abundance of life that owed as much to the world of the tree as it did to the human limbs that carried it. He had seen what he believed to be *Turch Trwyth*, the enormous boar that Arthur had hunted; a vast creature in its totemic form, it had run amok among the spirit poles of the dead, its spines brushing the canopy, its tusks scarring the trunks of the trees. It had run on, along the river, vanishing into the wood. This drama apart, the encounter had thrilled Wyn-rajathuk, since he had also seen the clan-warriors, an early group from the Iron Age cultures of middle Europe, whose violence and whose standard of the "wild boar" had given rise to the later fables of the "hunting of giant animals". One myth, human in shape, had been transformed into a new myth, animal in shape, and yet the essential story of repression, confrontation, and subjugation was the same.

To be able to talk about what he had seen! If only . . .

He pushed the thought aside, because there was something more important to contemplate.

Of all the creatures which had passed this place, journeying to the north, towards that inaccessible realm, Lavondyss—of all of them one creature had *not* been the product of the mind; he had been of the flesh.

Why he thought of a male, Wyn couldn't say, but he was certain that a man, a man like himself, a man from *outside* the wood . . . such a man had ridden past this river point. He had passed by before Wyn's time here, but perhaps only a few years before. Whoever that man had been, it was he who had left the Tuthanach behind, and the ruins, and much else besides, he who had scattered this part of the wood with his own mythogenic life-force.

Now, though . . .

Now *another* such was coming.

Wyn-rajathuk could sense its approach with every murmur of his intuition. Again, he saw the new arrival as a man and he was alerted by his old-age common sense to the nature of change in the forest; this was not part of his shamanism, his journeying into the spirit realm. He was just quite *certain* of the approach of one of his own kind, one from outside . . .

He stared into the distance, where a brighter light filtered drowsily through the forest canopy.

Who are you? he thought. *How long will you take to get here? How will you get into Lavondyss?*

He was suddenly aware that Morthen was standing, watching him. She looked startled and nervous.

"What's the matter?"

She glanced along the river. "I heard something. I think someone's coming."

"Quickly. Into the rocks . . ."

The girl scrambled into hiding behind her father. There was silence for a few minutes, then a sudden disturbance in the trees and birds went swooping and screeching through the clearing. A moment later three riders came galloping through the water from the shadowy green down-river, kicking up a great spume of spray. A fourth rider emerged from the wood and rode down to the river's edge, close to the spirit poles. The first three had uttered loud cries—war-cries, Wyn imagined—as they had swept into this part of the river's course. Now they stopped, turning their horses where they stood, a nervous action as they stared at the totems with their ragged shrouds, then searched the land and the wood around. The leader seemed to stare directly at Wyn and the old man cowered lower in hiding.

The riders were all of a type: tall, broad, dark-cloaked for winter travelling. Their beards were red and had been combed into a great spray of hair. They wore leather caps with loose cheek flaps and their faces were striped with black paint. The trappings on their huge, dark-maned horses were very simple; the saddle cloths were of a dull, broad check pattern.

One of them rode savagely at a totem; a bronze sword flashed briefly; there was the sound of wood cracking and the top of the pole, with its raggy remnant, flew twenty yards across the water. The four of them laughed. The sword was sheathed. Reins were whipped on withers, flanks kicked by leather-booted legs, and the riders stormed off, away from this place of the dead, crashing through the shallows up-river until they were lost from sight.

Slowly, cautiously, Wyn and Morthen returned to the water's edge, looking thoughtfully after the wild troupe.

"Were they the skogen?" Morthen asked.

"No."

"Then who were they?"

"It wouldn't mean anything to you if I told you."

"Try me. I've understood strange things before . . ."

"Later!" Wyn hissed at her, suddenly almost urgent in his actions. "Come on. I want to see what they do when they reach the marshes."

"Marshes? What marshes?"

"Don't keep asking questions. Come on. Let's follow them . . ."

Wyn found a turn of speed which delighted his daughter. Although she ran ahead of him, her father was never far behind. Sometimes she led along the tree-line where the bank was clear, at others along woodland tracks when the giant trees, which had slipped into the river, made passage along the edgewood difficult. Wyn used a staff to help support his body, but he was energised, excited, and he rebuked Morthen for her glances of astonishment at his agility.

The sons of Kiridu . . . could they really have been Pryderi's early bronze-age precursors? So much of the great Celtic saga of Pryderi was lost, swallowed by the later romance of Arthur . . . but that he was legendary in the remotest of times was unquestionable. Wyn had seen so many parts of the cycle of tales, yet never the man himself. He had been *Kiridu*, in the old language. He had had four sons . . . in that old legend . . .

Could these riders have been those sons? Each and every one of them black-hearted, black-souled, doomed . . . ?

If so, then they would cross the lake ahead by boat! Wyn hastened his step, desperate to see this part of the myth-cycle which had so tantalised him during his years in the wood. The coming of the boatman would confirm the identity of the riders . . .

After a day the river became dull with mud. The woodland thinned. Alder replaced oak, then huge willows and stands of silvery thorn. A different silence hovered over everything.

"We're close to the lake," Wyn said.

"I've never been this far," Morthen said quietly.

"I come here often," her father murmured. "The lake is one of the natural gathering grounds for life in the wildwood. It's an impassable place; simplistically so, but memorably. There are a hundred stories associated with it, most of them very grim."

He looked down at the attentive girl. "Stories from the Boatman of the Dead to the burial barge of Arthur . . ."

"After my time," the child said pointedly, and with a wit which ought to have been utterly incongruous.

Wyn chuckled. "After your time," he agreed. "Come on! I'll show you four thousand years of your future in one muddy, miserable, misty, reed-racked wasteland!"

They waded through the increasingly dirty water; it felt heavy on their limbs.

A few minutes later it was Wyn himself who led the way through the trees to the wide marsh.

It was a desperate and lonely place, this. It was right to call it a wasteland, a wasteland of water, mud and mournful movement through the misty fringes of the lake. The far side of the marsh was lost in that heavy fog, though the tops of the bordering woodland were just visible. Tall rushes and dense stands of reed moved in the wind. The black shapes of water-birds darted and scurried in the thin, dirty water. Willows reached among them, their branches low, their roots sometimes forming bridges between islands of firmer ground.

It stank of rot here. The sky was grey and hazy. The water of the central lake gleamed dully, lapping softly at the land, swallowing all sound.

Crouching low they waded through the weedy shallows to a hard bank of earth. Morthen pointed out the tracks of horses, the broken reeds, the still-unsettled mud following the passing of the riders.

"Where have they gone?" she asked. Wyn shook his head. He rose from his crouch and carefully scanned the hazy willow wood and the dense stands of rushes. He tapped Morthen on the shoulder, calling her to rise and look. She saw the indistinct shape of a vast man-like creature walking out into the lake and slowly sinking into the water. A few ripples accompanied its descent, then all was silence. On the other side of the pool a dark back rose above the gleaming surface, thrashed, then was still. Two of the giant willows quivered with the movement.

The riders were here somewhere. Wyn became nervous, worried that they might have heard him and the girl and even now be surrounding them. But all was quite silent, all still . . . save for the sudden appearance of a wading flock of herons, which stalked and stabbed their way towards Wyn's hiding place, stepping delicately through the weed. The birds shrilled occasionally, one long beak raised to the sky whilst the others skimmed the water.

Morthen, who still had her fish hooks strapped across her shoulders, began to make a barely audible Tuthanach bird-hunt chant; she fiddled with the hooks, probably assessing which would be the best to use if she were to make a running hunt through the rushes and strike at the leg of the slowest bird to rise from the water.

Her eager anticipation was dashed. One of the herons suddenly screeched and began to struggle wildly, while the flock rose noisily above their doomed companion and wheeled away over the willows. Morthen gasped. Wyn watched fascinated.

A hundred paces away two patches of rush rose from the water, waving wildly. They resolved into human figures, one male, one female. They had tied the tall water plants all around their bodies, from their waists up; below this they were naked. The rushes stretched half a man's height above their heads. They were bound, probably with gut, around chest and crown, split to form vertical eye gaps; the woman had tied back the rushes over her chest to allow her breasts more freedom.

It was she who held the net, glancing uneasily in Wyn's direction as she slowly wound it in. The man walked out towards the struggling bird and raised a stone club to despatch it.

The blow never fell.

As quickly as they had appeared the heron-hunters had disappeared, sinking down into the water so that they were lost in the natural landscape of the marsh.

Between them and Wyn a horse suddenly struggled into view, its rider familiar to the old man. Beside it came a second, then a third. They struggled in the mud, the voices of the men raised in muffled irritation.

The fourth rider emerged from the reeds almost where Wyn was crouching, but like his companions he was intent on staring at the far side of the lake, where the wood was lost in haze.

"What are they looking for?" Morthen hissed.

"A fleet of black ships," Wyn answered in a whisper, "pulled by a gigantic man who walks on the surface of the water. It will be their way into the unknown region beyond the lake . . ."

Again, Morthen asked, "Who are they?" This time, Wyn, after the merest hesitation, said, "Indo-European raiders. Nomads. Their clan is called the *Alentii*. They are very savage, or rather were . . . two and a half thousand years before Christ . . . they raided the early farming settlements of eastern Europe before becoming absorbed into the earliest emerging Celtic groups."

Most of what he had said had been in English. Morthen looked grim, glum and annoyed. "It doesn't mean anything," she confessed.

He smiled, tapped her on the nose. "What do you expect? You're a neolithic savage. These people are sophisticated bronze age murderers. In fact . . ." He rose a little, to peer at the nervous riders on their restless horses. "In fact, I think they're the sons of Kiridu. They are seeking a way into the underworld to steal the body of the woman who guards the dark. To violate her. To bring up and control spirits from her soul."

"What will happen?"

"I don't know the full story. They will try to ride into the underworld, but they will be caught by a labyrinth which will form around them wherever they ride. I am uncertain as to the outcome. I don't know if they will ever escape . . ."

Morthen nodded as if she understood every word. She stared in fascination at the restless horsemen as they waited in the marsh, watching the misty waters.

"Then that's where they're riding now . . ." she said. "To the underworld. To Lavondyss . . ."

Wyn-rajathuk couldn't help laughing, although he kept the sound to a minimum. Morthen smiled uncertainly. "What's funny?"

"Nothing," her father said. "Nothing is funny. You are quite right. Everything and everyone who passes up this river is seeking a way into Lavondyss. They say of that realm that it is the place where the spirit of the man is no longer tied to the seasons. Lavondyss is freedom. Lavondyss is the way home . . ."

He was suddenly wistful. All he knew of Lavondyss he had learned from those mythagos with which he had been able to communicate. It was a place where time ran riot, perhaps where there was no time at all . . . and it was home. He felt this powerfully. To think of Lavondyss was to think of Oxford, and Anne, and a life which he had never fully forgotten. He should have tried harder to enter the heart-of-the-wood. He should never have succumbed to the frailty of his body, to his sense of age, to the wisdom that had told him to settle, to rest, to give up the quest.

He was a voyager who had turned back. For most of his life he had watched the spirit of adventure pass him by, folk of all ages, families, clans, even armies . . . all of them moving from the crowded spaces of a human mind, through a time of wood and leaf litter, to a place where they could find freedom . . .

He was about to whisper more to the girl when she grabbed his arm, her eyes wide with fright. She pointed across the lake.

"A man! Walking on water!"

The sons of Kiridu had seen the apparition also, and they became restless, kicking forward, deeper into the thick water at the edge of the lake. Wyn-rajathuk raised himself up to get a better look.

The boatman was tall but he was no giant, and the illusion of his walking was because of the sinuous movement of his body, twisting from side to side as he used a pole to manoeuvre himself towards the side of the lake. He stood in a shallow coracle, its sides scarcely an inch above the level of the water. He was not so much dressed as armoured in an odd framework of lengths of wicker tied about his body and his legs and covered over with leaves, mistletoe and water lily. In several places the wicker had snapped and stuck out from his limbs like broken spines. Around his neck was slung the carcass of an otter.

As he twisted and poled his way out of the haze and towards the waiting hunters, so, behind him, appeared the fleet of dark ships: five in all, high sided coracles, blackened, watertight, each large enough for two men.

Wyn smiled. He could think of a later story that would very much romanticise this particular basic image. A ferryman ferrying coracles: very sensible. Everything was practical, save that the ferryman himself had become fantasised: dressed in willow branches, decked with lily (the water) mistletoe (for winter) and broad leaf (for summer).

"Let me see . . ." Morthen hissed, struggling to stand, but Wyn had felt a sudden fatherly concern, recognising the menace in the movements of the sons of Kiridu as they dismounted and waded out to greet the boatman. He had the strongest of intuitions as to what would happen next and he forced his daughter down into hiding, despite her uncomfortably loud cries of protest.

His feeling had been right.

The ferryman was swiftly and savagely hacked down from his unsteady craft. He screamed three times, odd sounds, like the shrill cry of a bird. There was a flash of blooded bronze in the hazy light, then his body appeared floating into the reeds; the horses, disturbed by the smell of blood, shifted nervously through the shallows, panicking, protesting.

The sons of Kiridu fetched their mounts and calmed them, then tethered them to the five coracles. They destroyed the boatman's craft to make crude paddles, then began to cross the lake, quickly disappearing into the haze, seeking the place where the upstream flow of the river entered this wilderness of reed and mud.

Soon everything was silent again, save for the occasional whinnying of one of the horses as it was dragged into deep water, its master unaware of the fact that by their act of senseless brutality the sons of Kiridu had set in motion the disastrous conclusion of their journey to the underworld.

Wyn-rajathuk looked with different interest at the giant willows which grew at the water's edge, each one reaching out across the lake as if struggling to return to the more ancient land, beyond the marsh haze. The act of murder was a common one, he thought. The next time he came here he was sure there would be a new tree, growing from the mud where the boatman's mutilated body was slowly being wound around by the roots of the forest.

Sensing that it was safe, and that her father was shocked, Morthen slowly rose to her feet and peered at the empty lake. "Did they kill him?" she asked. Wyn nodded grimly. He had seen all he wanted to see, all he needed to see. He took his daughter's hand and led her back to firmer ground. But Morthen remained intrigued by the riders.

"Why did you laugh when I asked you where they were going?" she asked again, as they returned along the river, then followed a deeper track.

"I wasn't really laughing," Wyn said. "I was remembering the epic tales of my own time. It always seemed to be so easy to get into the underworld. You fought giant dogs or serpents, but mostly any convenient cave or well would do, you'd just ride right in."

He stopped for breath, sitting on the fallen, mossy trunk of an oak which stretched out across the river, caught by the branches on the opposite side. Morthen watched the flash and dart of silver finned fish.

Wyn said, "But you *can't* just ride into Lavondyss." He was talking more to himself, now, staring vaguely into the distance. Morthen half watched him, half watched the life in the river. "You have to find the true pathway. And each adventurer has a different path to find. The true way to the heart of the realm is through a much older forest than this forest . . ." He stared up through the canopy to the bright, autumnal sky. "The question is . . . how do we get *into* that older forest? There was a time when the power was understood, when the path could be found. But even by the time of your own people, the Tuthanach, all that was left were the wooden symbols, the idea, the words, the sham rituals of people like me . . ." He smiled at Morthen, who was twisting one of her plaits around her fingers and watching him through brown eyes that were intense with concern; perhaps she thought her father was distressed. Wyn said, "Shaman. That's me. *Sham*. Rajathuk . . ."

"Injathuk," she contributed, not understanding.

"Indeed. Injathuk. Wizard. Warlock. *Druid*. Scientist. I'm known by many names over the centuries, but they all mean one thing: *echo of a lost knowledge*. Never *guardian of the power*. Even as *scientist* that was true . . ." He stared away from the girl at the swirling force of nature, at the silent power of the forest. "Perhaps I'm wrong on that . . . perhaps science will find its own way into the first forest . . ."

Morthen interrupted him, her hands raised, signalling that she was becoming frustrated with this diatribe in two languages, one of them occult. "If it's so hard to get into Lavondyss, then why do these riders even try? If they can't get into the place where the spirit soars away from the seasons, then why do they try?"

This was a sophisticated question coming from a neolithic child of eight years of age. Wyn paused to appreciate his daughter, pinching her cheek affectionately and smiling. "Because that is the way of legend, of *myth*."

"I don't understand *myth*," she muttered grumpily.

"Source," he corrected, even though he knew she was only being petulant. "This finding of the way is what lies at the core of legend. The oldest animals came to the land to spread out and give birth, but they first had to find the land. The *rajathuk* roamed the world during an endless night before it found the oldest bone, whose life force it could feed upon, and grow, and reach its arms to the sky so that *injathuk* could be born from its fingers and sing to the hidden Sun, and bring light."

"I know all this," Morthen murmured.

"Well there you are. All things seek their place in the world. Seek. Find. Quest. Seek the path home. Seek the way to the first home of all. Adventuring . . . stories evolve to explore the *idea* of exploring the underworld. Those travellers are legends them-selves. They are mythagos. They are *dreams* . . . and they are behaving in the manner of the dream according to the memory of the dreamer. They can't do anything else. The man who passed this way before, the man who created your people, the man who created the marsh, he left behind a life that performs according to the way he remembered it. The sons of Kiridu could not have spared the boatman, because in legend they didn't spare him. What they get up to between times is up to them, but when the pattern of legend tugs at them, they are helpless. They are called. Only the man who passed this way before . . . and me . . . only the two of us are free of the calling. We are *not* of the dreamstuff. We are alive. We are from the real world. We make the world around us. We fill the forest with creatures. Our forgotten ancestry materialises before our eyes, and we are helpless to stop it . . ."

Morthen watched her father carefully. She was restless. There was a long way to go before they reached home. Wyn knew exactly what she was thinking, since she had described the sensation to him. His words were making sweet sounds in her head, and were creating ideas and images despite the fact that he often spoke of things beyond her understanding. But slowly she was becoming frightened. His words were spirits, and the spirits could not rest in her head, they were uncomfortable. They made her heart race faster.

When Wyn had been silent for a while she asked, "Did that man-who-passed-this-way-before ever reach Lavondyss?"

Wyn-rajathuk smiled. "That's what I'm wondering. It has only just occurred to me to ask the question . . ."

His daughter sat down on the rotting trunk, leaned forward and braced her chin on her hands. "I wonder who he was."

"A man destined to journey," her father said. "A man who was marked. A man seeking triumph. Any and all of these things. He could have taken the identity from any of the myriad ages that had preceded his birth. He could have disguised himself in the feathered cloak of a thousand legends. But in his heart, he was from outside. From the forbidden place. When an outsider enters the wood, change runs through the canopy like fire. The wood sucks at the mind, it sucks out the dreams—"

"Like Tig. Sucking the ghosts in the bones."

"Yes. I suppose so. But as it draws on the mind so it loses something of itself. It has to, because it is *fusing* to generate myth: like a spark and a quick breath, the two things unite in flame. Flame means change. That's what we have witnessed today, when we saw the totems changed, and the mortuary house so run down, and the hill covered with blackthorn. Someone from my world is close to us and the wood is leaning towards him, tense and nervous, bristling with power. Can you see it? Can you feel it?"

"No. Only the skogen."

"It's the same thing." He watched her carefully, wondering what she could be stretched to understand. She was bright. She grasped concepts with remarkable facility. He said, "The skogen is making contact with us because it is *thinking* about us. That means it almost certainly *knows* us. Strictly, I should say it knows *me*. It is making an unconscious link across a great distance, and the link is showing itself in an . . ."

He hesitated. The girl's eyes were wide, knowing, demonstrating the thrill she felt at being taken so much into her father's secret world. He was using more words from his language of power —English—than he had ever used before, and was carefully translating them for her.

But he would lose her now.

"The link is showing itself in an alteration in the mythogenic landscape . . ."

"Huh?"

He laughed. "A foreigner is coming. The animal spirits in the wood are restless. They foresee great change."

"Well why didn't you say so?"

They spent their second night in the forest, hungry, now, to the point of irritation. By the time they reached the territory of the Tuthanach, towards the afternoon of the following day, Wyn-rajathuk could see further signs of the change, further evidence that a skogen was approaching. Looking up the wooded hill he could see that the earth bank around the mortuary house was slightly lower. The shape of his hut, in its separated compound, had subtly changed.

Looking back towards the wood he saw wind-broken oaks, higher than the canopy, their branches like black limbs and horns.

These giant trees had not been in evidence a few days before.

Morthen went into the hut to prepare food—a fish which she had caught, garlic bulbs which Wyn had gathered, and of course there was an ample supply of ground wheat for biscuits. Wyn-rajathuk walked up the hill to the mortuary house and entered the decaying enclosure. The blank, dead-eyed skogen was taller, now. The new life on its vast trunk was more extensive, a tangle of leaf and twig growing out from the key points on the carved pole. When he reached to pluck one of the leaves the ground trembled. The mouth of the skogen seemed to have turned down slightly. The deep axe-cut which had fashioned that mouth—black for so long—now had a white edge to it, like freshly-hewn bark.

"Are you calling *him*? Or is he calling you? I wonder. I wonder where the power originates . . ."

The tree was silent.

Wyn-rajathuk turned and stood against the wood, hoping for its embrace, finding it cold. He looked up at the half circle of carved trunks. The eyes would not meet his.

He almost dreaded entering the mortuary house, to see if the bones of the dead had changed; but he did, and for a moment could see no sign of disturbance. Then his eyes grew accustomed to the darkness.

The boy had been back to the cruig-morn. The evidence was clear. He had scooped bone from some of the cremation urns. He had disturbed the drying bones by the entrance. He had not touched the remains of the woman he had once seemed content to call "mother". The jackals had worried at the flesh of the newer corpses, but it would seem that Tig had driven them off. There was blood on the floor, and a stone knife.

Wyn-rajathuk searched the lodge, then returned to the outside, standing in front of the entrance, his staff in his hands. Behind him birds entered and left the place of decay, but he waited now for the movement he knew would come from another direction.

Soon he realised that Tig had crept into the mortuary enclosure unseen. The boy's clothing could be glimpsed as he lurked behind the rajathuk which the Tuthanach—as people before them—called morndun.

When he peered around the totem tree, Wyn-rajathuk banged his staff on the stone lintel of the mortuary house, to signify that he had seen the child. Tig immediately stepped into view, his arms full of bones.

Angrily, the old man said, "You came back to the place of the dead, even though I forbade you to do so."

"I'm bringing back the bone," Tig said nervously. He had tied his long hair into a spiky top-knot, bound with a white fur strip. His forearms were covered with scratches; these might have been wounds caused by the dense blackthorn scrub, but Wyn-rajathuk was more inclined to believe that they had been self-inflicted.

"Have you sucked them dry?" he asked the boy.

Tig grinned, shuffled forward a pace or two. "The child was too little. You were right. There was nothing there. But I have sucked the ghost of five men, now. There is a lot of memory in the bone."

"Have you eaten enough for one day?"

"For one day, yes." The boy hesitated, elfin face pinched with uncertainty, sharp eyes restless. "Shall I bring back the dead?"

"Bring them here."

Wyn-rajathuk took the bones from the trembling boy. Now that Tig was full, now that he had exercised his odd, incomprehensible shaman rite, he was just a child again, aglow with whatever he had consumed . . . or imagined he had consumed. He had scratched spirals and diamond shapes on the bones, shallow marks reminiscent of the marks that the craftsmen of the Tuthanach used in the decoration of stone, wood and clothing.

"Come inside . . ."

Tig followed eagerly into the foetid gloom of the mortuary house. Wyn-rajathuk returned the bone shards to their positions; Tig knew where each had come from. That done they returned to the stone passage leading from the outside world. They crouched down, boy facing man across the incoming light.

"Do you intend to eat every ghost in this place?"

"Every ghost," Tig agreed. "It will take a long time."

"Who told you to eat ghosts? Have you been talking to someone in the wood?"

Puzzled, Tig shook his head. "It's just something I have to do," he said blankly, and Wyn-rajathuk smiled, knowing that that answer was the only answer possible.

"Eating ghosts" was a part of the forgotten story that was Ennik-tig-en'cruig (a name which meant "Tig never-touch-woman, never-touch-earth"). It didn't have to mean anything to Wyn. It had meant an enormous amount to the people of 4000 BC who had first developed the legend of the boy who ate spirits.

"If you are found inside the bone lodge by any of the Tuthanach they will kill you. Do you know that? Children are forbidden here. They will drown you."

"Of course. That's why I've been hiding."

Without really thinking about it, Wyn-rajathuk had come to accept the inevitability of Tig's presence here; there was no way to prevent this development in the small mythago's life . . .

"It is too dangerous for you to keep coming and going. You had better live in cruig-morn until you have eaten everything. If you can bear the stink, that is, and survive the jackals. But if a new burial comes you must be sure to leave the place and not return for two days. Is that clear?"

Delighted, Tig nodded agreement.

Wyn asked him, "Do you know what will happen to you when you have finished here?"

The boy shook his head. The man smiled and said, "But I do. I know all about you, Tig. As mythagos go you're quite a common presence in the wood. I've seen you before. I've glimpsed you. I've heard about you. I know your story from birth until death, although I don't pretend to understand what it is you do, why you do it, and how you *became* legend. But I know what you will cause to change in the Tuthanach . . . and what one of them will finally do to you."

Tig was wide-eyed, but he clearly did not understand beyond the sense of being threatened. "Have you heard all this from your rotting trees?" he asked grimly. "From their cracking voices?"

"No. I've heard it all from the voice of my own past. I created you. Did you know that? You were a legend in my time, a forgotten story; but you were still there, still in my dreams, and the wood took that dream and shaped you from it. Part of that dream is that the boy will bring new magic to the people. He will overthrow the totems of the old clan. He will overthrow the man who guards the dead. Another part of the story is that the boy will eat the bird-feather man's head. I don't intend to stay around until that happens."

"Your totems are already dead," Tig whispered. "I've listened to them, but they have no voice. Your bird feathers no longer fly. But I would like to eat your head, to see your strange dreams . . ."

"Finish the mortuary feast first," Wyn-rajathuk said with a shiver.

Tig crawled away into the darkness, between wooden pillars and the tall stones. Soon, all Wyn-rajathuk could see were his eyes, slanted, bright, frighteningly intense.

Morthen had caught a pike, using a bone hook and a great deal of nerve. She returned with it to the shaman's small, cluttered lodge, outside the earth enclosure of the village, and on her father's instruction cut the fish in half. She wrapped the head end in a pouch of fox skin to present to the old women in the long-house. The tail was for themselves and Morthen stewed it with berries, watching as Wyn-rajathuk made copious black marks on one of the sheets of parchment which he kept hidden in a stone locker at the back of the house.

After they had eaten, Wyn pulled his bird-spirit cloak around his shoulders and tied the cord at the front. He picked up his staff and laid it across his knees. Morthen watched him anxiously, eyes bright. Wyn was certain that she sensed the parting which was to come. He had noticed that she was wearing her "Sunday Best", the little ritual headdress which she saved for the spring fires and the summer hunts. It was a webbing of gut, laced through the colourful shells of land snails. It had taken her a week to make and covered her head and neck like a prayer veil.

"Have I ever explained the staff to you?" he asked the girl. She looked at the single row of coloured feathers that had been tied down the length of the wood, then shook her head. In the last few weeks her father had begun to trust her so much with the secrets of his life. She was at once excited and saddened, saddened because she could think of only one reason why he would want to start to instruct her *before* she spent her years with the women in the water lodge, learning from them, learning their wisdom.

Wyn pointed to the two black feathers at the bottom of the row.

"The feathers of a coot," he said. "They are black because they are the two years that I was alone and lost in the wood. Then, as I stumbled through the wild, I came across the tribe known in legend as the *Amborioscantii*. They were the people who first worked magic with bright stone ore. They bury their dead in ash urns, much bigger than the urns of the Tuthanach. They ride wild horses. They make knives out of the bright stone. It is heated in fire and runs like muddy water. It becomes hard again and is shaped and sharpened, like you might sharpen a wolf's bone to make a point."

"You've told me this silly story already," Morthen said, smearing her finger round the clay pot where the fish had been stewed and licking the result. "The stone which runs like hot water; only it wasn't like *muddy* water when you told it before. You said it was the colour of an oak leaf in autumn. A bright colour from a bright stone. You called it *metal*."

"You've remembered very well. I've clearly lost my poetic touch. Part of the later legend of the Tuthanach, your own people, is that they will be the first people to steal the secret of this strange substance, and give it an earthly name. It's an early version of the magic forge story, a sub-section of legend that is unutterably boring to someone like me . . . but your version will pass out of consciousness three thousand years before Christ."

He caught his daughter's patient impatience. His translation of certain concepts was clearly leaving a lot to be desired, and making his story meaningless to the girl. He frowned, struggling to remember: "Have I told you about Christ?"

"Ghost-born-man-walking-on-water-telling-stories-dead-on-tree. Yes. You've told me about him. Show me more feathers."

"Very well. After a time with the *Amborioscantii* I married Elethandian, a wonderful and tragic woman about whom I could tell you five fabulous stories, and about whom my own world has remembered—" he smiled sadly—"*nothing*. By Elethandian I had a son. My first. Her third. She had been married to a hunter, but that's another story. My son was called Scathach. This feather here, the red feather, marks the year of his birth. The feather is from an eagle which was sitting in an oak tree; it was the first thing I saw when Scathach opened his mouth and brought his voice to the world. I named him for the oak, not the eagle. You see? Some things never change. We always name for the moment of birth. Like Morthen—"

In the language of the Tuthanach, *morthen* was "the sudden flight of birds".

"What if you'd seen a wolf being strangled?" she asked. It was an old Tuthanach joke and Wyn acknowledged it with a generous smile.

"When you are born you change the world," he said simply. "I've always thought it an elegant custom that the naming of a child should be for the first changing thing that the parents see . . ."

He glanced at his daughter. "In my ghost world, we pick names out of *books*. Many people have the same name."

Morthen thought that sounded very confusing.

Wyn returned his attention to the staff. "These twelve white feathers mark my twelve years with the *Amborioscantii*, and my twelve years with Scathach. The black feather here shows the year he rode away, to find out whether his true heart lay in the world beyond the forest. Like you, he was half of the flesh, half of the wood . . ."

Anxiety made him hesitate. Morthen watched him, but she did not carry the same questing fire in her eyes that he had seen in Scathach. Perhaps his daughter would stay in the realm. Perhaps she would never need to know to which of the two worlds she belonged . . .

"These feathers," he went on, "are my time with the Tutha-nach. That grey feather, there, is *your* birth; a crane's feather. All in all, twenty-four feathers. Twenty-four years. That makes me seventy-four years of age . . . but for fifty of those I lived in the ghost land, the shadow world . . ."

"Your ghost daughter was called *Anne*," Morthen said brightly. "The land was called *Oxford*. You see? I remembered!"

Wyn looked at the dying fire. "I miss her. I think about her often. Poor Anne . . . so unhappy in so many ways. I wonder what happened to her?"

"Perhaps she met Scathach. Perhaps he managed to find her."

"Perhaps."

Morthen reached out and touched the red and grey feathers which marked Scathach's birth and her own. "But where is Tig? No feather for Tig?"

"*This* feather for Tig," Wyn-rajathuk said, and touched a feather two years removed from Morthen's own. It was white, like all the others.

"That isn't a birth feather."

"Tig had no mother, only the forest. He came from a forest more ancient than the forest in which you hunt. It's the forest I told you about yesterday. The forest is here . . ." He tapped his head. "It is exceptionally old; it looks like a net; it vibrates like wind-blown beech; it speaks; it sings. It is like lightning. You've seen lightning, haven't you? Striking down to the wood—but here, in *this* wood," slapping his head, "the fire strikes all the time, it is *full* of fire. That fire reaches out and strikes the wood around us, and the wood smoulders and bones form, and the flesh smoulders and the spirit forms, and in this way Tig was born. He rose from the damp clay and the rot of the leaf litter . . . but he came from the forest in his father's head."

"I came from my mother's belly," Morthen said.

"Yes. You did. But your mother . . . all of her generation of the clan . . . came from the wood, generated by the fire in the head of the man like me, the man who passed by this river years ago, and who stopped for a while . . . and slept. And made a dream."

He could see that Morthen was still having difficulty with the concept despite the fact that he had repeatedly educated her in the nature of the mythago. But if she were fully mythago herself she would not even have been able to talk to him like this.

Wyn-rajathuk rose unsteadily to his feet and plucked a yellow feather from the ruff of his cloak. Morthen stood too. She picked up the portion of fish in its wrapping as if sensing what he would say. And she looked sad when he spoke, but accepted his words.

"You must go to the water lodge and take shelter there, with the women. It is high time you did so, but I have another reason for sending you away. The skogen is thinking very hard about the mortuary house—that's why the changes in the land are affecting it—and it is dangerous for you to be too close to me. If the skogen is who I think it is, he will be very aware of your spirit. I don't want you to change, but there is wood in your flesh and he can influence the wood."

"Is it my half brother?" Morthen asked. "Is it Scathach coming home?"

"I'm sure of it. My son is journeying back. And I have a strong feeling that he is very angry . . ."

He placed the yellow feather at the top of the staff and used a length of animal gut to secure it. "This may well be the last feather on the staff. When you become Morthen-*injathuk* please take that feather to mark the first of your own years. Do you promise?"

"I promise," the girl said and stared down at the fur-wrapped package in her hands.

The skogen was close. Very close. It would arrive in the land at any moment.

When Wyn-rajathuk inspected the totem trees on the mortuary hill he found them to be black with rot, even Shadow-of-an-unseen-forest, which had recently sprouted new growth. It was dead, now.

All of this had two messages for the man who had—despite his intellect—become effective in the way of the shaman: firstly, that the source of the contact, which had so enlivened Shadow-of-an-unseen-forest, was now so close that the communication was unnecessary, and the visual signs of its approach had ceased. Secondly, that there was a new magic in the land. Tig's magic. The magic of the rajathuk was fading, in the manner of fable, not of history.

A new system of symbology, of harnessing the unconscious power of certain individuals in the society of the land . . . a new magic was emerging from the ancient mind-stratum that was the Tuthanach.

All through history, Wyn knew, such sudden, explosive changes in belief and understanding must have occurred: a conception of ego; self imaging; an understanding of nature; conception of afterlife; an understanding of conception itself. And all of these things, simple evolutions of thought, began with the children, the new generation: symbolised in *one* child: the prodigy, the gifted child, the holy child.

Tig was such a creature. Through him—*Tig never-touch-woman, never-touch-earth*—through this odd, violent child, a whole culture would be born, and a new concept of the afterlife would become imprinted on two thousand years of human life.

Tig would organise the construction of great earthen tombs; he would interpret the random symbols of the middle stone age and initiate their formation into an accepted and comprehensible system of stone and wood carving. He would, by so doing, be responding simply to a sudden alteration in the relationship between the human conscious and its unconscious counterpart. But in Ireland and Western Europe of the fourth millennium BC, it would be the underworld which spoke, and its voice would be manifold, and a more orderly system of nature worship would come into being, fashioned by a considerable degree of foresight.

Tig would begin all this.

He had never existed, of course, not as a real human child. He was myth. He was the interpretation, belonging to a later age, of how the new system of belief and practice had been born. Tig's life, his aggressive, ghost-eating existence, was due solely to the birth from imagination of a population eager to explain their origins.

But Tig lived as powerfully as any child. Because he lived in all humankind.

He was formed from archetype.

He was power.

And now he was more powerful than Wyn-rajathuk because he had performed according to legend: he had confronted the guardian of the old bone lodge and threatened to eat his head. The shaman would flee from the land. Tig would pursue him and kill him, and then return and summon the forces of the earth. There would be a death by burial for all among the clan, each and every man, woman and child sinking into an earth grave and arising renewed. Only Tig would remain unburied; he would remember the stories of the clan. He would become their memory. This was why he sucked the bones of the dead. These stories would be placed, renewed also, into the reborn people of the Tuthanach, and they would build the first great tombs, and for the first time communicate with their ancestors.

When all of this was done, the young man called Tig would be impaled upon a pointed stone and a carrion bird would eat his eyes, his tongue and his heart, nesting upon him until his ghost, too, fled the flesh.

Still alive, he would walk away from the people and live on, eyeless, speechless, heartless, ghostless, to remind them of their betrayal.

And even this was not the earliest form of the myth . . .

So far as Wyn-rajathuk was concerned, however, the head on
his shoulders was one piece of good eating that he fully intended to
carry into safety. But he could not do this until the skogen had
come . . . Because the skogen was his *son*, and it had been ten long
years since he had seen the boy.

If Tig was close to controlling the world of the Tuthanach, for
the moment at least he had his mouth full with the mortuary
house.

Yes, Wyn thought. Yes, there is time. I can afford to wait here
for a few days more.

Morthen will take care of me.

The decision made, the next steps were simple. He walked to
the settlement of the Tuthanach, entered the gate and stood,
watching the chaos that crawled, clucked, ran, hewed, washed,
stoked, thatched and screamed. His presence at the gate caused a
certain quiet to descend upon this ordinary life: the chickens
scattered; the whelps yapped and were ordered quiet. Morthen was
playing with a girl of her own age. She stared at her father, but
caught his eye and made no overt sign of affection or concern.

Wyn-rajathuk drove his feather staff into the ground, worked it
left and right so that it burrowed into the earth. Old-woman-who-
sang-to-the-river came out of the long-house, on the arm of her
son, the oldest man in the settlement and a man as grey and lined
as Wyn himself, despite there being twenty years difference in
their age. The other women came behind, and Jykijar—First-hog-
of-summer—with his boar's-tusk staff and his frightening look of
the hunter; he was bored, waiting for the time when his hunting
magic could again be demonstrated.

Old-woman-who-sang-to-the-river came up to Wyn and placed
a hand on the shaman's arm. "Why are you doing this?"

"You no longer need me."

"But who will protect the mortuary house? Who will chant to
the sun? Who will challenge the moon? Who will help me sing to
the river?"

"Listen to the voice of the young man," Wyn said. "He will not
touch woman. He will not touch earth . . ."

"Tig?"

"Tig. He has come among you. He is bringing a new voice to
your people."

"We are your people too."

"No longer," Wyn said. "I came from outside. I must return to the outside."

The old woman backed away, touching her ears, the sign of great respect. The other Tuthanach imitated her, even First-hog-of-summer.

Wyn-rajathuk unslung his cloak of feathers and hung it on the spirit staff. The wind caught the ruff, the yellow feathers bristling as if with unease.

He tore off his crudely-woven tunic. He kicked off his shoes. Quite naked now, he backed away from the stockade, from the community, from the ever-present eyes of the ten family totems; from his life.

Stripped of his power, an outsider, a man alone, alone in a world which functioned according to dream, he went back to the river, to the place where the dead said goodbye to the water before beginning their long spirit walk to Lavondyss. To this place where he so often danced while Old-woman-who-sang-to-the-river made the elementals spin and scurry with her strange chanting.

Here he sat, without food, without drinking, without sleeping . . . for five days.

He made a staff from a length of broken alder. He made a shoulder cloak from leaves. He washed in the water every day, excreted when he felt the need, baptised himself. He never drank.

When he was empty and dizzy with loss, he began to feel how close the skogen was.

He sang to the coming force. He sang to his son. He danced in circles when the moon could see him. He remembered all the calling rituals; he kept them alive in this dead place, alive despite the new magic of the boy. He was the last of the ghosts, the last bone that would contain power. One day, too, even Morthen's skeleton would be consumed by the new shaman.

But not his. Not Wyn's. Not ever. His ghost tasted of a dead place, the place called England. It would make no sense to the boy, Tig. It would interfere with his power . . .

Wyn-rajathuk danced. He sang.

On the fifth evening the sudden flight of birds from the canopy stopped him in his slow dance and brought him eagerly to the far side of the river, searching among the trees for the source of the furtive movement his keen ears could discern. Someone or something moved in the treeline. He picked up his alder staff, turned a slow circle, scanning the whole dusklit clearing, then returned to the location of the disturbance.

He walked towards the darkness with trepidation, with excitement. There was most certainly a figure standing there, tall, clad in furs, watching him . . .

He banged the base of his river-dancing-staff against a rock. "Come on out. I know who you are. And it hasn't been that long that you can't recognise me . . ."

The undergrowth quivered. The figure moved. It stepped into the light of the clearing and watched him cautiously. Wyn-rajathuk felt his legs go weak, but he stayed where he was, stayed strong.

It was not Scathach who stood before him, but a woman. She was tall, her hair long and flaxen, wild. Her eyes, wide-spaced and dark, watched him with an intensity which was alarming. Her face was very lovely, made remarkable by the warmth and the pain that it communicated to the man who stood before her, silent. It was marred, too, with an ugliness which Wyn-rajathuk had come to associate with all mythagos: an old scar, raised and white, ran down the line of her left jaw. She was a commanding and breathtaking apparition; literally; the stink that came from her was part woman and part the smell of horse: she had been riding hard for many weeks. The furs in which she was clothed were full of sweat, full of earth, the oils of the animal not leached from the skin, now rotting. She was no hunter, then.

She carried a bundle of wolfskin under her left arm, and over her shoulder had a group of masks, tied with twine; they were bark masks, very old, rotting. Their dead faces clattered as she moved, empty eyes, empty mouths reminding Wyn of the heads he had seen carved in stone on his long journey to this, his place of peace.

He knew at once what she was. The features of the two masks he could see were familiar to him. The same faces watched the forest from dead trees on the mortuary hill.

Abruptly, this apparition spoke. "Are you Wynne-Jones?" it asked, and the man rocked back, astonished to hear his secret name after so long. The name sounded alien. It was from another life, another world.

"I am Wyn-rajathuk," he whispered, teetering on his feet, dizzy with shock and hunger. Where was his son? He had been so certain that this arrival would be his son: the skogen . . . searching for him.

"I've been looking for you," the woman said. She was suddenly deathly white, very tired, the fire fading from her eyes as if she was suddenly at peace herself. "I'm trapped in the wood. I've been here for too many years. Thank God I've found you . . ."

"I don't . . ." Wyn stuttered, realising that he was losing control of his body, too weak to fight it. "I don't understand . . ."

He felt his legs begin to buckle. He had been so *certain* that his boy was coming home. Who was this woman? What was she carrying? How could she know of him? How had she learned of the masks?

He saw the sudden startled look in her eyes. He heard footsteps on the rock across the river. He heard the grunt of effort. He turned.

Tig was staggering, then straightening up. It was a fleeting motion, fleetingly caught. Then the stone hammer which he had flung at his father struck Wyn full in the face, sending him hurtling back, his consciousness draining in the moment of pain and loss . . .

The strange woman cried angrily.

Tig shouted in triumph.

Water splashed violently as the boy raced to his kill.

Wyn tried to sit but his body would not move. He could smell his own blood, taste it; it began to fill his eyes. There was a summer's warmth on his face, spreading. The canopy above him began to circle, a wild dance, a death dance.

Tig was astride him. Twilight gleamed on white bone and the knife cut savagely into yielding flesh. The pain was sudden, then there was no pain. The boy sawed frantically at the living head. His elfin eyes said it all: "I want to eat you. I want to suck out your strange dreams . . ."

A moment later he was yelping, a whipped dog. He was dragged to his feet. The woman held him firmly, gripping the wrist that held the bone knife. And a gentler pair of hands than the boy's cradled Wyn's head; fingers pinched at the deep cut. "I need a needle. Anything. A fish bone. Anything . . ."

The voice was one he knew. The man who held him bent to him and whispered, "It has been a long hunt. You are a wily and elusive animal. But I have you now . . ."

Wyn-rajathuk went into his dreams in peace, no longer afraid. The last he heard was a single word, a word which filled him with joy.

"Father . . ."

[THE SILVERING]

The Sudden Flight of Birds

Wide eyes, in a sharp, angry face, watched from between the bars of the makeshift stockade; the boy's skin gleamed yellow with the light from the fire in the enclosure. His fingers curled around the wood. His teeth sparkled, his lips drawn back in a determined gesture of challenge.

I shall escape. I will eat your bones.

Tallis came close, unafraid. Tig made no move but his slanted eyes narrowed slightly, small points of brilliance following her approach. When the woman crouched down and raised the first of her masks, Tig laughed, spat, then shook the bars of his prison with surprising strength.

He faced the Hollower. He stared contemptuously at Gaberlungi and laughed at the Silvering. But he became subdued when Tallis placed Falkenna across her features so that she watched the boy with the cold eyes and sharp face of a bird.

"Why did you try to kill Wyn-rajathuk?" she asked through the feathered wood.

He roared out his answer (he had not understood the question) in violent words of his own tongue. Tallis heard 'Wyn' and 'Morthen', but apart from that she was lost. One expression was repeated over and over again: *Wyn baag na yith! Wyn baag na yith!*

When Tig was quiet again, Tallis said the same words back to him. He watched her, curious at first, then amused. Reaching through the bars he touched the *flight of a bird*, poked a finger gently through the mask's mouth to the unknown and uncertain region beyond. Tallis tasted the sting of urine and salt on the finger tip, but she allowed the tentative probe to enter her mouth. The boy seemed pleased by this moment of trust.

Tallis removed the mask, touched the wet fingertip with one of her own and watched as Tig became an animal, prowling the confined space of the corral, batting his head against the ground and wailing as if with grief.

Abruptly he was back, facing Tallis. He beat the palm of his left hand against his left eye until it began to weep. He spoke words in his fragmented, chthonic tongue. Tallis listened in silence, aware only of the distress in the boy's voice, a sense of regret, interspersed with moments of intense frustration.

"I can't help you," she said, and the eyes narrowed again, watching her lips as they moved to make what were to him quite threatening and occult sounds. "I *need* the man you want to kill. And I know what *you* have to do, so I have to stop you. Your new magic must wait. You must wait to pick through his dreams; I need to pick through them first myself."

As if he understood, Tig shook his head. He tugged his long hair forward, twisted it into a rope and held it diagonally across his face, bisecting his features across the nose and the left eye. He took dirt from the ground and smeared the features of his left side. It was a slow, deliberate, threatening motion.

Tallis took a finger-length doll from the group which she wore around her shoulders and pushed it into the ground, twisting it: a watching wood.

"My eyes will always watch you—" she said, and picked up the heavy burden of masks as she stood.

Tig laughed and lifted his skins to expose genitals that were tiny and bone white, roaring loudly as he did so.

The boy had escaped by morning. There was blood on one of the points of the palisade. The watching-wood, which Tallis had buried, was broken in half, laid on the ground and surrounded by a circle of snail shells. The shells were perforated. They had come from Morthen's ritual head-dress. During the night of his escape, Tig had entered the long-house, where Morthen slept close to her dying father, and stolen the webbing which she had so carefully fashioned.

It was his way of stating power. He could have killed Wynne-Jones at that time, if he had wanted, but Tallis's own power had subdued him just sufficiently.

Defiance, then. But Tallis had threatened him and the fear was in the boy. The fear of birds, an old magic which Tig had not yet overcome.

A flight of cranes passed over the settlement as Tallis circled the broken remains of her watching-wood. She glanced up, into the dawn sky. One of the birds began to struggle on the wing, struck by a sling stone launched from an unseen hunter at the forest edge. It fell slowly, neck twisted back. Tallis heard the distant growl of a dog. The cranes veered to the north and there was silence again.

The crane-hunter stepped into the clear land which surrounded the settlement of the Tuthanach. Tallis crouched down and the strange figure, carrying its limp prey over its shoulders, moved swiftly to the east. The man had a crane's bill strapped, as a penis-sheath, to his groin. Skulls, feathers and the shrivelled carcasses of small birds decorated his neck and limbs. His feet were clad in reed boots. He was a marsh hunter too. His marsh hound followed him. The penis-sheath caught the new sun like a lance. Shortly before he entered the wood again, the crane-hunter removed this triumphal, ritual garb, making it easier for him to run the forest, in search of a place to build his fire.

The hounds—scrawny, blunt-nosed animals—began to howl, greeting the new day. Smoke was urged from embers, then flame. The sun was a pale glow, low over the forest, subdued by autumn mist. Tallis heard Scathach's voice, and elsewhere a woman coughing. A child wailed and a man laughed.

At once the silent enclosure was alive with sound. A man stepped through the weatherworn skins that kept the winter from one of the round lodges and shrugged on his heavy fur cloak, raising a hand to Tallis, a greeting, and watching her curiously as he walked to the earthworks, to crouch in dawn shadow and pass his soil.

Tallis picked up her broken doll and returned to the long-house, stepping down into the earth and ducking beneath the wooden lintel with its deeply incised charms. Light streamed into this place from two smoke holes in the heavy turf roof. Everywhere her gaze was confused with the stacks of furs, skins, poles, clay jars and bowls, frames for weaving, and totemic objects. Strands of shells, small stones, bones, root vegetables and dried bird-flesh hung from the blackened cross beams, rattling and shifting in the gusting breezes that crept in from the outside.

Human shapes moved through this gloomy clutter, gathering around the central fire where clay pots of water were slowly warming at the edge of the renewing embers. Ash streamed into the streaks of pale light. In the shadows the fur-clad women were stooped, shambling shapes, their alertness demonstrated only by the sparkle of dark eyes, watching the tall, strange woman from the Otherworld: Tallis.

She walked over to the far corner where Scathach and his half-sister, Morthen, were keeping vigil over the battered body of their father.

The old man should have been dying. Already the wounds to his face and neck were swollen and stinking with infection. Tallis had found curative herbs, unknown to the Tuthanach, and Scathach had demonstrated his considerable skills as a surgeon in cleaning and preparing the wounds for healing. But the conditions of this culture were so basic that by rights Tig's attack should have been mortal.

A deeper strength kept Wynne-Jones in the land of the living. Scathach talked to him, and during the days which followed Tallis, too, whispered her story to the unconscious man, urging him to return to consciousness, to retrace his steps from the spiral path that led into the vibrant, bone-filled earth.

On the third day of his living death, Wynne-Jones turned on to his side and began to paw and kick the air. It puzzled Scathach for a while, then Morthen understood. Tallis had sensed it from the beginning. He was running like a dog, like a hunting dog dreaming of the chase. He was deep in the wood, running on a wild track, seeking water. Towards evening, when the hounds of the Tuthanach cried at hidden ghosts, Wyn-rajathuk too opened his lips and whimpered.

The next day he began to make swimming motions with his body and his mouth opened and closed. He was a fish, swimming in crystal waters. He swam for two days. Tallis watched him through the Silvering but caught only a hint of the cold river where his spirit journeyed.

At last he was a bird. His head jerked, his eyes opened. His fingers parted; a wing, feathered. Wherever he soared, wherever he flew, in the long-house he remained stretched on the rush matting, only the sounds from his throat and the twitching of his muscles identifying the nature of his flight.

"A stork," Morthen said. "This is the final part of his journey between the two worlds."

"But is he leaving us or coming home?" Tallis asked quietly. "In which direction is he travelling?"

She couldn't get close to Scathach, not in spirit, although when she sat with him he often reached out and took her hand in his cool fingers. But his mind was far away, perhaps pursuing the animal guide that led his father through the underworld. His eyes remained fixed on Wynne-Jones. His breathing was slow and deep. He sipped water from a leather pouch, but ate nothing.

Tallis tugged a bone comb through his tangled curls. He let her make the gesture and murmured "thank you". He was a hunched, sad shape, all the physical power in him, the strength that had complemented her own for so many years, all of that energy pouring through his dark gaze in the direction of the dying man.

Tallis told herself that this spiritual distance was a temporary thing, that the man she loved would return soon. But an increasing feeling of melancholy over the first few days made her tense and unsociable towards the Tuthanach; she was beginning to grieve for a loss which had not yet happened.

Wyn-rajathuk's daughter saw this and it drew her close. The girl and the woman—opposites in so many ways—became friends. Tallis had been sharing space in the women's lodge, but her height (she was six feet tall by her reckoning) and her fair-haired, aquiline looks were such a contrast to the smaller, darker clan women that she was held in a mixture of awe and fear. She wore her tattered wolfskins for two days, then agreed to wear the woollen and otter-fur clothing of the clan. The women relaxed more with her, although Tallis entertained powerful and wistful memories of childhood, when dresses had felt as billowing and uncertain upon her unformed body as this loose fitting weave.

When she left the enclosure she immediately changed back to

her travelling garb. This alteration of appearance at the gate became an odd ritual, and a delightful one to the younger men. But Tallis was *injathuk*—the masks she carried were clear enough evidence of this—and all such workers with the voice of the earth were expected to behave strangely, and to have their private rituals of communication with the sky.

She was left alone, therefore, and free to explore the dense woodland that led, in one direction at least, to the river where she and Scathach had first emerged into the realm of the Tuthanach. There were tracks everywhere, mostly overgrown, many of them marked by animal skulls or feathered poles. So many great old trees had fallen that no path was clear enough to run along and Tallis found it wearying to clamber over so many rotting, mossy corpses, seeking the glades where yellow green light illuminated a clearing.

In such dells, invariably, the Tuthanach had built forest rajathuks. In the mortuary enclosure, on the blackthorn hill, there was a cluster of the great statues, but in the wood each was represented many times and each had its own tangled, silent clearing, its edges hung with skins, pouches, clay pots and the bones of animals: votive offerings, Tallis imagined.

She soon realised that the blackened totems were of the same genesis as her masks. The details were different and often hard to see against the glare of the sky as she craned upwards, towards the axe-hewn features. Different, yet uncannily recognisable . . . as if drawn from the same imagination. Falkenna and Silvering especially were similar to her own child-fashioned bark masks.

The most haunted glade of all contained the Hollower. It grinned at her; she could see traces of the red tongue against the white ochre face. Here, the trees were hung with the dismembered bodies of humans, although for a while Tallis could see no skulls, only long bones and rib cages, which looked oddly forlorn, impaled on broken branches. White rag was everywhere, and thick twines of human hair. The ground was lumpy; the skulls were below the earth. There was a terrible stench of rotten flesh here, and in the canopy above the birds hopped and flapped but were never to be heard giving voice to song.

Was this stinking place, with its rotting statue, the gateway to Lavondyss? Had Harry come this way, found this sad glade, and passed into the ferocious winter from which he had called back to his home, a world away? Tallis placed her own Hollower over her face. Spirits moved in the shadows; human shapes, restless and frightened, drew back into the dark wood. The statue leaned away from her, its bark splitting vertically and parting just enough so that she could sense the fluttering movement inside the trunk.

It startled her. She removed the mask. The glade was as before.

For eight years Tallis had opened hollowings, yet had failed to find the path she wanted. She knew why, well enough: she was missing the Moondream mask. But even so, her power was limited. After the stag had gone, after her *gurla* had so dramatically transformed itself into a feature of the land, she had never again felt as powerful as on that day when the fields around her house had erupted into a riot of root and stone from other ages.

She was growing old. She was more than twenty, by her reckoning. She was growing old. She carried the relics of a different ageing process. The forest, in its many ways, was sucking out her soul, her spirit. It was sucking out her dreams. It was draining her.

She realised with sudden, silent anger that she was sinking into melancholy again; she drew in a sharp breath, stood and slapped the side of the Hollower. One side of its grinning face seemed dead, she noticed, an odd difference from her own mask.

If the wood *was* draining her, surely something had happened, now, that would give her a charge of energy. She had come close . . . for only the first time . . . close to Harry. Outsiders attract outsiders. Now that she had found Wynne-Jones she was certain that she had reached a place where her brother's anima had caused a brief riot in the woodland before he had passed on, up the river . . .

She often went to the river during these first few days. She saw Morthen there twice but concealed herself, although she noticed where the girl, too, found security from passing eyes: a high stand of rocks, some yards from the muddy bank, that at first seemed sheer and solid but which on investigation proved to be hollow and a natural shelter. On the night when Wyn-rajathuk began to swim, on his journey, as a silver fish, Tallis came to these protecting rocks and curled up, to sleep through one night on her own.

She was woken at dawn by four dogs, gigantic hounds, barking and baying as they sniffed and splashed their ways through the shallows. One of them came up to the rocks, braced its forepaws on the high boulders and peered down at the crouching woman. Tallis raised her iron knife menacingly and the hound withdrew, chasing after its fellows. Tallis remained in hiding for a while. A man, cloaked, carrying a staff, walked by on the far side of the water, keeping close to the undergrowth and uttering a short, high-pitched chant every time he circled round one of the feathered spirit poles. His head was cowled, his face bearded. With a shiver Tallis noticed that he carried two wooden masks on his back.

He passed by swiftly, not lingering in this totem-ridden place of the dead. Tallis followed him on foot a long way up the river until the next stretch of water could be seen, a bubbling series of rapids streaming between the crowded, leaning trees. The caped figure stepped across stones at this point, passing from one dense thicket to another, not looking back.

"Everyone is going up the river . . ."

Even horses!

One came by her now, a black mare, its trappings and harnessing ragged, old and rotten. Metal had eaten into the creature's flesh and its hide was stained and stiff with caked blood.

"I don't remember you from the story books . . ." Tallis murmured as she made her cautious approach to the wary animal. It was not old, but it was weary. There was a great dark stain on the remnants of the saddle blanket which still draped its back, stuck to the horse by the congealed lifeblood of its one-time rider.

Tallis caught the beast and soothed it, then removed what she could of the man-made torment which bound it. When she walked back to the place of the dead, the black mare followed. Tallis's own horse had been killed by falling rocks, some weeks before. Scathach—after the loss of his Jaguthin friends—had taken to running through the wood and the wild tracks on foot, an expression of loss the reason for which he was unable to articulate.

"You could well be a welcome friend," Tallis whispered to the animal. "If you're still here tomorrow I shall assume I can ride you. But I won't name you, so you will always be free. But if I *do* ride you, expect to go into a strange region."

The next day Morthen made her boldest approach to Tallis, to establish friendship.

Tallis had been aware of the girl's furtive presence for some minutes before she finally crept into the spirit glade where Tallis was sitting and crouched in the shadows behind the older woman. Tallis remained quite still. She was surrounded by her masks, which she had laid flat and face up in a circle. The wolfskin pack which contained her special relics was placed neatly before her, but still bound. Aware of the girl she nevertheless kept her gaze upon the eyes of the wooden statue, seeking in its bizarre shape for the clue to 'Moondream'.

The Moondream totem was made from a willow trunk. The female aspect of the shape was evident, but the true beauty of the rajathuk emerged through the representations of earth and moon in the subtle flow of the carved wood, and the clever conjunction of those symbols with the human features. It had already begun to communicate with the woman from the far realm.

"Tallis?"

The girl's voice was quiet. She was nervous. Tallis ignored her for a moment. Her mind was adrift in a nightscape and the shape of the mask was close to her, almost formed. It was not like the previous moondream, the mask she had made after talking with Gaunt. How could it be? That particular expression of her deep unconscious world had been used and expended. When she had dropped the mask, when she had lost it, she had lost, too, that particular link with the female in the land . . .

She wondered, sometimes, whether her father, after he had picked it up, had destroyed it, or whether he wore it on moonlit nights; and if he did that . . . what did he see? What did he hear?

"Tallis? What are you doing?"

Morthen's English was basic and sometimes barely understandable. Her words were full of the particular palatals and diphthongs of the Tuthanach (Tallis was pronounced Tallish, for example) but her father had instructed her sufficiently in his strange tongue for her to make a little sense.

Tallis turned where she sat; her hair fell forward to cover her face and the scar on her jawline; it also hid her smile; when Morthen remained motionless Tallis beckoned her forward and the girl approached, walking in a peculiar, crouched way. Her hair was smeared white and tied down with a red-painted strip of cloth from which strings of bone and shell hung. Morthen reached out to touch the older woman's dry hair, the flaxen hair that so fascinated the Tuthanach women. Tallis remained quite still, neither irritated nor amused by this gentle exploration of difference. Morthen's impish eyes, full of wonder now, stared hard into Tallis's. "There *is* green there. It's true."

"There wasn't always. Only for the last few months."

She had already heard it commented upon in the settlement: that although she was injathuk, she carried no sky in the bone of her head, but the green woollen robe of the voice-of-earth was showing through; she was becoming rajathuk.

To Tallis, all this superstition was meaningless; what mattered was that she had a certain power. Although the change of her eye colour was a slightly worrying thing . . .

In belated answer to the girl's first question, Tallis said, "I'm making a new mask. The last of my masks. It will help me open the hollowings . . . oolerinnens . . . more easily. Do you understand what I'm saying?"

But Morthen was already thinking along a different forest track. She asked, "Is Scathach my brother? Truly?"

She had removed her touch from Tallis's hair and now crouched, drawn in on herself, as she might crouch around the fire in the height of winter.

Tallis agreed. "Of course. Your *half* brother that is. He had a different mother than you. Tig is your only full brother."

Morthen's childish eyes flamed with anger; she snarled, a brief and bestial distortion of her lips. "Tig is *not* my brother," she spat. "He had no mother. He came from the *first forest*." She tapped her head furiously.

Tallis smiled, understanding what she meant. Tig was a more recent mythago. Wynne-Jones's, no doubt.

Morthen's flare of anger died as quickly as it had been kindled. Tallis gathered her masks and looped the leather strap through the eyes, slinging them on to her right shoulder. Morthen prodded the other pack and Tallis gently tapped the inquisitive fingers away. She glanced wistfully at the willow pole, with its subtle moon features.

Almost. One more hour and I'll have you . . .

Then she followed the girl. They passed around the winding track which led through the densest wood towards the river.

Morthen was excited. "I've got something for you," she said on three occasions, as if urging Tallis to remain interested.

They came to the river. With a shiver of anger Tallis saw the black horse tethered to a low branch. The tether was in the form of

a noose around its neck. It had struggled, but was now calm.
Triumphantly, Morthen presented her gift.

"I caught it. It was alone."

Tallis stared at the animal, then cautiously established a touch
upon its muzzle. "I still want to ride you," she said, and the beast
snorted. Tallis removed the tether. "Go, if you want."

Black mare stayed. Tallis smiled at Morthen. "Thank you. For
the gift."

Unaware of anything more than that Tallis had wonderful
control over animals, Morthen slapped her own cheeks in delight.
"I've named her for you. You can ride her. Her name is Swimmer
of Lakes. That will be important. You'll see . . ."

Swimmer of Lakes. An odd name for a horse. Morthen clearly
knew more about the land than Tallis had imagined.

She made her final agreement with the black mare. "You swim
one lake for me, I'll swim one lake for you. This is Tallis's
Promise."

So she blanketed the beast, and made a harness that didn't cut.
She led it to the open land around the Tuthanach enclosure and
protected it from dogs.

In the meantime, Morthen delighted in showing Tallis what
she and her father had discovered in the woods around the river:
stones carved deeply with the images of blind, dead human faces; a
tower, its slate tiles fallen but the ornate and gilded furniture of its
prisoner still recognisable in the ruin, though its occupant, and its
meaning, had long since fled into the storm skies. What Morthen
called "the end of the wood" turned out to be the high wall of a
Roman fort, overgrown but still impressive. Tallis used the
latrine. It was a simple stone seat above a deep, dry sewer, but it
was a marvellous change from squatting over maggots. There were
grain stores here, and barracks, and graffiti that seemed as fresh as
if they had been daubed that day. Morthen found a sword, then a
pennant wrapped in leather. It showed an eagle and a helmet, but
tore as Tallis tried to hang it out to read the inscription.

In one of the grain stores there was a pack of rats, each the size of
a wild cat. Tallis was the last of the two to flee.

There were tombs, too: from ornate black marble mausolea, still
impressive as they rose above the choking wood, to earth mounds
and narrow entrances, lined by chiselled stone and leading deep

into the natural realm below the roots of the forest. The oddest piece of flotsam in that land was a horn, forty feet long and wide enough at its trumpet end for Tallis to stand inside and shout. It was carved from real horn and there was no sign of it being more than a single piece. Morthen tried to blow its narrow end. Tallis heard the breath, then realised that the girl's voice had been transformed into haunting words, not English, not Tuthanach . . .

They left the horn behind them but noticed, for a day or more, that the woods in that region seemed active, as if something had come to disturb the peace.

Wynne-Jones was flying as a bird. Tallis had been in the settlement for five days. "Is he leaving us or coming home?" she asked. Morthen laughed, but Scathach slumped forward by the sweat-soaked palliasse. The vigil had sucked away his vitality. He was flesh and blood but his spirit was beating against the gate to the unknown region. His father was there, but he could not himself enter and lend his strength to the old man's journey home.

Finally, Morthen took Tallis up the river to the mist-shrouded lake, with its marsh creatures and giant willows. Swimmer of Lakes was strong and bore the double weight with ease, but when Tallis urged the beast into the muddy shallows among the rushes the horse drew back. Tallis dismounted and returned to dry land. She would not force her new-found friend to cross this place just yet.

But it was to the marsh that all the travellers came, and all of them would have to cross its still, grey waters. Beyond the lake was the land which called to ghosts—and Harry was there too!

So Tallis spread her masks around her and placed the Hollower on her face. Morthen stood behind her watching apprehensively as the woman undertook a ritual which she did not comprehend. Her apprehension turned to outright fear when the sky darkened suddenly and the waters of the lake were lashed into a fury. Dark roots coiled like snakes into the air and formed a sinister tunnel. The willows around the lake leaned and creaked, shedding birds from their branches like a myriad of swirling flecks of black ash. A storm wind flattened the rushes and a great gusting swirl of snow poured from the hollowing, sending Morthen screaming back to the shelter of trees.

Through the arch of roots Tallis saw a steep-sided winter valley.

Oaks and thorns clung to the rocks, their branches shedding snow. Dark fingers of stone poked against the pale, dead sky, a ragged palisade. The river thundered over boulders and the woman who watched could see the sharp angles and straight lines of stones that had fallen from whatever ruin had once guarded this narrow way.

The hollowing collapsed into the swirling water of the lake. Like animals, the trees withdrew their sinuous fingers from the shallows. Where the wind had dispersed the fog, Tallis could see the distant wall of forest and the broken cliffs behind it, where the river flowed out into the flats to become so still, so silent. Then mist closed in again and the rushes stirred with a life of their own, straightening up and quivering, although there was now no breeze.

Tallis gathered up her masks, found Morthen's ashen shape huddled in the protecting limbs of a thorn, and led her back to home.

Perhaps because she had been frightened by what had occurred, Morthen drew suddenly away from Tallis and began to spend more time in Scathach's presence, sitting for hours in the long-house, close to the hearth, staring at the grim-faced man who was her half brother. Whatever he wanted she was always the first to fetch it. She took every opportunity to reach out to him, touching his arms, his hands, his calves, brushing her fingertips along the light beard on his cheeks. She acknowledged Tallis but lowered her eyes when they met. Tallis felt very sad about this.

Two days after the incident at the lake Tallis saw her lean forward and lick Scathach's cheek, below the eye. She said, "You are a real brother. Your skin tastes of flesh." She licked him again. "Tig is not real. Tig tastes of dry leaves. You are my real brother from the wood . . ."

Tallis was shocked by this, although she had no reason to be upset. But it came home to her almost as a painful blow just how deep was the affinity between the two half-woodland creatures. She had simply not noticed it before. There was an attraction that was strong and utterly exclusive. His affection for his sister showed quite clearly in the comfort he felt in her presence, in the look he gave her, in the way the two of them murmured together as they nursed the dying man, effortlessly complementing each other's actions. For the first time in all the long and painful eight years she had been with the young warrior, Tallis felt isolated from him. The feeling in her body was distressing, but she was torn between her own need to come closer to Scathach again and her understanding that something important was occurring in the long-house . . . perhaps something in the way of a legend's detail . . .

She picked up her bundle, her precious bundle of wolfskin, and left the house, returning to the protecting rocks by the river, to pass another night alone.

She was certain, now, that Wynne-Jones would not recover consciousness. In her life in the wood she had known death on many occasions—the loss of Gyonval being the most awful—and the ferocity of that neck wound, and the terrible hammer blow to his skull, could surely mean nothing more than a slow, sleeping descent into the embrace of the underworld. But she would do nothing until the man had truly gone. In the meantime she had whispered her brother Harry's name to him; she had described Harry; and she had told the man all the stories, and especially the story of Old Forbidden Place.

And she asked him the question: "What does it mean? How do I get to Lavondyss? If you are high on the wing, can you look ahead and see the way?"

At dawn she glanced in at the long-house, on her way back from the river. She had come to a decision during the night, a decision that was very painful for her. She left her masks in Wynne-Jones's small shaman's lodge, but still carried her relic bag.

The enclosure was stirring with life, mostly of an animal nature. The wind was chill, that ever-present scent of snow that followed her from summer to summer. A fire was being rekindled, probably in the small house where the children slept. The smoke smelled sharp on the clean air, and mixed strangely with the sweet odour of the new hides, stretched on their frames and lining the way to the elder's lodge. The sound of the woman who blew life into the embers was interrupted by snatches of her song.

Crouching at the entrance Tallis peered into the gloom, to the far end where Wynne-Jones lay. For a second she watched the unconscious man, then with a great pang of anger and hurt she saw Scathach emerge from below his bearskin blanket and feel for his father's pulse; a second body remained below the blanket and Tallis caught a glimpse of clay-white, ringleted hair.

Without a sound she withdrew from the house. Clutching her

bundle she made her way through the forest and emerged among the dense blackthorn on the low mortuary hill. Her mind was very clear, but she felt cold; cold like death. She closed her eyes and tried to will away the great clawing sense of finality that gripped her heart and made her stomach feel like lead.

It's over. It has to be done. I know it has to be done. It's over. This is the right time. This is the end. I can't go on unless I do it now . . .

She stumbled up the hill, the emptiness in her heart drying the tears before they formed. She followed the rough track to the summit and scrambled over the collapsed earth wall, between the rotting pillars of the gate. Then she turned and stared out across the forest.

Somewhere in that immense and ancient land, Harry was a solitary voyager, but Tallis felt closer to him now than she had in eight years, even from the time when he had called to her through the first of her hollowings.

"I have to get rid of *him* before I can come to *you* . . ." she whispered to the distance, to the far peaks, to the unknown region. "Because you are the same. You are the same. I always knew you were . . ."

She stared across the wood. It had swallowed Harry, then breathed out Scathach. It had filled her head with legend, then sucked her in, a fish sucking in a fly. And somewhere beyond that land was her home. On occasion, on a certain type of night, she could almost imagine that the lights which shone among the trees were the lights from her house, and if she walked through the undergrowth for just a few yards the garden would be there, and the woodshed, and her mother, and Gaunt, and her father in his dressing gown . . .

Don't go child. Don't leave us! Tallis . . . don't go . . .

"I won't be gone long. Just one week . . ."

One week!

She had never stopped her self-recrimination for having been so naive, so stupid. One week, she had said. That's all I'll be away.

But the wood had closed behind her; then Broken Boy had left her, a bizarre and terrifying end to their relationship; and Scathach, for all his promises, had become lost too. They had been following the river for years. They had no conception of what lay at the end. Only occasionally could Tallis open a gate and though they had passed through them they had always ended up at the river again.

I have to get rid of him. I have to get rid of my tie to him. I have to make myself free.

Tallis stood outside the mortuary house for a moment, uncertain, concerned. Then she ducked below the stone lintel and entered the dark, narrow corridor. When she came among the bones she was confused. By the faint light from the gaps in the turf roof she could see that an animal had been here. A half decomposed corpse was scattered and shredded over the floor. There were small burial urns, piles of skulls, and piles of limbs. They were all set into niches below the roof. Tallis stepped among them, peering into the darkness, trying to let the thin shafts of sunlight paint a picture of the mortuary chaos. Birds shifted restlessly in the roof. Dirt dribbled on to the stone floor. Tallis straightened up, then looked behind her and up into the gloom. And cried out with shock as a dark shape swung down from a cross beam, appearing suddenly and frighteningly and hanging in front of her, inches away.

Tig's strange eyes watched her hungrily.

Then he dropped to the floor, walked around her and crouched in the exit tunnel.

Tallis waited until her heart had stopped racing with the sudden fear. Then she looked round, saw a part of the house where a stone cist was dimly illuminated. She went there, placed her bundle on the ground and unfurled the wolfskin. The bones of her son lay exposed at last, the sad wood which they had become crushed and broken after many years of being dragged through the forest and buried beneath her other goods.

Tig was curious. After a while he edged towards her, still on his haunches; an animal, approaching warily. He gasped as he saw the tiny bones. He reached forward, then hesitated, glancing at Tallis who remained expressionless and still. For years she had carried the death of her firstborn with her. Now she tried to think of these relics as nothing more than wood, a broken statue, crumbling memory. The child had lived only five months . . . he had not been real. Had he?

It was impossible to forget his cries. To forget the look in his infant's eyes. To forget his sudden quiet when the birds of the wood began to agitate the trees at dusk. It was impossible to

forget the feeling that the child had been *aware* of its own
fate . . .

Tig picked up a fragment of the broken skull. It crumbled
between his fingers, into dust, into splinters, yellowing shards of
the stuff of oak. He reached for one of the long bones, raised it
quickly to his lips, sucked gently, then shook his head. He looked
very concerned as he watched Tallis. He shook his head again,
then reverently placed the bone among the others.

"Ah well," Tallis said. "His dreams are still my dreams."

She wrapped up the bundle and gave it to the boy. Tig took the
burial package, looked around, then carried it into darkness.
Tallis heard a stone being shifted, scraping as it was moved aside;
then the sound as it was returned to its proper place.

A moment later Tig crept back. Tallis was puzzled to see that he
was still holding the bundle. He looked confused, perhaps distracted. He fiddled with the shafts of sharp bone that penetrated
his rough clothing and young flesh. He was inducing pain and it
showed in his eyes. He stood and walked to the exit from the
mortuary house. Tallis heard him sniffing at the air, a violent
sound. He too was crying. When he came back he was holding
some dry grass and two flints. He sat down again and made a small
fire.

He picked up the dry wood bones, one by one, and placed them
on the kindling. Soon the flames made shadows fidget among the
dead. Brightness gleamed in the boy's eyes as it must have shone
with unsteady radiance upon the tears that moistened Tallis's
cheeks. They sat in silence as the dead wood cracked and gasped
its way to the ash-grey light of another realm.

Towards the end, Tig drew a piece of dry fish from a small pouch
at his belt, impaled it on a bone and singed it in the flame. It gave
off a sudden and pleasant smell. When it was burned Tig licked it,
sniffed it, then passed it to Tallis, who accepted the gift and ate it,
choking with grief more than with the heat of the food.

She had thought it a part of the ritual of the dead in Tig's new
world—consuming the life-fire of her dead child on the fired flesh
of a swimmer to the unknown region—but Tig skewered two
pieces for himself and licked his lips eagerly as the fish grilled over
the flames.

Tallis became drowsy. In the fading firelight Tig's eyes watched her through bright lenses. For a while she felt the need to keep awake, in case he should become violent. But a more reasoning voice began to whisper to her, and she let herself drift into sleep. She felt the boy's gentle touch on her face, the small fingers pressing against the bone of cheek and skull. Images and memories began to flutter nervously, as if being called reluctantly . . . a mask slipping from her hands . . . a man stooping to the water of a stream, his red dressing gown soaked . . . her name, cried in despair and grief . . .

A voice shouting "Faster! Through the hollowing now! Come on, Tallis!"

Her own voice crying, "I can't *ride* this fast. I've only ridden ponies . . ." and the sense of unbalancing as she turned in the crude saddle and saw her father's face, huge in her vision, the mask clutched to his chest . . .

Then a sudden closing of the wood around him, like the shutting of foliage gates, the cutting off of summer.

Biting wind . . . Autumn on the wind . . .

A canter, then a fall, Scathach laughing, then guiltily remorseful, helping her to her feet, fussing at the cut on her leg, helping her back on to the horse. He swung up into the saddle with her, gave her a quick kiss, his arm around her shoulders. "I'll keep you safe until your legs grow longer. You'll be back before your father has time to dry his tears."

But she hadn't expected him to *see* her go. That was so unfair. That was so cruel. Now he had seen her she should go back. She should explain. The horses cantered forwards. She cried bitter tears, angry tears.

"Go back. Take me back . . ."

Scathach and his friends, though, were riding as if caught on a wave, following the current, drawn deeper into the wood, the broken, limping stag running before them, antlers clattering against the low branches. Sometimes it rose up the ridges of hills; sometimes it moved cautiously through shallow waters, disappearing into the heavy fog that often gathered above the river. They were compelled to move inwards, inwards away from the fields of the Keetons' farm.

Tallis followed because she had no other option.

How dense the forest became, how silent. A stifling stillness settled over all the green and yellow land below the canopy. Water whispered; trees protested at some unfelt breeze, short snaps and cracks of movement. Sharp light danced on the moist surfaces of fern frond and mossy rock. Even the stag became silent, leading the way through the gloom of the undergrowth, across rivers, stumbling on slippery crags of grey stone, ducking and twisting its great body as it weaved a path into the heart of the forest.

It became cold. Flights of birds disturbed the silence. Their movement let strands of brightness fall into the green half-light of the glades and dells below, clearings which led one upon the other, a trackway through the ancient realm.

Stretley field . . . street field . . . this secret path had been known for thousands of years . . . but did it ever turn back upon itself, did it ever lead to home?

Days and nights: Tallis lost touch with the passage of time.

She had not been here as much as a week, she thought, but she was dizzy with tiredness, with riding, with claustrophobia and with anxiety. Was he still standing there? Was he waiting for the woods to part again and for his daughter to come splashing triumphantly home along Hunter's Brook?

I want to go back, she whispered to Scathach.

One glance at the grim set of his face was enough to tell her that such was a luxury now lost. He shook his head. He looked wilder; fear was etched on his handsome features, now. His eyes were restless and he too felt the confining force of the forest, the bearing down of branches, the crushing weight of trunks and great rocks as they followed Broken Boy at the edge of the shallow, through narrow defiles of rock and into deep, echoing caverns, through restless alderwoods and stands of choking holly and oak.

We may be away a little longer than I thought, he said to her. I had expected to emerge into a snow landscape, not here. I don't know this place. I'm just following your *gurla* . . .

Broken Boy will lead me safely back, she thought.

But Broken Boy had a final irony to lay at Tallis's cold and water-sodden feet.

The stag started to run. The horses quickened to follow. Gyonval was nearly unseated as his roan mare bucked, then cantered, striking its rider against a low-slung branch. Above the canopy, the dawn was alive with the sounds of birds. They had been riding for only a short while, summoned from sleep by the roaring of their animal guide. The beast's antlers, more broken now than ever and stripped of their ragged velvet, seemed to glisten with dew. Its haunches steamed. It raced through the wood as if pursued by ravening dogs. Tallis slipped from the saddle and only Scathach's strong arm stopped her from tumbling below the hooves of her horse. "Ride better!" he snapped. She gripped the long hair of her mount's mane, but as the animal weaved through the river, stumbling on muddy banks and slithering and sliding over the fallen trunks of rotting trees, so she was bounced and thrown. Soon she was crying with pain and fear. Her masks clattered over the saddle, but they remained in place.

Suddenly they were in a misting dell. The streaking light which fell from on high was almost divine, shafting radiance. The fog swirled, gleaming yellow; leaves shimmered. There were a myriad colours here and the whole place seemed to tremble. The mist seemed to flow from the dark trunks of trees. The dell was awash with ferns and sapling growth. Broken Boy turned and faced the breathless riders.

He watched Tallis.

He shook his broken head. Strands of saliva dripped from his open maw. He shook as if with pain, or fear . . .

The stag appeared to freeze; its limbs turned to wood; its head tipped up and back, as if in a final moment of pain. As its jaws parted, the dell filled with a deep booming cry. Almost too fast to follow, the shape of the stag changed, enlarging, expanding, growing tall towards the trees whilst the broken antlers widened, becoming huge blades of bone. The legs, braced apart, stretched swiftly, thickened, formed a gateway through which a swirl of snow entered the cool dell.

The horses bucked. Tallis slipped from the saddle again, but was held in place by strong arms, Gyonval's this time. He grinned at her. Her masks swung heavily around her neck. Her head ached with the roaring of the dying beast.

The great elk faced them, higher than the trees, antlers lost in the foliage. Its body dripped water, as if rain were falling on its back and running from its flanks and belly. Ivy grew out over the trunk-like limbs, sprouting, shooting, reaching its way in seconds until the elk was swathed in green. Bushes of holly burst from its skin. Roots of trees crawled through the cracks, trembled across the enfoliated hide.

Soon there was silence, save for the murmur of wind above and the rustle of the new growth. A gigantic and rotten wooden gate, Broken Boy transformed now showed them the way to the heart of the realm. The forest beyond was in the deep of winter, and Scathach wrapped his furs around the shivering form of Tallis before he followed Gyonval and the others through the hollowing and into the frozen land.

If he was aware of Tallis crying, he said nothing.

Are we lost?
Yes.
You said you would get me home . . .
I don't know how to do that any more. I can't seem to turn. I can't retrace our steps. I'm being drawn deeper, to my own home . . .
What am I going to do? What about my parents?
I wish I had an answer for you. I don't.
Harry will help me . . . I know he will . . .
Then the sooner we find your brother the better.

(Tig's fingers moved across her face. Dreams oozed from bones, crowded her drowsy mind, tumbled out of order, sharp and painful; vivid memories of the years of being lost, the intense loneliness, longing for home, missing her parents, missing the hot summer days, and her room, and her books.)

But Scathach drew closer to her. He took her hunting, racing through the woods in pursuit of small game. He taught her use of the bow and the sling; she was never able to use them well. But her body grew, extending like the stag's, and she soon was an ungainly young woman, tall, twig-thin, bulked out only by the patchwork fur clothing and cloak garments knitted together with crude leather strands and fastened by bones at the throat.

She carried her masks and learned to use them, glimpsing the world in different ways as she peered through the eyes of a child, or a fish, or a hunting hound. The wood was alive with strange creatures. The lost band crept their way inwards, aware of the eyes that watched from the darkness and the gleaming armoured figures which sometimes kept pace with them for hours before dropping away into dense undergrowth.

They kept to rivers. Tallis fashioned a crude tent from hides, taken on the hunt. She regarded it as her own lodge, the seer's lodge, and she huddled within its wigwam space, watching the men as they sat around the fire and talked, or skinned their kills.

During the years, she extended the size of the tent and one day, after running with Scathach for hours through the wood, pursuing a small pig, they returned to the tent together, made a small fire and huddled close, feeling the heat on flushed skin, watching the light in each other's eyes, on each other's lips. Tallis felt suddenly very close to her companion. It was a time of change for her; her agony at being lost lessened as she discovered the man, and the secret strength in the man; and discovered the feeling in herself that was satisfied by his company, and his laughter, and his body pressed close within hers.

—and pain. Such pain. The river running hard; a fire burning; deep night, and Scathach beside her, wiping the sweat that poured from her face. Gyonval, hunched and concerned, watching from beyond the fire, his face so pale, his long hair hanging lank, his hands toying with the small doll which Tallis had fashioned and which he had agreed to hold, to help absorb the agony.

"Hold me . . ."

Scathach leaned down, pressed his lips to her cheek and wrapped his arms tightly around her. There was movement. The woods became restless with the swirl and scatter of birds, disturbed from their night's stillness. Her cries became wild, shattering the night. She clutched at Scathach's arms, then forced her head back, rising more to a squat, knees stretched apart. She sucked the warmth from the fire. Gyonval grimaced as he grasped and shook the doll, but the pain remained in Tallis until, like a rotten tree splitting in a storm, she opened, parted, and hot, fresh life flowed from her, giving her release . . .

—the child is dead.

I know.

A hand on her shoulder. Fresh falling snow blotting out sound. Whiteness all about her. The river frozen. The child in the tent, still wrapped in furs. Scathach crouched behind her, hands on her shoulders. She let her head drop. He leaned his face against her neck and the shaking of his body told of his grief. She had cried all night, while Scathach had been away, hunting, further inwards. She had no grief left. She stood up, looked down at the saddened man, his hair still bearing the green and brown dyes with which he had disguised himself for the wild pursuit of game. She touched the hair, his cheeks, his lips. He held her fingers close to his mouth, then shook his head, unable to find words to express his feelings.

I'll bury him, he said at last.

I'll carry him with me, Tallis said. He means too much to me.

—no sense to the seasons. Sometimes winter, then summer, then spring. They journeyed through the zones of the land, adapting their hunting to the forests they found, spending weeks in any ruin that could sustain them, trying to find some pattern to the wilderness; they left marks and camps, hoping to rediscover them, to bring an order to their aimless journey inwards.

—how many years have we been here? How many years? How old are my parents now? Have they forgotten me? Can my father see me through the mask? Can he hear me through the rough wood of the mask I dropped? Is that his voice?

Yes! He's calling to me. My father. I can hear him . . . he's calling my name. *Tallis . . . Tallis . . .* he sounds sad. No . . . he sounds *excited.*

Tallis. Tallis!

He's coming for me. My father is coming for me. He's shouting my name . . . he's found me . . . he's *found* me . . .

[MOONDREAM]

All Things Undreamed Of

"Tallis! Tallis!"

The girl's voice was very distant. It might have been shouted in a dream. Tallis glanced towards the exit from the mortuary house, then frowned and looked around. The fire was dead. Tig was nowhere to be seen. Since the embers were cool, Tallis imagined that she had been sitting there for hours.

She stood up, on legs that were stiff and aching, and limped from the cruig-morn, massaging circulation back into her flesh. She stepped through the sinister half-circle of rajathuks and saw Morthen, standing uneasily at the entrance to the enclosure. The girl's face darkened slightly when the woman stepped into view. She seemed angry, or perhaps discomforted.

"Hello, Morthen."

"My father," Morthen said, without greeting. "He's come home to us."

"He's awake?"

"Yes." There was a dull tone to her voice. She was definitely distancing herself from the older woman.

As Tallis began to move past her, Morthen caught her arm. Her dark eyes were fierce. The snail shells, formed into a loose net over her hair, clattered slightly as her head lifted. She said, "He is *my* brother. I've been waiting for him all my life. You must let *me* look after him now."

Tallis tried to smile, but the girl's fierceness froze the gesture. So

she said simply, "I've been with him all of *my* life. I shan't let him
go that easily."

Morthen made a sound like a wild animal, turned and ran down
through the blackthorn. Tallis followed glancing back at the huge
carvings, their grotesque faces watching her, some compassion-
ately, some with mocking expressions. Sinisalo—child in the
land—seemed to leer at her.

They passed through the gate to the settlement, weaved between the new hides stretched on their frames, and ducked into
the long-house. Morthen stayed by the door. Across the gloomy
interior, Tallis could see Scathach crouched by the straw mattress,
his arm around the back of the old man's head. Glimmering light
caught Wyn-rajathuk's eyes as he watched his son and listened to
Scathach's softly spoken words.

Tallis moved quietly round the house and came up behind the
hunter; she sat on the rush matting and hugged her knees,
listening to what was being said.

Scathach had been telling about his first journey through the
wood. ". . . the Jaguthin are always called away. You were right
about that. But the way of calling differs. For a while I rode with
one group who were summoned by a crone, guarded by giant
hounds. She emerged from the centre of the earth, surrounded
by black dogs. But the Jaguthin who became my close companions were summoned at night, during the full moon. Their
calling came in the form of a night spirit, a wraith. It drifted
through the branches of trees and lifted the spirit out of the man. It
was both strange and terrible to see the ghosts of each of my friends
leave their bodies, then to watch those bodies rise and run into the
nightwoods, in pursuit of their souls."

In a wheezing, faint voice, Wynne-Jones said, "They would be
reunited . . . body and soul . . . at the place of the deed to be done
. . . the great battle . . . all quest legend is like this . . . first thing
is to find the inner self . . ."

Scathach hushed the old man, who was struggling to keep the
flow of his words. "I lost them all. All my friends. Gyonval was the
last, just a few short seasons ago. His loss distressed Tallis more
than any of them. He seemed to resist the calling, perhaps because
of his love for Tallis. There was a special feeling between the two
of them."

Tallis went icy cold. Sweat touched her eyes and face and her heart thundered. She had not known that Scathach had known, not been aware that he had seen. It brought back a flood of fear and an almost unbearable memory of loss, the body of the warrior Gyonval fighting with the wood, impaling itself on a sharp branch as if that might keep the soul from parting.

An empty, broken corpse, it had walked past Tallis, stepping through the fire; above the trees the wraith was twined about the ghostly image of the man, dragging it across the canopy, even though it struggled for flight back to the woodland camp.

Only Scathach's restraining grasp had stopped Tallis following Gyonval into the wood, to try to bring him back. She had been silent, resisting Scathach powerfully but uttering no sound.

"He's gone," he had whispered. "We've lost him . . ."

My loss is greater than you realise, Tallis had thought bitterly; but that is a knowledge I shall spare you.

Now, in the long-house, she realised that Scathach had been fully aware of the special pain she felt.

"I was sad to lose them," Scathach said. "Three of them, Gyonval, Gwyllos and Curundoloc were still with me when I reached the forbidden world and found the shrine in ruins."

"Oak Lodge," Wynne-Jones breathed, and repeated the name as if savouring the sound of a place he had once known well. "A ruin you say. Not inhabited, then . . ."

"It was overgrown by forest. The trees had entered every part of it. The wood will never let it go, now. But I found the journal. I read it as you asked, but rain had made the magic blur. The symbols were hard to interpret. It was very confusing."

"Was there any reference to my departure . . . into the wood?"

Scathach nodded. "Yes. It was written that you had discovered the oolerinnen. You became obsessed with the opening of gates into the heart of the forest. It was written that one day you returned smelling of snow and very ill from winter. A week later you returned to that place of winter and never returned."

There was a moment's silence. Wynne-Jones's breathing slowed. He was staring vacantly across the lodge; Tallis leaned forward slightly to watch him, but he didn't see her.

"I passed through," he murmured. "It took me very much by surprise. It was in the oak-thorn zone, near to the horse-shrine. We had explored the area very thoroughly. We had mapped the energy of the ley-matrix. Oak and thorn always made powerful generative zones, and oak-thorn is a prime genesis zone for mythagos of a very primitive origin. Many of them were more animal than human. The oolerinnen must have set a trap for me. I passed through and I could not get back . . ."

Again Scathach hushed the man, raising a beaker to his lips so that he could sip cool water. Wynne-Jones sighed and his hand, gripping his son's wrist, fluttered like a flightless bird, then found a new, more reassuring perch upon the stronger limb.

"And Huxley himself? What of my friend George? What of the old magician himself?"

"His wife was dead. He created the mythago of a girl and fell in love. His eldest son came home from a great war in another land . . ."

"What was she called? The girl . . ."

"Guiwenneth."

"Where was she from?"

Scathach dipped his head in thought for a moment. "A wildwood princess of the Britons. I think that's what I read."

Wynne-Jones shuddered; Tallis thought he was coughing with pain, but he was laughing.

"The quietest man I knew . . . engenders the fieriest of women . . . Vindogenita herself . . . Guinevere . . ." he rasped with amusement for a moment longer, then relaxed.

"As far as I can tell," Scathach said, "father and son contested the love of the girl—"

"How predictable."

"And that's all. No resolution. No final passage. I cannot tell you what occurred after."

There was silence for a while, only the old man's breathing breaking the stillness with its catching, painful rhythm. Then he asked, "And what of you? How far were you able to travel from the edge of the world?"

"A full day on foot," Scathach answered. "Then a terrible pain began in my head; and dizziness and a feeling of fear. The world seemed dark even in daylight. I could see the shadows of trees on a land that was as bare as naked rock, and there were ghosts behind the trees, taunting me. I had to return to the area of the shrine. But I spent a year in that shadowland. I disguised myself in the clothes of the people. I worked on a farm. I helped to build one of their houses. I was paid in coinage. I asked about you, and about

Huxley, but I found nothing. Then, when I returned to the shrine—to Oak Lodge—I realised that the Keeton girl had been making contact with me."

"Later," the old man said. "Later . . . tell me of Anne . . . my daughter Anne. Did you manage to see her?"

"I used a telephone. I spoke to her from a great distance. She was still living in Oxford, as you mentioned. It was easy to find the way to call her. I told her my name, who I was, and that you were old, but in good health, and had journeyed very far into the wood. I told her of my mother Elethandian, your wife, and I would have told her more but she began to scream at me. She called me a liar. She was very angry. She said that I was a fraud. She said the police would come to take me into the stockade like the cruel and wild animal I was. I told her of the dead snake that you and she had found once, and which had been your special secret. How else could I have known about it unless I was your son? But she stopped speaking. She went away without leaving a message for you."

Scathach gently rubbed his father's wrist. "I'm sorry. I truly am."

The news had deflated the old man. He sighed with disappointment and lay carefully back on the straw pallet. "Never mind . . ." he whispered, and closed his eyes. Soon he was sleeping.

Tallis stayed with Scathach for a while but found the atmosphere in the long-house increasingly uncomfortable; it was smoky, and her lungs became choked. It was cold, too, an icy wind sneaking in through the thatch and through gaps in the mud wall. There was the smell of bitter herbs and of Wynne-Jones's incontinence, and soon the idea of the crisp outside world became attractive again.

If Scathach had wanted her to stay she would have stayed, but he remained distant, not responding to Tallis's touch. He slumped, then turned slightly, staring through the gloom of the house towards the north, as if he could see through the walls, through the wood, to that place of battle, that cold place, which lay northwards and to which he and Tallis—as everything that passed this way—seemed to be moving.

Morthen slipped into the lodge, circling Tallis warily and keeping her eyes averted. She seemed nervous at first, then almost resentful of the older woman's presence. Tallis resolved to remain for a while, but turned her gaze away. The girl whispered to her brother.

"There are *tamers* in the valley. They've cleared a trapping ground, half a day's tracking to the south. There are only a few of them, but they have several horses."

"Tamers?" Scathach asked indifferently. "What are tamers?"

"Tamers of horses," Morthen said excitedly. "Their weapons are poor. Their stone points are very crude and we can cut their nets easily. They're big men, but stupid, covered with clay streaks on their bodies. We should subdue them easily."

"You're just a girl," Scathach murmured, and Morthen looked shocked. Her brother was less than interested in her information, but Morthen seemed determined to win his favour. "All I will do is cut the tethers. First-hog-of-summer and others of the hunters will do the raiding. I'll bring you back a horse. I'll name it for you."

"Thank you. Be careful."

Morthen reached out and rested her hand on her brother's face. "I will soon be older," she murmured. Tallis grew aware of the girl's angry gaze towards her, then Morthen had slipped away, leaving a swirl of grey smoke where her body had passed by the hearth.

Tallis left too. She already had her travelling companion, Swimmer of Lakes, and if she thought of the wild horses in the valley at all it was simply to wonder about the legend of the tamers: to subdue the spirit of the wild animal; to be permitted to ride upon its back; yes, magic would have been necessary in early thought, and cult legends certainly would have grown around the hunters who snared the fast, proud creatures.

She returned to the mortuary house. Tig was nowhere to be seen. The fire had been kicked over, though, the ash distributed around the floor. From the earth bank outside she looked north; soon she saw the bulkily-furred figures of Morthen and three of the hunters; they followed the edge of the wood, round to the south, and were soon lost to sight.

But to the north: there was just greyness, a swirling mist; and perhaps the hint of mountains and winter beyond. It was hard to see detail; the canopy of the forest grew black and shapeless, only the shuddering elms reaching gigantically above the sea of foliage. She heard her name called again, and again she emerged as if from a dream and found that time had passed. When she looked down the hill she saw Scathach making his way slowly towards her, through the dense thorns. He carried Wynne-Jones on his back; the old man beat at the thorns with his stick, one arm held tightly around his son's neck. They came into the enclosure. Wynne-Jones rammed his stick into the ground then eased himself down from his mount. He slung his cloak of feathers over the staff and Scathach helped him to sit down in the slight shelter that this garment offered. He was facing the rajathuks. His good eye glittered as he stared at them. But Tallis, as she came down the bank, could see that he was frightened. His white beard was ragged. A blue line had been daubed across his forehead and round his short white hair.

Scathach had entered the mortuary house. He came out again. "No sign of Tig."

"Keep watch for him," Wynne-Jones said sharply, anxiously. "He can't be far away . . ." Then he turned to smile grimly at Tallis, adding quietly but audibly, "And I don't want that little killer anywhere in slingshot range. He's too accurate."

Man and woman exchanged long, searching stares. "Tallis . . . you are Tallis . . ."

"Yes."

"You spoke to me in my sleep. You told me tales and adventures. You asked me questions."

"Yes. Can you remember that?"

"As if in a dream," he replied, then beckoned her over. She went to him, crouching down on the cold earth. When he took her hands she felt the tension in him; he was shaking. The shadow of Tig masked him more than the ferocious wound that had blinded his left eye and decorated his cheeks with scars. Wynne-Jones ignored her worried look and continued to touch her, cradling her face in his hands and touching her lips with his fingers.

"How old were you when the wood took you?"

"Thirteen," Tallis said. "But the wood didn't take me. I went in with Scathach. I didn't intend to stay very long."

The old man found that amusing, but he said, "Can you remember much about England? About your life? About the world?"

She said that she could. "I'll tell you what I know, though I was a bit of a reclusive child . . ."

"Later," he said. "I'll hear about it later. First there is something I must show you, something to encourage you. Then I need to think about all the strangenesses that happened to you as a child; my firstborn son has already told me something of your life, and of the questions you have for me."

His words made Tallis look sadly towards the mortuary house, a last shiver of loss making her huddle into her furs.

"Are you all right?" Wyn asked, his voice concerned and kindly.

"A few hours ago I burned the remains of my own first born," Tallis said.

"Ah . . ."

After a while Wyn asked, "How long did the child live?"

"A season or two. A few months." Tallis smiled. "I still try to remember the old way of measuring time."

"How many children . . . how many altogether?"

"Three. The others were never properly born."

"Were they my son's?" Wynne-Jones asked.

"Yes," Tallis said quickly, but she couldn't help dropping her gaze as she told the partial lie, and when she looked back Wynne-Jones was not smiling.

Suddenly he reached out and tugged a small, black feather from the fringe of his cloak. The cold wind blew his cropped white hair and made him shiver violently, but he resisted Tallis's attempt to tug the cloak around his shoulders, instead pushing the feather into her hand.

"Rites and rituals in late Neolithic Europe," he said with a wry grin. "A black feather to show my sorrow. Tomorrow you should bring it to the shaman's lodge and we'll burn it with bird fat, honey and a strip of the dried skin of a wolf. In a hollowed stone, of course, and you must scratch your body-mark upon the stone so that I can decorate it later." He was almost laughing, his eye narrowing with humour, the look in it one of knowingness, a shared joke between people from an advanced culture. "It will help the spirit of the boy to travel on. Or so they believe."

Tallis shrugged. "Perhaps it will, though. Things do seem to work in this world. Magic things. Psychic things."

"That's very true. And it still frightens me. It frightens me how a child can be made of flesh and blood but decay to wood. What biological process is at work? Scathach and Morthen are the only two children of mine who survived out of a great number. Oddly, I realise that that means there is *more* of the wood in them than flesh. My son found it almost impossible to leave the edgewoods and explore the farmland around Ryhope . . ."

"I know."

"And I'm afraid your own fate was sealed from the moment you entered the forest with him. Once he had been to the forbidden place—for him, England—and once he had succeeded in returning, he would have been taken by a tide, a powerful current drawing him back to the heartwoods. You are only allowed one journey into hell . . . He could not have returned you to England no matter how hard he had tried."

Tallis nodded grimly. "I had expected to explore the wood for a month. I have been lost here for eight years."

"Be prepared to be lost here for the rest of your life."

"I won't ever accept that," Tallis said sharply. "I shall get home somehow."

"You will never get home. Accept that now."

"I will find my brother. I *will* get home. I accept nothing else."

"Ah yes . . ." Wynne-Jones said, a fleeting smile on his lips. "Your brother. Help me up. I want to show you something."

He was unsteady on his feet, leaning heavily on Tallis. He used his stick and pointed up at the grim-featured totem-poles.

"You recognise them of course."

Tallis stared at the wood, experiencing the feeling of familiarity. She shivered, uncomfortably close to an understanding. "Yes and no," she said. "They remind me of my masks."

"I've seen your masks," the old man said. "I saw it at once. That one is Falkenna . . ."

"The flight of a bird into an unknown region."

"And the one with the new growth upon it is Skogen . . ."

"Shadow of the forest," Tallis breathed. "I have always felt a strange affinity for that one."

Wyn laughed, a wheezing sound. "It was how I knew you were coming. It changed. Skogen is the *changing* shadow of the forest. I thought that my son was doing it, changing the totem because of the way he was reaching towards me. It was you, though. You are the skogen. You are the shadow of the forest . . . like Harry before you. It is in those shadows that you will find him."

He looked up again, pointed to the rajathuk which Tallis knew better than all, because of her own obsession with the wood . . .

"Moondream."

"The eyes that see the woman in the land. I lost that mask. I dropped it when I left for the realm. My father has it, now." She smiled. "I sometimes wonder if he is watching me through it."

Wynne-Jones seemed alarmed by what she had said, though.
"You must make it again. If the masks have remained of
importance to you, you must certainly fashion it again."

"Important to me?" Tallis shrugged. "I use some of them.
Others I hardly ever use. They seem to work, though. I see things
through them . . ."

"You miss the point of the masks," Wynne-Jones murmured,
stroking his grey beard and watching Skogen. "Perhaps you are not
yet ready to use them correctly."

"I use the Hollower whenever I wish to cross a threshold . . ."

Wynne-Jones chuckled. "Of course. What else would you use?
But Tallis . . . listen to me . . . in *legend's* terms, the masks, like
these rajathuks, are the facets of an oracle! The voice of the earth
speaking its vision through the shaman: that's me; or you; or Tig.
You cannot use the masks as an oracle if one of them is missing."

He turned to stare at Tallis, who pulled a face. "But they still
work."

"They work to an extent. But they could work much better.
Think of each mask alone as being on a chain. That chain leads
from the mask, when you wear it, deep into your mind. There
are many concealed places in your mind, many *forbidden* or *forgotten* places. Think of each mask as reaching to one of those
locked parts of the mind. The patterns on the masks, the shape of
the wood, the touch of the wood, the smell of the wood, any smell
you have incorporated, the bright colours, or the dull shades . . .
all of these are part of the essential *pattern*, the essential *knowledge*,
the unknowing knowing that is at the heart of magic. Each mask
unlocks lost memory when you look at it; each mask gives access to
a lost talent: it opens the door, if you like, and lets the legends *out*
. . . or perhaps *in* across the threshold. So if that is the capability
of *one* mask at a time . . . think of the power of all ten!"

Tallis said nothing, frightened by the old man's words. He
simply shrugged, tapped her on the shoulder with his staff, then
pointed again at the rajathuks.

"Think about oracles later. For the moment, look closely at the
faces of *my* masks. Do you see? They're lopsided. One eye on each
seems to be ruined. One side of the mouth droops. Do you see?"

Understanding blossomed in Tallis's mind. She began to shake
in anticipation of Wynne-Jones's words.

"Years ago," he said, "a man from outside the realm passed up the river towards Lavondyss. The wood sucked out his dreams to make mythagos. He made everything you see, the Tuthanach, the lodge . . . the totems. There is only one thing I can tell you about that man, since he has left the clue in the fashioning of these totems. He had a mark on the left side of his face. It was a mark that controlled his life. He was obsessed with it. Disease, perhaps, or a wound? Deformed?"

"Burned," Tallis said. She stared at Skogen. Suddenly its dead face took on life. Wynne-Jones was right. The shadows there were shadows of Harry, not the forest. It had seemed a cruel and empty face; now she saw urgency and sadness. Had he gone into the wood to find a way to cure the blemish?

Burned in the war. Shot down. Burned. He had come to her in the night.

I shan't be far away. There is something I have to do. A ghost I have to banish.

The ghost of his burning; an ugly mask—fire, fear and evil—a mark that had spread across his face; it had not covered him completely. But a mask is what it was, and he had hated the mask; and unlike Falkenna, Sinisalo, Hollower, it could not be used at whim. It could not be removed.

All this Tallis expressed to the shaman, Wyn-rajathuk, who listened in silence, his hand on her arm, his eye on the face of Harry which watched from the pieces of dead wood.

"Then it was Harry who passed up the river all those years ago, ahead of me. He is years ahead of you, but he is there. Those years may sound like frustration to your quest, but that is not necessarily the case. Time plays strange tricks in the wood. I've been lucky: Scathach has returned only four years older than I expected him to be." He took a breath, squeezed Tallis's arm hard. "But equally, when you get to Lavondyss you may find that Harry is a million years away. I do not understand the laws which govern Lavondyss. I say this only because of what I have gleaned from the living myth of the wood. But be prepared for it."

Tallis helped him sit again, sheltered in his cloak. The wind was growing even colder. "Winter is coming," Wynne-Jones said.

"A terrible winter," Tallis agreed. "It seems to have been following me all my life."

"What little I know of Lavondyss has left me in no doubt of one thing: it is a place of snow, of ice, of winter, of an age past when the land was frozen. Why this should be of such importance in the minds of you and me, and all the others from the world of the nineteen-forties I do not know. Later myths make of the Otherworld a place of endless hunting, endless feasting, endless pleasure . . . a sunny place. A bright realm. It is reached through caves, through tombs, through hidden valleys. But that is wish fulfilment. Adventurers have quested for Lavondyss since the beginning of time. I wonder how many of them knew that they would find a barren world, a place of death, of cold . . . no magic in Lavondyss . . . and yet the memory is there. There is *something* there, something that calls. Something that engages."

"My brother travelled there, I'm convinced of it. He called to me from the place. He is trapped there and I have made it my promise, Tallis's Promise, to release him. If he went up-river, then that's where I shall go."

"And what will you find there?" Wynne-Jones asked with a smile.

"Fire," Tallis answered without pause. She had learned of the place from an encounter some years ago. "A wall of fire, maintained by the fire-makers of an older age than even these Tuthanach. I shall pass through the fire and into Lavondyss."

"You will burn," the shaman whispered pointedly, shaking his head. "No-one passes through the fire. No human. I have heard of mythagos which have succeeded, but they are *part* of the myth that says tumuli and fire guarded valleys are the way to the Otherworld. For you, the route certainly lies in another direction entirely. It will take you through a forest far stranger than this tiny Ryhope Wood."

"Harry got there."

"*If* Harry got there," the old man said, "then he got there by finding his own path. He certainly didn't pass through the fire. And nor can you . . . Because, like me, you are human. We don't belong. We are voyagers in our own living madness. Around you are your brother's dreams, later modified by myself, recently modified by you. What *we* have that these wretched creatures around us do not, is freedom. The freedom to choose. Oh, I know Scathach has chosen for himself, for a while . . . but look at him, touch him, feel his mind . . . I was awake for just a little while and I could tell—"

Alarmed, Tallis said, "Tell what?"

"That the *wood* in him is being called. That the *legend* in him is being summoned. That his time with us is fast coming to an end. He must go to Bavduin, to be reunited with his knightly comrades."

Tallis felt sick. She looked up to the skyline, where Scathach's tall form was a silhouette. He was looking to the north, away from the river.

Tallis said, "I once had a vision of your son. I saw him at the very moment in his life when he *earned* the name Elethandian gave him: the boy who listens to the voice of the oak. I am not ready for him to achieve that moment of glory. Not yet . . ."

She would have talked on, but Wynne-Jones had suddenly pushed his hand against her mouth. She jerked back, surprised by the anger on his face, then reassured by the apology she saw there. The hand lowered.

"I beg your pardon," the man said. "Like you, I'm not ready to hear or know my son's ultimate fate. It would tempt me to interfere. If we interfere we become involved. We become trapped . . . I have discovered this over many years."

Tallis leaned forward, suddenly excited by the old man's words. She was thinking of her brother, of being trapped, of being caught . . . "Then is it possible that Harry interfered with legend? Is it possible that he found the way into Lavondyss, changed something, and is caught *because* of it?"

"Very much so," Wynne-Jones answered simply.

"Then how could he have called to me?"

"To answer that," the old man said, "I need you to tell me the story of your girlhood. Your memories of Harry. And everything that has happened to you in the way of learning. I dreamed something about a castle made of *stone which is not stone* . . ."

"Old Forbidden Place," Tallis said. "Or at least, a part of the tale. I whispered it to you while you slept."

"You must tell me again," the scientist murmured. "It may be that I have seen this place. A long way from here, but a place that is familiar from your whispered words."

Her heart missed a beat. "You've *been* to the castle?"

But he shook his head. "I've only seen it from a great distance. It is well defended; by a storm that would surprise you. Before I settled among the Tuthanach I wandered further up the river, crossing the great marsh. But it was too cold up there, so I returned. It was too far. Too remote. There comes a time, for people like you and me, when the mind has been stripped of all that is mythic. It's hard to describe the feeling: it's a kind of tiredness, of exhaustion . . . of the spirit. I felt vigorous; my work fascinated me; I remained handsomely potent—" He smiled and shook his head at his own unspoken memories. "But something had returned to the earth, and it took me with it. So I came back here, to the Tuthanach. They are an earth people and their legend is horrific, dramatic, almost senseless. Each and every one of them will undergo death by burial and rebirth renewed. They are part of the legend, of course; you and I wouldn't survive it."

Scathach called from the other side of the enclosure. "Tig is coming up the hill, from the south. He's carrying an axe."

"Take me back to the lodge," Wynne-Jones whispered. "I'm tired and cold. You can tell me your stories in the warmth of my hut. And I want to hear *all* the stories."

Tallis smiled. "I was asked that once before. It seems like a lifetime ago."

"There are old truths in the memories of childhood," Wynne-Jones said quietly. "Make that journey for me . . . then make Moondream again. I'll give you what help I can . . ."

At dusk an eagle began to swoop and soar over the village. The children imitated the bird's behaviour, arms outstretched. The young men stripped and painted themselves in black and white imitation of the feather pattern on the predator: bringing the hunting eye of the eagle to the clan.

While all eyes were on the majestic bird above them, Tallis had seen the fluttering movement of a more sinister flock, in the high trees around the river. One of the birds flapped towards a tall, dead elm, whose limbs had been stripped by fierce winds until only two remained, like gnarled horns, rising from the top of the trunk. Black against the sky, the black stork, too, was a silhouette. It perched on the elm's horns and soon several others followed it. When they launched themselves into the dusk they seemed to fill the sky to the north for long minutes, and their cries reached as far as the village.

Scathach had seen the storks as well. He approached Tallis, drawing his fur cloak tighter round his chest. He smelled strongly of woodsmoke after his long hours in the lodge, nursing his father. "Are they an omen?"

Tallis turned to glance at him. She saw affection and concern in his eyes, but imagined that the love was gone, the intensity of the gaze, that knowingness that she had shared for so many years as they had fought to find this place through the forest.

"I don't know," she said. "But they disturb me."

He watched the birds again. "Everything is going north," he murmured. "Everything. I feel impelled to follow . . ."

Tallis nodded her agreement. "That's where I must go too, if I'm to find Harry. But first I have to make Moondream again."

Scathach frowned, not understanding. Tallis had always kept her masks to herself. "To allow me to see the woman in the land. Your father says I should carve it again. I hadn't thought it important, but perhaps my power to open the hollowings has been affected by its absence."

"I'll help you make it," Scathach said. His hand was on her arm. Tallis wrapped her fingers round the welcome grip.

"What about Morthen?" she asked pointedly. The girl had returned earlier, and prematurely, from the hunt, but was not around as far as Tallis could see.

"Morthen is my sister and a child. I am her brother from the wood, but until she gets older, that's *all* I am. And by the time she reaches a suitable age, I shall be long gone."

"Does she know this?"

"She knows it. Besides, what I do with Morthen I do because of the forest in my blood. What I choose to do with you I do because of love."

Tallis said, "I hadn't realised you knew about Gyonval."

"I knew that you loved him. But I never felt that you'd stopped loving me. So that seemed to me to be all right."

"Well," Tallis said, with a smile and a private thrill of relief. "I'm glad to hear it. And you were quite right."

She leaned towards the man and brushed her lips across the beard that grew unkempt from his cheeks. He put his arms around her.

Out of the corner of her eye she saw angry movement. Morthen was running from the enclosure, slapping the taut hides on their frames as she passed them, her clay-streaked hair flying free. She was making sounds like a bird: the screeching of a bird, defending its nest against intruders.

She knew what she would use to make the mask, but when she returned to the glade where, yesterday, she had visited the Moondream rajathuk, she found it quite destroyed. An elm grew there now. Its roots, earth-encrusted and massive, curled through the dense oak and hazel at the edge of the glade, lying lazily, snakelike upon the land, feeding freely on the forest. Its trunk was almost black; thick fungus and moss grew in the deep grooves in the bark. It rose into the evening sky; three odd, twisted branches tangled with the clouds, all that remained of the tree's broken limbs. The glade was silent. An overpowering smell of vegetation filled the air, drifting on a fine steam. The light was sharp, the sense of power in this woodland mythago almost terrifying.

Tallis circled the giant tree twice. She found a shard of the broken totem and picked it up, feeling its dry, dead surface. Scathach waited in the forest, his eyes showing his concern as he stared into the heavens, where black storks flapped and watched the earth from the bare-bone branches.

"Is it after you or my father?" he whispered to Tallis when she came back to him.

"I don't know. But it has destroyed the rajathuk. I was hoping to sit here and make my mask . . ."

"Do you have an image for it?"

Tallis stared down at the shard of the ruined statue and with a thrill of pleasure realised that she did: an image of the female in the land. An image of white moon. An image of horns, of horse, of the smile that knows, of a mother's kiss. An image, too, of blood. An image of a child's bones burning. An image of a wild rider, white clay on long hair, circling the pyre where her lover lay. An image of bone in flesh, a child's cut flesh knitted closed with bone, with sharp bone fragments, the wound healed, the blood dried.

And Gyonval . . . gentle Gyonval. He was in the image too, his laughter, his concern, his ready acceptance that he was somehow a ghost to Tallis; that he, like Scathach, was shadow, soon to be banished by a night whose coming could not be stopped.

Gentle when he loved her.

Even as his broken body had followed its spirit into the night woods, there had been something about him: his fingers flexed just so, as if signalling to her; a frown on his face, as if he was struggling to turn his eyes to the woman by the fire; a sparkle in those eyes, the dead eyes, the tears that said how he longed to stay.

Tallis looked up, met Scathach's gaze.

"Yes," she said. "I have an image . . ."

Fascinating to watch: how she smoothed down the shard of the totem to make it a circle, to flatten it out; how she trimmed and chipped to make the natural lines flow; how she scored out the eyes, the mouth; how she touched colour with her fingers to emphasise the woman in the land, in the mask; how the dead wood began to live and breathe.

Crouched in the shadows, Scathach watched, but his eyes were on Tallis, not on her fingers as they moved swiftly over the charm.

"You truly are possessed."

"Yes."

Red for cheeks, and green in subtle lines, and here the moon, made with white clay, and there the blood of the child. All from dyes and ochres used by the Tuthanach.

"Does it speak to you yet?"

"It has been speaking to me all my life—"

There, the spectre, the woman in the land. There the snow. There the memory. White memory, daubed, smeared . . .

The land remembers. There is old memory in snow.

And a gentle touch for the gentle dead.

I shan't forget you.

And it was finished. She held it before her, stared at its eyes, kissed its lips, breathed through the mouth into the unconscious region beyond the wood. Then turned it round and held it to her face.

"Don't look at me through the eyes . . ."

Tallis sat quietly, Scathach's words frightening her. She stared through the mask at Wyn-rajathuk, old, broken man, fascinatedly watching the process of creation. His eyes narrow, he glanced at his son-from-the-flesh-and-wood, then back at Tallis.

"Don't look at him."

"Why not?"

"Don't look at him."

"What will I see?"

"Don't look at him!"

She lowered the mask. There was a sudden wind and the small fire in the shaman's lodge guttered. Stones and shells, slung on twine, rattled. Sheaves of the parchment, on which Wyn kept his journal, fluttered. A brief moment of the winter which pursued her sent a scampering chill through the warm place.

Scathach had gone. Tallis heard him walk away from the lodge. Then the heavy skins which formed the door were still again, the fire burning more calmly.

She stared at the mask, her touch on the wet colour of its face like a lover's touch on moist, flushed skin. "I don't understand."

"He is going away from you," Wyn said quietly. He tugged at his sparse white beard, then drew his dark fur robe tighter around his bent shoulders. He looked very ill and frightened. Tallis knew that he was worried about the boy: where was his son? Where was Tig hiding?

At his words, though, she looked up sharply. Scathach going away? Wyn raised a finger to his lips and said, "I imagine he is afraid that the same spectre haunts him, calling him to Bavduin, that took his friends, Gyonval and the rest. He didn't want you to see it, perhaps because he doesn't want to know the truth as yet."

Puzzled, Tallis shook her head. She knew Scathach's quest was for Bavduin, but he was not himself Jaguthin; he had merely joined the band. Why should he be called like the others?

"He became Jaguthin when his life in the wood became inseparable from theirs," the old man said. He picked up his journal and leafed through the parchments until he found a certain sheet, then read it through in silence. For a moment he looked as if he would pass the script to Tallis, but he changed his mind. He stoked the fire so that it flared, then reached behind him for a pouch of thin leather which contained charred bones. He rattled the pouch. "Recognise this?"

Tallis nodded. Wyn-rajathuk shook the pouch, then banged it on the ground, then struck it against his shoulders; he chanted softly as he made the rhythmic movements, and the words were nonsense words.

Tallis recognised what he was doing immediately, and sensed the point of what he was trying to tell her. She flew back through imagination to the festival at Shadoxhurst, to the dancers, the nonsense words they often chanted as they went through their formations.

Jiggery, higgery, hoggery, joggery . . .

"The land remembers," she whispered. "Men dance and chant, they fight with sticks, and one rides among them on a hobbyhorse, striking them with a bladder filled with pebbles . . . we don't forget . . ."

"We just forget why," Wyn-rajathuk agreed. "There is no magic left in the festive practices of Oxford, or Grimley, or wherever —the Morrismen and Mummers—no magic unless the mind that *enacts* the festival has a gate opened to the first forest—"

That expression again. *First forest.*

"—but how many times have I stood and laughed as that man on the hobbyhorse, a fool, an outsider to the troupe, prances round and through the dancers? The devil. The joker. The wily one. Old Coyote himself. Trickster. Reduced, in our time, to a fool on a stick for a horse, waving the symbols of forgotten shamanism. We always see *that* aspect, but we forget that *first* he must have been a warrior too. He is outside the band, yet a part of it. As a hunter he will die in the forest to become a warrior; as a warrior he will die in battle, and be resurrected to become a sage. The three parts of the King. Remember your stories of Arthur and his knights? Arthur had been all of those things himself: hunter, warrior, then king." Wyn smiled, perhaps remembering those tales himself, or some connection with them that he had witnessed in the wood. "Of course my son is being called," he murmured. "He has been the hunter. When he entered England he died, in one sense. Now he is a warrior. His death and resurrection as shaman lies in his future. His flight on wings of song and dream lies many years ahead . . ."

"I will be gone by then," Tallis said. She leaned forward and passed her hand through the flames of the small fire, letting its glow and its heat excite the ancient in her.

First forest . . . where was the first forest?

She said hesitantly, not fully understanding how to frame the words, "Two beliefs war within me: I am convinced that I will find my way back home again. And I dream of dying in a great tree . . . burning . . . is that the first forest?"

"You are at the edge of the first forest," Wyn-rajathuk told her; there was something about the expression on his wounded face, the slight edginess of his good eye, that made Tallis suspect he was holding back. But she didn't comment. "All your life you have been at the edge. You have opened threshold after threshold and stepped closer and closer to the centre of the realm, to the heartwood—to Lavondyss. But you still have a journey to make

and it will be a terrible journey. It will bring you home, yes, but
equally it will take you further from home than you have ever
imagined. You will travel in two directions at once. You will
probably die. You do not enter the first forest for fun, for
adventure. When you go there, do not expect to return."

"Harry is there. In the unknown region. I promised to set him
free."

"You will never set him free. Not in the way you mean. There is
no return from that unknown region."

She was silent for a moment. Hunger clawed at her. Close by,
faint against the growing wind, a woman sang. Then came
another sound: a boy's voice, shrieking at the top of its lungs. The
shrieking sent shivers up Tallis's spine, and Wyn-rajathuk paled
even more as he straightened and stared, alarmed, through the
lodge walls, towards the mortuary hill. The boy's taunting turned to
laughter, drifting on the chill night air. It was possible to hear the
way he summoned the old man, calling his name in a mocking tone,
calling out for his dreams, calling that he wished to *eat* those dreams.

Tallis reassured him. "He won't enter the compound. He won't
come close to the lodge. All the families are watching for him, to
drive him off . . ."

Wyn shuddered violently and leaned down again, sucking at
the fire's warmth. After a while he seemed to relax and Tallis
prompted him further. "You seem to be saying that this first forest
is an *imaginary* place. You are saying that I will not *ride* there, or
open a hollowing, or step down through a cave, but must find the
threshold to a journey *inwards*. How do I find that threshold?"

"Through the story of your Old Forbidden Place. Through the
castle."

"Where is the castle?"

"You have already seen it. When you opened the hollowing.
Beyond the marsh. You have known about it all your life . . ."

Tallis was confused again, disbelieving; a strange response in a
world where ghosts walked and shadows cast effective spells. "And
by coincidence I have found it? I can't accept that."

"Not by coincidence. You have been looking for it for eight
years. You were bound to find it."

"Did I dream it then? How can I have dreamed it as a
six-year-old? Why did I see it in a story? Who were the gaberlungi
women who could tell me about a castle that it turns out *you* know

all about? How could I have seen your son Scathach in a vision, and named a land Bird Spirit Land out of my childish dreams, and arrive here to find that *you* know about Bird Spirit Land, and Bavduin? And your totems have the same names as my masks, but I *made those names up!* Why are *we* so linked?"

Wyn-rajathuk placed small sticks on the fire, letting Tallis's edgy, urgent questions settle in the air. His pallid flesh glowed. He smiled. "Why—through your brother Harry. Who else? I thought I'd told you earlier. You found Harry years ago! You found him and you entered him. Look around you. Everything is Harry. All of this. The wood, the river, the Tuthanach, the birds, the stones, the totems . . . The first forest that he imposed upon the world is the world in which I live and through which you are journeying. The world in which you and I exist is not nature, it consists of mind! You have been in your brother's skull for years. You have simply not learned to speak to him."

"But he's trapped," Tallis protested. "He called to me from a winter place. He called to me. I can find him again, his *physical* body, not just his mind."

Wyn-rajathuk thought about what she had said, then slowly agreed. "It's not a journey I would wish to undertake. But I am not you, and except for the shadow-elms I see little evidence of genesis from you—you are moving too fast, perhaps. But you are not yet sucked dry. Which means you have creative energy. Perhaps you *can* find the location of the earthly remains."

Frowning, Tallis asked, "The shadow elms? Those giant trees? You think they're *my* mythagos?"

"Certainly they are yours. An unusual mythago form. Old, of course; they represent fear of the forest; mythologies about the birth of birds; the relationship between earth and sky through the thick trunks of the wood . . ." he chuckled to himself. "No simple creatures of legend for Tallis Keeton—while the rest of us engender Robin Hoods and Green Jacks and golden-tressed princesses, you bring into existence the living earth. Just as Harry did. You are drawing upon a more ancient and powerful source of memory than me, or Huxley, or the boys, his sons, Christian and Steven—and God alone knows what happened to them."

He prodded the fire, forcing warmth into the hut. "But that is all beside the point. You and your brother Harry . . . in a way you are the same. It's the only way I can think of to explain the coincidences in the tales you've told me. You told me that the gaberlungi women were your grandfather's mythagos. I think that can't be right. The broken stag had been known for years. *Harry sent it!* It was a fragment of his own mind, designed to journey to the edgewoods, to find his rescuer. Your brother himself seems to have led you into the wood. But such spirit journeys are costly. He sacrificed strength to send himself to you in that way. His journey from the unknown region must have been terrifying—a fragment of his soul, running the land but without benefit of flight or fin . . . *and* he came too soon . . .

"Then those three women were his mythagos too, therefore *himself*, bringing images and talents from the primitive age in which he had become lost. You must remember that the gaberlungi are *real elements of legend*. They can only function in their legendary way: as teachers of magic. So you learn how to open the gate between ages and worlds, to cross the thresholds that have been the province of the shaman since the great days of the hunter. So you learn to make dolls and masks, simple oracles, simple earth magic.

"This is the only thing that makes sense. Harry has a link with you, through blood, through mind, through family. The women were made of Harry, but also a little of your grandfather and of you. Your grandfather was too old, but he knew what you came to know. That's what you imply. And why not? Harry left his mark on everything, on the totems, for example. His mythagos take a shape that *of course* you recognise. From the moment he left your home on his quest he has been leaving a trail for you to follow; not of pebbles, not of bread or coloured beads; a trail of memory, of image—like blood, like a scent; something that you have always known even though so often it seemed to you that you did not recognise it."

"What you are saying is that I am not so much searching for Harry, rather, Harry is winding me in, like a fish on a line—"

"Yes. It is the only answer which makes sense to me."

"He sent the women to show me what to look for. They arrived too soon because time is strange in this world. They waited for me. To show me what to look for."

Wyn-rajathuk rubbed ash between his palms and stared down at the smear of grey lines. "Yes."

"And Scathach? Your son? And Bavduin? Are they part of Harry too?"

Wynne-Jones frowned. "I don't see how they can be."

"Then how do they fit into what has happened to me? Why are *you* and *I* linked?"

If Wynne-Jones had an answer to that question, he was not given time to express it. Quite suddenly the world outside began to scream. He grabbed for his staff and a stone knife, his face melting with fear as he watched the skins over the door. "It's Tig . . . it's his magic . . ."

Tallis went outside quickly, alert for the boy, her own heart racing in response to the awful wailing from the woods.

The dead trees had edged closer to the settlement; they crowded in around the clearing and the blackthorn hill, with its bones and its wooden idols. The birds of the forest gathered in the antlers of those trees, clustered in the horns. From the dead limbs they cried at the moon, pecked at the wind-shattered stubs where winter had stripped the branches from these creeping giants, added their own anger to the screaming from the split and rotting bark.

The Tuthanach screamed back, rattled bones, beat drums. They ran around the wall of the village holding streaming fires. Twenty torches burned in the moon-touched darkness, a circle of defence. The women slapped strips of painted leather against the palisade. The children threw stones into the night. The air filled with the strong scent of herbs being burned to discourage elemental spirits.

Birds circled in the dark sky. The trees shook, their movement making the earth tremble. When the clouds thinned, and the bright moon shone through, the dead arms of the elms seemed to beckon. They were the raised arms of the first shamans; the broken horns of the first stag; the broken memory of the fiercest winter. It was only the clouds which moved, Tallis tried to tell herself. But as she thought of her Moondream mask, so it seemed that the elms were creeping in to crush no-one but her.

A screaming night. Wind of wings. The invisible flutter and swoop of black creatures, still furious with the woman who had once banished them.

She had been fleeing from winter all of her life. She had not realised how close the birds and the snow and the deadwoods had been behind her.

A small white shape darted through the line of torches and came swiftly to the earth wall around the village. It was Tig, of course. He was naked and the icy wind blew his hair wildly. He was chanting in his childish voice and whirling something round his head. The whirling action stopped and something clattered off the palisade. His body dripped blood from several self-inflicted wounds on his chest and arms. As he passed quickly in front of the flame, Tallis got the hint of scratches on his body, and she imagined he had run through the tight thorn scrub between the village and his purloined domain upon the hill.

He squatted down in front of the gate and smeared the soil from his body on the path. He laughed uproariously, an artificial sound, taunting despite its ineffectiveness. Then he was off again, in and out of the torches, the slingshot whirling, the missiles impossible to see as they sped into the compound.

He stopped where Tallis stood on the wall. She watched him across the points of the stakes. He passed his hand slowly and deliberately through the fire from the nearest torch, his eyes never leaving the woman. (He had been watching her in the shaman's lodge earlier! He had been that close! And she had told Wynne-Jones that he had nothing to fear. The boy was mimicking her own "play" with the fire. He had seen!)

Tallis was tense, ready to duck if he fired at her. But he began to chant in a sombre, sing-song voice. "Where are you my father? Come to me old rajathuk. I am hungry for your dreams, old man."

His voice rose steadily in pitch, at first almost lost against the wailing from the wood, then loud against it, then clear.

I am hungry for your dreams. Come to your son from the wood. Come now . . .

When Tallis went quickly to the long-house, where Wynne-Jones had gone for extra safety, she found him huddled in a corner, shaking violently, his body wrapped in skins and his bird-feather cloak. Cold sweat ran from his face; he had scratched at the wound which Tig had inflicted previously, and blood and yellow fluid seeped down into the feathered ruff.

"You'll be safe with me," Tallis said.

"Where is my son? Where is Scathach?"

"I'll find him. Keep warm, now. You'll be safe with me. I shan't let Tig near you."

Wyn-rajathuk smiled wanly, his good eye glittering. "Poor Tig. He is only doing what he has to do. But I have no dreams for him to eat. They have all gone. If he ate the earth he would get far more nourishment . . ."

Outside, Tallis called for the young hunter and Scathach called back, emerging from the children's lodge. He looked confused and quite alarmed. He had been searching for Morthen, to protect her from her violent half-brother, but she was nowhere to be found.

On the wall they watched as Tig circled the village again, running and weaving between the torches, his body like red-veined porcelain, almost translucent, almost fragile. The earth rumbled. Wings beat the winter air.

Tig became shaman. His chanting put fear into the hearts of the listening families as well as into the mind of the old and dying man who was his father. When Wyn-rajathuk slept, guarded by one of the Tuthanach, he shivered even in his sleep. His mouth opened and closed, as if gasping for breath, the dying struggle of an animal bleeding out its life through the sacrificial cut.

After a long while, watching the attack and listening to the screeching wood, Tallis had had enough. She found a heavy staff, hefted it and began to make her way to the gate, to go out and beat Tig back to his domain. But Scathach called to her and she returned to the wall.

A dark rider had emerged suddenly from the woods. It galloped towards the boy in silence, swinging a thorn bush from its arm. When it opened its mouth and yelled, Tallis recognised Morthen. She beat at her brother's head, causing him to screech with pain. He couldn't wield his sling. He raised his hands protectively and she whipped the pale flesh of his backside. When he clutched the torn skin of his buttocks, she tickled his belly, and soon the boy-who-was-shaman was whooping with anger, but fleeing back towards the hill, to the mortuary house and the safety of his bones. As he ran he grabbed a torch, and Tallis watched its flame bob and weave into the darkness, soon lost among the trees.

Morthen kicked the wild horse and galloped up to the earth wall. Her face was black. She had blackened her limbs and her shallow breast. Her hair was streaked white. She was wearing the rags of her old tunic, hanging in tatters from shoulders and waist. Tallis wondered if she had undertaken her own form of self-mutilation. She controlled the horse with a length of twine and she had authority over the animal, which snorted then stepped proudly round to the gate.

Morthen entered the compound, ignoring the shadow wings which beat around her head. Her eyes were fierce, watching from the black of her warpaint. She circled Tallis twice, staring down at her, not touching, not acknowledging her beyond the hard, contemptuous stare. Then she rode to Scathach, who stood with his arms folded and his eyes narrowed, watching his sister. She leaned down from the horse and he didn't flinch as she grabbed his long hair and shook his head from side to side. In fact, he smiled slightly.

"My brother from the wood!" she said loudly.

"My sister!" he stated flatly, watching her, still allowing the rough grip on his hair.

"Wait for me!" Morthen said in an angry voice. "*Will* you wait for me?"

Now Scathach frowned. "Where are you going?"

"To get *older!*" the girl shouted. "To catch up with you!" Her horse was suddenly restless, trying to step back, and Morthen kicked it forward again, wrenching back her brother's head to stare into his eyes. Still his arms were folded. "Will you wait for me?" she cried again, more a statement than a question.

Scathach said nothing, then reached up and detached her grip from his head. "I don't think I can," he said. "But we will meet up again, I'm sure of that."

Morthen hesitated, then struck at her brother's shoulder with her clenched fist. In turn he slapped her thigh and smiled at her, but she wrenched the horse away from him, swung around and, with a final cry, galloped from the compound. She rode towards the river, entering the trees, entering darkness.

Birds followed her into the wood.

A little while later the restless forest calmed, the night sounds died away and the air, for so long thick with wings, was clear again. Wynne-Jones ate broth. He had woken from his brief sleep, emerging out of nightmares that had left him drained and sickened. His hands shook as he held the antler spoon. Scathach crouched next to him, half conscious of his father, half lost in his own thoughts.

The old man had been deflated totally by the news of Morthen's leaving. She had gone to find a place where she might age more rapidly. Scathach, Tallis learned, had rejected the advances she had felt impelled to make to him. She had wanted to stay with her brother, but he had called her a child, he had referred to Tallis as the woman whom he loved, and Morthen had taken both statements to her young heart. She had blackened her body to signal the blackening of her spirit.

"How will she get across the marsh?" Tallis asked, and Wynrajathuk glanced at her, then cocked his head, gazing at the glowing hearth. "There is something of the bird in Morthen . . . perhaps she will fly across. Who knows? There are many ways to cross the marsh."

There was a shout from outside. The skins on the door were pulled violently open and the face of First-hog-of-summer peered anxiously into the firelit gloom.

"Burning. On the hill," he said.

Tallis helped Wyn to his feet and they went outside.

On the mortuary hill, fire streamed into the night; ten streaks of flame, licking at the clouds.

"The rajathuks . . ." Wynne-Jones breathed, shocked. "He's burning the totems."

Intrigued, Tallis left the old man for a while and ventured through the intervening wood. She emerged at the bottom of the hill and stared up at the brilliantly burning pyres by the cruig-morn. She saw Tig standing on the enclosure wall, his arms stretched out to the sides, his head thrown back. He was just a silhouette against the intense blaze, but she was certain that his mouth was open and that he was singing.

The fires burned through the night, signalling across the forest that the era of the rajathuk was at an end. A new power was in the land. It summoned its forces around it now and they played in the dying fires, kicked through the wood ash, spiralled into the heavens on the vortices of smoke; danced with the dancing boy.

The fires signalled to something else as well . . .

Shortly before daybreak Tallis was woken by the distant sound of a hunting horn. For a moment she was confused. Scathach was sitting beside her, his breathing soft as he listened. The horn sounded again, four blasts, answered by four more.

They were on their feet in an instant, waking Wynne-Jones,

waking the other men in the lodge, who gathered slings, sticks, spears and stones. Tallis led the way outside; it was still quite dark. Dogs barked and ran, excited by the sudden panic in the compound. Children, woken by their mothers, cried or wailed as they were hurried from their small huts into the main lodge, to hide.

First-hog-of-summer and others ran to the palisade and peered at the forest edge. Scathach went to the gate and made sure it was firmly closed. Tallis just stood quietly, cloak around her shoulders, iron-bladed spear held in two hands. She watched the great elms but saw no movement; they were quiet, now, though around them birds rose in short flight, then settled again.

There was stealthy movement at the edge of the wood.

The air hissed slightly as the Tuthanach whirled slings. Scathach called out, warning them to keep still. An uncanny silence covered the village; the voices of women hushed the children; dogs wailed but were muzzled. Only Swimmer of Lakes made any sound, a restless snorting, an anxious pawing at the ground. Tallis went to the makeshift corral and let the animal out, stroking his bruised face, patting his flanks. She led him to the gate. Scathach opened the heavy wooden door and Tallis quickly gave the horse its freedom, sending him trotting to the south, away from the disturbance. Soon the animal had entered the shadows of the trees.

The horn was sounded for a third time, a single blast, long and mournful. The Tuthanach whirled their slings again. Scathach flung his heavy cloak aside. He carried a bronze-bladed spear and a heavy Saxon long sword, which he had won in forest combat some years before. Most of the Tuthanach had weapons of bone and polished stone.

From the direction of the river, from the woodland there, a rider trotted into view. He turned side-on to the enclosure and watched the low defensive wall as he walked steadily along the edge of the trees, a few paces in one direction, then the other. As the light grew so Tallis could see his armoured helmet, crested by a fan of spikes, and the dull leather of his breastplate. He wore short chequered breeches and a reddish tunic; on his legs, metalled boots; on his shoulders, a short cloak. It was an all-too familiar garb to Tallis. She stared at him, then glanced at Scathach and smiled. The raider's spear rested across the pommel of his saddle, first light glinting on its long, polished blade.

Already Scathach was envying the look of the warrior by the trees.

After a few minutes of this silent contemplation the rider raised a curved horn to his lips and blew it three times.

"This is it!" Scathach shouted. Tallis felt her mouth go dry and her vision became suddenly intensely clear.

At once the canopy of the wood erupted into screeching birdlife, fleeing from the sudden disturbance below. Eight riders galloped from cover and came thudding across the cleared land towards the settlement. As they rode they made gruff, barking sounds; not war cries, just encouragement to their horses. They carried spears and axes. Only two wore helmets; metal armour gleamed on some; mail coats rattled; for the most part they wore an odd, ungainly mix of leathers, mail and furs. Fair hair streamed and tattered cloaks billowed as they spread to ride around the earthwork wall. There was not much colour to this raiding band.

Tuthanach slingshot whizzed and whirred, and two of the horsemen fell back over their mounts' haunches. Spears thudded into wood. Sharp, guttural cries accompanied the drum of hooves. The leader came towards the gate. His horse, a black stallion of large breadth, reared and stamped, the hooves striking down the gate.

He yelled once, kicked forward, and First-hog-of-summer ran to meet him. Slingshot missed and the rider's sword arm slashed. First-hog was on his knees, hands to his throat. As Tallis ran towards him she thought, with idle horror, that he looked as if he was praying. The leader had turned, swung again and First-hog was sprawling on his side, head opened above the ear. His dark buckskins shone with blood. The crested helmet of the warrior gleamed in dawn sun and he turned and rode down on Tallis.

The sight of him made Tallis freeze. For a moment she thought it was Scathach himself who came towards her; her mind was full of the vision from the oak tree, of the young man, identically dressed, bleeding out his life . . .

The black stallion was almost on her. The bearded face of its rider grinned. He was leaning down, his spear arm back, the gleaming bronze blade wavering as it came towards her. She was pushed to one side. The blade sliced her hair. The horse whinnied, turned and rose above her, but Scathach was there, wrenching the spear's shaft. Raider and hunter tussled, strength against strength, the one pulling up, the other down.

Around her Tallis heard the strike of wood on wood; a scream; yells; the frantic barking of the dogs as they ran through the confusion of hooves and legs.

Blood splashed her face: Scathach's. He was stumbling, the wound in his shoulder shallow but momentarily stunning. The point of the spear had slashed and caught him. As the red-tipped bronze blade continued round towards her, Tallis struck it out of line and reached for the booted leg of the rider, pushing up so that he fell over to the side.

He fell heavily. Tallis stood above him, spear aimed down, but a stone axe struck his head and his eyes dulled, his lips loosened. He sank slowly down on to his right shoulder. Scathach pushed her away, turning her in time to deflect the blow from another raider. A slingshot unseated this one and Scathach impaled him. When Tallis looked back at the leader he was slowly sitting up, reaching for his sword. Scathach walked quickly behind him. He used both hands and all his strength to swing his own sword and took the man's head with a single blow.

The gate was up, pushed back into place by two of the Tuthanach women. The four riders who remained inside the compound were unsettled by the dogs, which ran among their horses causing them to buck and rear.

Tallis felt wind on her face as a stone whirred past. She dropped to a cautious crouch. One by one the riders fell, not without causing loss themselves: three of the villagers lay in their own gore, and one had been blinded by slingshot in the confusion of the raid. But whoever these men had been, they had not expected stone and stone had won the day against the metal of their more ferocious weaponry.

Now Scathach stripped the body of the leader. Tallis leaned on her spear and watched him. He sniffed the breeches and wrinkled his nose. He tugged off the leather breastplate, then the tunic, and brushed at the blood. He removed the boots. He inspected the helmet, with its heavy crest and the circling ruff of fur around the rim; his blow had cut the ruff and damaged the cheek guard. But when he put it on, for a moment he looked like a prince.

He smiled at Tallis, then removed the helmet. He hefted the dead man's sword, then strapped the scabbard to his waist, over his heavy furs.

When he came over to Tallis, carrying the spoils, there was a

strange look in his eyes; he had been fired by the bloody encounter. He was aware of her, but he was envisaging greater battles still.
His breathing was almost the panting of a hunting dog. "This will
be more suitable clothing for whatever lies to the north."

"It will be colder in the north."

"This is for battle, I mean." He raised the soldier's clothes. "In
the heat of battle I shan't need fur leggings."

The Tuthanach had gathered their dead. Wynne-Jones, leaning on the arm of a younger man, surveyed the corpses, which had
been laid on their side, knees slightly bent, hands covering their
faces. There was an unexpected and odd silence. No wailing, no
beating of drums, no sobbing. The families gathered round in a
circle, staring down at the remains of their menfolk. Even the dogs
had fallen silent.

Tallis stared into the distance, where the sky was brightening,
a beautiful iridescent blue, dark hued; the new day, and her last
day here, she was sure of that now. Smoke from the burned
rajathuks still coiled into the heavens. Tallis suddenly understood
the eerie silence among the clan.

Wyn-rajathuk's power was gone; there was no way to bury the
dead. If they wished to bury them they would have to summon
Tig. Tig-en-cruig; Tig never-touch-woman, never-touch-earth.

He was the power now. He had stated so last night. Tallis,
listening to the silence, realised that Wynne-Jones was whispering
to Old-woman-who-sang-to-the-river. She was listening, her
face grim. Then she flung back her head and closed her eyes.
Her mouth opened and after a few moments a strange ululation
sounded, a despairing cry, a death cry.

Wynne-Jones detached himself from the supporting arm and
came over to Tallis. He looked down at Scathach's armour,
touched the small wound on his son's shoulder, then looked into
the young man's face; he saw the distance there, the faraway look.
Tallis asked him, "What will happen to these people now?"

Wyn shook his head, then glanced round at the circle of
villagers and the wailing old woman. "They are calling for Tig.
Before he comes we must be gone. If Tig orders my killing they will do
it. I've told them that my power is finished. I've told them that Tig
is the new guardian of the threshold. Whatever rituals he devises
will be their rituals. Until he comes they have no idea what to do."

Indeed, even as he spoke Tallis saw fleeting movement in the wood towards the hill. She thought it was Swimmer of Lakes for a moment, but her horse had already returned to open land and was quietly grazing to the east. This new movement was the boy.

He appeared on the grass. He held two tall staffs, one in each hand. His face was blackened, an echo of Morthen. Around his body were tied strips of greying cloth, and Tallis recognised the ragged shrouds of the decaying dead, before they were dismembered and burned. They hung on him loosely, like a tattered dress.

Tallis went into the long-house and gathered up her masks and Wynne-Jones's few possessions. It was too late to go to the shaman's lodge and fetch his precious writings. Wynne-Jones stood as if in a daze. Scathach slung the clothing he had looted across one of the horses which still paced nervously in the enclosure. He calmed the animal, quickly inspected it, then led it to a second, checked this animal too for wounds and led it to Wynne-Jones.

He helped the old man climb into the saddle. At the last moment Wynne-Jones seemed to come alive. "My work. My journal . . ."

"No time," Scathach said. "We have to get away."

Tallis ran from the long-house, arms filled with furs, blankets, cord and sacks of oatmeal and barley. Scathach led the way to the gate, pulled it down again and mounted his own horse. He clattered over the wood, reaching for Tallis's simple provisions. Tallis ran to Swimmer of Lakes and flung herself across its back, twisting into a sitting position and quickly flinging a simple rope harness around its neck. Tig took no notice of her. He was still motionless, standing at the edge of the wood, perhaps waiting for them to leave.

Old-woman-who-sang-to-the-river filled the dawn with her wailing and chanting. Scathach kicked his horse towards the river track, leading Wynne-Jones by the leather harness.

Wynne-Jones cried out, "My journal! My writing. Let me fetch my writing. There is no point, otherwise . . . my writing!"

"No time," barked Scathach again. Tallis rode after them.

As she entered the wood, following the narrow track towards the water, she glanced back.

Tig was standing by the gate to the enclosure, staring in through the earth walls, his dream-filled mind on other things than the old shaman.

[DAUROG]

The First Forest

(i)

They finally reached the edge of the ancient lake late on the second day of their journey up the river, and in company they had not expected to attract.

They had not been able to travel fast, Wynne-Jones finding riding hard and requiring constant rests. He was very weak and his body trembled and broke into sweats whenever he tried to sleep. Scathach, impatient to get on, took note of Tallis's cautionary wisdom. Wynne-Jones's knowledge of the woodland realm was far too useful for them simply to abandon him and race furiously for the north.

Wynne-Jones cried—cried for the loss of his daughter, Morthen, and for the leaving of his manuscript in the primitive village of the Tuthanach. A lifetime's work, he wailed, and Tallis soothed him. Scathach hunted and killed a wild pig. They cooked strips of its meat over a fierce wood fire, but the old man's appetite was small. He chewed and stared to the south, where his precious parchment sheets might even now be ash, blowing on the storm wind of the new shaman's power.

It was during this first day of the journey that Tallis realised they were not the only travellers moving north, towards the marshlands. At first she thought of wolves as she listened to the furtive movement in the woods to each side of the river. Whatever it was, it journeyed in parallel, slightly behind the three riders. When Scathach ventured into the forest, all sound stopped. He emerged, shaken and slightly puzzled, long hair filled with leaves which he brushed away. He had seen nothing. Yet as they continued on through the shallows so birds wheeled above them in alarm, and creatures shifted in the undergrowth.

As she rode, Tallis unslung Skogen—the shadow of the forest —and placed the mask against her face, tying it, then covering her head with her woollen cowl. Now, as she cautiously peered behind, she began to see the shadows in the trees, the gaunt and sinewy shapes of the mythagos which followed them, darting from shadow place to shadow place. She kicked forward and whispered to Scathach, "They're not wolves, they're humans. Or human-like."

Scathach turned in his saddle, scanned the skies through the tangle of branches which arched across the river. Wynne-Jones, slumped in the saddle, raised his head. Spears of light made his pale features glow. He sensed the movement all around, then saw Tallis's mask-covered features, recognised Skogen.

"What can you see?" he asked. "Are they green?"

The three of them rode to the bank of the river, dismounted, then slipped quickly through the underbrush. They found the ruins of a flint and pebble wall, all that remained of an old stronghold, perhaps, or the defensive wall of a village; perhaps a tomb place, or shrine. Beyond the wall there was nothing but the wildwood, a tangle of small oaks and patchy flowers, not yet destroyed by winter.

In the lee of this wall they crouched, horses tethered, weapons on the ground before them. Wynne-Jones constructed a fire and pushed cut fragments of the wild pig over the flames.

Through the eyes of the mask Tallis watched the shadows move. All Scathach could see was the forest and what appeared to be the flickering of light filtering through the thinning canopy. But Tallis saw human shapes. They hid against the thicker boles of oaks and elm, then moved away, following the autumnal leaf shadow, avoiding entering the lancing beams of grey light from above.

And they came closer to the wall of flint where Wynne-Jones waited, breathless with anticipation.

"Do you know what they are?" his son asked.

"I've only ever seen them from a distance," the old man whispered. "I've heard them, though. Everyone has heard them. But I've never been this close before . . ."

There were five of the creatures. One seemed bolder than the others and came so close that it began to enter the realm of ordinary vision. Distantly, the sound of movement in the river suggested that a sixth was coming to join its companions. The wood began to fill with an eerie chattering sound, almost birdlike. There was a human quality, too, to the noise, as if several women were clicking their tongues at great speed. Odd whistles made birds flutter nervously. Tallis could see how invisible feet kicked up the leaf litter, broke and trampled bracken. It was a movement so subtle that it seemed to occur from the corner of her eye. A movement, then nothing; but the signs of the creatures' passing still quivered and calmed.

The nearest of the mythagos came into view, stepping away from the tree shadow, standing at the edge of forest light. Scathach gasped and reached for his spear. Wynne-Jones put out a restraining hand, eyes fixed on the slender creature that stood before them.

"Daurog," he whispered. "Green Man. Becoming Scarag . . . winter aspect . . . be careful. Be very careful . . ."

"It's a Green Jack," Tallis said, amazed. "I remember seeing them in churches, carved in stone. Old men of the forest. Leaf-heads."

"It's an earlier form than you've seen carved in churches," the old man counselled her. "There is nothing jolly or mediaeval about the Daurog. These are *old*, and they were made in the mind at a time of great fear. In their winter aspect they are exceptionally dangerous . . ."

"Green Jack," Tallis said to herself, and as if the sound of the fanciful name from folklore had attracted its attention it took a quick, awkward step forward, sinewy body cracking like old wood underfoot. It stared at her, bristling . . . rustling . . . It had stepped into a strand of light which played off the darkening face but caught the remnants of the leafy green which swathed the skull, the shoulders and the upper torso.

Its fingers were long, many-jointed; twiglike. What Tallis had taken for a forked beard she could see, now, were curved tusks of wood growing from each side of the round, wet mouth. The tusks branched, one limb reaching up to the leafy mass on the head, the other reaching down, becoming tendrillar, tendrils curling round the torso and the arms, then down the spindly legs, supplying lobate oak-leaves as a covering for the scored, scoured, bark-like flesh below. The creature's member swayed as it moved, a thin, thorned length of tendril that flexed like a worm between the rustling thighs.

It was carrying a three-pointed spear in one hand and a rough cloth sack in the other. As it watched Tallis it began to sniff. Flat nostrils opened in the bark of its face. It was growing rotten, this thing, this Daurog, and was shedding summer's growth. The face was something like a skull, but the contours were wrong. The bone swelled and curved in the wrong places; the angles were unfamiliar. The eyes were very close together. The Daurog didn't appear to blink, and streams of sap ran from the edges of the eyes. When it opened its mouth a slow drip of slime curled from the wet void; the mouth-tusks glistened. The teeth it exposed were greened with mould, and sharpened.

It sniffed the air again, then focused on Tallis, leaned towards her, made another awkward, hesitant step forward; sniffed again and exhaled, a sound like a breeze, a sound of puzzlement. Wynne-Jones reached out and clutched Tallis's arm. The pig sizzled on the flames, spitting fat, startling the Daurog for a moment.

"It smells your blood," the old man said. "It lives on sap, but it smells your blood."

"And not yours?"

"It's male. And I'm old and you're young. It smells the exudates from your body: blood, sweat, filth . . ."

"*What?*"

"And mind-sap too, I think. It smells your mind. It can probably see the way you are manipulating the wood . . ."

Tallis glanced at Wynne-Jones, frowning. Me?

He said, "Of course. You are creating life every second. Mythago-genesis. You are very alive, very active . . . you just travel too fast to see the end result. It begins with a fluttering in the mould and rot of the leaf litter. *You* only recognise it when it rises in bodily form, like the Daurog itself. But the Daurog can probably see the smallest activity. It seems frightened. It is trying to understand us. Stay very still."

Slowly the Daurog placed its spear and sack upon the ground. It circled the small clearing warily, catching the light and jerking as it did so, moving quickly into shadow. As it walked so browning leaves fell from its body. When it came slightly up-breeze of Tallis she noticed the appalling stench that emanated from its form: marsh gas and the smell of death which she remembered from her time in the mortuary house.

But the old Daurog came closer. Its companions hovered in the borders of light and shadow, hidden against the oaks. Their chattering, clicking conversation had diminished. Scathach stretched forward and rested his hand on his spear. The Daurog was nervous and eyed the human warrior cautiously. It stepped slowly towards Tallis, crouched with much rustling and snapping of sinews and reached a long, tapering twig-finger to touch her hand. Its nail was a rose thorn; she allowed it to scratch at her skin, making a faint red mark. The Daurog sniffed its own finger, then licked at the glistening nail. Tallis thought a lizard had emerged from the creature's mouth to bite at the thorn, then realised she had seen its tongue. The Daurog seemed pleased by what it had tasted. It spoke words; they were high-pitched and meaningless: bird chatter; the creak of a branch; more chatter; the rustle of leaves in wind.

Tallis realised with a start that the Daurog's body was alive with woodlice, some of them as large as leaves themselves.

The creature rose and backed away. The leaves on its back were being shed in lines and a skeleton of furry creeper and black, gnarled wood was showing through. It picked up its spear and its sack, then called to the shadows. Its companions emerged and approached the small fire, but stayed warily at a distance, more afraid of the flame than of the humans who had kindled it, Tallis decided.

Two of the Daurog were young females, one with skin made of holly leaves, the other silver birch. Their eyes were smaller than the males', sunk deep below forehead ridges of vine. The branch-tusks from their mouths were a silvery grey. They wore "jewellery" of sloe and hawthorn berries, blues and reds hanging from thorny crowns.

The two males were young also, one skinned in willow, the other hazel. Their tusks were gnarled and they differed from the older Daurog in one remarkable and savage aspect: ridges of long, black spikes grew from the fronts of their bodies; the central, vertical line of thorns ran down on to the twisting, restless sex organs that hung from their rotund bellies.

At last the sixth member of the group arrived, and Tallis almost smiled as she recognised the type.

Not a cloak of feathers, but a skin-cloak of every leaf imaginable. Broad limes on his head, a beard of holly, tufts of pear, shoulders of whitebeam, a chest of browning oak and elm, belly of ivy and brilliant yellow autumn sycamore.

Dogrose wound about his arms; red berries hung in lazy bunches. His legs were impaled with a thousand needles of pine and hemlock; hemlock cones and crab-apple were strapped to his waist. From his head grew a fan of spikes of rush.

It surprised Tallis to see, as her eyesight penetrated the mask of leaf and wood, that this shaman was young, as young, perhaps, as Willow-jack and Jack-hazel. He carried a sharpened staff and five decaying, woody heads had been impaled upon it. He waved the staff and the dead branch-tusks of the severed heads clattered.

"It's known as Ghost of the Tree," Wynne-Jones whispered. "A shamanistic function."

Tallis smiled again. "I'd noticed," she whispered back.

"Skogen reflected this ancient form. Your mask. My totem . . ."

"Everything is older than we think."

The Daurog group now crouched at a cautious and respectful distance from the fire. The elder among them opened his sack and spilled berries of many different kinds on to the ground. There were nuts, too, and acorns. He looked at Tallis. Tallis cut several strips from the sizzling joints of the wild pig and reached forward to toss them closer to the Daurog. Ghost of the Tree moved forward in an awkward crouching fashion, watching the humans suspiciously. He picked up a piece of the flesh, sniffed it and tossed it down. He pointed to two discarded bones and Scathach threw them over. The shaman *broke* the bones with his bare hands, and used the jagged edges to scratch at his bark. He passed one fragment to Oak, the elder.

Tallis rose and walked over to the pile of nuts and berries. Everything was here, dogwood, holly, cherry, buckthorn, sloe and even strawberry. She selected from among them, knowing that they could eat very little of this forest feast.

Trade having been done, they settled to take a meal, to eat, to indicate their good intentions. The Green Jacks were disturbed by the fire, but Wynne-Jones placed pieces of flint on their side of the flames. This symbolic gesture seemed to satisfy them.

Darkness, then a bright moon. The fire glowed and Wynne-Jones kept it fed. He and the old Daurog remained awake, watching each other across the small space. At one point the fuller figured female—Holly-jack—came up to Oak-elder, crouched, staring at Tallis, who had been alerted from her drowse. She spoke to her leader in her woodland chatter. After a while she came over to Tallis and bent down to peer at the human. Tallis was conscious of an overpowering and putrid odour, of sap running in streams down the silvery branch-tusks, of young eyes, of young power. The female Daurog sniffed the air then whispered words. She came even closer and emitted a sound like laughter. She touched a finger to Tallis, then to herself, trying to communicate in some way.

Tallis touched her own fingers to the sharp holly on the female's belly and something fluttered in the wood-flesh, causing the mythago pain. The black fungal mass of her sex quivered, and odd sounds came from the Green Jack's hollow mouth, like whistling gasps.

And in her body, the struggling of wings . . .

Holly-jack drew away, moonlight on evergreen causing her to shine among her fading friends.

He recognised the mythago form (Wynne-Jones whispered to Tallis in the silence of the night) from stories he had heard about them. They were far older than the Tuthanach, probably engendered by the association with the first post-Ice Age forests of the Mesolithic period, ten thousand years or so before the birth of Christ. By Bronze Age times the 'green man'—Green Jack, or Hooded Robin, the mediaeval 'wodehouse'—had become a solitary forest figure, partially deified, reflected in and mingled with such elemental forms as Pan, and Dionysus, and vaguely remembered dryads. But to the Mesolithic hunter-nomads they formed a forest kingdom, a race of forest creatures, saviours, oracles, and tormentors all at the same time; they arose in the mythogenic unconscious both to explain nature's hostility to the people's actions, and to express the hope of survival against the unknown.

All he knew of the early Daurog myth was the creation myth. He summed it up for Tallis:

With the coming of the Sun a cave opened in the ice, as far down as the frozen earth. In the cave in the ice, lying on the frosted soil, were the bones of a man. The Sun began to warm the bones.

The man had eaten a wolf before he died, all other animals having fled the winter. The bones of the wolf lay within the bones of the man.

The wolf had eaten a bird before the man had hunted and killed it. The owl had been cold and slow and had been a poor meal for the wolf. The bones of the owl lay in the bones of the wolf in the bones of the man.

The owl had eaten a vole. Its tiny bones lay there too.

The vole had eaten seeds and nuts and because it sensed the long winter to come it had eaten a little of everything: acorns, hazels, haws, hips, sweet catkins, sour apples, sharp sloes, soft blackberries. The seeds of the forest lay among the bones of the vole and the owl and the wolf and the man.

The Sun warmed the bones, but it was the seeds which grew, feeding on the marrow in *all* the bones, which had cracked with the frost. The life that grew was half tree, half man. It had the speed of the wolf. It had the cunning of the vole. Like the owl, it could lose itself in the forest.

In spring its flesh was clothed in white flowers. In summer, oak leaves shivered on its body. In autumn, berries burst from its flesh. In winter it grew dark and fed on the sap in trees, or the blood of animals. Then spring again, and with the greening of the land the creature gave birth to birds before waiting in the deepest thicket for the call of the Men who were hunting and gathering from the forest. In spring, summer and autumn it grinned at them from the greenwood. Only in winter did it snap their necks to gorge upon their warm sap.

Each year the painful birth of birds brought more seeds, more bones, more wolves into the forest. Soon there were many of the Daurog. They copied the form and ways of Man, but saw how Man was clearing the forest and saw how this destruction released elemental spirits from the earth which had once been frozen.

So the Daurog spread out to mark the limit of the *heart of the wood*. No Man was allowed to enter into that heart and live. But outside the heart of the wood the Green Men brought berries and fertility in the form of birds to the villages and farms of the people.

Only in winter did the wolf emerge to stalk the snow wastes and
the bare forest for prey. The people called them Scarag.

In this way, Man and Daurog lived in uneasy harmony for many
generations, each keeping to their realm, each finding power in
the other, each recognising the other in themselves . . .

There was more (Wynne-Jones went on, after a pause for breath
and thought) but it was fragmentary.

Tallis was concerned that these Green Jacks had come to kill
them. "We're in the heartwoods, after all . . ."

Wynne-Jones thought not. These Daurog were going north;
they were themselves adventurers. And the presence of Holly-
jack—evergreen woman among the slowly transforming Scarag
—was familiar to him; there was a story-cycle about her, but he
didn't know the details. They might find out more during the days
to follow.

During the night Tallis woke to the sound of wind in branches.
Scathach was curled up asleep. She sat up abruptly, confused and
still dizzy from slumber, and a hand reached out to silence her.
Wynne-Jones was alert. He pointed into the faint moonlight on
the far side of the glade and Tallis felt a moment's shock as she saw
what was happening there.

Holly was astride the supine form of one of the younger males, it
was hard to tell which. She was on her knees above him, back
arched, body shaking, hands held to her head as if to block out
pain. She rocked slightly. Moonshine on the holly leaves showed
the way she twitched and jerked as the blackthorn spines
probed deeper into the soft moss of her womb. It was she who made
the sound. It was clearly pleasure.

The male was silent, watching his mate with an almost curious
indifference.

A few moments later, Holly-jack flung herself down on to her
lover's blackthorn chest. She stood, slowly turned, and where the
spines had penetrated her she oozed bright sap. She watched
Tallis, then touched hands to her mouth, running her fingers
down the bifurcated branches of her tusks. And then she was
gone, into the nightwoods, towards the river.

A few minutes later there was a human scream; the night, for a
while, was filled with the sound of birds.

Stunned by what she had seen, Tallis was silent for several

minutes; then she turned to Wynne-Jones. "Are they mine? *Are*
they mine? Have I created these creatures?"

"I would think so," the old man said, but he was not sure. "They
seem to recognise you. Something about you attracts them.
Holly-jack at least. They seemed fascinated by you. Yes, I would
think they have formed from a pre-mythago pattern in your own
mind . . ."

The copulated male was sleepy. (Tallis saw now that it was
Willow-jack.) On his paunchy torso a spined snake curled and
flexed as if in ecstasy, slowly shrinking.

Ghost of the Tree appeared suddenly in the moon, holding his
staff of heads. Tallis could not see clearly but he seemed to be
pushing something on to the staff, working it round until, with a
crack, it slid into position. Then he was quite still, staring at the
humans. Watching him, Tallis soon could not see him. He had
become a small tree. He was forest darkness, rustled by breeze.
Only the slight flexing of his left hand gave him away, this green
man, nearing his winter death.

Disturbed by this strange and brutal event, Tallis found it hard to
get to sleep again. She must have succeeded. She woke in the early
dawn and peered around her blearily through the heavy mist that
filled the wood. Everything was very still. The fire had died,
though its smell mingled with the odour of the forest, the sharp
scent of the undergrowth. She looked for the Daurog, but they had
gone—or so she thought. There was a tight thicket of new, thorny
growth in the clearing, a bird darting between the branches
picking at the red and blue berries that hung from the twigs.

The bird, a small creature, abruptly fled. The thicket quivered,
then moved. It dissolved into six human forms, each taking on the
attributes of head and arms and limbs.

In the centre, Ghost of the Tree stood alone, his arms around
his skull-staff, his head bowed.

The Daurog moved about their business, eyeing Tallis with the
same shivering caution as the evening before. Scathach stirred, sat
up and rubbed his eyes, blinking at the dawn, scratching his beard.
He shook Wynne-Jones who murmured in his sleep, then began to
weep. But Tallis had no time for the old man and his sad, bad
dreams of lost possessions, lost knowledge. She watched the
Green Jacks. Last night there had been six, then one had gone

away . . . now there were six again. She recognised one of the females—Silver Birch—but there was a second female, now; and like the female of the night before, she too had holly on her breast and back.

She wore the same red berries. Apart from being thinner, and less obviously female than Holly-jack, she was the same.

Indeed, as the Daurog elder scooped nuts and berries and held them out to his family, Holly-jack came over to Tallis and stretched her branch-tusked mouth into the semblance of a smile. She rubbed a hand over the leafy belly, then plucked at the growth, tore it gently open, as if parting the folds of a shirt. Tallis felt slightly sick as a glistening space appeared in Holly-jack's torso, with the gnarled shaft of a backbone clearly visible at the back; ribs like curves of polished mahogany gleamed. The hollow in her stomach was filled with scattered feathers. She took some out and let them drift away, still stretching the soft lips of her mouth with delight. The silvery tusks trembled.

Holly-jack had shed her burden of birds, Tallis realised. In some way this had freed her. She had sent new life into the forest, and now she was young again, and hollow. It had not been her head which Ghost of the Tree had worked on to his skull-staff the night before. As Tallis focused her gaze on the young magic-man she could see that the newest skull was a blank-faced mask, crudely chipped out of a circle of rain-softened bark.

She raised Skogen to her face and through it she saw Ghost of the Tree turn a quizzical and penetrating look upon her. In the damp dawn mist he radiated green light, tendrils of luminescence which reached from the points of his body into the canopy, and down to the earth. The soft light bathed him, poured from him; the trees seemed to suck it in, like water.

The Daurog prepared for their journey. They gathered up their few possessions and almost melted into the wood, close to the river. But now, Holly-jack and Silver Birch kept themselves in human view, and called and chattered as they ran, keeping pace with the horses of their new-found friends.

Tallis rode with Wynne-Jones, who watched the antics of the Green Jacks with growing interest. They were certainly drawn to Tallis, he suggested to her. Something about her, some quality, some sign, had made them trust her. He could not see, nor think what that link might have been, beyond what was an evident fact to him: that they were mythagos created by Tallis, and were responding to the mind which had engendered them. They were not Harry's creation: they were too recently generated to have been from him.

Holly-jack—because of her evergreen skin—seemed set to be the one who would persist in winter as the human's friend; she would be the oddest of primitive heroines. There was no ivy-jack in this Green Jack group. Holly and ivy, the green leaves of winter . . . the thought of it made Tallis sing the carol, and Wynne-Jones joined in, adding his cracking voice to the melancholy memory of Christmas festivity.

As for the males: they were only days away from their final shedding. The transformation would be rapid. The sap in their bodies would dry, and with it the intelligence in their strange-shaped heads. They would become animals, ferocious, feral, fervent in their lust for the sap of life to sustain them through the cold.

"We must have abandoned them by then," Wynne-Jones warned.

"We'll cross the marsh with them," Tallis agreed. "Then force a departure."

They reached the lake a few hours later. Tallis thought it was about the middle of the day. It was chill and overcast. She wrapped herself more tightly in her furs and hood and trod carefully with Scathach across the natural platform of reeds and rush. He had not been here before and he was alarmed by the vast expanse of water that now stretched ahead of him. His fur leggings became saturated as he paced around the edge.

Tallis, too, was taken aback. The willows had crowded closer to the shore, a swamp of them; their branches formed a vault. Their thick trunks leaned heavily towards the middle of the lake. There were so many more than when she had been here with Morthen.

The Daurog began to whitter and make shrill noises. They were splashing through shallow water, between massive, brooding willow trunks. Tallis and Scathach followed them. The source of their excitement was a broken barge, shaped like a small longship. Whatever had been on its prow was now gone, sheared off when the sleek vessel had been driven among the trees. It was shallow, draughted, tapering at prow and stern. The mast had come down, but rags of the canvas sheets remained. They were white, decorated with a red emblem which Scathach thought might have been a bear. It was too small for a Viking longship, not sufficiently decorated for the ship of a king.

Or so Tallis thought at first.

The hull was holed in several places and the vessel was awash. But below the rags of canvas—which Scathach deftly cut and rolled—were garments, belts and brooches. Some of the clothing was black. Capes and cowls, and a dress with traces of gold filigree that had been woven along its edges. Tallis rolled these too. All clothing could prove useful.

She found bronze cloak pins, clasps, bead amulets and hair-combs. There were cut locks of hair, too: tight, black curls, some of them from a beard.

"Three women and one man," Wynne-Jones decided, as he sifted through the artefacts. "And there's blood on the hull, do you see? The man was dying."

Tallis stared back into the wildwood, puzzled as to the fate of this craft's enigmatic passengers.

The Daurog pushed the boat upright. The two males climbed aboard and worked on the leaks in the hull, using bundles of rush, which the females gathered. Ghost of the Tree and Oak-elder crouched on the swollen roots of a willow, watching the repair, occasionally singing.

Wynne-Jones had been afraid of staying too long in the company of these changing spirits of summer. His anxiety could now cease. Though the elder, oak leaves bristling as he faced Tallis, invited them to share the vessel to cross the wide lake, she shook her head. The boat would never have borne the weight of the three of them, plus the horses. Indeed, as the Daurog clambered aboard so further splits appeared in the decaying planks of the hull. The vessel wobbled. Holly-jack chittered and watched Tallis curiously, a girl again now that the haunting of wings had gone from her—for a while.

Ghost of the Tree rattled his skull-staff and the loose branch tusks of the dead clattered their challenge to the spirits of the lake. One of the males used a length of cut hazel to pole the craft out of the willow wood and into clear water. Holly-jack waved, then pointed ahead of them to the north. Mist, distance and the lake claimed the green men. Tallis wondered if they were aware of the fact that they were moving further into winter . . .

Now she created the hollowing, the threshold to the north. She wore the Hollower to do it. Scathach held the horses. Swimmer of Lakes was quite calm, but the raiders' mounts, perhaps still missing their masters, were restless and nervous, pulling against him, pawing the rushes and the dirty water below them. Wynne-Jones crouched behind Tallis, fascinatedly watching the way space changed before her, gasping as the first vortex of darkness announced the coming of the threshold into a new geistzone.

Her masks made a circle around her. Water rose through the eyes and mouths. She had placed Morndun—the passing of a ghost into the unknown region—at the front, aware that she wished to travel and that in this realm she was the ghost, as was Wynne-Jones, and a part of Scathach. The masks spoke to her with the voice of the past. She held each one before her, staring at the patterns and the shape. She felt each one unlock her mind. As she knelt there, water soaking into her furs, it seemed to her that the masks were singing to her. As the threshold came closer, Falkenna soared above her—

I will give you wings to ascend the castle walls
—Silvering struggled in a shallow pool—
Swim with me, through underground rivers, through streams
—Cunhaval, the great hound, sniffed at the air—
I know the best forest tracks. Run with me. I fear nothing
—Moondream gleamed—
Castle stone by moonlight; the castle is breathing; beware, beware
—Lament sang to her in old familiar melodies, and Tallis recognised the words and she felt chill—
A fire is burning in bird spirit land. My bones smoulder. I must journey there

"I am journeying," Tallis whispered. "I can't go any faster."

And Morndun howled at her, its spectral presence insinuating cold fingers into her mind, a tentative probing of the darkest region of her unconscious—

Release the ghost from your bones. Ghost follows ghost into the realm of ghosts. Release the life from your bones. There is no other way into the unknown region

"I shall do what I have to do to find my brother. There is no point in dying."

Sinisalo's voice was the calling of a playful child, running between the trees, hiding, teasing. It too called—

Bring out the ghost. Bring out the ghost.

Angrily, Tallis blocked her ears. A fish jumped in the water. A tree root flexed, then was still. Through her fingers Tallis could hear the horses protesting against the growing, icy wind. The platform of rushes vibrated, almost unbalancing her.

The hollowing formed!

The transition was so abrupt that it took her by surprise. As her mouth opened to gasp her shock it filled with snow and dead leaves. She spat violently. Water rushed over rocks. A storm wind raged against the dull sky she could see, trees flexed and bent like flowers. The sides of the valley were steep. There was too much snow for her to tell whether this was the place she had seen before, with the stone walls of the castle rising among the thick, frozen trees. But it was the same deep gorge—and it was on the other side of the lake!

She gathered her masks and stepped towards the hollowing, fighting against the gale that blew into the quieter realm of the marsh. Behind her, Wynne-Jones scurried forward. Behind him, Scathach tugged at the horses. Tallis stepped across the threshold and screamed as the true cold struck her. She was knee deep in a freezing river, and the bank was yards away. She turned and helped Wynne-Jones through into the gorge. He blinked his good eye and looked up, looked around, a half smile on his lips. Snow drove against him, but he just brushed it aside. He was experiencing something utterly new for him: his first controlled passage into a geistzone under the guidance of an *oolerinnen*; his first safe transit of the threshold for so long guarded by the bone, wood and bird-wing magic of the shaman.

Tallis screamed at Scathach to hurry. The man appeared at the gate; he looked shocked and shaken. He had passed through hollowings before, but never into a realm of such ferocity. Branches cracked from trees and plunged into the turbulent waters behind Tallis, who clutched her cloak and cowl, holding them tightly against the tearing wind.

"Hurry!"

The gale threatened to blow her into the water. Scathach tugged at the crude bridles of the three horses and the beasts, terrified by the transition from tranquillity to rage and protesting loudly, stepped through.

Tallis took hold of Swimmer of Lakes, tried to calm the animal and succeeded. She led the mare to dry land, then reached a hand to help tug Wynne-Jones from the surging river. Scathach wrenched the two other animals to safety; and the opening between worlds faded, winter darkness replacing the light from the lakeside.

"We are north of the marsh," Wynne-Jones said through chattering teeth, "But not as far north as I would have hoped."

They hastened into the shelter of rocks and wood, wary of falling branches but aware that they had little choice but to seek refuge from the storm in the wind-shadow of great trees. It was almost night. They had very little time. The snow was blinding but had blown so hard that it had not yet formed a blanket on the land. Scathach slung canvases between trees that surged and shuddered. Tallis tethered the horses, backs to the wind. Wynne-Jones eventually succeeded in starting a small fire.

They huddled together, wrapped in the canvas from the beached craft.

By early morning the ferocious wind had dropped. A fine snow fell for a while, then that too ceased. A welcome calm descended. The horses ceased to struggle and Wynne-Jones slept. Scathach came close to Tallis and they curled up together, her face buried in the fur collar of his clothing, his arms reaching into the warmth below her cloak.

The creation of hollowings had become a difficult and energetic process, leaving Tallis weary for hours after. When she was fully rested they ate a meagre meal, conserving their supplies of meat and berries for the arduous journey ahead, then mounted up and began to pick their way carefully through the snow tracks in the wood. They kept their path as close as possible to the river. Occasionally Tallis, masked in the Silvering, scanned the waters, but she saw no fish. Through Falkenna she glimpsed grey geese, but Scathach—expert with sword and spear—was an inaccurate shot with sling. Only through Cunhaval was she aware of life in the forest and it was not a life-form that encouraged them to slow down and set a trap.

They were wolves. They were close behind. They were following steadily through the black winter woods.

The thought was never spoken, but the identity of the pack seemed obvious.

(ii)

On the second day of their slow ride up the river they found traces of Morthen, a snail-shell hair net, slung from the branch of a tree close to the cold remains of a fire. Had the girl known they would follow her? Tallis unslung the net and fingered the broken shells thoughtfully. Everything about the odd relic suggested that Morthen had left it as a deliberate sign.

Wynne-Jones took the net and folded it carefully, tucking it into his clothing. He stepped down to the water's edge and smelled the air hard.

"She always used to leave little warning signs when she was younger," he said as he came back to the horses. "If we were hunting, or exploring, she would always go ahead. She would warn me of animals, or ruins, or mythagos . . ."

"Is this a warning sign?" Scathach asked. "What is she warning us of? Winter?" He smiled.

"Spring, I think."

"Spring!" Tallis said, amazed, looking about her at the dark, snow-striped land.

Wynne-Jones laughed. "Can't you smell it? It's in the air. The seasons are in flight. This is the strange storm I warned you of . . . Come on! We're getting close to a place that's very important to you."

Spring.

It burst upon them almost between one bend in the river and the next. The trees were in fresh bud, the air crisp but brighter, now, the water less fierce. They rode through spring—it took two hours or so—and entered summer. And by dusk were back in autumn; it seemed sensible to make camp in this gentler land-scape, but during the night an odd wind fetched up and snow fell, followed by an appallingly humid heat.

Confused by it all, Tallis found it hard to sleep. She sat by the guttering fire and watched creatures move along the river. At dawn they were in autumn again, and as they rode on, they came back to winter.

They journeyed for four days, and in each day they crossed the seasons twice. But Wynne-Jones began to show unease. Indeed, the wind was very strange, its scent and sounds confused, quite odd.

Scathach used the periods of summer to hunt for food, and gather edible plants. They rode hardest in spring and autumn. They spent most of their time in winter, simply because travelling through the icy storm was so difficult.

When they stopped, sometimes at the junctions between seasons, Tallis could feel the flow of time, the great spiral storm that curled around some focus a few days' riding to the north. Wynne-Jones drew a diagram with charcoal on bare rock.

"It's like a hurricane. It has an eye, and around that eye are the circular flows of the seasons, moving very slowly in a number of distinct zones. Because we are riding across them we are experiencing the seasons in very short order. I have been through such a storm before, and it is the *gusting* that is most dangerous.

A day later, with the valley walls steepening, the gorge deepening and the river widening, Tallis found out what he meant. Towards dusk a ripple of colour fled through the summer woodland, a widening band of golden brown sweeping through the green. It happened so fast she could hardly follow the change with her gaze. One moment the forest was rich and lush, the next it had turned golden, then the leaves blew into the air, almost as if there had been an explosion.

The riders stopped. Scathach's horse panicked and he shouted at the creature, which stamped in the water, twisting and tugging with discomfort.

Behind the leaf-fall came a gust of budding, the black branches sprouting new growth in seconds, the growth bursting into leaf. The woodland shimmered, was still—a moment's stifling summer silence, then the howl of the new season, a freezing wind bringing death and shedding so that for the second time in two minutes the land was drenched with fallen leaves and snow.

The journey through the zone of gusting time was terrifying. Heads low, they pressed on, galloping whenever there was a moment's calm and heat, turning away from the ice-laden wind when the ferocious shards of the glacier came at them like insects.

After a few hours the speed of change slowed. They found a pocket of spring/summer oscillation and camped overnight there, conscious that just yards away a biting winter was flaring and dying, the trees sprouting, then blackening again, as if the buds were tiny creatures, grasping and snatching at the light, then quickly tugging back into their wood-bark holes.

They came to the 'eye' of this storm, below a sullen, winter sky, and at once Tallis began to recognise the deep canyon which she had hollowed those days before, with Morthen.

"It's here," she whispered to Scathach. "We're coming close. This is the place . . ."

The young warrior brushed frost from his straggling beard and searched the steep sides of the valley, his breath misting. "I feel it too," he said. He seemed alarmed, his horse turning nervously. "Listen!"

Tallis heard the howl of wind among trees, the clatter of stones. She glanced at Scathach, frowning. He had a half smile on his face and his green eyes were suddenly alive with excitement. "Battle!" he said. "Can you hear the battle?"

She shook her head. "Only the wind . . ."

"More than wind! Sword strikes . . . horses at the gallop . . . shouting. You *must* hear it." He still stared at the cliff top. "It's up there, beyond the woodland. And my friends are there too . . ." He turned fierce eyes on Tallis, then reached to hold her arm. "Now *there's* a link between us. Your castle, my field of battle, close together . . ."

Wynne-Jones too had begun to recognise the dark and frozen place. Their movements echoed here, the sound of the river loud, though only Scathach seemed able to hear the distant cries of fighting. The canyon walls came close together as they rode in gathering darkness. Above them, jutting fingers of rock and branch almost obliterated the sky: stone ruins overgrown with black trees, the broken edifices of the ancient place covering the canyon, seemingly hewn from the stone itself.

Among those ruins, among the blackened oaks and thorns, fires burned.

Now, when Tallis listened hard, she could hear a drum being beaten as a warning. It was a familiar sound to her. And perhaps the drum beat had been the noise which had excited Scathach. When she looked into the dark she saw corrupt towers and crumbling walls, high on the cliff, the rooting place, now, of gigantic trees. Black shapes moved there, some huddled below the leaning walls, others flapping against the grey skyline.

"It isn't as I saw it in my dreams," Tallis said. "The gorge was wider. The castle was less ruined. Any youngest son trapped here could easily have escaped."

Not listening to her, Scathach said simply, "This place draws me. It tugs at my ghost."

He stood in the crude stirrups of his saddle and smelled the air hard, seeming satisfied. "The smell of battle! It's unmistakable. Bavduin is close. I'd recognise that smell anywhere."

"If only I had my journal," Wynne-Jones complained. "Something to write with, to record this."

"Look around you," Scathach hissed suddenly as they came round a curve in the river, riding slowly. He turned in the saddle, face shocked. "Look everywhere! Everywhere around!"

White rags fluttered in the trees. Light glinted on armour. Figures moved slowly in the darkness. Tallis gasped as she saw the bones of men and horses piled by the river and flung into the branches, grim remnants of those who had not won the day. Warriors crouched by the water, some drinking, some just staring. Tallis smelled blood and the more offensive stink of ordure. A horse skidded on ice, whinnying loudly as it fell to its side. It recovered, struggled to its feet and galloped away up the canyon, riderless, trappings flying.

As her eyes grew more accustomed to the hellish gloom, Tallis could see how *many* of these forlorn corpses were gathering on the north bank of the river. They ignored each other in death, though sometimes they crouched no more than an arm's reach away from each other, even touching as they slipped on the ice. They had eyes only for the journey downwards, now, and battle-fervour, love and pride had long since been sucked from them, leaving them soulless husks: in bronze, or leather, fur-cloaked or bright trousered. Helmets gleamed, some with tall plumes, others decorated with animals, others plain. The shoreline bristled with the spikes of spears and swords, rammed into the hard mud, no longer needed.

"Bavduin is a timeless battle," Wynne-Jones said as he surveyed the sombre gathering of the fallen. Bones slipped from a tree, clattered to the ground on top of rusting armour. Tallis noticed shields impaled on broken branches, standards fluttering raggedly where they had been flung. A cluster of decayed heads, slung by the hair, shifted in the wind, slack jaws singing silent laments, dulled eyes following the journey of their ghosts into the unknown regions of their age.

On the cliff-side, on ledges among the crumbling ruins: a

scattering of fires. And there were fires, too, on the skyline above them, while on the wind came the mournful blast of a trumpet.

Scathach cried out and raised his sword, then sheathed the weapon and slumped in his saddle, saddened, perhaps, by thoughts of his friends. Tallis remembered his fragmentary account of the battle of Bavduin, his incomplete memory of the legend that was ensnaring him.

A river flowed near to Bavduin, and each night the dead came to the water on their journey back to the cold earth of their own times and lands. Here they summoned the gods and guardians of the dead of their own people, and the ghosts mingled in the air, like mad beasts, fighting and destroying as if blind.

When she placed Morndun across her face and peered through its ghostly eyes she saw the air shimmering with elementals, sharp-faced, wraith-like, coiling and twisting above the river, streaming out of the mouths and eyes of the men by the water and from the piles of skulls by the trees. Horned shapes, scaled figures, shapes with the features of insects and spiders, birds with the faces of young women—it made Tallis shiver to witness this silent gathering of the supernatural forces of so many ages.

"Show *me*," whispered Wynne-Jones, but when he looked through the mask he could see no more than the darkness. So Tallis described what she could sense, and then they moved on through the silent and deathly place, watching the dying and the dead with caution. They arrived at the bottom of a winding cliff path which seemed to lead to the fortress and the forest on the land above—to the open land where a strange, timeless battle was being fought beneath the dusk sky.

They stole fire from a dead man, his limed hair, torque, bare breast beneath fur-lined cloak and cloth kirtle marking him as Celtic. He had ended his own life, but in the cold had remained crouched, his hand resting on the hilt of the blade which he had pushed into his heart. Twined about the fingers of his free hand were long strands of a woman's hair. His tears had frozen so that his cheeks and eyes continued to gleam with ice. Scathach dragged the stiff body back into the trees and laid it on its side. Then he straightened, sighed, and stared up the slope. He whispered the names of the Jaguthin, and his fists clenched with pain.

"They'll be there," he said quietly to Tallis. "They'll be there. All of them. I must go to join them."

"Don't abandon the old man yet," Tallis said. "Give me time to go to the ruins and look for a sign of Harry."

"And pass through to Lavondyss? And leave me waiting for ever?"

"I shan't pass through. Not until I've seen what's there and taken your father's advice on what to do about it."

Scathach still seemed uncertain. She pinched his cheek. "A few minutes in the ruins. An hour at the most. I don't intend to be as rash as you! Then we can say a proper farewell."

She put her arms around Scathach and he tugged her hard to his body. Their furs were too thick and they could feel very little of each other, but Tallis unfastened his cloak and quickly kissed the cold, taut skin of his throat. He responded more passionately, and for a second the faraway look in his eyes was replaced by knowingness and humour.

"A proper farewell," she repeated, eyes stinging. "Even in this cold. Wait for me . . ."

"I'll wait for you," he agreed softly, and glancing at the dark river valley he added, "I'll find food, if I can. Enough for several days. We could eat mythago-flesh . . ."

"No!"

He grinned. "Then I'll find something with a thicker hide and tougher meat. Be careful on the path. And avoid anything that sounds like fighting—and anyone who looks dead. And don't be long . . ."

A steep path, leading away from the river, wound up between low, stark trees. A path made dangerous by loose stones and snow. A path cut precariously into the valley side, sometimes only as wide as an animal's body, sometimes passing through the cliff itself.

When Tallis rode up this narrow track she sent stones tumbling to the glittering water below her, and at a certain height she stopped to listen to the sound, recognising it from a time in childhood, from a time when she had summoned images of another world, and Harry had called to her for help.

This *was* the place. It elated her to realise the fact, to recognise the echo of her horse, struggling on the icy path, to hear the drum, to smell the wood of the fires, the crack of the crude hide tents that had been erected outside the arched gate of the ruined fortress.

Eyes watched her from the thorn woods. She rode past the fires.

These people had lived here for years; the places showed all the signs of long habitation. Only the children were courageous enough to step out of hiding and watch her. They were dull-eyed and fur clad, with hair bound up into a bunch at the crown and the rattle of bones and polished stones around their limbs. They were like the boy she had seen at Oak Lodge . . .

The drummer was a woman cowled in black, who watched from a low tent, half obscured by hides, furs and wooden carvings. Tallis saw a gaping split in the cliff wall, and the small fire that burned deep inside, illuminating the cluster of wooden statuettes, some standing, some dangling from twine, at the entrance to the cave.

She rode on, ducking below trees, shivering as she passed the guarding statues at the crumbling gate. They were beasts, not men, but they had about them the features of nightmare, of ghosts, and though she recognised the animals of the forest in limbs, teeth and eyes, what struck her most powerfully was the element of madness in them.

All things in this world were born from the minds of men and since all men were mad, they were mad creatures, madly running . . .

So Tallis at last entered the stone corridors and galleries which had once led Harry to the first forest, and a forbidden land in whose winter embrace he had become lost. The cold stone whispered to her. She climbed stairs and peered through wide windows at the canyon and the forested land that stretched away to south and west. She entered small chambers, stood at the side of a great hall, its roof decayed, dark creatures flying through the sagging beams, the falling eaves. She knew this hall well, with its huge fire and its marbled floor. She went to the place where the King had sat. She stood where she had seen Scathach in the story, his face now indistinguishable from the young man with whom she travelled. She remembered again the anger in his eyes as he had faced her across the table. And she realised that the anger had not been directed at her at all. He was looking at her for help—he was pleading, through his fury, for the assistance of his sister . . . it was just that, in his youth, he could not control the emotion in his face, and she quivered with the imagined rage, only now recognising the desperation in his eyes.

Who was I? Why do I feel so old? If I was his sister in the story, why do I feel so old, so cold?

If only she had looked more closely at his eyes. In them she might have seen her reflection. She might have understood by now.

There was something comfortingly familiar in this maddening ruin, this mythagoscape, generated by a burned airman many years in the past, created by him as he journeyed to the innermost and most ancient place of all. Glimpses of her stories made her smile. Echoes of Harry made her sad. Although her body was cold, she felt enclosed by warmth, as if her brother's arms were around her, and she was snug and safe against his chest. She touched the stone of the walls as she might have touched a cheek, deliberately and lingeringly. It was so dark, so strange. There was damp quality to it, an odd stickiness. The patterns in the hewn rock were evocative, thin traceries of crystal, she imagined, beautiful whorls and arches, as fine to look at as the fine lines on a mother's face.

She recognised the stone for what it was, but the thought did not engage her, did not surface. It was stone which was not true stone, and she continued to question that oddity, even though the answer to the slight conundrum was obvious and all about her.

Wandering aimlessly, she ascended towers and followed twisting galleries deep into the cliff. Dusk was giving way to night and the fires outside the gate burned brightly. Fine snow fell and transformed the image of the wood. Wind gusted through the empty skull of the fortress, the ragged breathing of a dying man. And in one room she found the tattered remnants of a standard, white, emblazoned with the image of a bird.

From this room she could see out through a wide window into a dense stand of woodland, which seemed to crowd together, not quite hiding a track leading to a small cave. She was high on the cliff, here, and the ledge was close to the darkening sky. She imagined that to walk that track, and to climb the rough hewn rock around the mouth of the cave, would bring her to the top of the canyon. From such a vantage point she might see across the land forever—to the edge of the wood in all directions . . .

The room felt homely, cold and damp though it was, and dark. She walked around its edge. She tried to imagine Harry being here, huddled by a fire in the centre of the space, staring at the cave, reaching to the first forest, drawing the Ancient close to him.

Pale moonlight lanced through winter skies, the clouds

withdrawing for a moment so that the bleak, whorled stone gleamed silver, reflecting back the cool rays.

Something in the stone . . .

She crossed the room, reached to touch the glistening object embedded in the rock. It looked as if the rock had flowed *around* the pistol, curling strands of stone that gripped the barrel and the trigger-guard. But the shape of the revolver was clear to see, the metal now corroded, the wood quite rotten. Yet not so rotten that it had obscured the carved initials at the base of the grip.

H.K.

Harry Keeton!

Her brother's pistol, then. She thrilled to see it, to touch it. She could not dislodge it, but she stood there, staring at the weapon. Its barrel pointed to the cave. Its presence occupied the room.

Following by instinct, following the trail of mind and memory that he had left, she had surely and with great purpose come to the final place of Harry's death—

From here to rebirth was just a single step . . .

So she stepped out through the wide window, towards the cave. To her left the land dropped away to the river below, sheer and terrifying. She could see a flicker of fire, Wynne-Jones's fire. The river sparkled by dusklight.

There was a sound from the gorge, a strange whirring. She saw a dark, circular shape rising from the depths, ascending the sides of the canyon. It was like a dark wheel, flecked with white. It chattered . . . Fascinated, she watched as this object rose towards her, and only after several seconds did she realise that it was a screeching flight of birds, whirling on the updraught towards the freedom of the skies. She crouched as the great flock screamed past her, wings humming; some of them tangled in the trees, a few panicked as they shattered themselves against the stone of the fortress, or flew frantically in the confined space of the room; but most of them circled above her head, then streamed away to the south, lost against the fading luminescence of the sky.

This sudden, panicked flight interrupted the mood of closeness to her brother. Teetering on the sheer cliff, Tallis peered down at the river. She heard her name called from below, the sound distorted as it echoed from the depths. She grew instantly concerned and retraced her steps to where she had tethered Swimmer of Lakes.

Leading the animal by its reins, she descended the steep path towards the place of tents. She skirted the fires, seeing no sign of movement, then realised that someone was running through the dark trees towards her. The figure came up the path and into the sparse firelight, stopped, chittered, then darted on, arms waving as it ran.

"Holly-jack!" Tallis called, and as if it had understood its name the Green Jack stopped a moment, stared sadly at the woman with the horse. It was certainly the evergreen jack, her holly skin torn and ragged, now, her thin body shuddering. She looked as if she had been attacked. As Tallis watched her, so several prickly leaves dropped from her chest, and the creature touched the broken stems as if in pain. Then she turned and ran on, towards the gate to the ruins. Perhaps she was aware of what lay above her, or perhaps she just ran blindly.

Then Tallis realised that Holly-jack was running out of fear.

A wolf bounded into the place of tents, stopped and straightened like a man.

Swimmer of Lakes panicked and reared. Tallis dragged the animal down and soothed it, stroking its muzzle and whispering soft words. The Scarag stood, half visible in the dim light, swaying slightly and working its wet jaws. The stink of beast and forest was strong. It took a rapid step to the side, deeper into shadows, then turned its skull features to stare up the path. As it moved it creaked and crackled, an old tree moving over crisp leaves. Skeletal arms lifted, one pointing; eyes that were just holes in maggoty wood seemed to seek compassion from the human. A mouth that trembled and opened to expose pointed thorns for teeth seemed to work to speak; over all, the shape of the woodland creature was that of a wolf, but a bare boned wolf, its fur gone, its flesh shrunken on to the jutting bones of its body.

It dropped to its forearms and padded slowly to left and right. It sniffed the air. It uttered a doglike howl, then raced past Tallis, moving so fast on its hind legs, bent forward, that she could hardly follow its motion. It had entered one of the tents, but a moment later emerged and raced at Tallis, light reflecting in dull eyes. She was carrying a small spear and only just had time to raise it and thrust it at the Scarag. The point passed through its body as if through tree fungus. But the creature stopped. She withdrew the weapon, struck at its head and it staggered. She impaled it through the ribs a second time and the point took and held, and this time when she jerked the Scarag to the side it came with her, clutching at the killing wood.

Wolfish cries, a sharp wail, a barking death cry; then Tallis had swung the winter monster across the ledge. As it tumbled through the air it stretched out its arms. She thought she heard an owl cry, and the falling shape, black now and only just visible, seemed to sweep suddenly to the left, soaring, then falling, turning a round and white face to glance at her as it vanished into the gloom.

Let free, and panicked by the Scarag, Swimmer of Lakes had bolted. She could hear the animal below her, struggling on the icy path, and she followed it down. When she came to the river the horse was standing there, head hung as if abashed. As Tallis approached it whinnied loudly, then stamped and backed into the trees. She realised that it was not shame that made it cower, but further fear.

She looked along the river to where Wynne-Jones's fire burned. She could see a single horse, but no sign of men. Something, though . . . something tall, something like an animal . . . quite motionless . . .

She approached it cautiously.

What she had seen was a Scarag, impaled through the jaw and hanging limp on Scathach's lance, which had been driven into the ground. The creature twitched, then was still. Its long fingers curled in agony, then relaxed. The fragment of an oak leaf, brown and dead, quivering on its neck, let Tallis know that this had been the leader. A second Scarag's head lay by the fire, its mouth stretched open, wolfish features hardly recognisable. The corpse lay on the ground, arms and legs detached from the body. Tallis noticed that the beginnings of feathers had sprouted from the dry-bark skin, interrupted in their growth by the sudden death of the creature.

Where was Scathach? Where Wynne-Jones? The snorting of a horse drew her attention to the right, and she saw Scathach's stolen mount, roughly tethered. Behind her, a stone fell into the river and she turned, glancing up at the fires on the cliff and the dark clouds above the crags and ramparts of the fortress.

Movement . . .

It was all around her. She swung back, weaponless and frightened. She reached for the fire, intending to pluck a brand, but something grabbed her arm and swung her round. Teeth sank into her cheek. She screamed and struck at the wolf. A spear point cut through her fur robes, pierced her skin, then drew back. The wolf had become still, then it sagged. It fell in her arms, lay on its side. Scathach had impaled it from behind, the point going too far and penetrating Tallis. She rubbed her belly and touched her face tenderly, smearing the blood and pressing the shallow bite wound. Scathach said nothing. Tallis said, "I killed one on the cliff. Holly-jack was fleeing . . ."

"Then only the shaman remains."

"Will it attack like the rest?"

"It needs life. It will kill for blood." He looked around urgently. Tallis stood by him. The smell was overpowering as the winter green decayed faster around them.

"Where's Wynne-Jones?"

Scathach said, "He took his horse and returned south. He said he couldn't live without his journal . . ."

Tallis was furious. "You let him go?"

"He *went*," Scathach said bluntly. "There was nothing I could do. These creatures probably killed him a day ago . . ."

A day ago? But she had only been on the mountain for two hours, three at the most. What did he mean? When she asked him he seemed astonished by the question.

"You've been up there for two days. I've been *very* patient!"

"Two days!"

Her shock seemed to mollify him. "A lot longer than you promised. And now it's my turn. I *have* to go to the field. My father has made everything clear to me. The Jaguthin are there; my friends . . . my whole life. I must meet them again, fight with them, be rejoined with them. That way I can be liberated from them, receive my freedom."

"And what will you do then?"

"Return to your world. Continue my father's work."

But you'll die, she thought sadly. You'll die beneath an oak. You'll be burned on a pyre. There is only one freedom to be gained by travelling to Bavduin. The freedom of violent death.

Tallis was dizzy with the pace of events. Wynne-Jones had begun the return journey to the land of the Tuthanach. But she

wasn't ready for him to leave! Now that she had found the place of
Harry's entry into Lavondyss, she wanted the old man with her.
She wanted his advice, his insight . . . even his help! And how
would he cross the marsh? He had no talent for opening the
thresholds, the hollowings . . .

"He'll die. He'll never make it home. Not without help."

She glanced at Swimmer of Lakes. Had the horse really understood her promise, she wondered? If it had, if such magic worked
in this realm, then Swimmer was the old man's only hope of
returning. And if he returned safely to the Tuthanach, then he
might survive the boy Tig long enough for Tallis to return and
question him after whatever journey she might soon take, through
the highest room of the fortress, through the cave: in Harry's
footsteps.

She told Scathach what she would do. "If he has this horse he
has a chance. But don't leave me. Don't go up the cliff until I
return. I want to come with you to Bavduin. I want to be there
when you find the others."

"Then *hurry*," the man said. "I've waited two days for you. The
others will be looking for me. We must enter the battle together. I
can't let them down."

"Wait for me," she urged. "And watch for the Daurog shaman.
He was young. He'll be dangerous."

"I can look after myself," Scathach said grimly, and nodded to
the twitching corpse of the Scarag leader, still dangling from the
spear.

Tallis mounted Swimmer of Lakes and returned to the south,
kicking the horse, challenging it, urging it to run faster through
the night, back towards the swirling zones of seasons.

She found Wynne-Jones resting in the overhang of a rocky
outcrop, exhausted, wretched, starving. She caught a bird,
plucked and cooked it, fed the meat to him in slivers. She made a
broth from the bones, using roots that flourished in the summer
season, and after a while he had recouped some of his strength. But
he would not be dissuaded from his task. He would not come north
again.

"What point is there in finding the site of my son's death? I
know it's coming. I don't want to see it. You have your own
journey to make, I have my own death to avoid. But I would
sooner have my journal and fight against Tig than die, frozen,

wolfmeat, without anything to remind me of the pure *pleasure* I've had during my life. And those accounts are important to me."

"Tig will have burned them," Tallis said. "He burned your rajathuks."

"Yes. He will have burned some of the parchment sheets. But I've been in the wood for many years and there is a lot more to read than what I keep in the shaman's lodge. Those few pages will have gone, but the bulk of it is hidden. Only Morthen knew where . . . dear Morthen . . ."

He looked sad. "If you find her, bring her back to me . . ."

"I'll try. And I'll bring you Scathach too."

"How can you? You have already seen his fate."

Tallis smiled. "A wild rider, a woman, was reaching to tug him from the pyre. She seemed to love him. Perhaps he wasn't dead as yet. But as you said to me in the lodge, he will be reborn after his death as a warrior. So it's a question of recognising him . . ."

Wynne-Jones's hand closed round her wrist. "I wish you luck. I hope you get there. I hope you find Harry."

"I've found him. I found his pistol. He was there, in the castle. That *is* the way to Lavondyss. There is a cave there. All I need to do is find how to open the threshold through that cave."

Wynne-Jones smiled wanly, scarred face warm. She did not fail to apprehend the knowing gaze in his good eye. "What is it?"

"As you follow him through the first forest," he said, "Remember this, if you can . . . keep asking yourself the question: why did he *fail* to return. What trapped him? Don't make the same mistake. Don't follow too fast. Keep watching for signs of winter, of wood, of birds. Somewhere in all of the confusion of image and story which you have carried with you is the reason for Harry's *failure* to return." He settled back. "I wish I could help you more. I can't. But I am certain that the mistake he made is somehow lodged in your stories. You must enter Lavondyss as a child, not a woman. Watch and hear with a child's senses. You may see the mistake he made, and manage to avoid it . . ."

"Thank you for the advice," Tallis said. "My gift to you, in return, is my horse."

"But I have a horse."

"My horse swims lakes."

"Ah. That could be useful indeed."

"She's yours. Treat her kindly."

"Look after my son. Look for my daughter. Don't grieve."

"If I can work events right, I shall rescue Harry *and* save Scathach. I shall have it all ways."

"I like your determination," Wynne-Jones said with an affectionate squeeze of her arm. "I was pessimistic before. I thought you were doomed to fail. Now I'm not so sure. You are creating faster than the realm is destroying. You created stories. You caused change. Perhaps you *do* have the magic in your winter songs and odd chants to achieve a satisfactory end to your journey."

Tallis kissed his cold, thin lips, stroked a finger over the savage mementos of Tig's attack upon him.

"Ride well, old man."

"I will. And you—don't forget. Let the child ride *with* you."

"I shall."

In her heart, Tallis had known that Scathach would not wait for her, but it still came as a shock to find that he had betrayed his word to her. The fire had been dead for more than a day. She kicked the ashes and howled her anger and her grief. "You should have waited! I could have saved you!"

Through Skogen she could see nothing but shadows of a summer that had once flourished in this gorge. Through Morndun she saw writhing spirits and running ghosts that drifted back into the trees as her haunting gaze fell upon them and they became aware of being watched. The dead were everywhere around, bleeding into the cold water, waiting to begin their own journeys.

She could see no sign of the man she loved.

He had hunted the woods on her behalf, though. The quarters of a small animal were wrapped in a leather sack and tied to a tree's branch. She snatched the food down, threw it across the river shore, but on second thoughts rescued the precious meat and tied it to the slim horse that was now her steed.

The animal, restless, cold and hungry, responded to her sudden soothing. It stamped a foot and snorted briskly. Tallis fed it a meagre handful of the oats she carried. It was thin, fading fast like all horses in this bitter land. She might get a few days riding from it, but it could not survive for long.

On the steep path to the fortress the fires still burned. Tallis watched them, then let her gaze wander along the stark crags and jutting masonry walls. Holly-jack had fled there, and perhaps still hid, terrified, in the cold and draughty rooms. Harry's ghost called to her from the stone skull of the castle. Images of that winter, and of the summer wood, taunted her . . . called her . . . The way to Lavondyss was a short climb away, and all she needed was to resign herself to the journey, to abandon Scathach.

But she couldn't. She had seen a woman ride from the dark woods, screaming her grief, her clay-streaked hair streaming; the woman had ridden around the pyre. And then—and the memory was fleeting, but it had grown over the years—then she had *reached* to the boy . . .

What had she been about to do? Rescue Scathach from the fire?

A woman who loved him . . . a woman who had followed him . . . long hair and face coloured with white clay. Tallis had not made Moondream at that time—the mask to allow her to see the woman in the land—but she intuitively knew who she had seen, how she had reached through her vision to this very day, perhaps, in her own future. She had haunted herself all her life. If she had had her Moondream mask she might have seen it more, she might have distinguished between Harry's presence in her childhood life, and her own . . .

Let the child ride with you. Watch and hear with a child's senses.

She reached into her saddlebag and drew out a small cloth containing white clay which she had taken from Wynne-Jones's lodge and which she had used in the making of Moondream. It had hardened slightly and she moistened it with icy water, kneading it until it shed a film of white liquid. This clay exudate she smeared across her face and streaked into her hair.

Just a little, now. She would add to the clay as she journeyed. In the act of decoration there was both a love ritual and a death ritual. She climbed into the saddle of her restless horse and kicked it up the path, towards the fortress and beyond.

(iii)

Soon the forest closed around her, so dense and dark in places that even as the new day broke she imagined herself still to be in a midnight realm. The character and nature of the wood changed with every furlong's riding, and the traces and butchery of battle with it. In the woods of oak she passed glades where cowled men chanted over carved wooden heads or walked about the piled armour of dead warriors. She saw oval shields, with boars and stags brilliantly gilded upon the slashed leather, broken swords, highly coloured cloaks and small chariots of wicker, broken or burned, in each of which crouched the naked form of its dead rider. There were heads hanging from branches in these places, which gleamed as if oiled. The chanting of the priests seemed to summon wings, though as Tallis skirted these Celtic shrines she could see nothing; and only heard the raucous pleasure of the crow goddess.

A ragged legion passed by her as she huddled in a thicket of thorn and holly, her hand gently covering the muzzle of her horse. She watched amazed as the broken ranks filed past in utter silence, silence save for the dull rattle of equipment. She recognised the warriors as Roman, but had no knowledge of the arms they bore, nor of the type of uniform which would distinguish one legion from another. Their dull helmets seemed to be fashioned from iron; their cloaks were long and red; some carried shields, huge ovals with prominent bosses and the shape of an eagle painted upon them. Horsemen rode among the infantry, and waggons clattered through the forest, butting against trees, being forced through marshy ground and over fallen trunks. What mind had created *this* mythago, she wondered in astonishment.

As she rode further into the changing forest, she found the remnants of their defeat . . .

The woods were almost black; sheer trunks of pine and fir, some of huge dimension, crowded on the land, towered high above and blocked out light; they reduced the world to silence, and the depths of fallen needles below her feet made every movement quiet; even the snorting of her horse sounded dull, sucked into the black wood. Tallis became frightened. She could see fires occasionally, but when she approached them she found men strapped to stakes, burning. There was movement around her. Horses galloped too fast for sense through the black forest; she caught glimpses of their riders, tall men, yellow haired, their helmets crested with crescent moons, or spikes, or down-curved horns. Their speech, when they cried out, was guttural.

The forest opened into a large clearing and she gagged as she saw the slaughter within. Heads were piled in the centre of the place. Around them, in a sun's corona, severed legs and arms. The torsos of the dead were impaled on trees, a circle of greying flesh, mockingly decorated with tattered cloaks and kirtles. Shields were propped against the boles of the pines; broken spears rested by them and helmets, the dull iron helms of the lost legion, had been nailed to the bark.

Four thin, wooden gods watched the rotting dead, each made of twisted lengths of birch-branch, no thicker than an arm but twice Tallis's height. Roman hair had been plaited to make hair for these gods. A skull topped each pole. Pairs of hands had been nailed down their lengths; and in the centre of each watching wood were the shrivelled greying sorrows of severed sex. Blood, blackening now, was the paint on the birchwood gods.

Huge carrion birds gorged on the flesh. They rose in panic as Tallis blundered into the shrine, but settled again, crying loudly, too bloated to fly far.

Tallis moved swiftly through this place of forest shrines, and after a while the nature of the wood changed again. She struggled through holly thickets, forced through dense stands of winter blackthorn, still shrouded in dead leaf. Towering mossy oaks led her to the edge of the wood, and soon she could smell the smoke of a fire, and sense the open field ahead. There was none of the clashing of iron, or stamping of horse that she had come to associate with both skirmish and battle, only an odd silence, save for the distant and familiar sound of a storm wind, and the voice of a flock of birds, coming closer . . .

She led her horse to the very edge of the woodland, and peered out through the scrub at the rise of land before her. Oh yes, she knew this place, she remembered it, she could recognise all the details. She knew just where she stood, as seen from the twisted, ancient oak on the skyline. The tree was in silhouette, but there seemed to be flames in one of its branches; flames that licked high, then guttered and were gone, only to flare again . . . as if a fire was coming and going . . . as if the fire was not of this time, but spent brief minutes in the tree, then flared in another world, before revisiting the winter branches.

There was no-one below the tree. The field ahead of her, across the small stream which flowed here, was darkening below the storm. It was strewn with corpses. This was the end of the battle that she had seen. These were the dead whose stink had touched her when a child. Those were the broken spears and spinning, shattered wheels of chariots whose mournful death had so affected her as she had tried to protect Scathach from the Scald-crows.

The swirl of carrion birds would be behind her, above the forest, out of sight. Perhaps even now they were beginning to circle, to weave around the field, stretching out into a thin and malevolent line as they spiralled in to gorge . . .

Only to be thrown back by the magic of the fire in the tree, the tree spirit, herself, flickering through time, watching, watching for the clay-haired rider.

The pyre would be to her right. She was too late to save him. She knew this with a sickness and sadness that could manifest only as a cold feeling, a dead feeling inside her. She knew she had ridden from the woods, screaming her grief . . . but she felt no grief, only a terrible inevitability, only cold acceptance. Where was the passion she had witnessed, as a child, in her angry figure? Where was the sorrow? Where the determination to honour her lover's death, as he burned in Bird Spirit Land?

Only ice. Only knowledge. Only acceptance . . .

Then to her right, a woman screamed. Tallis was shocked for a moment, and remained quite still. A terrible thought had flashed through her mind. There was a fast and furious movement in the woods, the sound of a horse stretched to exhaustion, the slap of leather against flank and the dull sound of hooves on blood-soaked turf. Tallis ran from the treeline. Her steed trotted after her.

Smoke from Scathach's pyre was black, rising high into the dusk. The flames licked around the wood, around the corpse. The arms of the dead warrior seemed to flex, moved by heat, twisted by the consuming flame. A figure in black was just disappearing into the wood. Tallis thought she could hear the creak of a cart . . .

Then a woman on horseback burst from the wood, stumbled through the shallow stream-waters and struggled on to the field. She rode around the blazing pyre. Her black cloak streamed behind her. Her clay-stiffened hair took the yellow of the flames. Her body glistened, red streaked arms, white-and-black streaked face. Her cries of sorrow and anger were like the fleeting cries of dawn birds, banished from this forbidden place of battle, this Bird Spirit Land . . .

Morthen reached for the foot of the corpse and dragged Scathach's body from the funeral mound. She flung herself from her horse and smothered the burning body with her black cloak.

She shrieked his name. She cradled him in her arms. She kissed his lips, brushed at the burned flesh, slapped his face to try to wake him . . . but her brother from the wood was dead, and she leaned down, sobbing silently, furling him into her body like a dark bird gathering in its chick.

The girl was now a woman; she was years older. Tallis could recognise this fact even beyond the mask of clay. For a few minutes she stood in shocked silence; she had been so sure that the rider from the woods had been herself . . . but now, realising that the lover she had seen had been Morthen, she felt angry and upset. And yet, she could not apply that anger to jealousy, she could not storm out across the field and challenge Wynne-Jones's daughter for the body of the man they both, in their own ways, loved.

Suddenly Morthen seemed to sense the watcher. She turned slowly to look towards Tallis, her eyes fierce, her mouth twisted with fury. She was like a witch, a hag, all youthful beauty banished below the lines and hatred in her face. She stood, reached for the clumsy metal blade she now carried, flung back her cloak to expose patterned nakedness, threw back her head, howled Tallis's name, then Scathach's, then her own, then looked again, silent, furious, to where Tallis hovered in the shadows at the edge of the wood.

Tallis was prompted by this insult into an action that she knew she would regret. She walked out into the open, drew her dagger, shouted, "Leave him, now. He's mine. I'll take your brother to a proper place of burial."

"He's *mine*," Morthen growled, her voice more feral than human. It rose in pitch. "He's my *brother from the wood*. I've aged for him! I've sought him for years. I've found him, and you have put a magic on him. *You* have done this . . ."

"Don't be stupid. I've been with him since you left. He rode away from me a day ago. I've done nothing. *I* didn't desert him . . ."

Morthen turned and ran for her horse, swinging across its bare back and violently twisting its head to face Tallis. She rode forward, kicking the beast's flanks to make it gallop. Tallis stood her ground, and then was shocked as Morthen's blade slammed against her jaw, almost completely following the line of the old scar. Tallis fell, feeling no pain, only a sense of numbness and unreality. The blade had been used flat. There was no cut.

She stood and faced Morthen again. How the girl had grown! She was almost as tall as the outsider. Her eyes were as beautiful as ever, even through rage, even through the warpaint. Her hair stood like spines about her head, white, fierce, stiff with clay. Her breasts were naked as she threw back her cloak again and let the winter ice make her flesh shiver. A fully grown woman, the muscles on her arms and legs as thick and obvious as a man's. Tallis, huddled in her furs, watched this naked apparition as it stalked towards her. She fielded two blows, then felt her left arm cut as Morthen struck swiftly, savagely; then her left leg, so that she collapsed in a heap, struck three times on the left side of her body, bleeding, left to die.

Morthen slashed through the bindings of Tallis's cloak, stripped the woman as she lay there gasping for breath and life, mind awhirl with confused thoughts, with loss, with fear . . . with need. She felt the icy wind on her body. Morthen wrapped the furs around her own body, tugged on the wolfskin trousers, brushing at the bloodstain where her blade had slashed.

"He's dead," she taunted. "And the earth knows, I regret that. But you will die too, and that I do not regret at all. Now I shall return to my father. From his own first forest I shall find my brother once again. Scathach will come out of the wood . . . I haven't lived my life to fail. For you: the cold. Only the cold."

Her crude blade sheathed, Morthen wrenched back Tallis's head, then kissed her lips before flinging her down again.

She took me so easily. She could have killed me if she'd wanted to . . .

Tallis stared at Scathach's burned and blistered body. As she began to feel faint she reached for his smouldering cloak, the short red cloak he had taken from the raider. She tugged it off the body. Scathach's half-opened eyes watched the heavens. His lips were swollen with the heat, ugly to look at; the line of burning began on his jaw and his fair neck was wealed and raw. She tugged off his patterned trousers and the leather jerkin. She eased them on to her body, cutting out a part of the cold. Her horse came close and watched her. She crawled closer to the funeral pyre, rejoicing in its warmth, and slept. When she woke again only a little time had passed. She found a glowing ember and used it to close her wounds, then forced herself to stand.

Morthen had gone. Having dragged the body of her brother-lover from the pyre, she had abandoned him, returning south, Tallis imagined, to find her father again.

She had gone from Tallis's life, then, and so the final link with Wynne-Jones was severed. Tallis was on her own for the first time in her eight years or so in this unimaginable land.

The thought disturbed her and brought her to her knees by Scathach's scarred corpse.

Did you find your friends? Was he there? Gyonval? Were they all here? If I search the field, will I find them all again?

Now she regretted stripping the clothes from his body. She stared at the puckered, shrivelled flesh, its scars closed, all colour gone, save for blood like crude paint, its limbs without energy or force, its face without vitality. She had insulted the proud warrior. He had called to her in his dying moments, and she had thrown him a fragment of her white nightgown, which he had clasped with hope, and kissed, and kept as a precious icon. Now she had rudely stripped the corpse, and at no time during the action had she thought of that strip of white fabric . . .

She prised open the body's right fist, and there, charred at the edge, was all that remained of the nightgown. Linen. Roughly made. Cheap to buy, yet how precious it had once been.

In all her time with him she had never told him the details of what she had seen, that day one summer. Had he grasped this shard of hope with any real understanding, she wondered?

She rode to the tree. Scathach lay over the withers of her horse, his arms dangling; there had been no way to arrange his butchered corpse with more dignity.

She rode to the tree. She looked up.

Bare branches, winter-stripped against the fading sky. And yet when she had peered down at Scathach's body she had looked through leaves, through summer. There was no fire there, now, no sign of life, nor of the spirit that had once shrieked at the local folk who had emerged from the fortress demesne to loot and honour the dead: Four black-robed women and one man, robed in grey, a greybeard: he had understood the mythology of stone. The grey stone lay there now, chipped by his blade, cold on the ground, marking the place of rescue.

They had carried the body away on a rude cart. But they had built a pyre for Scathach, and in so honouring the man they had indicated their recognition of him.

She looked up. She dismounted, then climbed the tree, tugging and hauling herself high into the branches.

Go into Lavondyss as a child . . .

This was not the tree as she remembered it. Had she positioned herself here? Or over here? Which of the various branches had been the branch along which she had lain, and watched the dying Scathach? The tree was not the same in this world. She could only approximate the position.

So she found a place in the old tree which gave her a familiar view of the land. There she lay, cold and wounded, clutching the branch and staring at the corpse of Scathach, limp over the black horse.

There was no romance here, only the sickening remnants of battle, the dead looted, some still lying, waiting for the carrion eaters.

Night came close.

Scathach had lain just so . . . and she had been here . . . and had seen there . . .

And so, if she twisted round, perhaps she could see back to her own world, to the meadow . . . what was it called? And the stream . . . it had had a name once, but she couldn't remember it. And that wide field. Windy Field? And the house, and her home . . .

Perhaps she should fetch her masks. Perhaps one of them would allow her to see more clearly: the ghost in the land, or the child that she had been, or the old dog, or the rooks in the tall trees, or the woman . . .

She twisted on the branch, the wound in her leg hurting very much, still bleeding. She ignored the pain. She stared at the winter world through every aspect of this old tree. Somewhere below, only a few minutes away but in another world completely, she was running back to the house, Simon in hot pursuit.

What did you see? Tallis! Tell me. What did you see?

Somewhere close, somewhere—yes! just minutes away!—somewhere she was a child again, and Gaunt was pottering, and her father was getting angry with her antics . . .

And it was summer, late summer. Mr Williams was walking in the countryside, listening for odd songs, looking for that magic to be found in a new song. The festival would soon be under way. The dancers would dance, the mannequin would shiver and give birth to the green girl. The antler and noose would be used in the mock

execution of the Morrisman, and the wild jig would bring everyone on to the green, laughing and screaming in the hot, summer
night . . .

But there was only winter. And the field of the mythical battle
of Bavduin, or Badon, or the Teutoburgian Wood, any of the
names which had characterised this mythical confrontation to end
an era, to end hope . . . This was the centre of the field, and a tree
marked that place, and to this centre one hero among heroes
always came . . .

She had seen Scathach.

She might have seen . . . who? Any of a thousand princes who
had crawled away from the fire to shed their blood and start a
legend . . .

*If I jump from the tree I will be home again. I can start again. If I
jump . . .*

Temptation seduced her. Her horse reared as she fell and
Scathach's naked corpse slipped from its insufficient bindings,
falling awkwardly, an ungainly mass of pale flesh and bone, head
turned up, eyes dull. She had not passed into another world.

Tallis tugged the body back on to the animal, then climbed into
the saddle behind it. There was nothing for her, now, nothing
apart from Harry. She did not believe that she could bring
Scathach back to life, but he could at least be with her in the
fortress as she made her journey into the first forest, as she went in
search of whatever it was that had ensnared Harry, made him a
prisoner in Old Forbidden Place.

She returned through the black woods, past the shrines, to the
narrow defile which marked the nearer barrier to the castle. She
rode down the steep path, then up through the collapsed gate and
into the area of the pinnacle of land on which the fortress had been
constructed. On the way she placed her masks in the shrine cave
by the tents, where the fire burned.

And after giving the horse its freedom—perhaps a cruel act in
this severe winter—she dragged Scathach's body through the
empty corridors to the room where Harry's pistol marked the place
of his final departure.

She propped Scathach against the ledge of the wide window,
then made a nest in the middle of the room, furs, clothing, rags
and tatters of standards. Exhausted, Morthen's wounding cuts
hurting her, she remained seated here, watching the cleft in the

cliff over the gaunt and grimacing features of the man she had once loved.

She waited for Harry to beckon to her. After a while she fell asleep.

An eerie light woke her. The room was warm. She rose and walked through corridors, noticing how the stone walls seeped moisture. When she touched the stone she found it to be sticky. She ran her fingers over the tracery of pattern, following the curls and rings . . .

The light changed. Sometimes as she moved through the rooms and hollows of the ruin the light was yellow; sometimes green, sometimes tinged with orange. It grew warmer. A heavy and pervasive smell began to fill the place, choking her. The walls of the fortress seemed to close around her, stifling her.

When she returned to the top room, where Scathach lay, she found that the wall had almost completely absorbed Harry's corroded pistol. Tendrils of stone had wrapped over the metal and the butt; there was a fine hair on the stone, like a plant's roots. When she touched them they quivered. The stickiness remained on her fingers. Tasting it, she discovered it to be sap.

For only the first time, now, did she comprehend the nature of the stone from which the fortress had been constructed. As she returned to her nest, looking around her, she could see it so clearly that it made her laugh.

Petrified wood.

Looking carefully she could see the fragments of the great trees whose fossilised trunks had been carved to make the blocks. One great stone, spanning the nearer wall, was crossed with hundreds of lines, rings, marking the enormous age at which the forest giant had died.

The sap oozed and ran, pooling on the floor, slowly flowing along the incline. The room was warm, cosy. Green light flowed like the liquid, coming through the stone itself, although outside the night was dark, the winter harsh.

She closed her eyes for a moment only. When she opened them, Scathach's sad body had corrupted to bone. The walls were alive with branches, running over the stone like veins.

She closed her eyes. Images moved inside her. Seasons flew. Birds came and nested, then went to the south. Herds roamed, snows came. She opened her eyes. A holly tree grew from the place where Scathach had lain. Entangled with its branches were shards of human bone, crushed now, gleaming in the glistening green. The holly shivered. Around Tallis the room moved, tendrils of tree spreading along the floor, the ceiling, up the walls, reaching into the air. She became caged in wood. A gentle touch on her cheek, then her arm. Fingers ran through her hair, stroked her throat, gently probed her mouth. She closed her eyes and raised her arms, and the old fingers, gnarled yet soft, stroked her skin, then gripped her gently.

She was lifted. She hung in the room, strong arms around her waist, strong fingers around her legs. Leaves protected her, their broad faces covering her like skin. Berries trembled against her lips and she licked them, swallowed. The fortress grew around her, stone into wood, rooms into glades, fortress into forest. Her body was squeezed as if between great trees. The pressure began to hurt her and she cried out and the sound set bright birds to flight in the canopy around her.

She was lifted, turned, twisted and absorbed. In the preternatural green light she watched oak and elm slide into vision, growing at a fantastic pace, their branches reaching, entwining. Hornbeam moved as smoothly as a snake, creeper twisted, ivy writhed about the mossy bark, reaching towards her, its soft and furry touch tickling as it wound about her skin.

Then a harder, rougher feel, her legs forced open, rough bark serrating her flesh, butting against her, harder, bruising. She squirmed with pain, but was helpless in the grip of the renewing forest, and she felt her body entered, a single motion that never stopped, just filled her, swelled out, tearing her apart inside, fingers of pain, shards of agony, curling snakes of pressure that reached inside to the tips of her toes, her fingers, up her spine and round her ribs, rising higher, filling her stomach, then her lungs, then her throat.

Stretching her eyes open to see the light, bulging with the strain, Tallis helplessly experienced her rising gorge. She was going to be sick. Her stomach churned. The feeling of movement in her throat was torture. It crept towards her mouth, inch by inch. She retched and failed, squeezed, tried again, tried desperately to choke out the stodge that blocked her.

It came suddenly. She stretched open her mouth, screamed,

then spewed out the great twisting branch. It came like a hard, brown snake. It flowed from her. It divided into two, then curled back on each side of her head, bursting into bud, then leaf, to wrap around her skull. Her lips split, her jaw cracked as the branch thickened, then was still.

Something fluttered inside her, like the tremor of a heart. It was still, then moved again. The forest was silent. She was in its heart. The light was an intense green and she could tell the passage of sun and seasons above her. Sometimes a fine and fluid mist filled the forest. Sometimes a breeze blew and everything shifted, trembled, then was still. The light faded, leaves fell, and a fine snow drifted through the air, vanishing below her. Then green again.

Inside her, the movement became restless, almost urgent. Sometimes it fluttered high, towards her throat; at other times it seemed confined to her stomach. Tallis was idly aware that she had none of these organs left. The bones of her skull rotted around the branch. Her flesh fell away and only the impression of her face was left upon the wood. The sap flowed easily through her veins. Insects crawled beneath her skin, burrowed into her and were pecked out by flitting birds, which crossed her forest vision in a fleeting moment, came to her, and were gone, their beaks a brief sting upon her bark.

A tree fell. She watched its slow collapse with sadness. Its branches caught in the arms of its neighbours. Seasons passed and the tree slipped lower. A dense moss grew across its trunk and it sagged, then cracked. A high wind disturbed the primal land-scape, and the tree had gone. Bright flowers bloomed, were drowned with snow, then shoots of oak twisted into the new light, grew serenely upwards, fought each other like beasts, tentacles entwined, one overpowering its companions, crushing them, then looming large in Tallis's view. Its leaf tips touched hers and she soaked its energy, communed with the giant.

She grew older. Her bark split, her branches fell. Lines of painful rot began to rise along her legs. The movement inside her filled her completely, an endless fluttering of wings, intense and urgent pecking of beaks.

One day she felt her stomach rupture. The oak trunk opened, cracked by the forces of the earth. The pain was unbearable and she screeched in the voice of the forest. She was forced back as the bark opened and the hardwood below parted like a wound. The black birds struggled out, a thousand of them, bright-eyed, bright-beaked, anxious to find carrion. The sudden birth of birds left her exhausted, watching as they fled and fidgeted through the canopy, upwards, to the brighter light. When they had gone she felt fulfilled, emptied, at peace.

Great creatures roamed the forest, some like bears, others like cattle, reaching up on hind legs that were as thick as oaks to chew leaves and berries from the tops of the trees. Tallis had seen nothing like them in all her life, their hides so thick, their fur patterned in blacks and browns and whites, infested with parasites. Odd horns and protrusions covered their faces. Tongues licked leaves into mouths where teeth grew at all angles. There was other movement, slighter, quicker. Bands of monkeys roamed through the canopy, sharp eyes glancing at her, small hands picking at the bark of her face. A stag butted against her legs, far below. Then a great elk passed by, trapped in the tangles of the wood. In its panic it broke its antlers, shard by shard, tine by tine. Its cries of distress saddened her for years. Its corpse lay at her feet, slowly sinking into the moss and mud.

It grew cold. The green light became grey. Screens of holly and ivy sheltered her from the deepening winter, but now the forest became a black and frozen place. Wolves prowled below her, fought each other and consumed the dead. The wind became relentless. Ice formed in her branches, seeped into the wounds in her body, expanded and cracked her.

She felt the strength in her body go. She began to lean. She broke suddenly, crashed into the arms of her neighbour and lay there, sinking into his branches. Here she remained for what seemed an eternity. But the winds became so fierce that the whole forest shook. She slipped further and the lover-giant's grip upon her gave. She struck the ground. He shed his leaves to cover her. They fell through the light for years. Snow covered her, finally. Small animals used her as a shelter, burrowing into her rotting bowels.

There was a sudden movement. A grey shape passed across her vision, came back, peered down. She sensed human sweat. Saw elk-hide and wolf-fur.

Bright eyes in a pinched, cold face caressed her with their look. The boy's hands ran over her face, his head cocking this way, that. He touched her eyes, her mouth, her nose, and Tallis understood that he had seen the hints of the face within the wood.

He smiled; his broken teeth stung in the icy wind and he clapped a hand to his mouth in pain, his eyes watering.

He drew a stone axe from the belt at his waist and made tentative cuts around her neck. He shivered with cold. He was hungry. There was frost on his hair, on the fur of his hood, but soon, as he hacked at the tree, his skin began to glow and a fine, warm moisture gleamed on his face. Tallis felt the warmth from him and loved it. He cut and chopped and she felt herself detached from the rotten wood. He heaved her upright. She was taller than him. He caressed her body, peered at her face, used his axe to snick off bits of twig, loose bark, the bulging scars of old wounds.

Small though he was, he carried her over his shoulder, passing back through the frozen forest to the snow field beyond.

He had come from a miserable place.

He lay Tallis down in the shelter of tents. They were slung between trees, closed over, roofed in, with a mean fire burning inside.

There were other grey shapes. They spoke softly. They drank thin soup and shivered. The snow drove at them fiercely. From where she lay Tallis could see the skulls and bones in them, the faces of death creeping close to the surface. The tallest of the grey people, a man, came back with frozen roots. They were in despair. There was no hunting. The winter had caught them by surprise.

The wind reached into the tent, blew the fire, blew ash. They struggled to keep the winter out. The trees rocked. The sounds of animals were distant, great roars of dying elks, the barking of wolves. Each time this sound came the man ran from the tent with his knives and spears, but he came back, huddled and weeping.

His skull poked into the day. His lips drew back. He was so near to death that even his eyes were like caves into the underworld.

The boy came over to Tallis and began to work on her with a knife. She felt her eyes opened wider; he parted her lips. Through nostrils she smelled the fear and the death in this wretched band more powerfully.

She could see the family clearly, now. A father and a mother. It was the youngest child who hacked at the wood. There were two older children, both boys. One had a wild look in his eyes. The other was a dreamer. He kept his mother happy by telling her little tales. He made her laugh. The father, black beard full of snow shards, watched the youngest son, watched him work. Tallis could hear the way his belly rumbled.

The boy had finished. Tallis was raised up and five faces stared at her, some smiling, some too dead to show emotion. The boy carried her out into the snow and pushed her into the ground, turning her so that she faced the tent and the cluster of trees that formed their crude and failing shelter. The land glittered with white. The sky was utterly grey. There were no features, save mounds below the snow, and the black of trunks. No animals moved on this forbidding land. Nothing grew. This family was doomed.

Below her was the corpse of a woman. Tallis had seen the grimacing features as she was carried to the grave. Now, as she impacted with the body, she felt the bones stir. A sap rose in her, human warmth in the veins of the wood. The dull, meaningless sounds of the family became clearer to her. The family kissed the wooden image of their grandmother. The woman cried, then rubbed her tears into Tallis's eyes. The man scowled at her. The youngest son looked proud. His touch was the touch of an artist, inspecting his work, his craft, rather than honouring the dead woman. The dreamer smiled at her. Fierce eyes watched her coldly, then nodded, then stared beyond her, at the denser wood. Then sniffed the air. He was behaving as the hunter he would soon become.

The storm came and drove them into their flimsy shelter. Tallis watched the winter with awe. She had never seen anything like this. The snow drove across the land for days. Trees cracked and fell. Through the blizzard she could see the constant effort of the family to keep their crude tent intact. Snow piled against it, threatening to destroy it, but this helped to protect it eventually, as the snow wall hardened and compacted.

The blizzard eased. A greyish light to the north told of ice. Nothing moved on the land.

The youngest son came to the totem, to Tallis, and straightened her after the blizzard had made her lean to the left.

"Grandmother Asha, send us food. Please send us food. Where are you? Are you in the warm woods in the south? I made you from oak. I used the bone knife you gave me. You told me it has a special spirit. The deer was drowned in a lake. Its bone made my knife.

My knife carved your oak. This storm has killed the oaks, but you are in a warm place, where the leaves are green. Grandmother Asha, send us food from that warm place?"

The woman came to Tallis and embraced her frozen bark. Death grinned through the woman's skin. She fingered her necklace of shards of antler. She rattled the bone to draw the old woman's spirit from the wood.

"Mother . . . mother . . . I lost the child. It would have been a girl. It came out of me without blood. I have no blood left. Tell me what to do. The rest of the clan are too far from us. Most of them are frozen to death. We have been too slow. This winter will never go away. My sons will never see themselves as fathers of the tribe. What do I do?"

The dreamer came and crouched before her. His hair was reddish below the hood, which he swept back despite the freezing of ice on his lashes and brows. He was handsome, with dark eyes. He had survival in him. He contemplated death, but was thinking of life. He called on Grandmother Asha through the oak statue that was Tallis.

"You are a part of the first forest. You have seen all things. You have lived through all times. You are bone and wood, Grandmother, so you must know how to save us. Please send us food. There are no birds here. Please send them back to us. Please show us the path to the warm place, and the warm forest, show us the path to the light which is green, and the leaf that hides the bird. I have a song for you, Grandmother . . ."

He sang in a child's voice that was beginning to break, so that it was tuneless, the register awkward, the pitch uncertain. It sounded like the song of a shaman. He sang, "A fire burns in the warm forest where the woodcock flies. My bones are burning with the thought of that warm forest. Help me journey there, to that bird-filled land. I will always sing of this winter, and your laughter, and of my journey to that land in the warm forest, away from this cold place of bird spirits."

He drew a stone blade and carved a sliver of wood from Tallis's arm. The shard was sharp. Watching her, staring into her eyes, he opened his furs to the breast and cut four lines with the wood, marking himself. A pale, feeble line of blood seeped from his starving flesh.

"With this mark I take your spirit with me. With this mark I promise to remember your life, so that your life will always be remembered, Grandmother. With this mark I *will* find the wings to fly to the warm place. With this mark I will tell the life of our family, and our hunts, and this life will *always* be spoken of."

He went away. Fierce eyes came and pushed her aside. An icy wind howled and a great wall of snow bore down upon them. He scrabbled in the snow for the rotten corpse. He tore flesh from his grandmother, but tossed it aside.

"We should have gone with the others. My father was wrong. Now we are alone and the next blizzard will kill us. There is nothing left in this land. Grandmother, you *knew* the great winter was coming, but you said nothing. When you died I was glad. But now I wish you were alive. So that I could kill you and suck the warm blood from your neck. You *knew* the great winter was coming from the north. You said nothing to my father. We hunted. We journeyed. We should have been running south!"

He struck Tallis a hard blow with his fist. She leaned further.

This eldest boy seemed remorseful for a moment. "You taught me many things. You showed me what to look for in the tracks and trails, to know where to hunt and where to follow. You prepared me to lead a family on a long journey. You prepared me for triumph. Now the great winter is drowning us. *You should have prepared me better.*"

The snow struck and drove him back to shelter. The wind tore at the land. The ice struck with glittering fists. The land seemed to howl with pain for days. Something gigantic waded past during that long night. By the time the family had become aware of it, it had travelled too far south. The mother keened her anger while Fierce Eyes danced his fury. Game had passed and they had slept, huddled, more aware of cold than of the hunt.

Another time of darkness. A wolf skulked past, sniffed at the totem, scrabbled in the hard snow for the corpse of the grandmother and dragged out one of her arms, limping into the night with this meagre feast, to find some place where it could chew its way to the frozen marrow.

At dawn the father came out of the ragged tent among the trees. His body was wasted. His arms were wrapped around him, his body's breath so cold that it hardly frosted. He stepped through the deep snow towards the grave where Tallis stood her silent guard. He came down on his knees before her and hung his head. He said only, "It has to be done. Forgive me, Asha. It is not the way of our clan, but it must be done. Forgive me."

He stayed there for a long time.

Soon the youngest son emerged into the grey light of the winter land and came silently towards the totem. His eyes had dulled. He was almost dead. There was precious little flesh on his bones now. He carried his bright bone knife and seemed to become more cheerful as he came closer to his art.

He was aware of his father, glancing at the frozen man whose darkly bearded head still hung as if with shame, his body hunched, the cold seeping through the bear and wolf skins. The boy ignored him, though, and came up to the wood.

"I must open your mouth. Then you might speak to us. It came to my brother last night, in a dream. He told me I must open your mouth."

He raised the bone knife to the wooden lips and she felt the first gentle cut.

Behind the boy the stiff figure of the man suddenly rose to its feet. Grey light glanced off polished and sharpened antler. The movement was swift, soundless. Soundless except for the dull crack of the axe against bone. The boy's eyes glazed. His hood was tugged back and the axe struck again. The brains and blood splashed across Tallis. The axe was used again. The head of the boy came away. The axe struck. The arm of the boy came away. The man worked furiously. The snow absorbed the blood and the sound. Clothing was discarded. Animal entrails drawn. The man buried his face in the steaming soft mass of an animal's liver. He gorged. There were tears in his eyes as he turned his face to Tallis. His black beard was stained red. His lips were slack, his mouth still full of food. He swallowed quickly, then like a jackal went back to the carcass, gulping down the soft tissue, sucking air and blood through his nostrils, choking with the violence of his ingestion.

When he was full he leaned back on his haunches and looked at the mess of blood and flesh. A moment later he turned to his right and was violently sick. He wept as he released his son, and choked, then rubbed snow on to his face and in his beard. Somehow the sound was deadened.

Though wind disturbed the tent, no-one emerged.

After a while the man stood up. He was shaking. He looked at the stains on his hands, then at the murder beside the totem. Quickly, glancing back to the tent, he gathered up the limbs and torso, wrapped them in the discarded skins, tied them crudely and gathered them into his arms. There was scant eating in the meat, but it would sustain him for some days, assuming he could keep the scent away from wolves.

He staggered upright and carried his youngest son into oblivion, journeying towards the south, lost in the bleak and frozen wilderness.

The lame wolf returned. It sniffed the air. It could not believe its fortune. It nosed against Tallis, then turned and ejected a tiny, stinking drop of liquid from its shrivelled glans. It chewed the bloody snow, gulped the entrails and the gore, growled in its throat as it worked at the tough tissues. When the flap of the tent was disturbed it began to shudder, but hunger was now so powerful a force in its life that it could not bring itself to leave the stench of the kill. It shovelled snow and food into its maw, turning to confront Fierce Eyes and Dreamer, too torn between the delight of meat and the fear of attack to make a move.

Fierce Eyes' spear took it in the shoulder. It howled and leapt, but was knocked aside. It leapt again, at Dreamer, raked the young man's face with its claws. Dreamer fell, clutching at his left cheek. The wolf was struck again. The knife cut its throat. The axe bludgeoned its life out through the holes in its skull. Its skin was stripped and rolled. Fierce Eyes chanted with triumph as he dismembered the scrawny animal, ignoring the gore-marks of his youngest brother.

The woman came from the tent. She fell to her knees by the head of her youngest son, cradled it, yet did not lift it from the snow. She cried loudly, a sound that lingered. She forced the sad and crushed skull below the snow and piled the ice above it. She reached out and ran her hands through the blood-snow, dragging it towards her, lifting the stained ice to her chest, to her face, smelling and licking the discarded life of her youngest born. Fierce Eyes watched her, chewing on the meat of the wolf.

He said, There's meat here. Eat it. Get strong.

Dreamer went to crouch by his mother.

Fierce Eyes kicked snow at him and laughed, then backed away, to guard his meat. Dreamer watched him. Fierce Eyes taunted him. There's meat here, but not for dreamers. We have a long journey to make to the south. Take your dreams to the ice in the north.

I don't need your meat, Dreamer said.

You'll die, said Fierce Eyes, and chewed at the freezing wolf-flesh. He threw back his head—he was a boy—no more than ten—a boy—he threw back his head—he laughed like a man —he chewed the ice flesh.

Tastes good, he said. It will sustain me. It will sustain our mother. Fight me for the flesh.

I will eat snow.

Eat snow then.

Dreamer crouched above the place where his father had lost his youngest son. The red mush had frozen in the snow. Dreamer used his knife to cut the red snow into blocks. He held the blocks and stared at them, small, cube-shards of his dead kin, like coloured stone, yet not stone. His mother crouched beside him. He gave her a son's kiss, then ate a piece of his brother. She picked a block of the red ice and watched her dreaming son. She gave him a mother's kiss and ate her son. The act was done. Fierce Eyes was subdued. He chewed the wolf, then backed away, running into the tent, to shelter from the driving cold.

Dreamer and his mother ate the wolf until they too were sick. They chewed small slivers of the rancid meat and cried, and Tallis watched all of this from the oakwood, and in her oak mind, through the brain sap that flushed through her body, she remembered a time of childhood, and a question from an old man.

What is a mother's kiss?

The kiss of acceptance. The kiss of knowing. The kiss of grief. The kiss of love. There was no such thing as a mother's kiss. It was a kiss for all things. A son's kiss, too. It signalled the *rightness* of a deed. It signalled acceptance. It signalled love that goes beyond the love of a kiss. Yes. She knew it now.

The two boys stayed in the tent. A fierce blizzard raged for days, but through it Tallis saw the mother slip away to the south, carrying weapons and a bag. She was like some bulky animal, bent low against the storm, layered in furs. She had been sustained by the stray wolf. Tallis knew where she was going.

Later the woman returned. She carried a bundle in her arms. She was exhausted. She flopped through the snow, stumbling, picking herself up again and walking on. She almost walked right past the tent, then saw the statue of her mother and brought the sad remains of her son to lay them at Tallis's feet.

There was blood on the front of her fur.

"Mother," the woman whispered, her eyes screwed tightly shut. "The man is dead. I killed him with this . . ." She cast the broken antler-axe to the snow by Tallis. "I found the green sapling strength of my youth to do it. The green child in me slipped from the old woman. I have killed the man who was your husband and my father. I have killed the man who was my husband and the father of my sons. I have brought back his heart, because before this great winter his heart was strong for me." She took the greying mass from the furs and held it out. She placed it down again and sank a little into herself. "And I have brought back Arak, my youngest-born. It was my dreaming son who told me how to do this. There is a spirit in the boy which is wiser than I am. There is a spirit in the boy which can see further than I can. There is a spirit in the boy that has smelled other forests. He will remember what has happened here. The memory of this snow will grow old with the people. Nothing will be forgotten."

Later, through the snow, Dreamer returned to Tallis and watched her with more knowing than before. Again he sang the song: *A fire burns in the forest where the woodcock flies. How my bones smoulder to join that fire. How I long to fly free . . .*

Tallis felt a surging flow of sap; her bark ached for this young man. Her wooden lips longed to cry her recognition, to call to Harry's spirit inside the boy who had been marked.

Harry!

Dreamer said, "I long to fly south, Old Silent Tree. But there are no birds to carry me. I long to fly south. But there is no birdsong to inspire me.

"Old Silent Tree, once you gave birth to birds from your branches. Bring a winged dreamer to me now. Help me journey to the south, to see the way. Arak is dead. He had knowledge of the land. He was close to the silent trees. He could read the air and the stars. My brother is a hunter. He can see tracks. He can trap and kill animals. But we need birds to show us the flight to the south. Where are the birds? Without them I cannot release the restless spirit in my bones. My bones smoulder to join the fires of the warm forest."

He was quiet for a long while, and the snow blew against his huddled body, piling up. At length, he lifted his face again.

"Old Silent Tree, there is a spirit in me that is restless. There is a ghost in my bones that struggles for wings. I shall make great magic in my life. I shall remember this snow. But the ghost asks for freedom. It is a bird spirit that longs for freedom. I dream about it. I see it high in the air. Its wings are huge. It is above the cloud. It gleams. It roars as it flies. It is a strange bird spirit. Old Silent Tree? My mother tells a strange story. When I was born two voices cried from my mouth. One cried with the voice of a bird. When my youngest brother was born, all the birds went away. We journeyed through a land without wings. No birds to show us hope. No birds to eat. No birds to follow.

"Old Silent Tree . . . do you remember? When this happened you said that I should call on the spirit of the wood. That I should summon the spirit of the oak. You are here. I am here. Our spirits are together. But you must show me what to do next."

He came close to Tallis, his red hair curling from below the fur hood, his eyes wide and searching. The scars on his left cheek seeped a pale blood. He kissed Tallis on the lips, then watched her eyes.

He said, "My brother carved you well. You are more than a grandmother. You are the spirit of my dead sister. You are the spirit of woman in this frozen land. My brother carved you well. If only you could speak. I am marked by the wolf. How can I be both wolf and bird? You could tell me. You would have understood . . ."

He returned to the tent. Later, the woman came through the driving snow, staggering before the howling wind, huddled in upon herself. Her sons came after her. The three of them fell to their knees before Tallis.

"Mother . . ." the woman greeted.

"Old Silent Tree," murmured Dreamer, knowingly.

"Old *dead* woman," sneered Fierce Eyes.

The woman said, "My youngest son made you. Your spirit is in the wood. Now my dead son's spirit cries to join with you. Together you can return to us from the frozen forbidden place. My dreaming son has found the way."

Dreamer came up to Tallis. "You will be the fire burning in Bird Spirit Land. Your flame will break the spell."

Fierce Eyes scowled. "Get this over with. If we follow south fast we can survive. Then you can tell this story until you die, brother. But if we don't go soon we will go nowhere but into ice."

Dreamer came up to Tallis and tugged and twisted her from the frozen ground. He carried her in his arms, through the raging storm, into the freezing place within the tent. Somehow they had kept a fire smouldering here. They lay Tallis across the dull flame. Fierce Eyes blew upon the embers until they flared. Tallis felt the nip of warmth. The fire drove the water from her. She sizzled and singed, then the fire began to take a hold and flames leapt across her skin. The three of the family warmed their hands. It seemed to Tallis that she had smouldered for a long time before finally the fire had taken hold.

The woman took her dead son's bone knife and held it in front of Tallis. On her side, Tallis watched the sadness in the woman's face. She drew the antler necklace from her neck, unslung three fragments of tine. She picked up the sheet-white leg of her murdered boy and warmed it by the fire. Then she flayed the white skin from the flesh, drawing it carefully back, a silky, glistening sheet of human rag. As it came away from the cold flesh, so she cut it into strips, and she wrapped each strip of skin around a piece of bone. When the horn was robed she threaded back the leather of the necklace and gave it to Dreamer, who put it round his neck and tucked this frail memory of the broken boy into his furs.

The woman gave the knife to Fierce Eyes, who held it up, a grin of delight on his gaunt, ageing features. The polished bone caught the light. He held it like a sword, perhaps imagining the gutting and the killing he could perform with this weapon which had once been used to carve the image of a woman in the land.

His mother said, It was fashioned from the bone of a drowned beast in the water. When you are old, it must be returned to the water. It belongs to the realm of beasts.

I will do it, Fierce Eyes said.

Dreamer watched him, smiling through the pain of hunger and cold. He held a hand to his chest where he carried his brother's memory. The fire ate deeper into Tallis.

The woman used long needles of bone to stitch the parts of her son together again. The brothers dropped their gaze as the gruesome task was done. The body was incomplete. White bone through grey flesh made a lifeless puppet. The mother cradled it in her arms. Then she placed it on the flames.

Fierce Eyes went out into the storm and returned with the grandmother's grizzled skull, the hair frozen into spikes which he broke off and cast on to the fire, where they sizzled, cooled, then flared. The skull was placed among the bones of Arak, and through the heat and the smoke Tallis watched the watching eyes, three cold people from an ancient day, remembering and honouring the dead.

Soon she was aware that the snow had stopped. The crude hides of the tent ceased to billow and bulge. The fire below her ceased to gust and roar. Fierce Eyes went outside and came back excited. He found a lure, tested its strength, then went outside. Dreamer went too. The woman pulled back the flap of the tent and Tallis, dying, saw a pale sun in the fields of snow. Fierce Eyes was whirling the lure around his head. It made a rhythmic sound, a pulse in the still air. Soon it began to create the steady whine that she had come to associate with this strange instrument. Dreamer stood beside his brother, watching the heavens. There were specks of black, coming closer.·

Tallis heard cries. Bird cries. The birds returned, invaded Bird Spirit Land and flocked and swarmed above the funeral pyre.

Fierce Eyes and his mother used nets to catch them, stamping on their heads as they struggled in the loose, confining space. When they had killed twenty they laughed together. Other birds stood on Tallis, pecked at her, pecked at the charred flesh of the youngest son.

The hunters of birds piled their catch and the moment of elation passed as the woman came into the tent space to watch the death flight of her youngest born. In the beaks of birds, he went to whatever place would entertain his spirit. As each black creature fluttered and flapped away into the greying sky, she watched it, tears in her eyes.

"Goodbye Arak," she whispered with each of them. "Goodbye Asha . . ."

It was night. The fire had burned low. Tallis was charred wood, hardening, still aware through this gate into the first forest of what was occurring around her. Dreamer came to the fire and brushed among the ashes. He lifted Tallis in his hand, the small fragment of coal that she had become. He kissed her, held her to the breast where the skin of the youngest son was warmed by his own skin, and the horn of the stag kept the life and the memory of the youngest son alive.

She watched from the burned wood. The shards of horn stood out starkly against the snow-cloud sky. (*An image from another life: lying below Broken Boy, looking up at the summer sky through the broken reaches of the creature's antlers. It had been a sexual feeling. An intense feeling. A recognition of the link between herself and Harry . . .*)

Dreamer went out into the still night, wading through the snow. If there was a moon it was behind clouds, causing brightness without form, a glow in the heavens, life struggling to pierce the confusing fog. Birds came and flapped around the body. He remained still and one of them settled on his shoulder, hopped to his head and reached a yellow beak to peck at his eyes.

The bird pecked and pecked.

The boy's blood flowed and he was blinded.

Tallis fell to the snow.

The spirit in the boy lifted from the bones, from the flesh, through the furs. The man was there. Tallis remembered the way he had looked. He gleamed blue-yellow in the night. He was naked and there was no longer a burn upon his face, but he was the brother she remembered. He was gaunt. She could see Dreamer through his insubstantial form.

Dreamer spoke to her, but the words were in a different voice from the boy's.

"We all have our own ways out of the first forest," Harry said. "I was trapped. You trapped me. Now you have released me. Thank you. I shall not be far away. I shall find you again. You are not dead. You have simply journeyed. I shall not be far away."

There was the sudden sound of wings. The elemental presence seemed to shrink. It rose into the air and was dark against the moongleam through the clouds. Dreamer sang a shaman song, a chant of journeying, a celebration of release into the spirit world.

Crow-Harry circled, came close to the charcoal shard that was his sister, winked, then rose and was gone, flying to the south, to home, to warmth, to freedom.

Dreamer fell to his knees, blind, bleeding, journeying on wings of song.

But he was smiling.

He flailed around on the snow. He found Tallis and lifted her. He kissed her blackened face. He hugged her charred body. He stared at her through eyes that saw the shadows of many lands. He had absorbed Arak, and could see the shadows of forests. So he was vision maker, now, as well as memory. Fierce Eyes, with his bone knife and sense of triumph, would lead them safely to the warm. There would be stories told. The family would never be forgotten. All the world would know what had happened here.

Arak journeyed to the forbidden places of the earth.

But after he had been lost he was brought home again.

Goodbye, he said to Tallis.

The woman was packed up. Dead birds, plucked and dried, were slung from her belt. The cold would keep them good. They would eat the carrion of the carrion eaters as they journeyed south, out of the forbidden place. Fierce Eyes was impatient. He began to walk away. His mother, his woman, followed.

Dreamer summoned them back.

He took the tiny bones of the stillborn girl from where they had been buried in the ice. Sightless, seeing all, he placed them by the bones of his brother. He had the remains of the wolf. He found a fragment of his grandmother. He placed berries from his hidden pouch beside these shards of life. He put the skull of a bird on top of it all, then impaled the heart of his father on the beak of the bird. He piled up snow and covered the remains. All this happened in the area of the tent, the warm place that had been their haven. He pressed the snow to make a mound, a burial mound. Fierce Eyes and his mother made a wall of snow around the mound.

Dreamer placed Tallis on the snow, facing south, facing home.

Then he sniffed the air, took his brother's arm, and allowed himself to be led away.

Somewhere, in an unknown region, his spirit, his lost ghost, flew above dark forests.

The long winter came to an end. Tallis sank through the snow, nestled among the bones. The snow melted. Tundra covered the land. Animals walked there, the vibration of their passing stirring Tallis from her earthly sleep. Small plants grew upon the tundra, and then the seeds buried with the bones hatched.

Thorns and holly grew where Tallis lay, absorbing the marrow
of the wolf and the crow, sucking the sad life of the stillborn
infant, tapping the memories of Old Silent Tree and the grandmother skull that nestled by it. Out of the earth came a scrubland,
and this scrubland grew and became a wood. The first tree in the
wood had been holly, wrapped around with ivy. Shaded by
prouder trees, Tallis waited in the stillness, watching the movements of summer through gleaming green and spiky leaves.

The Daurog formed. The holly shuddered. Sap drained in
strange directions. Leaves curled to form flesh; branches twisted to
shape bones. The holly tree shrank, then burst out again, swelling
into the shape of a woman. It detached itself from the thicket and
reached rose-thorn fingers into the hard earth. It moved aside the
earth and found the petrified wood that was the heart in the forest.
Black, because it had been burned a thousand years ago; it still
showed the shape of the face impressed upon it. The Daurog
opened her belly and placed the stone inside. At once it began to
hatch. Warm, seeing through holly-eyes, heart beating like the
frantic flutter of a bird, Tallis went with Holly-jack, deeper into
the forest.

She was alone. After many days there was a movement behind
her and she turned to see a strange-shaped man, crouching,
watching. He wore necklets of forest fruit; his skin was a confusion
of leaves; rushes grew from his scalp. Tallis-Holly recognised the
Daurog shaman. He stood and came towards her. Leaves rustled.
He lay down, smiling, his serpent's member twisting, rising.
Holly-Tallis felt impelled to straddle the force of magic, and knelt
above the grinning wood and let him enter, let him feed upon her
and fertilise the growth of birds.

She went with him through the forest. He danced in moonlit
dells, shivered in thickets, pranced at the edge of the wood,
grinned at travellers from the green of the bush. There were others
with him, gathered on his journey: a leader, and two warriors, and
a woman. All their leaves were different. They passed silently and
swiftly through the rankest, wettest wood, feeding on the soft
fungus of the bark of trees, sucking at the dampness in the rotting
litter, chewing the lichen from mossy, greying stones.

When they came to the river they stopped. Tallis-Holly
watched and soon three riders passed from the human world, an
old man, a young man, a woman with a face like stone. Tallis

smiled. Holly-Tallis followed with the others. The encounter came at dusk.

At some point during the evening, Tallis-Holly went to the crouching wary form of the woman, and watched herself watching the Daurog, and saw the fear and the tiredness in her eyes. She could not tell the human who she was, but she remembered the feeling of affinity; she tried to indicate that affinity, a finger pointed to holly and to human flesh, but the blank look remained in that fur-wrapped, pale-faced Tallis. The feeling between the two females was strong, however, and Tallis-Holly smiled to recognise it.

They shared food. Holly-Tallis gave birth to birds. The pain was very great. Released, she joined the others. They went up the river together. At a great marsh Holly sailed with the other Daurog in a battered craft, entering the mist for days, helping to propel the ancient boat across the stinking, shrouded waters. She had felt sad watching as Tallis had slipped behind her, a figure on the shore, watching with concern but without understanding, since she had failed to place her Moondream mask across her face, and thus could not see the woman in the land.

Winter came and the Daurog shed their leaves. The wolf emerged, sometimes the bird, and Holly-Tallis huddled, alone and unloved, her evergreen skin a challenge and an irritation to the others.

Soon they came to a place of ruins. The wolfish appetites surged. The Scarag attacked. One of them turned on Holly-Tallis and she fled up the path to the gate, passing a woman she knew well, remembering her earlier shock at this unexpected encounter. She watched from the gate as Tallis killed and discarded the Scarag. She hid in the silent, stony rooms and watched Tallis secretly when the woman came into the castle, dragging with her the body of a man.

She watched the ruins take Tallis, the walls and the stones becoming trees again, responding to a glow of green that radiated from the woman as she sat within her nest of rags. They took the man as well. Bodies crushed and absorbed, Tallis-Holly herself became trapped in the quivering, silent forest that filled the stone place.

So she went into the room, pushing through the foliage, and found the place where the woman's corpse had rotted down. She lay down and a sweet slumber came. A long night. She dreamed of childhood. She remembered Mr Williams. She sang old songs, and giggled at remembered stories.

When she woke she had shed her leaves, and the wood-bones lay discarded and piled around her. The trees had gone, absorbed back into the stone, which shimmered with a last remembered green, oozed a final sheen of sap.

Tallis was cold and she fled the place. Her naked skin puckered with a dust of ice. She went among the people of the tents and found dark clothes, and furs.

She stayed here for several days. The people lived both on the edge of the world and on the edge of the battle. Sometimes they looted the dead, sometimes they honoured them. Their tents covered the cliff ledges, hugged the trees; every cave was used. One cave was a shrine.

Tallis left her masks there.

After a while the pain of what had happened to her went away. She had entered the first forest. Wynne-Jones had been right. It had been no simple journey.

Her hands had aged. She could hardly bear to look at them. They were like gnarled wood. When she finally looked into clear water and saw her face, she wept bitterly as she greeted the old woman who stared back at her.

"But I found Harry. I saw my brother. Didn't I? I released him from the tomb. He called to me. I came. I did what he needed. He flew away. But I saw him. Perhaps I can expect no more."

[LAMENT]

Ghost of the Tree

She returned to the settlement of the Tuthanach, a journey of countless days and great difficulty. At the beginning of the great marsh she found the Daurog's boat. Although it was awash, she could see how they had repaired the leaks with rushes and she made the patching good again, launching the frail craft with all her might and throwing herself into the shallow hull, lying there, exhausted, as it drifted through the fog and the silent water.

She felt almost sick with apprehension as she followed the course of the river and came to the spirit glade where she and Scathach had first found Wynne-Jones. What would she find? Was the old man back? Had Scathach, too, undertaken a journey through the first forest, only to return, aged but triumphant, from the underworld?

She followed the overgrown tracks. She had already seen how the spirit poles by the water were rotten, encrusted with fungus. Emerging into the clear space around the compound she could see at once that it had fallen into decline. A thick scrub wood filled the clearing. The palisade had fallen, the earth had slipped. The houses of the Tuthanach were broken, the thatched roofs gone, the daub walls melting under rains.

It was deserted. But among the new trees making their mark upon the land were enigmatic mounds, in the shapes of crosses. Tallis walked among them, prodded them with her staff. When she shifted a little of the earth from one she shuddered to see the grey flesh of a man, face down in the ground.

They will go through a death by burial, and rebirth.

There was smoke from the hill where the mortuary house guarded its legacy of bones. And Tallis could hear a thin piping sound from that direction. Odd, pleasing notes, catching the drifting air, fading in and out of hearing like a sea-tide. As she came closer the notes resolved into a tune, and with a half-smile and a beating heart she echoed the tune from Sad Song Field, humming the simple melody.

Why she had expected to find Wynne-Jones she couldn't say; perhaps because she associated the tune with Mr Williams, and so she had climbed the blackthorn hill with the image of an old man at the top, crouching in his furs, piping her back to his life.

She found Tig, of course, and the young man lowered the bone whistle and watched her through his pale and terrifying eyes. When he smiled she saw filed and sharpened teeth, two of them quite broken off. He had made a fire pit where once the proud rajathuks had stood. When he rose to his feet he was tall and his loose hide cloak fell away from his body, which was taut and muscular, covered with scars and blisters and the old and fading patterns of ochre, copper-salts and blue berry juice. He was a painted man, skin wrecked by mutilation but body hard and ready for the years of survival ahead of him.

"You've come to see Wyn-rajathuk," he said in a hoarse whisper, emphasising the shaman-term, sneering slightly. Tallis was astonished to hear him talk in English.

"Is he here?"

"He has been here for some time. I'll fetch him."

He went back into the crumbling cruig-morn, ducking below the sloping stone lintel and crawling along the dark passage. Tallis crouched down, shaking her head. She had not the slightest doubt of what Tig would bring out to show her—an armful of bones, perhaps; his skull. But the old man coughed at the exit to the bone lodge, eased himself out and stood. Tallis cried out with delight as she saw Wynne-Jones's familiar features. He was grey, his face stiff with cold, and he had difficulty smiling. The eyes that watched Tallis through the white-bearded flesh were bright, though, full of intelligence. His sight had come back.

"Hello Tallis," he whispered hoarsely.

"Wyn . . ." she said, but she felt her heart grow cold. The old man shuddered. His face wrinkled, collapsed. A tongue probed through the grey lips.

"Hello Tallis," Tig mimicked in a high pitched voice. He raised a hand and detached the soft flesh-mask from his face, letting the old man's features crumple in his hand. He shrugged off Wynne-Jones's fur cloak and was naked again.

Tallis felt like crying. Above her head a bird circled suddenly and Tig jerked back, his moment of triumphant trickery suddenly banished. The bird was huge, black-and-white-feathered. It was long necked and had a vicious, curved beak. Tallis had never seen a creature like it. It spiralled up on warmer air, then cried out and dropped swiftly to the north, vanishing among high trees.

The sudden flight had unnerved the young man. He watched the bird until it was well out of sight, then scratched at his seeping, savaged skin, mouthing silent words.

"Why did you kill him?" Tallis asked, and Tig's impish face turned back to her.

There was no smile, no taunting when he said, "It was what I had to do. He knew it. That's why he came back. I only needed his bones, so I carved and kept the flesh."

As if suddenly sorry for his trick he held the face towards her. "You may have him, if you wish. He's inside, all of him. I used oil and resin to keep the flesh whole. The bones are there too. I don't need them any more. He was a rich meal."

"No. Thank you," Tallis murmured, feeling sick. She looked behind her, out across the wood to where the Tuthanach lay buried. "Did you kill the people too?"

"They're not dead," Tig said. "They are simply touching earth. All manner of wonderful things will be happening to them. Old spirits are flowing through their bodies; new spirits are whispering in their heads; wolf-birds, and bear-stags, and frog-pigs are dancing in their chests; long-forgotten forests are seeding in their bellies. When they rise up again they will be mine. I have the knowledge of the people. That is why I ate their dreams. Where you stand now will soon be a great monument, with painted stones and carved stones, and a single way to the heart of the mound where the sun will shine among the dead; it will be the way, lit by the earth's light, into a wonderful land."

Tallis watched Tig and thought of Wynne-Jones's words. You

don't enter the underworld through caves or tombs. That's the stuff of legend. You have to go through a more ancient forest . . .

She smiled wryly as she realised that Tig *was* the stuff of legend. Henceforth, for the Tuthanach at least, the way to Lavondyss would be far easier.

How safe am I, she wondered? She had made herself crude weapons from wood, but Tig had stone axes and knives, bone spears, hooks, slings and stones. They were scattered around the compound, where the rajathuks had once stood. Tallis suddenly realised that they were spread out as if for defence from different angles. Now that she looked carefully she could see the deliberately placed piles of stone, five spears at regular intervals, and the fluttering, feathered carcasses of birds on poles on the earth bank.

Tig had made Bird Spirit Land! He was afraid of birds and he had worked his own magic to keep the predatory creatures, and the carrion eaters, away from his bone house, away from the remains of his people.

Tig was frightened. He was under siege. Would he be glad of Tallis's presence, or hostile to it?

She decided that a blunt question was her best recourse. "Are you intending to eat *me*?"

Tig laughed sourly. "I *thought* you were afraid." He shook his head. "There is no purpose to be served. I have all the dreams of your *England* that I need. It feels such a terrible place, so much barren land, so little in the way of forest, so much crowding in the villages, so much shadow and rain . . ."

Tallis smiled. "Wyn-rajathuk told me once that I would never be able to return to that 'terrible place'. I assured him that I would. But I had expected to be taking my brother with me, and all I have done is glimpsed him. He is still here, still around. If I go back to my own land I shall never find him. If I stay, perhaps I shall stay until I die. I would have liked to question Wynne-Jones about these things," she sighed. "But he made a feast for you, and a cruel mask to trick me . . ."

Tig grinned and patted his hand on the ground before his crouched body. "But you are forgetting something . . ."

A cry! A shriek of anger. It came from the wood, between the cruig-morn and the settlement. It interrupted Tig and he stood, ashen-faced, bleeding from his scars. He raced for a slingshot. Tallis went to the top of the earth bank and stared down at the tree line. Then her spirits rose. There was a woman there. She was tall. She was painted half in white, half in black. A cloak of feathers was wrapped around her, tied at the waist. Her head band was feathered too, long pale yellow tail-feathers.

"Morthen!" Tallis cried. Despite the anger at their last encounter, despite the wounding, Tallis wanted to know the girl again. Alone in this vast forest she needed to gather round her all the familiar things she knew, and that meant Morthen, who was the only possible ally she now had left.

Morthen screamed in her own language. Tig danced in a circle, then howled, a rising and falling cry of challenge. Blood literally burst from his body and he smeared it with his right hand, while in his left he crushed the skull of a crow.

Morthen threw back her head and laughed, then turned and ran back to the woods. Tallis followed quickly. She crossed the settlement area, following the traces of the girl, but suddenly, as she reached the river, she saw the footprints end. In the silence of the spirit glade she looked north and south along the water, but there was no sign of Morthen, although close by, above her head, there was disturbance in the trees.

She looked up into the branches, but could see nothing.

Dusk came as she waited there, and Tallis, cold and hungry, returned to the mortuary house.

Five fires burned on the earth wall. Tig ran between them, piping briefly at each, then finally uttering a raucous screeching sound, which Tallis took to be a challenge to the birds. He watched the skies nervously, and Tallis suspiciously. She entered the mortuary enclosure and smelled food being charred. Tig had speared several small animals and they sizzled over wood-fire flames.

Without being asked she ate some of the stringy meat. It was strong and unpleasant and killed her appetite. When she had finished, Tig came to the fire and ate a little, sucking his fingers. He smelled disgusting, now, and was shaking.

"Morthen is trying to kill me," he said. "I killed her father, the old shaman. She is outraged. She will try to revenge the old man. Then she will kill you too."

"She has had her chance to do that," Tallis said. "She struck me three times and left me to bleed."

"Is her other brother dead? Scathach?"

"Yes."

Tig nodded thoughtfully. "A part of me thinks 'good' when I hear that. But the other part of me, the old man, is saddened, even though he knew it had to come."

His words thrilled Tallis. She could hardly bear to speak for a while, but watched Tig as he tore a further strip of meat and chewed it quickly, gulping it down and glancing round.

"The old man is in you? Wyn-rajathuk?"

Tig smiled. She guessed that he had been waiting for Tallis to understand. He was canny as he watched her, and almost kind. "I told you earlier. I ate his dreams. I speak in his tongue, now. I can remember many things. Oxford. A friend called Huxley. A daughter called Anne. England. The terrible place."

"Not as terrible as the place which I've just visited."

After a moment's hesitation, perhaps as the swallowed dream that was Wynne-Jones came forward in the mind of the mythago: "You found the place of ice, then? You found Lavondyss?"

"I suppose so. I went through the first forest. I *became* the forest. I suppose I entered my unconscious mind . . . have never known such pain. I feel violated, consumed; yet I feel *loved*." She shook her head. "I don't know *what* I feel. All my life I thought that Lavondyss was a realm of magic. Cold, yes. Forbidden, yes. But I thought it was a vast land, with many aspects. I found it to be a place of murder. A place of guilt. A place of honour. A place of the birth of a belief in the journey of the soul."

"It *is* a vast land," the boy who was Wynne-Jones said slowly. "It *does* have many aspects. You entered only that part of it that is personal to *you*. It was personal to Harry too, of course. Each of you was born with memory of the same ancient event, and the abundance of later myths and legends that had developed from it. The closer you came to the place of Harry's entrapment the more your mind and the wood co-operated to create the route through which you would enter that shared, mythic landscape. Lavondyss for you—for all of us—is what we are able to remember of ancient times . . ."

"I begin to understand that, now," Tallis said softly, watching the blankness in the young man's eyes as his mouth moved to articulate the words of an intelligence more than five thousand years in his future. "I had been fashioning the place of our meeting throughout my childhood, following the pattern that Harry had established . . ."

"And did you find Harry there?" Tig murmured.

"He was trapped in the second son of a family. He had been trapped there since I created Bird Spirit Land from a vision of a great battle, Bavduin. It wasn't Harry who had interfered with his journey into Lavondyss, but me. When I banished birds from Scathach's grave I banished them from the snow world where Harry was a visiting spirit in a young, dreaming boy. He couldn't get away. They burned me and the magic broke. Birds came. He took wing and left. I glimpsed him for a moment, then I lost him. I didn't touch him. I feel I've failed."

"And how did *you* get back?" Wyn asked.

Tallis smiled. "You told me that the Daurog were of my own creation, not Harry's. You were right. About *one* of them, at least. I was Holly. I entered her and saw ourselves—you, Scathach, me—ride up the river. When I was in the first forest, millennia seemed to pass. I was an old wood. I watched odd creatures, extinct animals. Hundreds of years passed before I was carved into Old Silent Tree and entered the heart of the wood, the beginning place. Coming home, in Holly, time passed very rapidly. I remember the way she looked at *me* in the wood, when I was travelling with you. I remember how I looked at *her*. Holly and I were the same. I had made the mythago of my own journey home. Even as I was going *to* the realm, I was coming home. I find that a strange thought, even though you told me it would happen. You said, to travel to the unknown region is often to travel home. I would be journeying in both directions."

Tig seemed to sink into himself for a moment, then looked up. "It's what the old man had heard. He hadn't understood its true meaning."

He fell silent. He stoked the fire below the blackened carcasses of small mammals. Although he, like Tallis, had eaten little, there seemed to be no appetite in the air. The moon was bright through storm-laden clouds. The wind was crisp. Tallis searched Tig's gleaming eyes for a sign of Wynne-Jones, but the old man was simply a restless spirit, an elemental, fluttering in the branches of Tig's forest brain. His voice was an ancient wind. The dream would be fading fast. And Tig did not have the smell of survival about him.

Wings beat the air, then passed away. Tallis shared the young man's chill look.

"She is coming for me again," he whispered. It was Tig who spoke now.

"I'll help protect you," Tallis said.

"I'll drive her off. My work here isn't finished. There is a great deal to return to the people. I am the guardian of the knowledge of the way of the earth. She *must* be kept away until the task is done."

Tallis remembered Wynne-Jones's brief account of the Tig legend. His death, when it came, would be terrible. She remembered, too, Wynne-Jones telling her that Morthen would one day be Morthen-*injathuk*. Tallis was adrift in a world of magic. All around her, everything she encountered seemed to reflect that same magic. It was in Tig. It had been in Dreamer-Harry. It was in Tallis herself. Wherever Scathach was undergoing his resurrection, it was as a magic man. It would be in Morthen.

Tig was destined to die. He was also destined to pass knowledge back to the resurrected tribe of the Tuthanach. Strange vision, old memory. There was old memory in the land, and Tig was the "human" carrier of that memory. If he died, the Tuthanach would not pass into the next generation. Unless it was through Morthen?

Was Wynne-Jones still there? She called softly for the old man.

He came forward, rattled the bars of his woody cage and made the young man smile. "He's here," Tig whispered.

"What did I witness? What was Lavondyss?"

"Tell him what you saw . . ."

Tallis recounted the transformation and encounter.

"You witnessed not a legend but the deed of murder that *caused* the legend. That is the nature of Lavondyss: it is the place, made from mind out of memory, where the first stories lie, the deeds that *generate* the myths, through the memory of children. Dreamer survived to tell the tale of that terrible time. It may be that the rest of the clan, those who had gone ahead, perished. The summer land was filled with the descendants of the family who had been left behind. Dreamer's tales, enlarged and remembered, became the stuff of legend; a son murdered, his corpse stolen, becomes —in story—a son denied a castle except in a forbidden realm. A grandmother who teaches a child to carve, then witnesses his death at the hands of her son, becomes Ash, teaching a lame child to hunt in strange realms, only to witness his death at the hands of something—the Hunter—that she has created herself. When Harry called to you for rescue he used all the versions of the story. He had entered the *deed*. He had entered the *memory* of the deed. He had entered the nugget of fact that lies in every mind. He became trapped there. He reached through the forest of his own mythagos, to his sister . . ."

Tallis closed her eyes. The words ran around her head in circles. She had come to find Harry, and had only released his spirit. Something . . . something irritated her. It was the question she had asked before, and even as she spoke it now she began to see the answer.

"But *I* trapped Harry," she said. "And I trapped him *after* he had contacted me. If he hadn't called to me I wouldn't have learned the hollowing; if I hadn't learned the hollowing, I wouldn't have seen your son, Scathach. If I hadn't seen Scathach and wanted to protect him, I wouldn't have made Bird Spirit Land. If I hadn't made Bird Spirit Land, I wouldn't have trapped my brother Harry by denying him the bird in which to leave the unknown region . . ."

Tig murmured, "When you made that Bird Spirit Land, you affected time, you affected Harry's journey. You changed things. You changed the details of the first murder. Bavduin, the battlefield, was just a later echo of that event, connected to the past through your two minds."

"I understand that. All my life I've known that you should never change a story."

"Your creating of Bird Spirit Land was the *beginning*. Harry reached to you through a confusion of time and ages. He arrived too early."

"That I understand too. But *why* did it begin? It began with Scathach. Why? I made the spirit land *after* I had seen your son arrive in the world of England. I made it a *year* after his arrival. It was your *son* who started all this off. *Scathach* is the beginning. He inspired me to hollow his future and his death. By interfering with that vision I trapped my brother . . .

"But *how* could I do that? *Who was Scathach? Why* is he the link?"

"He was the old man's son by Elethandian of the *Amborioscantii*," Tig said slowly.

Tallis asked, "And who was Elethandian?"

"She was Harry's daughter. She was only half of the wood." Tig grinned. "You are Scathach's *aunt*. That is the link between you."

Tallis sat slowly back on to aching legs, shaking her head and breathing steadily in the chill air. Tig cocked a head, watching her peculiarly. It was hard to tell how much of the boy was present, how much of the old man.

"You knew all the time, then. But why didn't you tell me?"

"He didn't know it until he was almost at the site of Bavduin. Your question of linkage had been disturbing him. It came to him suddenly. He returned here as much because of that knowledge as for his journal."

"Why?"

"Why? Because Elethandian herself would have been there. She is part of the same legend cycle. She is the mother who goes to the place of her son's death. There she finds the spirit of her father, disguised as an animal—"

"Me!" Tallis said, understanding. "I was the spirit of Harry. And she was the old woman in the black veil . . ."

"And she sacrificed her own life to give a new life to her son. He couldn't bear to see that."

For a moment Tallis watched the young shaman; the words of the old man, murmured in the old tone and accent of the boy, fluttered restlessly in her head.

"Then Scathach may have come home too?" she said, hardly daring to hear the answer from the old man's eaten bones.

"He'll be there." Tig grinned. "You told the old man of the protection of his son's body by stone—"

Leaf Man and Leaf Mother—

"Yes. I hung them over the body. Leaf Mother and Leaf Man."

"You became Leaf Mother to return. You summoned the Daurog. You travelled as the Daurog Holly-jack. You shed the Daurog like a skin."

Leaf Man. Shaman. The Daurog that had escaped the winter killing. She had travelled with Scathach too, his own spirit returning from the unknown region of Lavondyss in the woodland form of Ghost of the Tree. Perhaps it should have been she herself who had travelled in that particular form! They had not recognised each other, and yet an affinity between them had sent them to the ground in a lover's embrace within moments of their finding each other.

Tig struggled within himself. His eyes were on the heavens, frantically searching for the creature that haunted him. The fire made the sweat and seepage on his naked body gleam. Tallis realised that she was losing Wynne-Jones. The boy was over-powering his eaten memories of the man.

She rose and left the mortuary enclosure, walking uneasily down the hill, back to the silent settlement, the river, and the passage north again. Behind her she heard Tig piping and chanting. It was a desperate sound.

Somewhere—to the west, she thought—a bird screeched loudly. Then the air was disturbed by the sudden flight of giant wings, beating towards the boy on the earth wall of the old charnel house.

She climbed the steep path to the ruined castle, passed through the gate, found the room where the forest had taken her. The remains of Holly-jack were on the floor, crushed, rotting wood, disturbed by wind. A few green leaves remained among the bones.

By the window to the ledge were the remains of Ghost of the Tree. Tallis crouched by them, fingered the wood, the dried leaves, the crumbled skull. If these remains had been here when she herself had returned from the Otherworld, she hadn't seen them.

Her masks were still in the cave. She sought among them. Which should she wear? She placed Morndun across her face, but there were too many ghosts and it disturbed her to see what occupied the same air, but on a different plane.

There was no mask with which to search for Scathach.

She moved about the cliffs, the woods, the ledges. She sought among the shuffling figures at every fire. She lifted cowls, turned faces to the light, tried to find a language that could be understood. She searched for days.

If he had been here he had gone. He had not lingered. Perhaps, like Tallis herself, he had decided to return to the Tuthanach. They had passed on the river, during winter, perhaps, and had not seen each other as they had braved the storm.

She was wrong.

She returned to the shrine-cave, hungry and cold, and there

was a man there, crouched over her masks, feeling them with gnarled and shaking fingers. He straightened a little as she approached him from behind. He looked round slightly, listening to the sounds she made. His hair tumbled grey from the scalp. The skull in his face poked through shrivelled flesh. His eyes were open, but there was no fire there now.

She placed her hands on his shoulders and leaned down to kiss the top of his head.

"Ghost of the Tree," she whispered. "It's good to see you."

He sighed, let his head fall, a gesture of intense relief. He smiled and cried, shaking his head slightly, reaching up to cover her hand with his. He was silent for a long time, his breathing ragged as he began to accept that his time of waiting was at an end, and that Tallis had come home to him.

"Where have you *been?*" he asked.

"Walking in the woods," she said.

Coda

I dream in my dream all the dreams of the other dreamers,
And I become the other dreamers.

Walt Whitman
The Sleepers

The pain had ceased, but her head still felt light. She lay among the furs of her bed, face half-turned towards the glancing light from the small window of her hut. There was a strong wind outside, and she could smell snow. She hoped the coming storm would not be too ferocious. Year by year the mound of earth and stone that covered Scathach had been worn away. Soon there would be nothing left to go and kick. She visited Scathach every day. She kicked the earth. *You should have waited longer. I needed you more.*

He had been too old. His journey into Lavondyss had been too demanding. It had taken too much from him. But those several years had been good ones, even though she'd been the eyes for both of them.

Was that the sound of horses? She struggled to sit, but failed. The wind blew the hides that covered the window. The young woman who tended the fire, and nursed the old-woman-who-was-oracle, glanced up, but was too lazy to come and help. Everyone knew that Tallis was dying. Everyone knew that the oracle was dying. Everyone was afraid.

Thank God the pain had gone away.

She lay back again, stared at the ceiling. She was hungry, yet not hungry; she was anxious to walk to the shrine cave, yet content to lie here. She wanted to talk, but needed silence.

It was odd to be dying.

Horses? It *was* the sound of horses. Distantly. They were struggling up the path. She could hear the drum. They always beat the drum for new arrivals.

The young woman who was her lazy nurse began to sing. It was a familiar lament. It brought back memories of Ryhope. Tallis cried without tears, laughed without smiling, called without sound. This was familiar indeed, but she was too weak to go and smell the air.

She had thought a great deal about Ryhope recently, memories pressing forward as if sensing her imminent death and urgent to be a part of the journey to come. She had thought especially about her father, saddened again, all these years on, by the image of him, his forlorn, hopeless figure, standing in the stream and clutching *Moondream*, that shard of his daughter's life. And she had thought fondly of her mother, too, though she had realised something recently that made it almost painful to think of her mother's silent sadness, the deep loss that must have haunted the woman through all the years that Tallis had been alive with her.

Two blue ribbons, tied around the antler shard, hidden in the treasure trunk—blue ribbons for her dead sons.

Two boy children (born in wartime!) who had not survived, remembered in strips of their own christening robes, blue edging tied around the lace of Tallis's dress.

Tallis was the youngest child—her story, of the King and his three sons, the youngest sent wildly into the Otherworld, was a reflection of her own life, known to her without her truly knowing.

She closed her eyes, but soon opened them again as she heard the boy, the child, the pest. His name was Kyrdu. She liked him, but he was always asking questions. She would be glad when he was older. He called "Grandmother Tallis. Grandmother!"

He burst in through the hides on the door, letting cold air gust across the floor and blow the flames. He approached Tallis cautiously, rose above her, peering down. His face was full of concern. He had been unhappy at the old woman's recent decline. He had tried to share her pain, but he could not use the right magic.

He tugged at her shoulder as she lay there.

"I'm awake," she said. "What is it you want?"

"Riders coming," he whispered anxiously. "They're still in the canyon. Five of them."

They had sounded closer. Her ears had remained keen after all these years. She smiled at Kyrdu. Pain lanced her chest, squeezing tears from her eyes. The boy cradled her head, looking concerned.

"It might be Harry," he said brightly. "It might be Harry at last."

"How many riders have passed through the shrine?" Tallis whispered to him. "How many each year?"

"Lots."

"How many have been Harry?"

"None."

"Exactly. I found Harry ages back, when I was just a girl. I found him in spirit. I've told *you* the story and you alone, but I didn't expect . . ." she coughed violently, and again Kyrdu cradled her, helplessly watching her. "I didn't expect," she went on breathlessly, "that you would plague me with your *sightings*, and your *keenness*. You drive me mad. Go away. I'm feeling strange."

"There's something else," he said as he laid her back. He brushed aside the hair from her eyes. He looked so like his father as he watched her.

"What now?"

"Your cave. Your shrine . . . the oracle . . ."

"What about it?"

"A girl's voice. It called out. I looked hard, but I couldn't see anything. But there was a girl's voice in there. And a funny smell. It smelled sweet. And hot. Like a hot wind . . ."

Tallis watched him. Her heart raced so hard that the pain came back, and with it the dizziness and the feeling of being sick. She reached out and touched the young boy's hand. He had known winter all his life, and would know no other season. But Tallis knew what he had experienced, and she tried to smile through the shaking of her face, and the sudden sense of finishing . . .

"Summer," she said. "You smelled summer. I remember that summer well . . ."

It was Harry. It *was* Harry. He was coming. And the voice in the shrine cave was hers—herself as a child, listening to this very moment in the ferocious winter. Perhaps, after all, there was a way back, back to home . . .

Her body strove to rise, but she failed. She drove the boy away.

She sent the woman away. She lay on her bed and shook, and sweated, and tried to *think* the pain away. Her head felt like exploding. There was something rising in her throat and she swallowed it back. The furs were warm, but a wetter warmth slipped from her, upsetting her. Her chest seemed to rattle. She could hear the drum, the whicker of horses. She clutched at the furs, tried to keep the cold out. She stared at the roof of the hut. She counted the rushes, the slats. She tried to see each detail of the roof.

Hurry.

Pain and the fluttering of wings.

Hurry!

Breath bubbling in her throat. A darkening . . . was it night? The light seemed to slip away. She couldn't feel her hands. Her feet were numb. Were there birds in the roof? Is that why everything seemed to spin?

HARRY! HARRY!

"I'm here. I'm here by you . . ."

He had entered without her realising it. She could feel warm wind on her face. His hands took hers, raised them to his lips, kissed them. Her vision was suddenly clear. He was handsome, as she had known he would be. There was no burn-scar on his face. He was armoured for war and long rides, leather-clad, fur cloaked, his hair tied back with an iron ring. He smiled broadly, his fair eyes sparkling. He was so young!

"Harry . . ."

"Tallis. You look so lovely."

"I'm an old woman."

"You're no such thing." He leaned and kissed her lips. "It's taken me a long time to find you."

"I was supposed to rescue *you.*"

He laughed. "Well. That's the way it goes. It's my turn now. I have to get you home."

"Home is a long way," she said.

"Not that far. Can you walk?"

"I don't know."

"Come on. Get up. There's no point in not trying."

She felt the furs taken from her body. She had expected to be embarrassed by the smell of her incontinence, but her legs were suddenly strong and the air was scented with snow. She took

Harry's hand and he pulled her to her feet. He led her outside, laughing. Thick snow covered the land. They ran through it, Harry leading, tugging her along. Her old legs felt strong again. She felt the wind on her face.

"Come on. Come *on*," called Harry. "Home isn't that far away."

"You're running too fast," she cried, knee deep in the snow. They pranced through the snow like horses, laughing as they stumbled. They ran up the rise of land, to the woods at the top. There was warm air there, and bright trees, in full leaf.

"*Wait!*" Tallis cried irritably. Then laughing. "I can't keep up. Your legs are longer than mine."

Her brother tugged her, swung her round, holding her by both hands. She swung so fast she felt her feet leave the ground. She giggled. It always terrified her when he did this, but only because she imagined he would let her go. He never let her go.

Strong against the Storm was on the hill. They ran towards it and again he lifted her, swinging her high and planting her firmly on the lowest branch. He stood below her, grinning.

She sat carefully, afraid of unbalancing. "Take me down."

"I don't think I will," he teased.

"Harry? Please help me down."

He cocked his head. She remembered the way he had always looked.

"Look behind you . . ."

She turned on the branch. She was staring through dark woods, towards open land. She saw a man's figure standing out on that open land. All she could see of him was his silhouette. It disturbed her. The man was standing on the rise of ground, immediately beyond a barbed-wire fence. His body was bent to one side as he peered into the impenetrable gloom of the wood. Tallis watched him, sensing his concern . . . and the sadness. His whole posture was that of a saddened, ageing man. Motionless. Watching. Peering anxiously into a realm denied him by the fear in his heart.

Her father.

"Tallis?" he called.

Without a word she jumped down from the branch of the tree and stepped forward into the light, emerging from the tree line and stepping through the wire.

James Keeton straightened up, a look of relief upon his face. "We were worried about you. We thought we'd lost you."

"No, Daddy. I'm quite safe."

"Well. Thank God for that."

She went up to him and held his hand. He led her home.

The freezing wind could not dampen the fire. They burned her on a fine pyre, opposite the shrine cave where her masks hung, twisting slowly in the sheltered place. The boy Kyrdu wailed. He was inconsolable. When his mother shouted at him he simply ran, he hid. But he came back and crouched near to the place where the masks dangled. He had always liked Sinisalo. It was a child's mask. It was from the child's lips that he had heard the voice of the girl.

He gave her no thought, now. Grandmother Tallis burned on the wood. The smoke that rose from her found wings and flew away. The lament followed her. The sad song, chanted by the woman who had nursed her, drifted high into the winter sky. Like the smoke, it seemed to curl and turn, streaming to the west, to the place where Grandmother Tallis had always said her *real* home lay. The drum was beaten.

The riders were growing restless. Four of them stayed on horseback, leaning easily over their saddles, waiting for their leader to finish with his grief.

He was tall, that one. He had command. He was old and wore not just the cloak of the hunter, but the weapons of the warrior and the skin-paint of the shaman. He was all things. Now he was distraught.

Kyrdu watched him through his own tears. The big man passed around the pyre. Fire made his face gleam.

Suddenly he shouted out her name, giving vent to all his grief. "Tallis! Tallis!"

The horses reared and backed away, their riders struggling for control. His voice was filled with sadness, filled with desperation. And longing.

And love too.

"Tallis!" he cried again, a lingering cry . . .

And from Sinisalo came the girl's eerie voice, whispering in the strange language of the old woman on the pyre. "Harry. Harry. I'm here. I'm with you."

Kyrdu forgot his tears. He watched the dead wood of the mask. It clattered against its neighbours, blown by the gusting wind. Its eyes were guileless. Its mouth was pure. Sweet smells, and warmth, came from it.

The man on the ledge had not heard the voice from the mask calling to him. He had given in to grief, thrown back his head in bitter self-recrimination. "I've lost you. I've lost you. And now I've lost everything!"

"No," whispered the ghost in Sinisalo, and Kyrdu shivered as he heard the magic words. "I'm here. I'll come to you, Harry. Wait for me. Wait for me . . ."

There was a way to another land through the shrine cave, a way to the land of Grandmother Tallis's birth; that warm land. Kyrdu watched the mask, remembered Tallis's tales and tricks. There was a *hollowing* there. His father had once spoken to the old woman about it. Grandmother Tallis had laughed. You *will* go there, she had said. You will go through the shrine to a strange house. You will go with your wife and your son, Kyrdu. The house will be ruined. You will all be very frightened. You will see a *rajathuk* there, a small girl, terrified. But you will not recognise it. Only Kyrdu will be able to see the woman in the terrified face of the young girl, as she runs for the light and for her own father.

Kyrdu knew that his mother longed to journey out of this terrible, icy place. Perhaps he could use the masks to find the magic for such a journey. Grandmother Tallis had always said that there was power in the child. Perhaps she *had* meant him.

The riders had gone, clattering up the path to the castle and the woods beyond. But long after the pyre had burned to ash the boy was still crouched within the shrine cave, following with his gaze the trail of the drifting smoke, out across the forest, to the distance, to the setting sun, to the unknown regions of the west.

He wondered how to journey there.